Swe   union

A Brick Winslow novel

First in a series by Ray Knight

https://knight-moves.com/

Printed in the United States of America

Knight-moves publishing
Knight-moves.com
Ray Knight

ISBN: 978-17350589-0-0

First Edition

Dedication

For the past 40 years I've had a partner and companion. She has been; my confidant, lover, co-conspirator, nurse, financial consultant, and best friend. We don't always agree and are very different people in approach and problem solving, but we always seem to find a way to work things out. Without her love and support, this book and my amazing life would not have been possible. She deserves more than I can express and should receive the credit she's earned.

My Wife and the magician behind the curtain, Harriette Manis.

There needs to be a blank page here

.

One

It started with a tingle.

One secret he never shared. It began in his balls, built, and spread faster than a virus until he thrummed like a tuning fork. He felt lightheaded and empty, merely the husk remaining. Blessing or curse, the jury was still out.

He'd spent years trying to get a handle on it. Premonition was a possible definition of course; he couldn't ignore the energy, but it was always unfocused and non-specific. The physical sensations were overwhelming. It left him weak and shaken. Aren't premonitions supposed to be spot-on? Intuition perhaps? But how to explain the physical invasion? Besides, wasn't that a chick thing? He finally settled on spell, just spells. Even if he had someone he could talk to, how to explain? He tried to remember the last time and couldn't. This one was unmistakable, signaling something significant, soon.

He set his cup on the hall table and explored the vast deck surrounding the house. It was early dawn and sunrise brought rosy red tentacles brightening the sky in sharp contrast with the dark shadows that enveloped the grounds. Daylight patiently penetrated the old-growth hardwood trees; the oaks and maples still held winter's remnants inhibiting the spring buds and didn't do the roof any good. The sun and icy tentacles playing peek-a-boo. No winner yet established. He hadn't adapted. His bare feet burned from the cold wood planks of the deck and his breath froze inches from his lips.

He wore the burnt bronze of a deep-water tan covering his chiseled frame. His face unlined and smooth, belying a hard forty. The aqua eyes mimicking the warm waters of the Caribbean, like emeralds, calm until riled. The sandy blond mane bleached near white from salt water and sun. Almost pretty until you got a close looks at the eyes. The clothes hid the damage.

The tingling spread and focused on sound, hearing amplified, blocking, extracting the kernel needed. There … a faint hum growing into the distant distinct throb of an American V8, the steady whap, whap, whap of hot skins chewing up asphalt. Michelins he thought, good rubber. The car was approaching too fast and he willed it on, but his gut recognized the lie. A screech of brakes as they made the turn on the dirt road, although road was a stretch, more a twisting trail through dense undergrowth. The car traversed a hundred yards before breaking in the clearing. At fifty yards he could make out the sight of it drifting through the trees, a giant manatee, lazy, rolling on soft suspension, a fat sea cow. Speeding up, it became two jackrabbits humping. It bumped through the rain-filled ruts; the last vestiges of slush, dirty and frozen, slanted the road.

He couldn't help a grin—this slapstick clown cop shtick couldn't be for real. Drunk kids in a stolen car or old farts lost? Still, he retrieved the big Kimber and slipped it in the back waistband of his jeans. It seemed unlikely that a serious threat would present itself as a joke, but … He donned a windbreaker to conceal the gleaming .45.

Assassins didn't drive boxy soft American technology.

The driver realized the error of his way and was cautiously moving along. He poured another cup of Joe and strode back to the rail.

As the car broke into the clearing, the driver accelerated stopping ten feet short of the house. He braked hard, pushing the lumbering beast in a skid that churned grit and gravel, spraying the lawn furniture and peppering the porch at his feet. The sun still at a low angle, it glinted off the windshield obscuring the occupants.

It sat there, a giant grey worm spewing effluent in a plume of vapor staining the morning sky.

"A hookah-smoking caterpillar."

The door opened. A slick hunk of raven hair obscured her face; it didn't matter.

She exited in a fluid, practiced sweep designed to be effortless. She looked somehow the same, yet different; she wore the years well. She was dressed for Rodeo Drive or Worth Avenue. A blue-black print dress that shouted designer. The black hair sleek, shimmering in the sun as it kissed her lily white shoulders. A necklace of white gold inlaid with small diamonds circled her slender neck dangling a blood-red ruby the size of his thumb.

The pricey ensemble enhanced her perfect figure. He searched her face and body looking for flaws or extra pounds. She still made his blood rise and his heart flutter. He dreaded to hear her speak; those pouty lips weren't familiar with truth.

Bonnie and Clyde on the job. It looked like Bonnie would pull the heist while Clyde sat, an inept wheelman. Smart. He couldn't handle them both.

The smile he forced never reached his eyes; his blood pumped rich in adrenaline.

She stood cloaked in her Californication with the stink of LA scrubbing the shine off the newborn day. Her posture was ramrod straight as she squared her shoulders; her eyes swept the surroundings, taking inventory. She didn't look up to where he stood. She had a thing about having to look up to anyone. A haughty trait inherited from her mother.

"Logic and proportion have fallen spooky dead."

He felt like he was in a surreal documentary depicting real life in a hallucinogenic dream, as if he'd fallen down the rabbit hole.

"Hello Brick," she said, looking up into his face. The heavens parted, pigs fell from the sky, and she smiled. A real smile. The old smile. The one that lit her face, lit the whole clearing. A genuine smile that said volumes. Like an old lover who was truly happy to see him.

His heart melted.

She did the unthinkable. She chuckled in a self-depreciating way and said, "It's colder than I thought and I appear to be sinking. May I come in?"

Her come-fuck-me shoes were inching into the mud like quicksand. And she shivered.

She had said and done all the right things. His muscles relaxed in groups starting at his shoulders. His smile filled the void between them. A civilized call at least. "Hello Cassie. Of course, come in before you catch cold. The weather seems unpredictable lately."

Neither mentioned the car's driver, who sat motionless behind the wheel.

Jonathan Wingate was her husband's name; he insisted on being called Jonathan. That's why Brick called him Jack. At least when he was trying to be civil, he called him that.

Demurely she acquiesced and ascended the eight stairs. When she drew even with him, she looked down at his bare feet and said, "You're cold too. Is it warm inside?"

For an answer he opened the front door and beckoned her in. She peered past the foyer into the interior of the warm house and took in the décor. She kicked off her muddy shoes before entering as if it were natural. A show of respect he knew.

He scanned the horizon hoping his paranoia didn't show. Then with a last hard glare at the idling worm, he turned and ushered her into the hall and down two steps to a vast sunken living room richly furnished with deep-pile Persian carpets, fine-crafted oak and maple tables, hutches and cabinets with comfortable fabric easy chairs, and a long wide cozy couch all arranged with style.

"Have a seat," he said.

She acted like she hadn't heard him and instead began a slow, careful inspection of the room. Wandering, her hands gliding over furniture and art. Her eyes calculating a quick appraisal. The shrewd banker performing a final inventory before repossession.

"I read about your folks, sorry."

First blood, typical. Rip off the scab; let it bleed.

Icy fingers gripped his heart at the thought of his mother. His dad, not so much.

Brick knew she could be sad, for a minute. His parents had liked her, bought the act. She didn't say anything else. When dealing with Cassie, it was best to keep her off her rhythm; it made it harder for her to utter the carefully choreographed dialogue she'd rehearsed. He had lived with this woman long enough to know the drill.

"I don't know how you found me, but you want something."

"Cindy gave me your address and obviously I want something. I have to ask … I'm a little desperate and it's been a long time, so I have to ask."

"How would Cindy know my address?" He was clueless.

"She said she got it from some Playboy Bunny bimbo."

She just couldn't help the bimbo part, another little jab. He remembered it now, a lonely drunken email sent to Dawn one night when he was depressed and needed to reach out. Dawn was his special friend from Oregon. Two months earlier, she had sent him a letter. He must have given her the address.

Still, this didn't compute; he couldn't connect the dots and make sense of this new crazy. He'd been so careful with his location and now it seemed as though everything was unraveling and spinning out of control. The gun pressing against his back was uncomfortable; he was following her as she moved through the house.

"I'd offer coffee but you won't be here that long." He looked out the kitchen window; Jack was still in the car. He moved the gun to his pocket, still not sure. She had adroitly moved him to his private quarters.

"What do you want, Cassie?"

She averted her eyes the way she always did before she told a lie. "Well, my son, John Jr.... You remember Johnny, don't you, Brick?"

Another dig; he didn't bite.

Still smiling he said, "I haven't seen or heard from you in ten years. You've concocted some new scheme in that wicked little mind. Cut the crap and get to the point."

Her eyes betrayed her irritation; this wasn't going according to plan.

He said, "I remember everything."

Cassie left him seventeen years ago and he'd been devastated. She was his childhood sweetheart and, if he was honest, it still scorched. They were only teenagers, kids really, when they started together and were married when Brick was twenty. She's a year younger. When she left, he thought his life was over and in a way it was.

Brick was a sweet guy and crazy smart, with an IQ in the 140s and an almost photographic memory. Hard worker, he tried to be a good provider, but it wasn't enough. She wanted more.

Jonathan was twenty years her senior, married with two grown children. When she started working as a salesclerk in the clothing store that bore his name, she was still in high school, seventeen. Old Jackie set his sights on her from the start. Brick never will forget or forgive him for taking her away.

In reality, Cassie was the cheat. She tore Jonathan's family apart. She worked at it, at him, until his marriage was shredded. Cassandra destroyed his family faster than a tiger tore through tissue paper. And she was there for Jonathan to the end, loving with humid passion, milking his fantasies.

After it was all over, Brick changed. He left the dark blue suits, firm handshakes, and phony smiles. Left the guile and lies. Screw the other guy as your foot pushes off his head on the way up the ladder. You leave little pieces of yourself on that journey, and when you arrive you find the real you has vanished. This place was his sanctuary. He hid here and healed. Found himself once again after a long time lost. But now his sanctuary was in jeopardy. If these two could find him, so could others. This could mean an end.

The last time he ran into Cassie was at Cindy's birthday party ten years ago and it was enjoyable. Brick had a hot little thing along who clung to him like a leech in a bloodbath. He flaunted her and got a little retribution. Cindy had been a friend since school and Cassie's best friend. She's an adventurous woman who loves to embarrass with sexual innuendos. He especially liked her husband, Gary, a nice guy and funny as hell.

"Money, I need money and you've done well for yourself. You can call it a loan if it makes you feel better, but I won't pay it back. You can afford it."

"This is probably really stupid but I have to ask, why would I do that?"

"Because otherwise we're going to sue you on the grounds that you cheated me on the original divorce decree by trying to obscure the fact that you would inherit a small fortune from your grandfather in an existing will."

Brick laughed, "Sue me, go ahead." He thought of Bucky when he said, "I have a great attorney and I'll bankrupt you." Old granddad was still sprightly as a leprechaun and wiping his ass with hundred-dollar bills.

Cassie practically screamed in his face, "We're already bankrupt, you dumb fuck. Look at this place and all of this shit—you're worth some big money. I know people who drink and talk; you didn't get all this finery and pay taxes on it. I'm betting the IRS would get hard when they hear."

Honesty, refreshing for a change. He had to smile; he had had the same tingle and feeling the day he first saw her face. He remembered it well. They were at school. He had wanted to talk to her, so he walked up and asked if she had a pen he could borrow.

She was searching through her purse. Do women ever find anything in those cavernous bags? She seemed sorry when she came up empty.

"No worries, I'll borrow one in my next class. I'm Brick."

"Uh … Cassie," she stammered.

"See you around, Cassie." Two days later he called and they went on their first date.

Now, she appeared defeated for a moment and looked at him like she used to.

The look transported him back in time. They were Brick Winslow and Cassandra Thorpe. He, homecoming king; and she, queen a year later. She, head cheerleader; and he, captain of his class and the football team, star quarterback. People worshipped them—the prettiest couple in school, high achievers, destined for success.

What all the observers didn't know was that Cassie had a dark side and sometimes would lock herself in her room and not come out for days at a time. Her childhood convoluted with a father she never knew and a stepfather who was frequently absent, a long-haul truck driver who was morose and distant when he was home, never offering the love and support she so desperately needed. Her mother was a narcissistic, fat diva who wasn't interested in anything but her own comforts.

At seventeen Cassandra discovered sex. On a routine visit to the doctor, she was directed to wait in his office while they prepared her room. After rummaging through his desk, she nicked a prescription pad. She had studied his signature and the next day forged his name and her age on a prescription for birth control pills. Heading to a pharmacy in a nearby town, she left with the pills that would offer her freedom.

The next night she seduced Brick. They both were virgins, but Cassie soon exhibited behavior with the wisdom and knowledge of a seasoned pro. Her sexual appetite was limitless and she became a sensual athlete who took more daring chances as she grew more aggressive and pushed further into experimentation. He was shocked at her knowledge. Then she became enamored with public displays, testing the limits until it seemed certain they would be caught.

Life has a way of coming full circle. Before he knew what happened, Brick found himself sitting on the edge of his bed. She had somehow maneuvered him into the bedroom. Quiet, he didn't know what to say. So he said, "Fuck you, Cassie."

She changed track, smiling with that old beguiling, sultry demeanor. She lowered her eyes and said, "Maybe we can work something out."

He laughed and in spite of herself, so did she.

She had a low, throaty laugh that started deep in her chest and consumed her in a fit of uncontrollable glee. "My God, Brick, you are so hot when you're mad. I really am sorry for everything I've done to you, just a stupid greedy little girl who didn't know what she wanted—such a mistake."

This was a first. It rattled him. The guile was gone from her face and she reminded him of how it was when they were young. So beautiful … if only …

"How much?"

"Two hundred would help"

Brick reached into the front pocket of his jeans and removed a neatly folded wad of bills, peeled off two hundreds, and held them out to her.

She gave him a withering look, the one he guessed she used for the help. "Pocket change?" She laughed.

"So you waltz in and expect what? Two hundred thousand?"

In one swift shift of her body, she was on her knees at his feet, looking into his eyes, and in her bruised whiskey whisper said, "Take me to bed. You remember what it was like. I know you remember."

"What about …?" He trailed off, inclining his head toward the window and the still idling worm.

"He's afraid of you; he'll just sit there for an hour, two if you want."

She was so close and he could smell her now. A faint hint of something expensive with her underlying funk. The odor of arousal, sweet and musky, a promise of untold pleasure.

Then she was on him, smothering him with her body, mouth insistent on his, tongue probing, searching, gaining access. It was hot, smoldering. His hands were moving now, roaming, the stirrings impossible to ignore. She reached for him; he was hard, straining against the fabric.

She made a mistake and he saw it immediately. She couldn't help herself, the smirk. She knew she had him.

Suddenly brought out of the trance, Brick came back to the moment and laughed. He remembered all right, but he remembered it all, not just the brief good times. She had caused him too much misery to forget, but God he was tempted. He wished he wasn't. He couldn't deny her hold over him. Damn her, he still wanted her. He pushed her back, hard—too hard. She went down on her back and the momentum carried her legs to flip head over heels, commando.

"Sorry." He tried to help her up, but she shook him off. Now it was her turn to be pissed.

He ran out the door, out the house, and down to the car, leaving her lying there, very unladylike. He went to the driver's side window. Jack had the window down, straining to catch every word.

They could have gotten his number from Cindy and just called. Now they had exposed his new life, and he had to take measures for his safety once again. The past was gaining fast. He blamed Jack; of course, he always blamed him.

This time was different; Jack glared at him with hatred as he fought to gain control of his rage. If he had expected Brick to scream or get physical, he was disappointed. Brick stood in silence and looked the older man over from head to foot with obvious scorn.

Jack shrank back into the interior of the big beast as far as possible, visibly frightened as Brick leaned in and rested his forearms on the windowsill. In a quiet, almost conspiratorial tone of voice, Brick said, "Look at you, man—you look like shit. You've got a fat gut, lost most of your hair, and you've got creases I could drive my four-wheeler through. Look at her; she's still beautiful, slim, and sexy. Do you really think you can hold her? From what she told me in the house, I think she's already fucking someone else. Is she still as kinky? Has she asked you to bring other men into your bedroom for her?"

Jonathan screamed, then threw the still-idling car in reverse and floored it. Brick thought he might try to run him down, so he moved closer to the trees. But instead of continuing backward, the car lurched forward before skidding to a stop in front of the porch. Laying on the horn, he yelled at her, "Get in."

She took her time descending the stairs, never taking her eyes off Brick, smiling in a knowing way that unsettled his nerves more than the simple gesture should have. She was disheveled and had made no effort to straighten her clothes. As soon as she was seated, Jonathan Wingate peeled out, gouging deep ruts in the yard as he sped off. Cassie's eyes never left Brick's face and her smile never wavered.

"And the white knight is talking backwards and the red queen's off with his head."

He sat on the porch steps for a moment, reliving the experience in his mind. The pain had found relief in some dark recess, but the memories were as fresh as a new cut, bleeding into the present as she forced him to remember.

He started to climb the steps and was struck with a bolt of vertigo that brought him to his knees. The light faded and grew dim, the trees leeched of color, and the landscape turned barren. He must have lost consciousness for a moment; he was surprised to find himself sprawled on the stairs feeling empty and adrift.

The tingling began in earnest, the vibrations giving him strength enough to stand. He staggered up the last few steps and into the house, locking the door for the very first time. He stumbled to the couch and passed out cold.

Two

I woke up feeling unbalanced with a bitchin' headache. The recent scene played over in my mind in slow motion like an old newsreel in black and white. Coffee and aspirin, my antidote for all that ails me. When I checked my watch, I was shocked to see that I had lost an hour. Slowly my mind began to clear, and I felt a little like my old self again. I refilled my cup and went back to the porch, unhinged to find the front door locked. The mid-morning sun cast a brilliant glow over the land, and the scene before my eyes was serene and calm once again without the dark recriminations of my past interfering. I kept shaking my head, still unsure of the recent episode and its meaning. *Goodbye Mrs. Wingate and I hope you suffer as I have.* I couldn't ignore the premonition, but hadn't a clue as to what was coming; if I did, I would have left right then.

I shook it off and started the deep breathing program I'd been working on. I was proud of myself. In the old days I probably would have yanked him from the car and beat him senseless. Maybe I am growing up, finally mellowing with age. I sure got to him anyway; it looked like he believed what I said might be true. I hope it eats him like acid in the gut.

"Remember what the door mouse said: feed your head."

I knew it was a scam from the beginning, but I had no idea of the depth of her thinking. It didn't matter—she was wrong again. Wrong to think I hadn't covered my tracks with the IRS and wrong to think I would give her a nickel after what she'd done.

Before the duo arrived, I'd packed plenty of ammo, spring water, granola bars, and now added half a thermos of coffee. Then I set off for the range. The day became spectacular as the sun rolled merrily across the sky on its journey to its nightly death. The air so clean and sweet I could taste it. The smell of fresh-cut pine and pitch a comforting cloud that permeated the land. A few wispy clouds were taking shape, making me think that this could be a special sunset. I wasn't in a hurry, as I needed to breathe away the tension.

I made frequent stops to fill the bird feeders along the way and sat awhile on an old stump, still trying to clear my mind. It's hard to shoot accurately with a fogged brain.

I started walking lazily along, thinking about the last twenty years and the fate that had worked its way into my life and changed me.

For most of those years I moved around a lot and found the world had shrunk. I had two long-term relationships and must have whored around with a hundred more women. They all left. I finally figured out whom to blame and she had just returned to torture me further. I gave up on finding anyone else about the time I quit working. Truth is, I stopped all enterprise. Calling myself an entrepreneur, I sold what I called commodities; you do the math. Although, I did clean up once selling security systems. It was a good ride but I felt too old for any of that shit anymore. Besides, I knew I'd been lucky. And there was Jesus always at the back of my mind, haunting my every decision. I had plenty of money and eventually everybody goes down. It seems I quit just in time.

As I strolled along, I would stop and try to see it the way Cassie had. The old cabin still stood at the foot of the hill. I didn't know what to do with it, but I couldn't bring myself to tear it down. It was a simple four-room square building but sturdy, made of pine logs and tar with a high-sloped slate roof and river rock fireplace and chimney. It was constructed in the early thirties to withstand the elements. There was this old cast-iron woodstove that cranked out heat like a blast furnace and the place was well insulated. I lived in it for the first year while we built the house.

The pole barn, garage, and storage sheds were all part of a complex that blended together with the natural landscape. It worked and I was proud of my creation. All that was missing was a woman's touch. Might never happen.

I continued my trek to the range, stopping to move a branch or smell a new wildflower and just to breathe the fresh sweet air. My shoulders had relaxed and I had that loose easy feeling when worry and tension take a vacation. Using a handgun didn't come easy for me. It took a bit of experimentation to understand the equation. I'm left-handed, but right-eye dominant, so it becomes an unnatural stance and grip. That's why I like it—I have to concentrate. It makes me forget my surroundings. I was trying to breathe my way into that relaxing shooters calm where I exhale as I squeeze the trigger as I strolled through the stand of red pines. The range is just on the other side in a clearing that faces a small hill. I was almost there.

That's when he shot me.

Three

I heard the sound before I felt the impact, the sharp crack of a small caliber rifle. It sounded like a .22 fired close by. I've been in gunfights before, most south of the border where the law's what you make it.

If you stop to think, you're dead. Move and drop down is the way to survive. I threw myself to the right, flat on my belly; my right arm became trapped beneath my body. It wasn't my shooting arm and that mattered because any delay could be critical. Reaching behind me, the pistol came free easy enough. I couldn't believe the dumb fuck shot me! You don't go after a man like me with a popgun; he should have hired a pro.

Looking up, I could see him stumbling through the trees like a drunken fawn, all arms and legs akimbo. It was Jonathan fucking Wingate III all right and he was walking toward me. Was he coming to finish me? Well, he finally grew some balls, but this was really stupid. Old and mellow or not, nobody comes after Brick Winslow with a gun, not if they have half a brain.

It was awkward shooting from this position—one-handed through the trees, unbalanced and sprawled sideways. That's what I blamed for missing my mark.

The shot took him high in the right shoulder and he went down hard. The money shot is center mass and that's where I was aiming. Of course it didn't matter. I could have hit him anywhere and he would have gone down.

The first rule of the jungle is bring a canon to a gunfight; bring something bigger if you've got it. I learned this early—Charlie taught me. The round I hit him with is the only one I use, a .45 caliber 165 grain Hydra-Shok. I knew he wouldn't get back up. The Kimber Gold Match pistol that I carry is amazingly accurate for a .45, and I'm usually pretty good with it. The hollow point expands with fragments, sending shards of lead in a wide pattern.

I rolled slightly to my left, freeing my right arm, and reached back to feel my ass. The bullet had hit me in the right buttock. I searched with my fingers until I located the wound. Not bad, the bullet entered the fleshy part of my butt and there was a small hole in my jeans trickling blood down my leg. I'd live; he might not.

Before getting up, I yanked my cell out of my right front pocket and called 911. It was connected to Summerdale emergency. This is the closest town with facilities, a few miles north.

"I'm twelve miles south on postal route 7 just off County Road 6, marker 647. There's been a hunting accident. We have two men injured, one pretty bad; you need to send help. Two ambulances if you have them."

"What's your name, sir?"

I hung up or they would have kept me on the line asking questions I couldn't answer.

Rising up a little shaky, I hurried over to Jack. Lots of blood but it wasn't spurting. He was shaking from shock. I knew he wouldn't last if I didn't stop the bleeding. Tearing my shirt off, I stuck it in the wounded shoulder and tied it as tight as I could.

I heard Cassie yelling something in the distance. Fuck her, I didn't have time for her bullshit and I didn't know what role she played in this madness.

I took off jogging back to my place, limping visibly; I could feel the bullet lodged against my pelvis. After picking up my emergency kit, I returned as fast as I could. Cassie was there, holding and rocking her husband and sobbing. Her dress was covered in his blood. Pushing her roughly aside, I talked as I worked. I removed the bloody shirt with my knife and replaced it with as much gauze as I had, wrapping the bandage around his body and tying it as tight as possible. I had to move him around; as I did, he groaned in pain. Fuck him too—I was saving his life and screw gentle. He would have bled out if I didn't act fast.

Cassie was screaming at me. When I finished with him, I shook her by the shoulders. "Stop it, you stupid bitch!" I yelled. "Listen to me. I called the cops and an ambulance. They'll be here soon. I don't know what you two were up to, but he tried to kill me."

I grabbed her shoulders again and shook her to get her attention, her mind focused elsewhere. "The cops and ambulance are on the way. When they get here, you both need to have your story straight. You don't know me. You were taking a drive and he got out to shoot squirrels. You didn't know this was private land, okay … okay?" I had to shout in her face. She nodded her head once.

"Now shut up! He'll live; he shot me first. Do you understand?" She nodded again and I hoped she would do what I told her.

She was still weeping when we heard the sirens. "Stay with him. I'll go out to the road and flag them in."

Having just made it to the entrance as they arrived, I waved my arms. The trek to the road had taken me a while as the limp became pronounced the more I tried to run. Covered with dust from the speeding vehicles, I was coughing and my ass had started to hurt. The sheriff's car was first. He knew me and skidded to a stop, spraying dirt in a rooster tail back above the roof of the car. Third time this morning and it pissed me off the first time. He rolled his window down and I was at the door …

"What the fuck, Brick?"

"I'm shot in the ass and there's another man down in the woods a piece, maybe a couple hundred yards; there was a hunting accident. He looks bad. I can lead you there," I said, pointing.

"If you're shot, I don't want you in my car bleeding all over the back seat," the sheriff said. I knew it was his personal car and that he didn't like me much. He's a miserable fuck. No love lost between us.

He didn't wait for me and took off fast down the rutted trail. I went back to the ambulance, which had just pulled up. They put me in back and a medic started fussing with the wound. I figured the sheriff could follow the sound of Cassie's wailing and find them easily enough. He could deal with the asshole bleeding out in the trees.

When the ambulance pulled back closer to where Jack was, the sheriff was out poking and sifting. There wasn't anything to find.

The medic treating me went to help his partner and when they saw the bandages I'd applied, they grabbed the stretcher and loaded him.

The sheriff pointed in my direction and said, "This one doesn't look too bad. Can you patch him up enough to ride to the hospital with me?"

Minutes later, I was in the back of the sheriff's car and we were headed to the hospital. I had surrendered my gun to the medic, who gave it to the sheriff. It sat on the seat next to the big man, riding shotgun. I kept my eye on the gun. I wanted it back but now wasn't a great time to bring it up.

"Okay, what happened?" he asked me.

I gave him my abbreviated version, stating that I didn't know much. "Just walking the property when somebody shot me," I said. "I was lying on my face and shot back to let them know that I was out here. Lucky I hit anything … hitting him was an accident." Everybody carries a gun in these woods and shooting back at someone who just shot you should be acceptable.

The sheriff was watching me suspiciously through the rearview mirror, but he didn't grill me further. He'd been leery of me since I moved here and I know he'd checked me out. "When they finish with you at the hospital, I'll want a written report," he said.

We rode the rest of the way in silence. We weren't friends and I know how cops think. He would grill Jonathan and Cassie, and collect evidence before he pushed me any farther, then try his best to catch me in a lie. The less I said the better.

At the hospital, I had to wait until they stabilized Jack before they had time for me. When they did, they gave me a local anesthetic and took the bullet out of my ass. Stitched the hole and administered some ointments and shots for infection, finally taping a large bandage over the wound. At least they gave me some Oxys.

I was there about four hours before I found out his condition. They had me on my stomach naked from the waist down for an extraordinary amount of time. The smell of disinfectant, alcohol, bleach, and death was making me nauseous. I thought at first they were just busy; after an hour I figured they forgot about me.

I was about to start screaming for someone when a cute nurse, petite and perky, sauntered in the room. Her name tag read Jeanie; she said she had to do a final examination. She began by massaging both of my buns, kneading and almost caressing.

"Say Jeanie, are you almost finished? Can I get dressed and leave?"

"You could have left an hour ago, sweet cakes."

"Why the hell did you keep me then?"

"I've been bringing the young nurses in for a look at that sweet, tight ass."

"How many?"

"So far ten, it's shift change. I let them stare for a few seconds or a full minute depending on what favors I can expect."

"You're a pervert, Jeanie."

"I know, ain't it great? If you get popped in the other cheek, I'll insist on home health care." She was grinning. I heard her laugh echo down the corridor as she walked away to continue her rounds.

23

The sheriff left word for me that we would talk tomorrow. Cassie must have corroborated my story. I stuck around for a while chatting up the girls on staff. They like me, so I flirted and squeezed out information, making it sound suggestive so we all laughed. Everyone in town likes me, at least most. I support local business. I'm charming. The girls tell me I'm good looking. But the real reason for my favor is that I buy a few rounds for the crowd at the local watering hole every time I come to town. I'm also an easy touch for local charities. I sponsor a high school football team and buy all their gear. In other words, I buy their affection and am not ashamed. Coming to a small town as a stranger isn't easy.

I don't think I'm a bad guy. I've done some bad things but always to people who deserved it. I've served my country, pay my taxes, and work at being a model citizen. But … down deep I know that I have been responsible for people I love getting hurt, and Jesus is never far from my mind and heart. Hence, here I am squirreled away from the ones I love doing penance for my transgressions.

Before I left the hospital, I found out that Jack was too traumatized to talk to the sheriff; he was heavily sedated on morphine, his shoulder a mess. He would need several surgeries to correct the damage and might not regain full use of the arm. He'd lost a lot of blood, so transfusions through the night were necessary. They had a chopper ready to pick him up in the morning and take him to a hospital in the Cities. I guess he was stable enough, if he could last the night.

In short, it would be a bitch healing and he would be in a lot of pain. Good. This last was a moot point. Finding what I needed to know, there wasn't any reason to stick around.

Just as I was about to leave, Cassie came down the hallway from the operating room, her face a mask showing no emotion or recognition. Her clothes were bloody and torn. I don't remember that happening—she was bloody from his wound, but when I last saw her the clothes were fine. Her face turned and she stared straight into my eyes. Her gaze never wavered as she approached and when she got close enough, she slapped me across the face as hard as she could, twice. It stung like hell but I refused to acknowledge it or retaliate.

"You bastard! You didn't have to shoot him—it was a mistake," she screamed and then she spit in my face. I turned and walked away.

One of my sometime girlfriends gave me a ride home and then wanted to stay and mother me. Her name was Mary (I thought of her as Mary Poppins—way too perky, like Jeanie); she was around my age. Nothing serious between us, just an occasional outing for dinner and drinks. Some comfort and release. What my granddad Artie called "a bit of the old slap and tickle." I convinced her that I was going to take a handful of the pain pills and sleep for ten hours. After a few minutes, she left. I didn't plan to take any pills tonight; it's a long drive and I need my wits for a while longer.

Four

It was almost time to act. I would wait another hour. I was concealed in the woods behind the hospital. Dressed in black from head to toe, invisible in the dark. Still hoarding a large stash from the old days, I had breached the hidden cavern in the woods behind my place and retrieved what was needed. It was in the black fanny pack that I wore in front. My ass was throbbing, but I tried to ignore it.

By 3:00 a.m. the shift had finished changing; it was a skeleton crew and they would be busy this time of night. I would slip in the back. I knew the layout and what room he was in—the girls told me earlier. The hypodermic filled with morphine was protected in cotton wadding in the pack; I was ready.

I couldn't let the asshole live. He would be reported as heart failure due to a massive chest wound, shock, and loss of blood. There wouldn't be an autopsy. Hick town, hick sheriff and resources, so there wouldn't be an in-depth investigation either. It would be another tragic hunting accident. I'll try to keep my name out of the papers. I should be in the clear.

He did come after me with a gun. The next time, he might hire a pro. No, this has to end here and now. Nobody hunts Brick Winslow with a gun and lives to talk about it. I might have mellowed with age and all that happy horseshit, but I still have my principles.

Cassie will find another rich dude. She's not old; she's still hot and always lands on her feet. Jack wasn't much of a dad to the kid anyway. He must be about eighteen by now. Kids are resilient at that age.

When this blows over, I think I'll take a little vacation. The woman Cassie referred to was Dawn, ex-Playboy Bunny and a sweet girl. She told me she had rediscovered her sexuality, and she extended an invitation for me to help her explore it. I admit I was enticed. I have good friends from the old days who live near her, around Bend. I can call … No … after what I did, better to show up unannounced. The thought of her blond hair and perfect body was more than enough motivation and I had to go somewhere to cool off. These good friends happen to be the loved ones mentioned earlier. The very people I was avoiding. Guilt.

Whatever happens, I'll stay in Oregon for a few weeks, take a suite in one of the resorts. If the papers in the Cities print my name, I'll need to get away from here and see if anybody else takes a run at me. I can rig the property so I'll know if someone was here. I used to sell security so I have the equipment. I'll be alright. I've been lucky so far.

Five

When Brick woke at dawn the next morning, dread and guilt settled into his bones the way a cold misty fog encompasses a swamp. He lay in bed covered with a sheen of sweat. He had spent the night at the old cabin—he couldn't explain why; it just felt right. As he collected his thoughts, he felt sick at what he'd done. He had handled it wrong from the beginning. Jack wasn't the enemy; it was about Cassie, the only woman he had ever loved.

As the mist cleared, he dragged himself to the bathroom and puked until dehydrated. On his knees staring into the putrid yellow of the porcelain throne, he was aware of his surroundings as never before. The tub was cracked and worn, the grout stained with mold. The floor tilted slightly to his left and Brick noticed the cracks in the tiles and the shabby ancient wallpaper, sagging torn and limp. What only yesterday he thought of as cozy and quaint now appeared decrepit and old, the way he felt.

The pain in his rump had settled like an abscessed tooth. He made coffee but couldn't drink it; even the smell made him sick, so he settled for cold water. The scenes of the previous day spun through his mind at warp speed and he had trouble accepting the truth. What happened to him? All the inroads he'd made in self-improvement were ground underfoot with rage and hate. He thought he had put all that behind him over the last couple of years, but now he could see that it was still seething beneath the surface. All it took was his ex-wife to bring it back with a vengeance. *Why did they have to come here? Why did I lose my cool? What the hell is the matter with me?*

It took an hour before he had his breathing under control and started to think straight. He desperately wanted a pain pill but knew he couldn't afford to cloud his mind. Brick had a full day ahead and too much to do. He ate a piece of dry toast and drank one cup of coffee. He managed to choke down both and they were gurgling like sour wine in his belly. He showered, dressed, and was on the road by 7:00, headed to town.

The first stop was for the morning papers. Brick was relieved to see that he wasn't in the news. Next was the sheriff's office; he still had to file the shooting report and see about his Kimber.

Sheriff Welsh was still in a bad mood and said, "I was going to give you another hour and then head out to pick you up."

Brick was quiet and respectful as he filled out the report and signed it. He waited until Sonny was satisfied with the paperwork, then asked, "Could I have my gun back now?

The sheriff just sat there glaring at him for a little too long; finally, he said, "I received confirmation this morning that it's registered to you. I also saw that you have a license to carry a concealed weapon in Minnesota. I reckon it's up to me if I want to honor that here in Wisconsin. Maybe tomorrow on the gun; don't stray too far, you hear?"

Brick knew that Sonny was blowing smoke up his ass but he took a sincere tone as he replied, "Thanks, sheriff, whatever you need. I'll be around town for a couple of hours and then head back to my place; I've got some work to do. I sure would appreciate having that gun back. It cost me a month's pay and it's the only protection I've got out at the place. If I don't hear from you, I'll just come back tomorrow if that's alright?"

"I said come back tomorrow and I'll see." He didn't look up.

Brick cursed under his breath as he left. "That fucking hillbilly better give me that gun or I'll take it from the fat fuck." Of course he had an arsenal at his command but the Kimber was special, a thing he had about luck and fate. He'd had a gunsmith rework the action and set the trigger pull right at three pounds; it was worth over four grand. When trouble started, that gun was the reason he was still here. He bought it well before the action started—the action being the real reason for the rabid attachment. Brick felt that gun as an extension of his left hand.

He tried to push it from his mind as he went about his errands. He had already formed a plan and needed supplies. He shopped the local hardware store for over an hour and loaded a couple hundred dollars' worth of gear in the back of his pickup. Next he stopped for a haircut and over tipped the dude as usual. Just before leaving town, he bought a couple days' worth of groceries and headed back to his spread. It was noon by the time he returned and realized he was starving. Wishing he would have stopped at the Broken Wheel for a burger and a beer, he made two salami sandwiches and settled for water to drink. Brick was finally feeling human again and the wheels in his head were turning; he knew that survival might require several quick moves ahead on the chessboard of life.

His ass was still throbbing and was making it hard to think straight. He gave in and took two pain pills, then started his preparations. His truck was a two-year-old Ford F150 extended cab, solid black and filthy. Brick bought it new and hadn't washed it since. He wanted anonymity, nothing flashy or bright, so nobody would notice or remember it later. Even so, it was top of the line with all the bells and whistles. Four-wheel drive with black leather interior; captain's chairs, CD and iPod, Bluetooth, radar detector, GPS and police radio.

He spent another ten grand having some guys he knew in Denver add the extras. There was a false bottom below the truck's bed that slid out and had enough room to carry his small arsenal of weapons. There were also two hidden safes, one in the back cab and the other under the driver's seat. They were both invisible unless you knew they were there and both had fingerprint-recognition locks for instant access. He kept cash in the back and the Kimber up front. While the Denver guys were at it, they added an extra security precaution in the form of an ignition cutout. If anyone tried to steal the truck, it wouldn't start without the code.

He could and had lived in that truck.

He spent the rest of the afternoon setting the security perimeter. Motion detectors and carefully secured cameras strategically positioned earlier needed to be activated with fresh batteries. Everything was wireless; they fed monitors in a closed entertainment center in the living room. From there the alarm was wired into his bedroom in the form of a flashing light, no sound alarm. He was back in the old cabin, as this was still where his first line of defense was formed. He would leave the main house brightly lit as a diversion.

Brick bought the place because he had relatives from his mother's side living nearby. Back then he had good reason to be paranoid. During the last year he had become lax about security because the abundant wildlife on the property kept setting off alarms in the night, interrupting his sleep. Now sleep would be a luxury.

Two of his cousins helped him with the work he wanted done. He trusted one of them as much as he trusted anyone. Digger was smart and could build anything. He was a well digger by trade, but in the current economy work was scarce and his equipment was mortgaged to the hilt. He had a wife and two kids, so the work Brick offered was more than welcome. They sweated like pigs for four months, but when they were finished Brick rewarded him with a generous bonus in addition to the escalated salary he had promised.

Digger was a fine family man and as reliable as a Swiss watch. He stood five foot ten and went a rangy 185 pounds, straight black hair and soulful brown eyes. His hands were huge in proportion to the rest of him and heavily callused from a lifetime of toil. His given name was Percy Patrick; Brick could never understand why anyone would name a kid

Percy. But then again, there were reasons folk didn't use that handle. He was a gentle man but when leaned on could erupt like a whirling dervish. His wife, Lisa, was a distraction. At first she would bring lunch for them all, but he had to halt that practice. She was hot as hell and the work suffered.

Tim Scallion, better known as Slide, was a different animal—6'3" and 245 pounds of muscle overlaid with a generous coating of fat. His long, stringy black hair seemed perpetually greasy and hung in his face. He had squinty little black eyes and a flattened nose. He was lazy, but strong as an ox. Brick didn't understand why his wife stayed, probably for their little girl. Slide was a worker bee but had a big mouth.

While Digger made the plans and crafted the work, Slide did what he was told but couldn't wait for quitting time and his first drink. They made for a strange couple, but Brick could understand Digger's loyalty, as he possessed the same quality. The three of them labored over the summer to finish the work Brick had envisioned. An extra benefit in working for Brick, he always paid in cash.

Now, Brick tested all the equipment and, with a few minor adjustments, finished by sunset. He threw a frozen pizza in the oven and opened a beer. He started to write a contingency plan on a legal pad, meticulously going over each step, making minor corrections as he went. He fell into a deep sleep by 9:00, confident that he would be alerted in the night if intruders approached.

The sun was still in hiding when Brick started the next day. First thing he did was drive to town and stop at Annie's for a paper and breakfast. It's the place to be for comfort food, open seven days a week and serving from 5:00 a.m. to 9:00 p.m.; the café rocked for most of the day. Located along Front Street in the middle of town, it was tucked into a block of interconnected buildings. There were ten counter stools and twenty or so tables served from a pint-sized kitchen in the back. Both restrooms were one-holers so there was usually a line; go easy on the coffee or do the dance by the door.

The décor, if you could call it that, was rustic—cutesy gingerbread with platitudes framed and hung from floor to ceiling. The smell of fresh ground coffee and grease blanketed the town.

Annie worked the front days and manhandled her customers where and when she wanted. No requests, go where she said or out the door. She was built like a fireplug, wide and swarthy, standing just tall enough to lean over the counter with her thinning brown-streaked grey hair and scream orders at the cook a foot away. She was comic relief and played to the crowd. Smiling at Annie's was mandatory. If you're in a shitty mood when you walk in, you'll still somehow leave in stitches.

Buried on page four of the local section of the *Minneapolis Tribune* was the article entitled "Man shot and killed in rural hunting accident."

FUCK!

"Are you okay, Brick?" Dory, the waitress, was standing at his table; a deep frown creased her forehead.

"Sorry, just something in the paper that took me by surprise. I apologize for the outburst."

Still looking concerned, Dory said, "You look white as a sheet— are you sure you're alright? It's not the food, is it?"

"No, it's good; could I have some more coffee?"

"Sure, coming right up."

Dory always worried about Brick. She was Slide's wife and she mothered him because he was so alone; plus, he always found some work for her slacker husband.

They had published his name and gave the location of the town, said it happened on his land. It couldn't get any worse. Brick's death sentence was signed and staring back at him. He was fucked. The problem with the past—it always shows at a shitty time. Got to move. He pushed the food away and downed the coffee, left money for his bill and a big tip on the table, and rushed out. It was time to stop fucking around.

Circuit judge Oliver Patrick, his uncle and friend, was in chambers before court reading legal briefs.

"Hi Uncle Ollie," Brick said, as he stood in the open doorway. "Have you got a minute?"

Looking at his watch, the judge said, "About five minutes at most. What can I do for you this morning, son?"

Entering the chambers, Brick gestured to the chair.

"Sure, have a seat," the judge said as he leaned back and folded his hands on his belly tucked beneath the desk. Judge Patrick was a tall slender man with luminescent blue eyes and a shock of full snowy white hair. He had a regal stature and grace. A thin, wistful Colonel Sanders.

Brick hesitated, then said, "The sheriff told me I wasn't charged with anything in that poor fellow's shooting … I mean it was an accident. I really want to get my pistol back and I was hoping you might put in a good word for me. The sheriff doesn't seem to like me much."

"Old Sonny doesn't like anybody all that much, but he's a good lawman and we get along." Ollie smiled as he said this; Brick knew that the judge would never disparage an elected official. "I'm going to see him later this morning in court. I'll have a word with him."

Six

He knew he should gather his supplies and head out, but he wanted that gun and he had other obligations. He returned to round up the goods for an extended trip and to retrieve some cash for later that day. Revisiting the cavern on his ATV, he entered the cave with a battery-powered lantern. He was impressed by all he had accumulated, admiring the craftsmanship of the space.

He loaded two 12-gauge shotguns, an MP5 submachine gun, a sniper's rifle with scope, and two more handguns. Threw in plenty of ammo for all and felt he had as much firepower as he could use effectively.

He counted $100,000 in $100s, $50s, and $20s; Brick always kept $200,000 in cash in the cavern. He put $30,000 in his pocket; the other $70,000 would go in the truck safe. He would need most of the cash later. If his trip became extended, he could access his numbered accounts in the Caymans from his laptop. Money wasn't an issue, more of a worry. He had too much.

The cavern itself was a natural cave recessed into the base of a large outcropping of rock. Brick discovered it by accident when roaming his newly acquired property. After eliminating the large family of bats, he brought Digger to the site and explained his mission. It took some big equipment; the two of them worked for weeks to turn the cave into an amazing structure. Digger framed a two-inch-thick steel doorway into the mouth of the cave and engineered an enormous boulder to slide on steel rails, concealing the entrance. Perfectly balanced and featured a hidden release lock. Slip the release and move the boulder with one finger, and access the steel door with a fingerprint lock. It was exactly what Brick had envisioned.

Digger was the only person who shared the knowledge of not only the cavern but the hidden tunnel. Slide, along with a couple of other cousins, pitched in to build the garage and pole barn. A full crew had been hired to build the main house.

Brick's stomach lurched as he reminisced on their accomplishment. He swore to himself that he'd return. With reality jolting him back to the present, he loaded all the gear into the ATV and headed back to the cabin. He should have left then.

Packing economically, he loaded the duffle in the bed of the truck, adding dry food stuffs and a few extras; he settled the weapons in the under-bed compartment and the cash in the rear safe. The truck's bed was covered with a hardtop and locked, but this could be burgled, so only expendables went there.

It was after 3:00 and he still had to visit the sheriff. He drove straight to the office, but Sonny wasn't there; Brick waited. At 4:30 Sonny finally sauntered in and gave him a hard stare.

"So you talked to the judge about that gun."

"It just came up—he's my uncle and we talk regularly."

The sheriff reached into the drawer and withdrew the pistol; he laid it on the desk and said, "You better watch your skinny ass. I'm keeping an eye on you."

As much as he hated sucking up, Brick said, "Thanks sheriff, I'll take care with it; you can count on it." *Count on a boot up your ass, you prick.*

Lunch was a non-event and by now Brick was starving, so he stopped at the Broken Wheel for the cheeseburger and fries he craved— grease and alcohol combination lunch and dinner. The Wheel was dark and dank with the leeched-in odor of stale beer and cigarettes. A windowless cinder-block building set off on a side road, it was decorated in battered wood furniture and stained linoleum floors. The main feature was a long mahogany bar with old license plates, milk cans, and other junk hanging from the ceiling; sports paraphernalia plastered the walls. There was a preponderance of Packer gear, ranging from number four jerseys to helmets and autographed footballs. At the end of the bar stood a small bandstand that featured live local rock bands on the weekends. Shabby as it appeared, the Wheel was the place to be in this small town and always drew a large crowd. The food was surprisingly good.

He had an alternative motive for the stop other than nourishment. He wanted to contact his cousin's wife. She wasn't there so after he ate, he went to his house. Digger's truck was in the drive when Brick cruised by. She answered on the second ring. "Lisa honey, it's Brick. I need to see you right away and Digger can't know. Can you get away?"

"Alright, Julie. I'll be there in ten minutes," she spoke into the phone. Then he heard her call out to her husband, "Digger, my sister needs some help with her taxes. I'll only be gone for a while; watch the kids." She whispered, "Where?"

"Meet me in the bank parking lot around back."

His truck was out of sight from the road. Brick waited, nervously tapping his nails on the wheel. Lisa pulled in a few minutes later in her red Camaro. As she exited the car, Brick wondered once again what a woman like that was doing in the sticks. She stood tall and straight with a long blond cap of silky hair, deep-blue eyes, and proud features set in a flawless complexion. Dressed in skin-tight jeans with legs long enough to climb and a slinky black tank, she exuded sexuality. Having kids hadn't hurt her figure any; her pendulous breasts rode high on her chest, which tapered to a slim waist before flaring once again in shapely hips and those incredible legs. Where she traveled, men's eyes trailed close behind.

Her natural gait featured swaying hips and Brick admired her beauty as she opened the door and sat down next to him. Her face was lit with mirth as she watched him from her perch. She was Scandinavian pretty.

"Don't you want to know why I asked you here?" Brick asked.

She leaned close, enveloped in jasmine-scented aromas, and in her thick, husky voice replied, "You'll get to it."

Lisa worked as a real estate agent for the largest firm in northern Wisconsin and could sell flies to a mule. Her maiden name was Stark and she kept it after the wedding, claiming she already had business cards. Lisa was the smartest person around and Brick knew it. Property sales were in the tank, along with Digger's business; the current recession affected rural families more than most. But nothing seemed to dampen Lisa's spirit or humor. She sat at ease while waiting for a reply.

"How's the family doing?"

Lisa laughed. "You asked me out here alone in the dark to discuss the family condition?" She leaned in closer and, with her mouth touching his ear, said, "I thought you had something more intimate in mind? Don't you think I'm pretty?"

Brick squirmed in his seat and replied, "Digger might be one of the only friends I have left!" He reached in the side pocket of the truck's door and retrieved a thick envelope. Leaning away from her, he thrust it in her lap.

Lisa ripped it open and stared at it for a full minute before she spoke. "What the fuck is the matter with you!" she screamed. "I could have any man I want. I come on to you and you mumble some shit about loyalty and turn me down? Jesus Christ, Brick, I don't get you—this is more cash than I've seen in my life and you just shove it at me and don't say a fucking word. What am I supposed to think?"

"Sorry, I didn't handle that well. I don't think you're pretty—you're gorgeous, stunning really, and you are so hot. You make me fucking nervous, okay? Don't tempt me."

There were tears in her eyes as she shook her head and stared down at her lap.

"I'm trying hard to change, be better," Brick continued. "Digger confided in me; he said he was broke and was afraid he'd lose his equipment. He's too proud to take that money, so I'm giving it to you."

"How much is in here?" she asked.

"You can count it later; it doesn't matter."

"Goddamn it, how much?

"Twenty thousand but it doesn't matter. I need to go away for a while and this should hold you over until I come home."

"We can't pay you back."

"It's not a loan—it's a gift."

"Why, you don't even want to fuck me?"

"You are not to tell Digger; say you made a big closing on a mansion on Whidbey Island or something … And that's not true, about not wanting you; I just don't want to ruin lives again."

"This has to do with that man you shot, doesn't it?"

"Maybe."

"You're a mysterious dude, Brick Winslow. Men fear you, women want you, and nobody knows shit about you."

"What's to know?"

"You don't work, have tons of cash, and we don't know where you come from or why you're here. Sonny Welsh has been investigating you since day one and he can't find shit. You're alone most of the time. Those bikers busted up the Wheel, not your rodeo—you were new in town. They didn't even look your way, yet you told them to leave. When they laughed and came at you with broken beer bottles, you wiped up the floor with those assholes and never broke a sweat. You think we don't notice the slab of iron glued to your hip? How can you sit there and say what's to know?"

"I won some money, inherited some, worked for most, and the army taught me a few things. Any more questions? What about you? An intelligent, beautiful woman living in a small town when you look like you should be in Hollywood."

"Been there, done that."

She opened the door to leave and then paused a minute, thinking. She moved back close and said, "Let me get this straight—this much money but I don't get any sex, right?"

"Yes … I mean, you don't have to do anything for the money."

"It feels like I'm being cheated. I think I should get the money and a lot of sex. I mean, it's a lot of money. I'm really good if that's what's got you worried."

"No Lisa, I'm sure you are."

"Are you really that dense? When an older man gives money to a younger, married woman, he wants to screw her. She at least feels like she earned it. This is cheating me. I feel rejected."

"I'm sorry, not when the money is for the husband."

"Well, at least a little quick kiss then."

"Okay."

The kiss was neither little nor quick. He finally broke it and pulled back.

"Whew, that's what I thought. If you change your mind, I'll give you back some of the money."

"You should go home."

She looked reluctant as she slid back to the door. When she opened the door and got out, she turned back and said, "Make it a regular thing and I'll give all the money back." She smiled, flipped her hair over her shoulder, and gave a little hip bump as she walked away.

Seven

The storm was approaching out of the west and was moving fast. As the lightning raced to catch the thunder, huge raindrops pelted the windshield of the truck. Gestures of goodwill left Brick spent and weary. *Why doesn't it ever go the way I think? Damn Lisa.* It was easy in his mind—tell her about the trip, give her the money, she thanks you and you're on your way. He could still taste her; he smiled. She had a great attitude. *Women, I'll never ...*

Blinded by sheets of debris-streaked water punishing his vision, Brick finally eased into the garage. Too long, he should have been back hours ago. Almost midnight and visibility at ten feet, he desperately wanted to leave but things weren't ready. It was all moving so fast.

Slogging through the rain, he was soaked to the skin on the short jog to the cabin. It was stupid to leave and dumb to stay, his careful plan gone awry in the first phase. Decision made, he donned full rain gear and made four more trips to the truck, adding extras with every step. Shapes became blurred; he needed sleep.

Rigging the double-barreled shotgun was easy. He had perfected the triggering device last year; it was tested and true. With the gun loaded with turkey shot and aimed head high at the only door, he was ready for unexpected visitors. Two-second delay after the door opens, one trigger pull, another two seconds and the second trips. Should give him a couple of extra minutes; he hoped he didn't need them. They should go to the main house first and bypass the cabin; that's what he was planning for.

Brick lay on the bed fully dressed, his boots handy. The MP5 he retrieved was inches from his fingers and the big pistol under his pillow. The rain sloughing off the roof lulled him into instant sleep, the rest lasting three hours.

The alarm light next to the bed flashed incessantly for ten seconds before Brick sat bolt upright in bed and moved automatically; killing the lights, donning his boots and slipping into the rain-proof shooting jacket, pockets overflowing with magazines and ammunition. It was ten after three; he moved silently to his monitors in the main room of the cabin and noted that four had been tripped at 100 yards out—should give him seven minutes if they were cautious, less if they weren't.

With nerves taut as piano wire, Brick's mind cleared and the training and adrenaline took charge. His movements seemed choreographed as he pulled the trapdoor open under the throw rug in the kitchen floor. Descending the narrow stairs to the old root cellar below, with the Kevlar vest trailing behind him, he shot the bolt lock securing the trapdoor from the inside.

Working by flashlight, he slipped the jacket from his shoulders and donned the vest. Back in the jacket, he turned to the shelving unit against the far wall. The trip switch Digger designed worked the same as the one in the cavern and the shelf swung noiselessly aside. When he entered the tunnel, the shelf clicked shut behind him. Brick was in full combat mode; he knew it would be a fight for his life. He planned it like a military raid, one that Charlie would lead: be alert, don't try to get tricky, move fast, and assume your assigned position. Time is short; don't falter.

Brick moved along the confined tunnel in a crab-walk; it was too low to stand. At the end of his twenty-yard march, he stopped and waited. He removed the balaclava from his jacket and pulled it down over his head, leaving only his eyes exposed. An invisible ninja, black as night, crouched in the darkness at the foot of the short ladder with a hand on the panel above.

The illumination from his watch said five and a half minutes had passed since the alarm. The first shotgun blast was his signal; silently moving up into the soft rain, he stretched out on the ground behind a hundred-year oak and closed the lid to his hidden lair. A second later, he heard the blast from the scatter gun.

Excellent!

The diversion had accomplished its mission—focus attention on the interior of the cabin. His eyes sharp as he swiveled from side to side. The rain and wind subsided enough to have visibility to 75 feet. Faintly, he heard a whispering of Spanish.

His suspicions verified, it calmed rather than terrified him. It was time, inevitable really. Brick was tired of hiding; if he must do battle, he would be formidable. Only the final outcome uncertain, the enemy exposed. With a new sense of confidence, he ascended the big oak on the wooden slats that led to the concealed deer stand above.

Halfway to his destination, he froze. Automatic gunfire erupted inside the cabin—over fifty rounds exploded along with the sound of splintered wood. Brick realized his mistake; he should have known they would find the trapdoor. Now they knew he'd been there and found another exit. He began descending as two shadowy figures emerged on both sides of the house. They had discovered the only door was the front.

They signaled each other and started to fan out in positions on both sides of where he crouched above them. He fucked up once, but he couldn't be flanked. His left side was most exposed. Aiming chest and head high, he fired a burst from the MP5; the target dropped like a stone. Rolling left and back, he narrowly escaped a similar burst from the opposite side. Had to get off this deer stand. On the opposite side of the tree was a thick knotted rope. He reached out and snagged it one handed and slid down in a second. Knowing the terrain was an advantage and Brick moved to a slight rise in the thick wall of old-growth oaks.

Without knowing how many antagonists were still in pursuit, Brick held his position and let the enemy come to him. The air was eerily still and the rain had slowed to a slight drizzle when he heard movement back in the direction of his last pursuer. With all senses on high alert, Brick studied the landscape. He knew exactly what cover it would provide for an advancing attack. His gaze caught a sudden bulging at the base of a medium maple tree, as if the tree were growing a tumor at the trunk. Slowly the silhouette of a man became visible. Brick waited, forcing his breath into a slow, easy cadence and compelled himself into a patience he didn't feel.

As his confidence grew, the man emerged with his head and shoulders clearly visible in the rifle's sights. Gently squeezing the trigger with the tip of his index finger, Brick fired a short burst of gunfire. A scream pierced the night and the man crumpled like hot carbon paper. Brick moved back and then to his right and forward again because the natural move would be away from his victim.

Dead silence followed. He needed a better vantage point and retreated to his tree stand again. Brick climbed slowly, head swiveling from side to side. The rain erupted with a new fury, blurring sight. A stab of pain was followed by the sound of the rifle as Brick found himself airborne before landing on his belly, knocking the breath from his lungs.

From the pain Brick knew the shooter was to the left of him, but all was quiet as the water poured from above. He crawled on all fours around the tree's base and tried to locate the position of his attacker. Sight and sound were worthless in the face of the storm's wrath. How many were left? Brick thought two at most, but more likely just one or they both would have fired in unison. His best bet was to lie there and play dead.

Like divine intervention, a bolt of lightning illuminated the crouching figure running in Brick's direction. From his position behind the tree, Brick emptied a full clip at his target's groin. The man screamed in agony and collapsed twenty feet in front of him. As a punctuation point, the rain stopped. Brick snapped a fresh clip in the MP5 and approached cautiously.

Moaning in pain from a prone position, the wounded man was facedown. His gun two feet away. Brick regained his breath but the bruising in his ribs would follow him like a spurned lover for weeks. The vest had saved him from a possibly mortal wound and he knew his luck had held. He approached with the barrel of his weapon pointed directly at the man's head.

With the toe of his boot, Brick flipped the man to his back and said, "Nicky?" recognition registering in confusion. Nick Yablonski had soldiered with Brick and Charlie in Panama and Colombia. He was part of the secret mission that the squad had run for personal gain. His lower body was almost severed from the blast that caught him just below his vest. He was a goner for sure. Brick asked, "Why, Nick?"

With blood trickling from his lips, Nick managed a faint smile and said, "Sorry, man, but I needed the money. Fucking gun jammed or I would have taken you off that tree for good."

Brick asked, "Why would you work for that maniac?"

"Guy wants you real fucking bad—fifty grand worth. He'll keep sending troops, you know." He started coughing blood and it covered the top half of his chest.

"Yeah, sad you and I have to end like this; you should have asked me for the money." Brick raised the rifle and put a round in his forehead.

It couldn't have gone worse unless he was the one dead. He should have left; Brick knew if he kept making mistakes, he wouldn't survive. With new resolve he walked to the shed. The backhoe fired up on the second try. He hooked the cart up and started collecting bodies. Stripping

46

guns, cash, and wallets from the dead men, he dumped them unceremoniously into the trailer on top of each other. He walked through the yard very cautiously, making sure there weren't any surprises.

The trip took fifteen minutes, just off his property onto federal land. Digging in the soft soil with the powerful machine was quick and easy. With a building hatred burning him from the inside, he piled the dead bodies into the burgeoning hole and covered it while night slowly faded away and a glimmer of daylight shone on the horizon. He knew his past was back for the duration. Deep in his heart, he always knew it would come back. This was a wound that had festered too long; it was time to put an end to it now and forever.

Brick had to revisit the cavern one more time; this was war and he needed to be prepared. He liberated the Barrett 5.56 caliber machine gun with 10,000 rounds of ammunition and loaded that into the truck. By now, the dawn was breaking a rosy shade of coral and the raindrops glistened like tiny diamonds on the forest floor. Brick had one more stop to make before he began his long journey. But first, he set his booby-traps and made sure everything was shipshape. He thought he might have three to four hours before new troops were dispatched to his beautiful paradise and another five for the drive.

Eight

He drove slow without lights, listened and stopped, motor off. Quiet. His light knock on the back window brought the proper response and Digger looked out, coffee in hand, a goofy grin splitting his face.

"What's up, man?" the confused cousin asked.

"Digger, I need you to jack up my truck."

Digger looked perplexed but said, "Pull it around back. We can use the hoist; it's faster."

When they had the truck in the air, Brick lay on the floor creeper and slid under the truck with a trouble light. It took him less than a minute to locate the tracking device mounted on the chassis with a magnetic panel. His visitors had done what he would have and planted it before they breeched his cabin in case he got away.

Handing Digger the tracker along with a prepaid cell and his own phone, he said, "I want you to drive to Chicago as soon as you can, within the next hour please; this is crazy important. Here are two telephones, this first one I want you to keep. Drive to south Chicago with the second phone; do it early tomorrow morning, when they're sleeping. Find a house—it'll be a dump with a pit bull or some bad-ass dog chained in the yard, like a crack pad. Throw the phone somewhere it can't be seen. Throw the tracking unit in another seedy spot, and then drive back. It's about sixteen hours of driving round-trip. If you get tired, get a hotel room somewhere along the route, but only on the way back. Don't stop for long until you've gotten rid of both devices. Call me when you're done, please! I'm giving you $5,000 along with $500 for your expenses; that should cover it. There'll be a bonus of another five large if you can do this ASAP—like now."

"What the hell is happening, Brick?"

48

"Long fucking story, man. You don't want to know. I'm being hunted. It's the reason I'm here in the first place. They found me last night. These motherfuckers are bad news. I'm not going to bring any shit down on you and the family. Do this for me and be sure to stay away from my spread. Call immediately, I'll take care of you—you know that."

"I know. Stay safe—we'll say a prayer."

"Thanks."

Brick left before Lisa and the kids woke. He headed west by the northern route that he knew, taking I-94 through northwestern Minnesota, across North Dakota, and into Montana. At Billings, the interstate became I-90 and shifted north. At Butte, he'd need to make a decision and either veer north or south across the mountains into Idaho. He'd done it both ways and would decide when he arrived at that juncture. It was a long drive and Brick was in no hurry. He hummed along to the music as he drove, letting his mind wander. He thought back to how it all started and now the inevitable end. He wondered if he'd live to witness the conclusion.

Nine

The kid danced along the broad boulevard on his way home from school. He had a soccer ball he handled exclusively with his feet. Watching him was a pleasure; as he controlled the ball, he moved with the grace of a ballerina. He would stop, kick it straight in the air, and with his back to it switch from one foot to the next without ever missing a stroke. This was hallowed ground he cherished—he spent hours on this wide swath of lush grass.

He left the broad expanse of Summit Avenue, a two-lane street separated by an oversized median of grass and old-growth hardwood trees. It was lined with mansions beginning to end, including the F. Scott Fitzgerald home. There were many famous homes, as a plethora of the old robber barons converged here during the eighteenth and nineteenth centuries. What better place to keep an eye on their businesses of rail and lumber. Fur and commodity trade from the entire state passed by below the hill. He headed across the grounds to Ramsey Middle School. Closer to the playground, he saw there was a fight in progress. He kicked the ball up onto his shoulder and, holding it loosely with one hand, continued into the playground.

There were two kids fighting near the jungle gym. He loved to watch fights, in fact loved to fight—his whole family did. There was a tall, goofy looking kid who was being backed up by a much smaller opponent. The smaller kid had blood smeared across his nose and upper lip, but he was a tiger. The kid kept moving, jabbing, punching, and hitting hard, finding targets in the midsection. The tall kid tried to rain blows upon his head, back, and neck, but he was ineffectual. The smaller kid knew how to box; he took a stance and defended the blows.

Out of the side door, an older burly kid emerged. He looked over the situation and started to wade in; he was going to break this fight apart. Our spectator wouldn't have it. He stopped the kid with a look and a hand and said, "Let them fight it out." Then he turned to the two fighters and stared directly at the smaller kid. He said, "Kick the shit out of that wimp." Encouraged by the older boy, the smaller kid stepped in and delivered a left hook followed by a right uppercut that rocked the kid on his heels and may have broken a tooth. Then with a powerful left, thrown from the bottom of his feet, he connected with the tall boy's nose and blood poured down his face and shirt. He went down; fight over.

The burly boy who had tried to break it up led the tall kid back into the school. He was still bleeding and crying like a sissy. The burly one said, "We'll see the nurse."

After they left, the kid with the ball slapped the smaller one on the back and said, "It was a hell of a job; you're a tough little dude, aren't you?" Then without warning, the older kid dropped the ball at the feet of the younger boy and sprinted away; at thirty yards, he turned and said, "Kick it to me." The small kid was athletically gifted and made a perfect kick that descended lazily in front of the older kid, but it never hit the ground. The boy caught it with his toe and started moving down the street, juggling the ball in the air with his feet as he moved. He had a grace and rhythm seldom seen in any man, especially one so young. As he danced away, he yelled over his shoulder, "Hey kid, maybe I'll see you around sometime."

The next morning at school, Brick Winslow was a hero. The tale of his fight the day before would become legendary. It was all the other kids could talk about. The kid he beat was Jimmy Istmas, who was absent that day. Brick was called into the principal's office and asked to explain what happened. Brick was matter-of-fact as he told his story of beating out the other boy for the position of wide receiver on the football team. Then he explained that as they were leaving school, Jimmy came up behind him on the steps and hit Brick over the head with his full load of books, so Brick defended himself. The principal smiled after Brick left. He knew that Jimmy's parents would call, but he had heard what happened from his snitches as soon as he entered school that morning and knew Brick's account to be true. It was the last week of the eighth grade and these two boys would enter high school the following year; he decided to leave it alone.

Brick was bragging to everyone that if Jimmy showed his face around him again, he was dead meat. Jimmy knew he'd been shamed and no one was going to back him, so he clung to the shadows.

Even though he was riding high in the aftermath of the fight, Brick was perplexed: *Who was that older kid?* It didn't take long to find an answer.

His best friend, Mason, laughed and said, "You don't know Charlie McShane? He's going to be a senior next year at Central where we'll be freshmen. Charlie is the toughest kid in town; he has three older brothers and their old man is rumored to have killed three men. I can't believe you, man—you must have your head in the dirt along with your dick."

Brick reviewed every detail of the previous day in his mind. Charlie McShane, sure he had heard of the family, but Charlie was three years ahead of him in school and he'd never seen him before.

To Brick, an older kid like Charlie seemed to occupy an entirely different plane of existence. Brick didn't know it yet but he would start his growth spurt next year. For now, he felt small at 5'6".

Charlie must be well over 6' with corded muscles, long and lean. His hair was wavy brown, worn just over his ears, and his jaw was square. The nose was slightly beaked like that of a bird of prey. The eyes were hooded by a thick protrusion of bone, but the brown eyes were alert and intense. He moved like a ballet dancer, so light on his feet that he seemed to glide along attached to an invisible thread that beckoned him in a dance, to music no one else heard. As he grew older, he would resemble Matthew McConaughey, the actor.

Charlie was coveted by every coach in school. His athletic abilities allowed him to play any sport he chose with a sense of ease and grace. He tried them all and the coaches begged him to play everything and anything. They all felt that Charlie would be a superstar. Unfortunately for them, he wasn't interested. He loved gymnastics, but refused to compete.

Every generation has a segment of men born for battle. They know it young; they're the tough guys in school and are willing and eager to prove themselves. Vietnam was the first real test since the big one. Most of the dads had served—tough, quiet men who never spoke of the hardship to their family; they stayed stoic. These boys were the first to join and hungry for action. Boys fight the wars that the power structure creates and this was a controversial one from the start. It coincided with the new age freedom of love and peace. The war caused a rift in the generation with lasting repercussions.

Charlie was a warrior and knew it, felt it, and worked to be ready for the opportunity. He felt he was born to fight, born for war. Every move he made was to prepare him for that career. Too young for Vietnam, he readied himself for the next in line. He joined a local gym and boxed. He took karate and was a black belt by age fourteen; taekwondo and judo came naturally. No one intentionally fucked with Charlie. If some bully was stupid enough to try, he learned a painful lesson in tough that would follow like a second skin.

Two weeks after school let out, Brick walked outside his house one morning and Charlie was working his ball in the driveway. Brick was an only child. His father was born English, named Cary, and taught the subject at Saint Thomas, an expensive private college. He thought himself superior to everyone around him and was considered aloof and argumentative by most who knew him. He regarded his only son with an air of detachment. When he was drunk, as he was most nights, he would pontificate on his superiority over the American peasants and the tragedy of the imprisonment thrust upon him by his wife and son. He always spoke of the great novel he would write one day, but that day never came. Brick had learned to ignore him.

While his dad may have been a prick, he was a handsome one with strong patrician features and blond hair. Women seemed mesmerized by his accent and he could pour on the charm as he finagled them into the sack. Brick's mom, Katie, knew but quit caring long ago.

His mother was compassionate, loving, and gentle with deep concerns for her son's welfare. She taught world history at Saint Kate's college with an emphasis on American wars past and present. She possessed strong moral beliefs and tried to show her love for her son in all she did. She, too, was an only child. Her parents, Art and Dolly O'Malley, married young in Ireland and joined the hordes of immigrants to arrive and thrive in the new American Midwest.

Arthur O'Malley—Artie to his family and friends—a bricklayer by trade and a master of the craft, built a fine grand house for his new family. Dolly knew it would be a difficult birth from her doctor's warning; she made Artie promise that should they have a girl, she would be named Katherine. Katie, as she was known, was still in her mother's womb when the home was completed. Dolly never knew the pleasure of her dream for this home and family, as she died in childbirth. Katie and her father filled the grand house with love and humor; even at a young age, Katie strived to make it a home. Needless to say, father and daughter shared an isolation that bonded deep. But the loneliness soiled the daughter, made her brittle.

The O'Malley's prospered as Katie grew into womanhood. Artie was shrewd and built a fine business of quality homes. The demand was growing and he had a waiting list. As he became more successful, he branched out into developments and apartments. He had over a hundred employees. Art O'Malley was a wealthy man, but his daughter never got over the loss of her mother.

Artie was a high-spirited Irishman who loved his drink and female companionship. With the devil in his eye and the leprechaun in his heart, he cut a dashing figure as he made the rounds of his new world.

Young Katie never thought less of her father and was quick to his defense. She knew by her early teens that should she ever be blessed with a son, his name would act as testament to the trade that formed their lives.

Against her husband's objections, she smothered Brick to make amends for the father's neglect. They argued over most issues, including their son's name. He wanted Reginald; she wouldn't hear of it. She wore him down on all fronts.

Katie was a stunner. Her Irish heritage was evident. She was fine boned and buxom. Coppery hair and porcelain skin enhanced her proud features. She could have been a Hollywood starlet if she pursued a career that favored rare beauty. But her intelligence and drive craved more. She was a mature, striking woman and dominant leader of her profession.

Brick walked onto the back porch of the house and said, "Hi Charlie. Are you some kind of hot-shit soccer player?"

"No. Brick. I don't play any organized sports; do you swim?"

Confused, Brick just nodded his head.

"Well then, let's go."

Brick said, "I'll grab my suit and tell my mom."

Charlie countered by grunting and said, "Just tell you mom; you don't need a suit where we're going."

This exchange let both boys know that they had learned each other's names from other sources. It also established a pattern that would be the crux of their relationship from then on—Charlie and Brick communicated at an instinctive level. This was a test, Charlie's test. They both needed a friend and were testing the waters, literally and figuratively.

Charlie had a car; it was a piece of crap, but he was proud of his ride. It was a twenty-year-old Chevy, painted puke green with a brush. Brick later learned Charlie had painted it himself. He drove them across the border into Wisconsin to the Kinnickinnic River. They parked on a dirt road, off the beaten path, and Charlie led him to a ten-foot cliff overlooking the serene, crystal blue river lazily running downstream. A grotto sat on the other side of the river with a stretch of valley floor overgrown with wildflowers, alive with the buzzing of honeybees and hummingbirds. The early afternoon sun bathed the setting in a golden hue of bright luminescence. The smell fresh and scented.

In his typical fashion, without a word, Charlie stripped to briefs and made a beautiful and perfect swan dive into the cool waters. Brick hesitated for a minute, then removed his own outer clothes, and jumped feet first into the clear river.

The boys swam a long time, moving effortlessly up and down the calm stream. When they found a place where they could touch bottom, they had a water fight along the banks, laughing like hyenas as they became comfortable in each other's presence.

On the ride back to Saint Paul, Brick inquired about the soccer ball again. Charlie's answer was not what he had expected and would eventually reveal the true nature of the older boy.

With a solemn expression and a demeanor that was dead serious, Charlie said, "It's not about sports or the ball. I'm training my feet and legs to be more flexible, but that's just a small part of the equation. What it's really about is focus and concentration. I believe a person can achieve greatness in any endeavor if they can relax and concentrate."

The pattern was set and from that day forward, the two boys were inseparable. They spent the rest of the summer cementing the bond. Charlie taught Brick martial arts and Brick joined some of the same classes as his mentor, though not on the same level—it was difficult if not impossible to match Charlie as a warrior. It took a rare individual indeed to possess the same lightning-fast reflexes, flexibility, and strength and then to combine those physical attributes with a keen intelligence and animal instincts.

Unlike Brick, Charlie came from a very close-knit family. His brothers were kind but tough as nails. Franklin, the oldest, had been a semi-professional boxer when he was young. He now held a managerial position at the slaughterhouse in Austin, Minnesota. He was a big, happy Irishman, quick with his fists and first to the drink.

Sean worked with his father at the butcher shop and was shorter than most in the family, including their mother. He stood 5'5" and had amazing good looks; his dark wavy hair and piercing brown eyes combined with a loose and easy style that made most women, including the older ones, take a second look.

Jimmy was the charmer and ladies' man. He was probably the best looking in the family, standing 6'4" and weighed 225 without an ounce of fat. The brothers all fought each other like tigers when they were young, but any perceived threat to the family core brought them together as an invincible force. They were all devoted to each other, and their bickering and sarcastic remarks were taken in jest.

They welcomed Brick into their family as if he were born there. They seemed to instinctively sense that Charlie and Brick would be the best of friends for life, and they sometimes joked that a fifth brother had been conceived. For the first time in his life, Brick felt part of a warm and secure family.

Ten

Brick made it to Fargo before he stopped at a Red Roof Inn around two in the morning. The long drive, along with the events from the previous three days, had left him physically and emotionally drained and he couldn't stop worrying about Digger. It was a bad time to call, but he was afraid that his gentle cousin was in over his head. Brick would never forgive himself if anything happened to his loyal friend. He slept in bits and spurts, tossing and sweating until the sheets and pillows were soaked in a sour mixture of fear and funk.

Brick woke with the dawn, standing in a steaming shower until the water ran cold. After retrieving two large cups of coffee, he turned on the national news, keen for bits connected to Chicago, and was disappointed. He turned off the TV and stared at the hand clutching the phone. The fingers were white and starting to numb from the pressure. He forced himself to relax and started pacing the room like a caged lion.

The room was just a place to crash and he longed to be rid of the motel and Fargo, but wouldn't leave until he had confirmation from his cousin. If anything happened to Digger, Lisa would kill him and he couldn't blame her. At seven he was starting to think that maybe he should turn around and drive back. He was just getting ready to call when his new phone rang, he nearly jumped out of his skin; fumbling, he dropped the phone on the carpet and then scrambled to answer before it stopped ringing. As soon as he clicked on, he heard the laughing voice of his friend.

"You should have been there! It was beautiful, just like you said. I've never been to Chicago—wow, what a city. My wife went to her mother's for a few days so I think I'll stay here overnight and see a bit of the city.

Brick breathed a sigh of relief and said, "Good job, buddy; drive downtown and get a room at the Fairmont. Spend the day, use the services, and get a good night's sleep. Call Lisa and tell her you'll be back tomorrow. Thank you; I'll send the bonus."

Eleven

I left right after Digger's call and drove hard, straight to Glendive, Montana, about 375 miles from Fargo, almost six hours of easy driving on back roads. The journey worked as a cathartic balm on my nerves, and the more distance I put between the two points, the calmer I became. I remembered a nice resort in the area and plugged it into the GPS. As I made the turn onto the property, I smiled at the name on the sign out front: Big Sky Resort and Golf Club.

I strolled into the lobby around four that afternoon, dressed in blue jeans, sport shirt, cowboy boots, and a dark blue blazer with gold buttons. The jacket was buttoned and had been tailored to hide the big pistol. There were two other guests in line in front of me, so I took my time surveying the lobby and then focused on the pretty blond girl behind the counter. Her moves were efficient and pleasant as she accommodated the other guests. Her name tag read Laura.

I finally made my way to the front wearing my most charming smile. After introducing myself, I studied her as she checked for available rooms. When she said they didn't currently have a single room available, I apologized and said I was really interested in a suite. She checked her computer again and found one junior suite left facing the golf course and casually mentioned that it was $350 a night. "Perfect," I said, pulling out a credit card with the name, Richard Swanson. "I can pay cash at checkout. I had a client pay me in cash and I don't want to carry this much around. Someone could take it away from me, winking and flashing my best smile. Please call me Rick Mr. Swanson is my dad."

I recalled that Laura had given me more than a cursory glance when I came through the front door and I wondered if she was interested; now her facial expression told me that she was becoming intrigued. Later, in a more intimate setting, I would learn that Laura had a theory about men and admitted to herself that she always knew on sight if she would or wouldn't. But right now, I could only see that her cheeks were blushing as she flirted with me. "I don't think taking anything away from you would be easy." When three new couples began moving toward the counter, she appeared reluctant as she took my fake ID and matching credit card and handed me the room key.

Before walking away, I leaned in close and whispered a question in her ear. She replied in the same secret whisper without hesitation; she said, "Yes!"

I'd asked her what time she got off work and if I might take her to dinner. She said 5:00, but it was closer to 5:30 before she could get away. And now stood in front of my room, lightly knocking on the door.

I had showered and shaved and was dressed in loose cotton pants and an oversize tee. Laura seemed taken aback by this attire, so I apologized and said that I didn't know where we were going for dinner and wasn't sure how to dress. She entered the suite and asked for a drink. I made two from the mini-bar.

Laura hadn't been with a man in over six months and now she was in my room and thinking that maybe, just maybe … *An older man, he must be in his mid-thirties at least. Wait till I tell the girls back at school,* she thought. At forty plus I liked that—maybe I don't look ancient after all. That night, she didn't tell me about the six-month dry spell. I only learned that later.

Before going to the suite, I had returned to my truck and retrieved my suitcase and some extra security, leaving the rest in the truck—it was safer there. After unloading the bag, I stashed the MP5 under the bed and slid the Kimber between the mattress and box spring. I felt safe, but skittish.

The national news was on TV and Laura sat next to me on the sofa as we enjoyed the drinks and started chatting like old friends. Suddenly, I sat up straight and turned the volume up loud. The news coverage showed video of two rundown houses in a seedy looking neighborhood in south Chicago. They switched back and forth between houses. I watched with focused intensity as the talking head reported the gunfights at two separate locations that had occurred at almost the same time just after dawn. At first report from the police commissioner, it appeared that two rival gangs had clashed—presumably over drugs—and there were huge fatalities. The count at present stood at six dead and fourteen wounded, some critically. The anchor promised more details at ten.

I turned the television off and looked at Laura, who was staring at me with questions in her eyes. I explained my response, saying that I was from Chicago and couldn't believe the violence in the city. Laura was semi-reclined on the sofa and was staring warily in my eyes. More questions on her lips.

I excused myself and changed clothes without direction. Dressing in jeans, dress shirt, and blazer, I rejoined her and announced myself ready. When we were seated in the truck, I asked about the best restaurants in the area. She was hesitant until I insisted, "What is the very best joint in town?"

"It's Che L'Croix, but we can't get in. You need to make reservations weeks in advance; besides, it's ridiculously expensive."

"Lead me to it, fine lady, as I am in the mood to celebrate and expensive is perfect."

"Okay, but we won't be able to get in."

The place with the pretentious name was a freestanding tan stucco building constructed within the last ten years. Valet parking was a nice touch and spoke to class. It looked promising. The entryway was polished black stone and glass, a generous space with an intimate bar off to the side opposite restrooms; the main dining room was divided into levels, with a couple of steps adding elevation. It had the look of an authentic French bistro and oozed money. Candles and fresh flowers adorned the tables and the lights were dim. It was obvious that the restaurant didn't cater to locals; the tables were filled with wealthy tourists.

The maître d' was a tall, fit, swarthy man in a dark blue pinstriped suit with a vivid scarlet tie and crisp white shirt. Perfect. If you're savvy enough, you've seen the drill before and I had numerous times. The man is in his late forties, pompous, and self-important. Missed his chance and should be an owner by now. So he finds himself a Continental-style restaurant in a tourist town where he can act the big shot until he's forced out.

I decided he was arrogant enough, so I palmed a hundred. When I approached, I stuck out my hand and announced, "Rick Swanson, 6:30 reservations. I'm afraid we're a bit late."

He made a show of examining the reservation book as he snuck a look in his palm. I saw his eyes light up. He said, "Yes, of course, Mr. Swanson. I'm afraid I had to give your table away, but if you could wait a few minutes in the bar, I will set up a much nicer one. Jessica, please show Mr. Swanson and his guest to the bar and their first drink is on us, of course. Thank you for your understanding, sir."

Laura was duly impressed. "Wow, I've never been in a place like this. You're going to have to help me."

"My pleasure."

Jessica returned when we were halfway through our first drink and led us to four-top on the highest level of the dining room, the best table in the house. I knew I had read the man well.

Our conversation was light and easy. Laura was animated and energized and she said. "I don't know how you did that, but I'm impressed." As the dinner and drinks continued, she revealed a lot about herself: This was the first date she had in over six months, but that was such a fiasco that it was more like a year. She had a boyfriend in college and she thought they would get married and live the fantasy, but then she caught him screwing her roommate when she had a class canceled. Right in her living room on the couch. Asshole.

Then her mom got sick and she dropped out of school to take care of her. Now her mom is in remission and she's back in school in Billings and lives with mom during school; this is her second summer working at the lodge.

"Do you like it?" I asked.

"It's okay; the money is good and we live in a common house like a dorm they have for the summer employees. They feed us and the food is decent, but I'm bored out of my tree. We don't have cars and we work long hours, so town is a rare trip. There's nothing to do in your off time."

We rambled among subjects with no particular order. The food was incredible; she had let me order the works and had the best wine I could find on their list. She ate like a lumberjack and had a pretty good buzz going.

She seemed to be in a dreamy mood when I paid the check and over tipped the staff on the way out. The valet had washed my truck and had it waiting in front by the door; I slipped him a fifty. Although my truck is my home base and contains plenty of valuables, I didn't hesitate to let the valet park it. I just gave him the valet key that allows someone to drive it only a short distance. Laura was in the restaurant's foyer twirling to music in her head when I retrieved her and helped her into the passenger seat.

She quieted down on the ride back, kind of dreamy and thoughtful. When we were in the lobby by the elevators, I shook her hand and said I had a good time and thanked her for having dinner with me.

"Oh no you don't, Buster. You don't take a girl and give her one of the best times in her whole freaking life and then dump her in the lobby like old fish. We are going to your room, end of discussion."

"Okay, okay, one nightcap."

"We'll see."

As soon as the door closed, she was all over me. She pushed me down on the couch and straddled my hips, rubbing her body along my length while her mouth was hungry searching. Obvious.

"Look, I'm just passing through; maybe I gave you the wrong impression. I'm way too old for you and if you think you have to pay me back for dinner, forget it. I would have eaten there if I was alone. The money doesn't matter to me."

She grinned like the Cheshire cat. "You moron, I told you I'm bored and I'm horny. I decided when I said I would go to dinner. I think you're hot and I want to get laid. Are you going to screw me or not?"

I've been spoiled, not sure I deserve it. But I've been blessed with some pheromone, a scent or magnet that females find attractive. The women of my generation were burning their bras and marching for women's rights, demanding sexual fulfillment, and they were aggressive. I became a target, a prime candidate for their attention. They were exploring their sexuality and I was a foot soldier in their revolution. They were demanding orgasm, preferably multiple.

Making love to a woman for the first time is a delicate matter and needs to be approached with care. Women are very complicated and strange creatures—completely emotionally based. They have different

66

motors. Men have gas engines that burn hot and fast, ready to rumble at top speed.

Women are more like diesels, cold to start and require time and patience to warm. Once up to operating temperature, like a diesel, she will ride you to the ground.

The vagina is a wondrous multifaceted organ of superior design. It not only fulfills the basic housekeeping function of eliminating waste but is capable of expanding and giving birth to new life. It is self-cleaning, adjustable—a real one-size-fits-all. It's also self-lubricating and seals tight against unwanted invasion of water and debris. Sexually, females are capable of receiving stimulation from a wide range of pleasure centers. I've known women who could achieve orgasm with breast manipulation alone. Vaginal orgasm is more difficult for some women, but that's usually the man's fault. The clitoris is the most sensitive and the heart of the female sex center. Unfortunately, it is the most overlooked by men.

Men are so completely enthralled by their penises that they spend most of the time exaggerating sizes. A very wise woman once told me, "It's not how long it is but how long it lasts." Spend quality time with the clitoris and you will have a grateful and loving experience—and plenty of repeat business.

Oral sex is a prerequisite for a woman. Many reasons, but primarily women worry. They worry about being fat or not pretty. Some women worry about the smell or taste. Oral sex reassures them. You don't need to be asked; enjoy it. Tell them how good they taste and that they're beautiful. Now they can trust you.

If you are a sexually aware man and love women, you realize this practice offers a tenfold reward. My personal goal is two oral orgasms before insertion. You won't believe the results you'll receive for your efforts. This technique seemed to have the desired effect on Laura. She was a grateful and giving luscious young woman and I was honored at the gift of her body.

Before we drifted off, she said it was the best date she could remember and would one day be a shocker story for the grandkids.

Our past is an ethereal wraith that permeates our souls and haunts our subconscious minds with endless sound bites and images. It hangs on the fringes of our consciousness as a moist mist viewed through a gossamer veil—always just below the surface, trailing in our wake without pause or respite. It lives on the edge of sleep as an honesty filter. The dream descended from this land as vivid and raw as the moment frozen forever in time.

Twelve

They were flying over a verdant jungle nestled in the outskirts of Cali, Colombia, near the Panama border. Skimming the treetops, nerves taut, stomachs in their throats but committed. The flight was near end, and they came in fast and hot. Not even a star, the faint moonlight hidden. They were flying by radar and using night-vision optics to guide them. The incentive was the prize. Some were trying to figure their share. The frantic beating of the chopper's rotors was deafening in the gloom. Every man knew his job; they had prepared and trained for months and their fate would be decided within minutes. Using hand signals, they flipped down their night-vision goggles and the landscape turned a ghostly green as a large compound appeared, hacked out of the jungle with machetes.

Hey-sews set that big mother down light as a feather in the clearing, the men rappelling on snaking ropes. Their bodies thick with gear and the vests hot and sweaty. Smoke grenades blinded them for an instant as handheld rockets decimated buildings. Fragmentation grenades and machine guns spit tracers and hot shards of metal. Bodies flew, ripped to shreds like scarecrows. Nothing left but sparks and ashes. The survivors would shy away from questions, not able to acquit themselves of their guilt.

The forklift sat ready as the cargo was to be moved in the morning. The squad took advantage, loading the Black Hawk with the pallets. The mission took twelve minutes. All Brick remembered was Charlie leading the charge, machine gun and a k-bar dancing through the carnage. Mouth stretched like a Halloween mask of ferocity. His mission—planned it, trained the squad, executed the raid. He was a soldier and a damn good one.

The midday sun shined through the windows and reached the side of Brick's face; the heat woke him. The bedside clock read 12:15; he stretched—a long lazy bear, hibernation interrupted. He relived the previous night. The room was empty but Laura's scent lingered sexy and fresh. He couldn't remember sleeping like that before. The fact that he lived had a delicious taste. He was safe, the girl an undeserved gift. Tempted to stay. He'd be content with the break; it's a long way from here to finish.

Time seemed to melt away as he lingered over a hot meal and read the paper. It was 2:00 before he dressed in a tank top, running shorts, and track shoes. When he emerged from the elevator and stepped into the lobby, he saw Laura at work behind the counter, but she was busy with a customer so he entered the gift shop where he bought a bottle of spring water for his run and a dozen red roses for Laura.

She had seen him from the corner of her eye as he walked into the shop, totally ignoring her. What a fool she'd been, a shameless slut who jumped into bed with a man she knew about twenty minutes. He must think her the resort whore and look for the service on his bill. Her need had been greater than she realized, but now she sensed the danger that could burn her. She wasn't sorry though—Brick had shown her the most wonderful night she could imagine. Never in her wildest dreams would she have thought her buttons could be pushed, tuned, and stretched. Hot damn, she finally drew a live one.

Her reverie was broken when he suddenly appeared like an apparition, holding a bouquet of long-stemmed red roses. "You should have woken me before you left," he said with a grin. "Tonight I want to take you to dinner again, and this time I insist we go somewhere casual and talk. Pizza and beer kind of joint sounds great."

She turned a bright crimson and looked around to see if it was noticed. Fraternizing with the guests was strictly forbidden. She started stammering incoherently. All she could think to say was, "I don't know what to do with those flowers here at the desk."

His laugh was deep and reached his eyes. He said, "Call room service and have them bring me a vase and I'll keep them for you in my room. Now what time can I see you tonight and do I have time for a jog?"

The flowers were arranged with deep green ferns in a crystal vase sitting on the table when she let herself into the room with her master key. Brick wasn't back from his run yet, but then again she was early. She just couldn't stand working any longer and had her supervisor fill in for the last hour of her shift. Now that she was back in his room, her excitement was too intense for her to sit; she walked through the bedroom and allowed her mind to replay every detail of their lovemaking. She felt his hands again caressing and stroking every inch of her hot flesh. It was driving her insane with desire, so she went to the bathroom and splashed cold water on her face. She knew with certainty that if she was still here when he returned, she would be back in his bed in minutes. She wrote him a quick note saying that she had gone to her room to change and ran for the door.

At 5:30 Laura was ready; she didn't trust herself to be alone with him now. She slipped out the service door and walked around to the prearranged location of the truck.

The spot she chose for dinner was close and she could find it in her sleep; she practically lived at the pizza joint. Brick approved and they had a sloppy, fun, playful second date; he was a kick, and the beer was rich and foamy. Laura was relaxed, laughed big belly laughs, and got a bit stoned and giggly. It was a fun second date and at the end of the night she was back at her own place, not his bed. They also had some moments of real discussion. She told him about her plans for getting a CPA and starting her own accounting firm in her hometown.

He said, "You should do well—hot young woman with brains. Wear librarian glasses and the boys will flock around to have you handle their stuff."

"I bet they would—you're a dirty old man, you know. So … what are your plans and how long do you intend to stay?" she asked, shooting for indifference and missing by a mile.

"How long would you like me to stay?" he replied.

Laura laughed nervously and said, "Right now I wish you would stay forever, but after a bit, when I know you better, maybe I'll want you to leave."

There was a long pause as Brick pondered his answer, then said, "I guess we'll have to see in a bit."

For the rest of the week Brick's days were filled with rest, food, drink, and exercise while his nights were filled with Laura. As the week progressed, Laura became a sexual athlete trying to consume him and wanting as much as possible before he left. She couldn't help herself. He was the best thing to visit the resort since she started—hot, single, and available. She was too smart and ambitious to think it was long term, but for a summer romance this couldn't be beat. She romanticized the memories. On the final day before his planned departure, Laura took the day off work and they headed out for a picnic in the park and a walk along the river. She was thinking this the best story ever for her later years. When in her seventies, she would relish the time with her handsome stranger, but she was premature in this thinking.

They found a secluded spot about a half mile from the parking lot and spread out a large blanket where they sat with their lunch. Brick opened a bottle of wine and poured them each a glass. They were relaxing and chatting. Just as Laura was about to speak, there was a rustling in the bushes and three young men appeared and stopped at the edge of their space, way too close. Brick could tell that they were drunk, and he smelled trouble in their smirks and swagger.

Brick silently rose and stood facing the biggest kid, who appeared to be the leader, and asked if he could help them.

"You can drag your sorry ass out of here for starters."

Brick started walking forward, backing the boy up a touch—good start. When dealing with a bully, never back up. These childish brutes expect you to move back. Move in and it fucks up their heads. These weren't men; they were just older boys, maybe in their early twenties, delinquents who thought they were tough. But Brick wanted them gone, now, and wasn't in the mood for any bullshit from these assholes.

The leader's name was Billy McDermish. He was the town bruiser. His father, Big Ansel, ran the town's tow-truck service and garage. Billy, his only son, was the spitting image of his father. Dad busted his ass to improve Billy's young life and found constant excuses for the brutish behavior of his son. He spent time and lots of dough keeping the kid out of jail.

Billy was born mean; most people were so intimidated by him that they kept their mouths shut, fearing they'd make things worse. Have an argument with Billy and find your house burning or your cat dead.

Now face-to-face with Brick, Billy stopped and took a loose fighter's stance. He was a brawler and used his size to intimidate. His two buddies closed ranks and the three of them tried the hard look.

"We don't take kindly to strangers with our women, old man. Leave now while you still can."

"Okay kid, that's enough; you just toddle on your way now. We're trying to have a private moment here."

His buddies crowded up close. Emboldened by the odds, the leader asked, "Who's going to make us … you, old man?"

Laura spoke up then. "Just leave us alone, all right?" she said.

The kid looked at Brick with a smirk and said, "Shut up, cunt."

Stiff fingers found his throat; a shock, paralyzed look; eyes like bugs gagging without breath. Clutching his neck, Billy was sidelined. The lanky one on Brick's left threw a roundhouse at his head. Brick blocked it easily and with a right hook caught him in the middle of the guts, spun him with a quick rabbit punch to the kidney. The kid dropped to his knees.

The final boy rushed Brick like a linebacker intent on taking him down. Brick stepped aside at the last minute and tripped him with his outstretched foot. He landed hard. Brick snatched his right arm from behind, yanking it up and back until the shoulder dislocated. The scream never reached his lips; it died as he fainted.

A minute or so later, Billy had recovered; he regained his feet and came in low with a long serrated knife. Brick dodged the first thrust and shoved the kid off balance headlong into a tree. The boy screamed in rage and jumped back on his feet.

Brick calmly said, "So far none of you is seriously hurt, but if you continue I will put you in the hospital. That's a promise. Not hurt, but in the hospital, you fat fuck."

Too stupid to listen and furious with rage, Billy rushed like a running back overconfident in his bulk. Brick stepped inside between his arm and body, caught the wrist at its weakest arc, and snapped it like a twig, sending the knife flying. With a sidekick from his left boot, Brick exploded into the boy's right knee. Billy crashed to the ground. He was hurt but Brick was careful not to blow it out.

His breath still controlled, his features calm, Brick walked the short distance to the blanket, reached out his hand, and said, "Laura, honey, it's time to go."

She sat glued, the shock wild in her eyes. It all had happened so fast. Here they were having a lovely time, then as if in a dream the boys had emerged. Brick didn't appear afraid or concerned as he spoke to the leader, and Laura had been sure the boys would just leave. Instead, she watched in disbelief as the man she thought she knew erupted in a show of violence so quick and complete it took her breath away. He had been so loving and sweet with her that sudden savagery seemed impossible.

Brick led the way back to the truck as if nothing had happened. He carefully arranged their supplies in the back. Just as slow and methodical, he backed up the truck and started driving. The silence was deafening and after two minute, Laura exploded, "Who the hell are you? What just happened?"

Brick thought for a minute before responding. "I was military, Special Forces and extra training in hand to hand. After that dick brought you into it, I kind of lost it. They had plenty to deal with in me; bringing women and children into confrontations pisses me off. Losers who beat innocents in domestic abuse piss me off. I don't like fucking bullies.... Did I overreact? That cretin will kill someone—pulling a knife can get you dead. This fucker needs to be put down. He's still alive and when he heals, he'll have a new respect for the unknown, wary of strangers."

They drove in silence to the resort. Laura's mind was churning. He was leaving in the morning; she didn't know if she'd see him again. He'd explained it last night and she thought she got it. He'd said there were things he'd done and men who wanted him dead. She pushed, was pushed back to the wall. He was stern as stone.

He said he would be back if he could. He had appeared like a dream and would leave the same way. It was over as fast as it had begun.

They said their goodbyes and Laura had cried; it just seemed so sad and unreal, a wonderful experience ending on a sour note. He'd been hiding too long, tricking no one but himself. The time for running was over; finish this now or in ashes.

Thirteen

The sun was at my back and still low on the eastern horizon as I turned off the interstate after barely forty miles. From here I'd take back roads as I worked my way to Oregon. The thoughts raced backward with every mile as I returned to the places and people I'd been hiding from. There wasn't any reason to hurry. Not that I was afraid … but maybe a delay? No, I'm scared. I only made a couple hundred miles and stopped early at a small mom-and-pop motel perched on the bank of the Missoula River. They had a smattering of cabins separated by cottonwoods and slim aspens reaching straight as telephone poles blocking the last of the sun. Filtering light glimmered and danced across the riffles in the stream. The towering rocks claimed heritage, commanding their stance, and the river was forced to seek a new path as it diverted into three separate forces before regrouping, stronger for the interference. The lesson of the river: be flexible, adapt, survive. There are always rocks in the stream.

My cottage had a small deck facing the river with two worn rattan chairs and a lopsided matching side table wedged in the middle. I propped the table using matchbooks found inside. The sun faded, then dissolved in the trees. I closed my eyes and the images flooded in rapid succession and vivid detail. The truth I've denied stood out in stark relief against the harsh reality of my life. I fucked up. Not even sure how or when. We want to go back to the mistakes of the past and change them, fix them. How naive.

I had escaped a fierce attack; I'm running for my life. I needed a break, regroup; that's fine. I repeat previous behavior, even though I know better. I took advantage of a nice girl. Why? I tell myself that she seemed like she was friendly and I didn't want to eat alone. That it was innocent. It's a lie. I know what happens when I devolve into the flesh. Another reason I should be secluded away. No good can come from this; sometimes I'm my own worst enemy.

After high school, Charlie enlisted in the army and I attended the old man's college. I got a full ride. Between my grades and dear Dad's influence, I slid in easy enough. I suspected he had the dirt on some big shit colleagues, because I knew they hated his guts. He was a tenured professor, so he felt safe. It was like a twenty-year state or federal employee; you had to kill somebody to get canned.

I worked day and night studying and working construction, framing houses in the summer. Classes and flipping burgers at night during school.

We kept in loose contact, Charlie writing sporadically when he had the opportunity and me answering weeks later. The bond we had formed as children never weakening but in a holding pattern until the fates brought us together again. After two years, Charlie had risen in the ranks as his skills were honed to a razor's edge. He was a legend among the men. In hand-to-hand combat, he had no peer. Soon after basic training no other man, including hardened combat instructors, would willingly face him in training exercises. His physical stamina was tireless. His knowledge of wars dating back before Christ included obscure battles. World history became a passion as he strived to become a strategic master. The brass noticed and recommended him to West Point.

It was almost eight. Ruth had told me that they served a limited menu this time of year but closed at eight. I had meatloaf and mashed potatoes with beef gravy that was perfect comfort food. While I ate, Ruth's husband, Josh, joined us both in the deserted dining room and started chatting.

The proprietors were a friendly couple and I had a stock answer whenever people asked what I did. Like all good lies, mine was based loosely on the truth. I told them I was an investment banker and was currently on leave while mourning the death of my young wife from a tragic illness.

I'd graduated from Saint Thomas young. I started when I was seventeen and worked hard to move along fast. I earned a double master's in business and economics, then scored a job with Wells Fargo in Minneapolis. Investment banking division. The powers that be had me on the short list for Wall Street.

Cassie's tragic "illness" was her infidelity and subsequent betrayal. I never wanted that fucking business life, just did it for that bitch. She wanted money and prestige, and when it all seemed within my grasp, she just fucking left. Do I still sound bitter? You better believe it.

Ruth lent me an umbrella and I made my way back to the cabin along the twisted path in the downpour. I was shaken by an explosion that broke my concentration; I pulled the gun before recognizing the sound as thunder.

Jumpy!

I gave the fear and frustration of the last ten years permission to cry. Just sat in the downpour, my gaze to the heavens and let it all out. After the rain slowed I rose to my feet, lethargic from emotion, and stumbled through the cabin door. It was cold but I was too weary to start a fire. After stripping off my soaked clothes and pulling the heavy Indian blankets tight, I fell into a dreamless sleep.

Twelve hours brought a frosty morning. With one of the heavy blankets wrapped around my shoulders, I built a fire in the hearth. Showered and dressed in fresh clothes. Moved to the deck with a cup of coffee. The day broke crisp and clean with the sun warming the early summer day. The river rushed high, swollen from the heavy rains and I stretched like a big cat after a feast, cracked my neck and back, and realized I was grinning like an idiot savant. For the first time in years, I wasn't afraid and was done running. I would fight and wouldn't be alone.

When I returned to the cabin, it was toasty so I refilled the cup from the small percolator and decided to spend another day; I needed exercise and wasn't used to being cooped up in the truck all day. Today I would explore the trails and footpaths along the river.

Fourteen

Two hundred miles north and three hundred back, a lone figure drove in a black E-class Mercedes on the same approximate course as Brick, not knowing where he was, but guessing where he would eventually be. The man wasn't in a hurry; he rarely was—he danced to a different drummer, just a little off the beat. Tall and lean, a handsome man with sandy blond hair and piercing blue eyes. At one time in America, he would have been called a natty dresser. He favored Harris Tweed jackets and fine wool slacks with razor-sharp creases; add Italian loafers without socks. His freshly ironed white button-down oxford shirt was open at the throat. He secretly wanted to wear an ascot but wouldn't. Too poufy. One close look in his eyes and you knew that cruelty lived behind the mask; the eyes of a killer. Women found his accent charming and he had no intention to try to be more American. He relished his very proper British lilt; it held a sensuous, foreign tone.

Brick had a hard run on the trails that followed the rapid torrents of the spring melt. Walking the trail back, he stopped often to admire the natural beauty and wipe the sweat away. After a blind turn, he almost ran down a cute young brunet unloading a small trailer of blankets and folding chairs. She arranged the items around a fire pit built from huge river rocks. The origin of the work intrigued him. The stones had to weigh hundreds of pounds each. The charred surfaces of the stones indicated the pit had been in use for many years.

She felt his presence and her smile warmed his day. She stuck her hand out and confidently said, "Hi, I'm Beth. How you doing?"

Brick returned her smile as he studied her innocent, young face full of hope and promise. He was touched to see such honesty. Brick said, "I'm doing great! What's going to happen here?"

"Just a spring river party. Actually just an excuse to party; the spring semester is almost over."

In his peripheral vision, he watched a muscular young man on an ATV aiming their way. He was almost Brick's size, in fantastic shape. His bright open smile revealed a gentle warmth. When he got off the ATV, he walked toward them with a loose gait. Brick met him with his hand and they exchanged a fist bump and greetings; his name was Mark. After a few minutes chatting, the two young students invited Brick to their bonfire party that evening.

Brick left them to it as Mark hooked a trailer to the ATV and headed back over the dune to fetch a load of firewood. When Brick returned to his cabin, the fire still contained burning embers and a fresh log flamed in an instant. He took a hot shower and dressed in fresh clothes and donned a light coat to conceal the Kimber.

He decided to have dinner in town and pick up a few supplies. Finding a cozy little restaurant off the beaten path, he enjoyed a wonderful meal of fresh brook trout and a bottle of Oregon Pinot Noir. It was still light when he left the restaurant and he stopped at a convenience store where he purchased a Styrofoam cooler that he loaded with beer and ice.

Back at the cabin, he changed into jeans and a sweatshirt. He started to leave with the cooler but stopped. He had the Kimber in a shoulder rig under his right arm, but before he pulled the jacket on, he paused. After a reflective minute, he took the big gun off and studied it before tucking it under the mattress.

With a new sense of calm, he picked up the cooler and headed out—unarmed for the first time in ages. He wound his way down the path humming a tune he knew but couldn't place until the roaring, crackling bonfire loomed ahead. There must have been at least twenty college-age kids there laughing and chatting. Some were dancing to the beat coming from a boom box sitting on a log. He greeted Beth with a smile. She looked radiant, her fresh face flushed with excitement at the success of her party. When he opened the cooler, she yelled to the crowd, "Hey everybody, this is Brick and he brought beer!" This declaration was met with cheers and backslaps as the crowd welcomed him.

It was after midnight when Brick finally took his leave. The flames were still roaring and the drunken revelers were starting to couple up and move off. Brick's face was flushed and sweaty, and he could not remember having such a good time. Even though he was almost twice the age of his hosts, they treated him like one of their own. He played volleyball, skinny-dipped in the frigid stream, and became mildly drunk. God but he needed this respite.

The black Mercedes rolled smoothly into Glendive, Montana, about the same time Brick set off for the bonfire. The stranger checked into an upscale motel and went to find some local color. He cruised the bars along the central corridor and stopped at the one with the most parked cars. It looked appropriately seedy, so he entered the smoky atmosphere. It was loud and busy—mostly cowboy types in big hats, jeans, and boots. The jukebox in the corner blasted new country music at a deafening volume.

He was so overdressed and out of place that the locals ignored him as a harmless townie with too much dough and light in the shorts. He took a seat at the bar and asked for a single malt Scotch whiskey, neat. The only one they had was Glenlivit and he ordered a double with water back. The bartender said, "Its eight dollars a shot."

Gran said, "Wonderful, make it a triple."

With the whiskey in hand, he listened in on various conversations. He moved around the room inspecting the junk that littered the walls—old milk jugs, posters from the fifties, playbills, and really just shit the owner thought might look rustic.

The bar was long and straight, a shotgun with the biffs in back and the pool table hogging the center of the room. The Englishman didn't expect to find much, but he had a flair for dissecting conversations fast and was alert to the odd bit. There was a group of old farts gathered around the pool table discussing the recent thrashing of one miserable town bully.

"Billy ..." said a wizened old man in the shadows, "couldn't happen to a nicer guy; may he burn in hell." He moved to the outskirts of the group, waiting for another morsel.

The men were laughing. They obviously enjoyed the tale being told by a white-haired man in his sixties who seemed aware of untold details. The man said, "Yep, old Billy boy was drunk as usual, and he and his boys came on a stranger in the park with this young woman and you know Billy—he started a fight. I don't know what it was about, but the stranger put him in the hospital. I guess he's all fucked up, broken wrist and busted knee. Good news, right?"

The Englishman stepped up to the old gent and said, "Excuse me, sir, but I think I know the young gentleman in question. May I inquire as to the lad's birth name?"

Everyone looked at him; his thick accent threw them for a loop. The old man said, "It's McDermish; how would you know him?"

"My dear departed sister used to live in the area. I can't remember her husband's name but her son was named Billy. I believe his father was a shop owner."

"Couldn't be the same one. Billy's dad owns the garage and tow service in town."

"So very sorry to have bothered you; you're right, not the same man." With that he filtered away from the crowd and left for his motel.

Fifteen

Brick woke with first light breaking through the valley. He had fun last night. One of the kids had some good pot and they all got a little silly and laughed their asses off. He had desperately needed that release. Now he was refocused and it was time to make the call. He knew he was putting it off, which was stupid. He just had a hard time admitting his mistakes. He took his coffee out on the little deck and dialed the number embedded in his encyclopedic brain. It was answered on the first ring. He didn't know the man who answered, but the man knew him. It was a simple message: give him the new number. "Have him call me," he said; they both knew who he meant.

The Englishman was also up early. He checked out of the motel and grabbed a quick breakfast at the local diner. It was around ten o'clock when he circled the garage. Everything looked quiet. There was a single mechanic working on an old Dodge pickup in the far bay. He parked the E-class a block over in front of a vacant lot and meandered into the office of the garage.

A beefy man in jeans and work boots sat behind a scuffed wooden desk strewn with paperwork. He had the sleeves of his plaid flannel shirt rolled to the elbows and a scowl on his meaty face. A large, stinking cigar hung from a pouty little girl's mouth. The lean stranger walked into the office, turned without speaking, and locked the door, then pulled the shade covering the window.

"What the fuck? Are you crazy?" the man bellowed as he got to his feet.

"Excuse me, sir, but I need to have a private conversation with you," he said, his cold eyes trained on the older man's face.

The accent threw him off; it threw everyone off and this dandy was being nice. Big Ansel locked eyes with the stranger and said, "What do you want?"

"So very sorry to bother you, sir, but I heard in town that your son was beaten by a stranger and I have reason to believe I may know this man."

Ansel looked confused and again asked, "Who are you and who's this asshole?"

"My name is Granville and he is a person of interest to me. Tell me what you know of the situation, please."

Big Ansel stood up straighter now. He was a head taller and fifty pounds heavier than the strange man in his office. He balled his fists and said, "I'm not telling you shit, motherfucker. Who is the man who fucked up my son?" His huge fists were clenched tight as he moved out from behind the desk. He was backing the Englishman into the corner.

"No need for violence, my good man; let us discuss the matter like gentlemen." As he was talking to Ansel, he feinted left, then moved to his right with blinding speed. He caught the big man flatfooted as he drove his left fist into the man's sizable gut. He was able to spit the cigar out rather than in as the breath whooshed out in a huff of smoke. The Englishman's right hand flicked the blade up to his throat, drawing blood. The switchblade that appeared was red with a trickle running steady to the hilt. The pressure brought him up on his toes.

"You bloody fucking cunt! You so much as twitch and I'll cut your throat from ear to ear." At the same time his left index finger stabbed into the pressure point behind Ansel's carotid artery, and the big man went unconscious in less than a minute.

Gran let him down easy into the chair behind him. By the time he regained consciousness, his arms and legs were bound with the electric cord cut from his office lamps. He had a greasy rag stuffed in his mouth; he thought he'd gag.

"Be careful; you puke, you'll probably choke to death." Gran was sitting on the edge of the desk and had turned the chair around until it was only about a foot away. The switchblade was Italian made with a blade engraved with some script; the handles were red with buffed brass balusters and it was as sharp as a straight razor. He stuck the point into the brow over the right eye and drew a single drop of blood that dripped down, temporarily blinding his captive.

"Listen like your stupid life matters, you fat bloody fuck. I talk, you answer."

He pulled the gag out and immediately the man said, "Do you know—?" The gag was shoved back in deeper than before and the big man involuntarily retched and started choking.

The Englishman was staring as Ansel fought for breath and started to turn purple. Both hands moved together as Gran placed the tip of the blade inside the man's right nostril facing out. He yanked the rag with his left hand as his right wrist flicked from inside out, slicing Chinatown style, sending a cascade of blood down his shirt. Gran was fond of the scene.

The fear was singing from Ansel's eyes and his face was stretched into a mask of terror. "Shut the bloody fuck up and listen." Gran cupped his left hand over Ansel's mouth, his right hand clutching his hair. Mouth pressed tightly to his ear. "The man's name and heading?"

Ansel was choking; blood continued to run freely down the front of his shirt, pooling in an oblong puddle. He was crying and said, "Please don't … I think his name is Rick and someone said he was headed west."

"Easy when you listen. Truth is an ally, an insufferable bitch when betrayed." He stuffed the rag back and turned off the lights. Unlocked the door and disappeared.

Twenty minutes after placing the call, Brick was still on the deck watching the steam rising from the cup as his coffee cooled in the mist over the river. His phone rang once. "Hello Charlie."

"Talk to me, my brother."

Brick went through it all, starting with the letter from Dawn. Charlie never said a word throughout the narration. Brick told him of the visit from Cassie, the shooting, and the attack on his cabin, noting the death of their former comrade, Nicky. He even told him of Laura—what a fool he'd been—and the bonfire last night.

"The attack obviously came from the cities and the spic had to be responsible. That business in Chicago was your doing, so the big question is, who's behind it? I don't like to assume anything. You done good, brother. Wise to make a tactical retreat. We can sweat the Aussie and find an answer in Oregon," Charlie said.

"I heard you say 'we.' Does that mean …?"

"Of course, I'm on the way but three thousand miles takes a minute. Give me seventy-two hours and I'll meet you in Sisters."

"I can call when I arrive and tell you where I am."

"No, don't call again. I'll find you and I'll bring secure satellite phones. Weapons and gear will be waiting for us. What about GK? This is obviously tied to our old crew. Nicky's dead; that leaves three, and I'll have them checked. GK concerns me—you never know, but he must have heard. He keeps an eye on you, even if you don't know it."

"Christ, Charlie! I forgot about him—you're right, he can smell this shit."

Charlie's voice was filled with concern for his brother. This wasn't a time for wounded pride or sucking it up; Brick needed help and Charlie would wade through a swamp of alligators to help him. "Watch your ass, buddy boy. You two made that western run many times; he knows you almost as well as I do. Try to remember we own a security firm, and if you paid attention, we have resources.

"And Brick … be careful. We lost Jesus and I can't bear the thought of losing you. You stay cool and wait for the cavalry. You capish?"

"Charlie … thanks; it's good to hear your voice. I'll see you in three days."

Sixteen

The black Mercedes continued due west and Gran smiled to himself, *I found you bitch and I know where you're headed.* He chuckled and thought about the peckerwood with the split nose. He told him his real name, but the man wouldn't remember; they never did. Granville Harlow III was his given name, not all that uncommon in the British Empire, but in the Wild West these dirt farmers were as ignorant as gnats. Gran thought of himself as aristocracy, born to the upper class, educated at Oxford and Harvard; he thought of most Americans as peasants. The only question in his mind right now was, where was Charlie?

After finishing the call, Brick packed his gear and paid his bill in cash. At the first major road, he almost turned north but, heeding Charlie's warning, realized that others could have picked up his scent. Push on and fast. He drove hard that day, almost making the Idaho border, stopping only for gas and food. Late that night he slept at a nondescript motel and headed west again at first light. It was still early in the season and he had the Rockies to conquer. The mountain passes were still closed, so the fastest and easiest route was the major interstates of I-94 and then I-90 to Butte where he hooked up with I-15 south to Idaho.

At Pocatello he was able to head west again on I-84 and slide into Oregon at Ontario. The miles flew by; it had been an easy journey and his mind was filled with recollections of the past and plans for the future. After his conversation with Charlie, he was at ease for the first time since the visit from his ex-wife.

Their old crew played a crucial part in this drama. Neither Charlie nor he ever believed in coincidence. He had two quiet years and it seemed enough, had to be. He had been avoiding the truth but now it was time to face it. The old crew consisted of seven men and they had all made a difference in Panama and Colombia. There was the army's agenda and then there was Brick's. It was 1989 when these six men were handpicked by Captain Charles McShane for a reconnaissance team for the US Army Rangers. What the army didn't know was these men were also picked before enlistment; nothing was coincidence

Seventeen

After Cassie left our marriage, I worked at becoming the bank's best drunk. I wasn't the only one but I worked at being best. The business was boring and a little edgy. Not exactly illegal but questionable. The first time I heard the word *derivative*, I had to look it up. I studied them, as we were all expected to sell tons of the crap. It was a gamble at best, but no one questioned the big banks back then. It was theft pure and simple.

The longer I worked for these purportedly respectable bankers, the more I was reminded of the robber barons at the beginning of the industrial age. It seemed the type of scheme that would appeal to old John D. or Mellon and Carnegie. If I were to become a thief, this wouldn't be my way. As a junior executive in the big banks, I was at the bottom of the barrel. The trickle down from the billions would drip to thousands, maybe only hundreds before it reached this low.

In my free time I drank. Mornings would find me dragging ass to the bank in an imitation of a zombie. The hangovers were intense. My friends said they were worried. The women I courted soon tired of my shenanigans. I wasn't eating or taking care of myself, so when Charlie came home for leave I was a chocolate mess.

He was harsh. Charlie was the only man I needed respect from and he viewed me with scorn. He had two weeks' leave and during that time he never left my side. I didn't go to work or answer calls. He made me run. Every day with the sun, he would drag me from my bed and push. No alcohol, nothing, cold turkey. Each time I said I couldn't go on, he would kick my ass. No was not an option for my friend. He probably saved my life. We did weight work, calisthenics. Good food, healthy; plenty of rest and water. So fucking much water I felt like a fish.

At the end of two weeks I was a different man—clear eyed and sober for the first time in almost a year. I wasn't sure what was next. That's when he convinced me to join the army. With my education, I could be an officer and he had pull. We would be together again. I didn't have anything to lose. I could give it two or four years and grow up. That's what Charlie said: "Quit your whining and grow the fuck up."

Basic was a snap; under the booze I had been an athlete and my age was an advantage. I regained strength and flexibility in a hurry. The Rangers were tough but I had always had a great work ethic, thanks to my mom. Charlie was right; it straightened me up and it didn't take long to become a first lieutenant. He indeed had pull. A year more and he made captain stationed in Panama City. He requested me, so off I went.

Panama was a stone's throw from Colombia and a plan was forming. It was more than rumored that Joe Kennedy had made his fortune during a period in our country when some thought they could control the tastes of others in society. It continues to this day. Didn't work then and doesn't now. I laugh when people cry about the law—well it's against the law, you know. It's laughable, laws change. Men make the laws and men repeal the old laws and create new ones. It didn't take long before the Volstead Act was repealed. The population had more than a craving; they drank and were not going to stop. They say prostitution is the world's oldest profession and yet in America, it's still against the law. Drugs were currently against the law, but I was confident that would change.

The way I saw it, this was my prohibition and I would follow in Joe's footsteps to create my fortune. It was the Wild West in Panama in 1989. The government under Noriega was corrupt and easily circumvented. Charlie indeed had more pull than I had imagined. He was left free to command as he saw fit. Our government had its hands full with the crook running the country.

We handpicked our crew for their talents. I was second in command. Charlie trained us; it wasn't easy. He ran us hard but the duty was soft before things got hot. No matter how hard you trained and worked, Charlie worked harder. He ran us but he was in the lead so no one bitched. For first-time recruits, Charlie had a routine. He would kick in the door to the barracks when the men were still asleep and announce a twenty-five-mile march with fifty-pound packs.

Charlie and I wore aviator glasses so our eyes were hidden. We did the twenty-five one way. The first man to approach me and ask what Charlie thought he was doing, I would hit him with the glasses and say, "Why don't you ask him?" By the time we reached the clearing, the men were exhausted. All along the way Charlie would travel back and forth along the line saying, "Don't worry boys. Jesus saves."

You could see it in their faces. They thought they were being led by a religious fanatic. They were disgusted and ready to drop out. Charlie kept repeating, "Jesus saves."

When the chopper landed and the guys filed in to universal relief, Charlie would say, "Meet Jesus." And laugh his ass off. Charlie thought he was funny.

The Panamanian Army was a loose affair riddled with graft and corruption, but they had a few outstanding soldiers. One of the most reliable and intelligent was Colonel Jesus Montenero (*Hey-Seuss* in Spanish). In the interest of cooperation between the different cultures, he was ordered to serve in the 75th Regiment of the Army's Ranger division and assigned to Captain Charles McShane as a helicopter pilot. With this development Captain McShane felt embolden to make another unusual request. With prodding from Brick he requested Squadron Leader Granville Harlow of the British Royal Air Force to join the squad as communications officer. This was also approved as new president George H.W. Bush was a hawk with strong ally ties. When the queen of England calls the President of the United States to ask for a favor for one of her favorite soldiers the red tape disappears and shit gets done fast. Charlie and I were already brothers bonded in blood and soon the Panamanian would round out our command as officer of transportation. But first Charlie planned to take him apart—when the pieces were reassembled, he would be family too.

Eighteen

The weather in the high altitudes turned crisp, blue and bright, the sun bleaching the surrounding countryside the shade of weather-beaten cedar siding. Brick turned the heater up high and set the wipers to intermediate; a few minutes later he was climbing into the mountains. As soon as he started to gain some altitude, the weather turned nasty. The steel grey mist was biting the earth with stinging crystal needles, not quite sleet, thinner and longer than raindrops; it was like liquid icicles were pelting the windshield. It quit on a dime and all was serene once more.

The sparse late afternoon travelers were pulling off the road to stop for the night but Brick wanted to push on, hoping to arrive in Bend shortly after dinner. The light traffic was slowing and the vehicles were starting to bunch up. As he drove, Brick remembered the first time he met Jesus. Charlie and he were in a seedy little bar off the main path in Panama City, drinking shots of Sauza Conmemorativo with Dos Equis when a stout, ruddy complexioned man entered the side door. He stood maybe 5'6" in boots and had a slight belly; he wore mismatched clothes. His face was cratered with scars and pockmarks of severe acne. A broad spongy nose took prominence and gave him the overall appearance a fat, toady presence. He appeared to be in his forties but it was difficult to discern his real age, as he wore the miles well.

He stood in the entrance and scanned his surroundings. The smoky haze was pierced with a shrill whistle and a finger raised high in the air. The man with the devastated face walked to the booth where the two Americans sat. There was plenty of room at the wide booth for him but as he approached, Charlie hooked his foot around the leg of a chair at the next table and said, "Sit here." Then they both went back to drinking and ignored him.

Without a word to the Americans, the new man attracted the attention of the serving girl and spoke to her in rapid Spanish. She returned in record time with a bottle of the Sauza and another round of beers along with a fancy little crystal glass for the man. The three men sat in silence for at least ten minutes; Jesus was comfortable with the silent treatment, though he had been summoned to appear by Captain McShane.

The bar was frequented by military men from many nations, the Panama Canal being crucial to shipping worldwide. It was a humid, sweltering Saturday night in the middle of August 1989, and things were heating up between the United States and their supposed ally General Noriega, taking American money and siding with the Ruskies.

He'd been receiving a salary from the US since the 1950s, when he was an asset for the CIA. The ceiling fans spinning counterclockwise overhead in the smoky atmosphere resembled inverted beanies stuck to the tops of precocious children, while the air held a heavy, prickly sense of irritation and absence of patience.

Crowded in like cigarettes in a pack, the drunken mass of soldiers had an edge of volatility that needed only a tiny spark to ignite the fumes. An Aussie from the bar was staggering through the crowd in search of the pisser when he hooked his foot in the Panamanian's chair and fell across a table, knocking over the bottles and glasses. Instead of apologizing, he roared up swearing at Jesus.

"You bloody fucking cunt; what the fuck you sitting in the fucking aisle?" he screamed.

Like a lit fuse, Jesus went off swinging one of the beer bottles in a backhand blow across the intruder's face, the glass exploding and sending sharp daggers of piercing slivered shards like angry hornets into the Australian's face and neck.

Eerie silence permeated the crowd for a heartbeat before the spark tendered the powder keg of sweating humanity into chaos. Charlie and Brick were on top of the table using the high ground to defend their position. As the Aussie's mates began to swarm Jesus, Charlie's strong arm reached down and pulled their new acquaintance up with them. The three men stood with their backs together meeting all challengers with steel-tipped boots and bottles for clubs.

The fight was clearing at the entrance and Brick was the one to see the path and led his comrades on a Comanche run across the tabletops and through the door to the street. Once outside, they ran down a dirty side alley littered with condoms and broken glass and smelling of stale sweat and urine before the MPs arrived.

Charlie was laughing like the devil and it became apparent that when he made Jesus sit in the aisle, he expected no less than what transpired. Charlie grabbed the Panamanian in a bear hug and kissed him on the forehead. "You done good, you crazy fuck." The newly formed amigos jumped in a waiting taxi on the next block and Jesus gave the driver directions to a quiet local bar across town where Brick laid out his plans for after the invasion.

On Monday morning at 0600 hours, Charlie met Jesus outside the barracks, both men loaded in full packs, and set the pace for a ten-mile run, slowing the pace considerably for the older, out-of-shape Panamanian. After a couple of miles, Charlie stopped to let his new pilot rest. Jesus was sweating profusely and gasping for breath. Charlie said, "We've only gone two miles; do you think you can walk the rest of the way back?"

It was after 1100 hours when they made their way to the barracks. Charlie let him rest for an hour and then met him in the courtyard. "Hit me," said Charlie.

"What? Where?"

"Anyplace. Hit me as many times as you can; fight dirty but hit me—you know you want to. If you don't hit me, I'll beat you senseless," Charlie barked.

Like a cornered animal, Jesus assumed a clumsy martial arts stance and began circling, knowing he didn't have a chance. He started to jab and kick a little, to no avail. The warrior dodged everything effortlessly, finally tapping the old man's belly with just enough force to make him wince. Jesus made a great show of being hurt, then tripped over his own feet and laid sprawled on the ground.

"Get up," shouted Charlie.

Jesus rolled to his knees and as he started to rise, his left hand threw a fistful of sand into Charlie's eyes and his right hand, gripping a large rock that he had strategically fallen near, smashed Charlie in the temple.

As he was backpedaling, Charlie pressed his hand to the wound and it came away bloody. He was shocked, incredulous that the old man had managed to outsmart him. Charlie said, "That's never happened before—I like you better all the time. We're finished." That was the end of it. Charlie needed to know the strength and weakness of each man in his command.

.

Nineteen

The black Mercedes was falling far behind its quarry as it zigged north and zagged south; instead of finding the trail, Gran only managed to find snow and bitter driving conditions at the beginning of the Rocky chain. He smiled as he remembered his old mates and the early beginnings of the simple, yet fantastical plan that Brick had outlined for the squad once they were bonded together in Panama.

They had just arrived from Fort Benning, Georgia, and were meeting for the first time. He knew Brick and Charlie but the other men were all new to each other. They had been briefed individually but now their roles were defined and they began to concentrate on specifics.

If Gran was to be honest, this whole episode began as a child in his birth home of Manchester. Sir Harlow was fifty years old when he took the young Mary Ackerman, only twenty-two years of age, to become his bride. His only heir was born a year later and with the birth it appeared that the contract, for surly it had to be a contract, was terminated. When Gran was growing up, his father was more real to him in the news reels than in real life.

The prominent male figure in his sheltered life was the rowdy Irishman who served both parents as bodyguard, chauffer, and handyman and was known as Hugo Sullivan. The mansion itself was on a sprawling estate thirty kilometers from London and Parliament. His parents took residence in separate wings and mealtime was the most intimate and civil time the family shared. Of course, Sir Harlow spent most of his time in London, either in the flat or Parliament. It was a rare occurrence when young master Gran was in his father's attendance, and when he was, those periods were devoted to Sir Harlow's lectures on the social classes and their distinctions. When he had exhausted himself on the first subject, he further badgered the boy on his studies and homework.

It was little wonder that Gran couldn't wait to rush down to the garages and stables where the servant's quarters were housed. This was the warm comfort he was desperately seeking in contrast to the vast, sterile environment of the mansion. Mister Sullivan's quarters were tidy and efficient. No more than six hundred square feet but cozy enough for a rounder. He stood 6'5" with 250 pounds of chiseled muscle sculpted from a lifetime of hard, honest work and play. His features were angular with hard planes and a deep cleft chin and devilish brown eyes that bespoke a hidden joke. His curly black hair announced black Irish heritage but would never admit to membership in the IRA.

Gran was only twelve when Lord and Lady Harlow handed over the reins of the boy's daily duties to the swarthy Irishman. They both feared the boy was becoming a bit of a pouf and trusted their loyal bodyguard to "Make a man of him." Hugo took to this task with great relish, as he did everything. Every day after his schoolwork was completed, the lad would joyfully run to his new mentor where he would be assigned tasks that Hugo monitored with care.

He was given mundane duties such as washing and waxing the auto fleet, mucking out the stables, pitching hay, or whatever the big man said. To his credit, young Master Gran never complained and put his back to the yoke. As the first summer came to a close, the boy had packed on ten pounds of muscle and one hundred pounds of awareness. He always referred to his employee as Mister Sullivan and in turn was properly addressed as Master Gran.

The big man worked the boy hard, same as he had been worked, but developed a compassion for the lad as if created from his own loins. He taught him to hunt, read the wind, identify scat, and follow a game trail.

The boy was a natural with a gun, possessing excellent hand-eye coordination and rarely missed a shot. He taught him to fish and ride the big black stallion, Excalibur, which Mister Sullivan fancied and would let no other man touch.

Over the following two-year span everyone, including his parents, noticed the change for the better in young Granville. Sir Harlow invited Hugo to his study one afternoon to hand over a large bonus for a job well done. Strangely enough, after fingering the envelope, Hugo set it back on the desk and said, "No disrespect, Sir, but the pleasure of watching your boy growing into manhood is all mine and I'll not be taking extra pay for my pleasure. Thank you very much." In spite of declining the bonus Hugo didn't complain when he found his weekly pay increased by a third.

At the beginning of September of his fourteenth year, there was an electrical fire at the school and although the damage was slight there remained an awful acrid odor of electrical burn and so they closed three hours early. Gran as usual couldn't wait to get down to the stable and as he was running through the field, about fifty yards away, he saw his mother leaving Mister Sullivan's quarters straightening her skirt. She saw her son from the corner of her eye and blushed a deep crimson and mumbled some nonsense about the Bentley when she usually just called down to the garage for the cars.

At his age and well into puberty, Gran well knew the smell of semen and the scent in Mister Sullivan's quarters reeked of it. "So then, you shagging my mum?" he timidly asked.

Standing by the bedside wearing only his trousers with the suspenders hanging limply at his waist, Hugo was bare chested and sweat gleamed off his well-defined abdominals and pectorals. His mentor frowned at him. Then, quick as a snake, he crossed the room in two long strides and slapped Gran across the face with more force than he meant, and the boy was knocked to the floor bleeding from a split lip. "Don't ever let me hear you talk ill of your mother or so help me God, I'll take the switch to you and beat the hide off your back. Now get the fuck out."

Three days later Gran returned to his duties and the two never spoke of it again. The next two years flew by in what seemed an instant and the bond between man and boy grew stronger each day. His mother often asked about other boys at school and why it seemed he never brought his friends around. He would laugh and say they were all busy and that they saw plenty of each other at school five days out of seven. The truth was his classmates were afraid and thought him cruel and cold-blooded.

Hugo Sullivan was fond of knives—more than fond, almost obsessed. He acquired dozens of blades, pocket knives, sabers, throwing knives, hunting knives, stilettoes, more than fifty in all and kept them razor sharp. He had given Gran a pocket knife when he first arrived at the stable, saying that no gentleman was fully dressed without one. Duly armed, he was enticed into what Mister Sullivan called the game of fear, Mumbley Peg. There are many versions of this game played with pocket knives. The simple version is to throw a knife at the ground near your feet and the closest one wins. The more complicated version is to vary the throw each time—hold the handle, the point, off your wrist, off your nose, shoulder, elbow, etc.—and the first one to miss loses.

This is an old game of what was considered manliness, and of course, Mister Sullivan made it very manly indeed. His version contained all the elements of the various tosses, which is a highly trained skill in itself, but it was played throwing the knife as close to your opponent's foot as possible, barefoot. If you flinched, you lost; if you moved your foot, you lost. If the thrower hit your foot, he lost. Hugo played for money, lots of money.

Gran had been playing since he was twelve, that first year Hugo worked with him. For his sixteenth birthday, Mister Sullivan, dressed in his Sunday best and accompanied by young Master Gran, went into the village to Hugo's favorite pub. The boy had grown like a weed and now stood six feet tall with 165 pounds of muscle built from his four years of hard work. Mister Sullivan considered this the boy's rite of passage to manhood. His goal this evening was to get the lad drunk and laid, in that order. They took barstools and a crowd gathered as always when Hugo held court.

Once they were firmly entrenched, Hugo made a huge show of buying the lad his first pint and then produced the crudely wrapped package. When the paper was stripped, there lay an ornate walnut box, engraved in ivory, the letters GH shining forth from the middle. There was utter silence in the crowded room as all waited to view the contents. The box was hinged with a tiny release catch hidden in the left edge. Gran found it by intuition and when the cover snapped open with a click, there within the maroon velvet lining sat the most beautiful sight Gran had ever seen. The Italian-made switchblade that he carried to this day seemed to fly from box to hand. He felt the weight and power; it made his testicles clench. The slight pressure applied to the brass button made it spring to life. The Spanish steel blade with its engraved Gothic inscription reflected the glare of the bar lights. With a boy's sense of romantic illusion, he promptly named it "El Diablo" and he still thought of it by that name. It was and still is the most wondrous gift he ever received.

Gran felt like a king holding court in this smoky barroom with the laughing faces surrounding him. The alcohol cruised through his veins as he became lost in indulgence. Soon Mister Sullivan appeared out of the smoke accompanied by a voluptuous pale-skinned beauty with flaming red hair and swung her onto Gran's lap. "This gorgeous beauty is Georgina and she's a personal friend of mine, so be very nice to the lady. Give the birthday boy a little kiss then, love." She enveloped his mouth within her own and he felt her lips devour his as her tongue snaked in, thrusting into the hollow in his cheek.

She had her bountiful breasts pressed tightly to his chest and her hands wandered over his face and wound snugly in his hair. She had the smoothest whiskey voice as she cooed in his ear, biting and licking as she went, "Off to my room then, love." Rising from his lap and pulling him along behind her, the young whore led him up the stairs to whistles and shouts from the bawdy crowd.

The following morning was cold and drizzling rain with a strong easterly wind blowing as they made their way from the pub to the Bentley. Mister Sullivan was whistling an old Irish tune and was in extremely good humor. Gran never wanted the night to end, as it was the best of his life. He only slept for an hour or so and now nestled down in the creamy soft leather seat of the Bentley; he closed his eyes to the wet, windswept landscape speeding past the windscreen. Hugo was as proud as if the boy were of his own loins. He had performed admirably, not getting too drunk and evidently servicing the experienced Georgina to satisfaction. Hugo had won the knife in a long extended match of Mumbley Peg with an older former champion. He had already taken a thousand pounds from the gentleman and he wagered the knife against his losses. It was the grandest gift he had ever given anyone.

The following two years were exceptionally busy, as Gran was now expected to fulfill his role as the heir to an enormous estate and tremendous wealth. His father was in his late sixties and in poor health. After the years under the tutelage of Mister Sullivan, the boy couldn't bear the thought of assuming the musty, dull life of his family. He longed for adventure and fancied a life of service in the RAF. But, try as he might to relive those first four years of his youth, he was forced to spend most of his

106

time with studies and duties to the manor. Mister Sullivan's tutelage appeared finished.

Twenty

Snow began in the high country, shifting from light airy flurries to thick, heavy flakes that battled the wipers to submission and diminished the visibility by the minute. The E-Class Mercedes wasn't the best choice for this climate; its limiting rear wheel drive allowed the rear tires to lose footing and the car began fishtailing at any speed over ten miles an hour. Gran was forced to find shelter and wait until the skies cleared.

Brick had outrun the storm with his four-wheel drive and pulled into the outer limits of Bend just as dusk slowly disappeared in the shadows of darkness. He opened his laptop and searched for lodging. He booked a room at a small motel off the strip, then drove to the center of town and treated himself to a nice king salmon dinner. It was only a few minutes after nine and Brick was wired, so after driving aimlessly for an hour acquiring a sense of the town's new additions, he felt the pull of the past.

On the next block, the red neon's glow beckoned from high in the night sky. He parked on a cross street down the road. He turned the corner to a memory. The twenty-foot flashing neon sign read "The Red Shoe." The marquee across the front said, "Live Entertainment Friday and Saturday Nights."

It was Thursday; he entered the front door with his hat pulled low and eyes downcast. He climbed a stool at the end of the long circular bar that held at least thirty. It was quiet and all he hoped to accomplish was to get a lay of the land. Things hadn't changed much; it was almost all bar with twenty-five tables in the back room for diners, but most people came for the entertainment and weekends were standing room only. The bar was scarred from long years of cigarette burns and fight damage.

It was only ten years ago but seemed like a lifetime when the crew assisted the Hartwell family in their search for the missing daughter. Wyatt Hartwell owned the place, a small neighborhood joint called Wyatt's Corral. The crew was here converting assets at the ranch. Most people knew they were ex-Rangers and the story they spun was raising sheep for the Pendleton Woolen Mill in Portland. In reality, they were still moving tons of marijuana and cocaine throughout the country and England. Brick was the front man and brains behind the operation and became the face of the ranch. He was so charming and accommodating that the strangers were soon accepted into the community. They were generous to a fault, buying drinks and lending a hand where needed. Everything was too good to last and on a sullen stormy night in late November calamity struck.

Wyatt had two lovely daughters: Zoe, almost eighteen and already a minor celebrity with her gravelly voice and acoustic guitar, and Audrey, who was the apple of his eye. He wouldn't admit it of course, claiming he loved them equally, but it was clear in his face that Audrey was her daddy's little princess. She was only thirteen years old with golden flax for hair, green eyes, and a mile worth of personality. She spoke with a slight country lilt and sparkled like a bed of diamonds. She was there … and then she wasn't.

Brick's crew was notified and joined the search party in the early stages. There were over a hundred fifty volunteers searching the countryside day and night. They searched for three straight days before her broken, lifeless body was found between Bend and Redmond to the north. She had been brutally raped and her panty-clad body was otherwise naked except for one cherry red high-heeled shoe. To the family's knowledge, she never owned anything even remotely close to such shoes. The killer was never found and it remains an open investigation to this day.

The wife and mother had run off shortly after Audrey was born, so now brokenhearted Wyatt dove to the bottom of the bottle and stayed there until he died. That was two years ago and Brick heard about it before his self-proclaimed exile to his cabin. Zoe had assumed managerial responsibilities for the barely surviving bar and for her broken-down father a year after Audrey's disappearance. She proved to be stronger and more resilient than anyone would have thought. She renamed the bar "The Red Shoe" in honor of her little sister; she never wanted anyone to forget her or her horrific fate.

Zoe featured herself as a regular performer at the bar, and other entertainers and bands flocked to help her transform the place into a palace in the wilderness. She had an uncanny business sense and when surrounding property values went into the tank, Zoe bought up everything surrounding the Red Shoe. Bend prospered as a city and the Shoe, as everyone called it, turned into a very successful operation. Brick had been an early investor, not caring if he ever saw the money again. Zoe wouldn't take charity and paid back every last cent. She knew she could always count on him.

With her managerial responsibilities and all the details of everyday life, Zoe had largely stepped back from the stage and now only sang when she felt like it. Tonight, she appeared as magic by his side. She was smiling her thousand-watt variety when she said, "Hey cowboy, long time."

Brick was surprised, as he never felt her approach. She looked beautiful, no longer a girl but an incredibly attractive woman. She was a country girl from her long, soft brown hair to her matching eyes. Flannel shirt, tight, low-cut boot jeans, and hand-tooled lizard shit-kickers. Ready for the rodeo. "Man, I don't know what to say ... It is so good to see you—you look fantastic."

"You bet your ass I do," she managed with a chuckle. "But for an old duffer, you look pretty damn good yourself. You know I always had a crush on you, but so did all the girls, and you never gave me a second glance. I hope you're sorry."

"You can't imagine how sorry; want to go to bed?"

She broke into a thunderous, guttural laugh that started deep and turned into a belly laugh. "Why you taking it so slow? You always could make me laugh."

After her laughter subsided, he turned the conversation to a more somber topic. "Did they ever find the guy?" Brick asked.

"No, and it hasn't stopped. There are lots of girls gone missing every year. Some are runaways, but there are others that people swear would never run. Not just parents but friends and teachers who would know."

"Sorry, we tried. I know how it wrecked your family."

"I lost my sister and father that day."

"Is Casper the friendly ghost still sheriff?"

"That's mean, Brick."

"Be honest, Zoe. Casper couldn't find his ass with both hands."

"He retired last year. There's a new sheriff in town but he's just temporary. The city council hired a New York cop and he's destined to take over. He's smart and street savvy; you can tell when you meet him. The missing girls bother him and he might be our best hope of stopping this maniac. I sure hope so."

"Good … I hope so too."

She sat next to him and they resumed a lighthearted conversation, trying to fill the blank pages in both their lives. It had been a long time, but they fell into an easy rhythm as if they saw each other every day. They had a couple of beers; then Zoe slid off the barstool and said, "I want to play you a song. When I first heard this, I thought of you."

She went to the stage giving a little wiggle of her hips and looked back over her shoulder coyly at him to make sure he was watching. She turned on one spotlight directly overhead and adjusted the microphone on the stage. By the time she strapped on her acoustic guitar, she had everybody's attention. "Hey you all, I've got a special guest in the house tonight and I want to play this one for Brick." She then broke into a cover of Bob Seger's "Like a Rock."

She sang with such heartfelt intensity that Brick had tears in his eyes as he listened to the words; he knew he hadn't lived up to what she thought of him. He swore on his mother's grave that he would try harder to be the man people thought he once was. She had changed her last name simply to Heart—Zoe Heart—and Brick thought it appropriate; he didn't know anyone with more. He listened to her sing for another hour and when she wasn't looking, he slipped off the barstool and made for the door. He couldn't face her after that, but he knew it would be noted and soon many would know he was back. There were tears in his eyes when he left.

Twenty-one

Gran was furious—furious with the weather, furious with the roads and the car, but mostly furious with himself. He didn't take mistakes or miscalculations lightly, and he needed to lash out at something, preferably someone. He was stuck in this hick town and someone needed to pay. He had to beg for the last shitty room in the last shitty motel and his car had to be towed the last four miles and was being held ransom in the shitty little garage. "FUCK!" he screamed at no one. The rage was simmering and the pot was ready to explode, so he walked into town looking for trouble. *Goddamn it, I am a fucking aristocrat and I hate all this bloody fucking wilderness; it's not fair!*

He was in Caldwell, Idaho, just a sneeze away from the Oregon border, but the fucking roads were closed. He tried to find someone to take him back to Boise where there was at least an eyelash of civilization, but no luck. So once again he made his way to the shitty little bar where all the shitty locals pretended to have a life. The name was Friar Tuck's but he didn't even notice; it looked like the same one in the last town.

He walked in and headed straight to the pool table where about ten locals were gathered around and had taken over the tables and chairs in the corner. He stood next to the table until the man missed his shot and then announced, "I'm not from this country but I understand that I can pay my way onto the table, is that correct?"

The man shooting next said, "There are three ahead of you. It's five dollars to get on." And then he lied and said, "We're playing for twenty dollars a game."

Gran said, "Stellar, alert me when this is gone." He threw a hundred-dollar bill on the rail and strutted to the bar. "Innkeeper, whisky neat, the finest you have."

This small-town crowd had no way of knowing that Gran grew up playing with Mister Sullivan on the ocean table at the mansion. They played nine ball and rotation, but the most challenging of all was Snooker and Gran was a master. These boys were playing eight ball and didn't have a chance. Even worse, Gran was a hustler and would miss on purpose, leaving an impossible shot for his opponent, barely winning every game. Why? It's simple: he was gunning for a fight; someone would pay for his frustration and shitty attitude.

After winning two hundred and eighty bucks from these chumps, Gran was tired of it. Playing with such inferior opponents was boring and some of his anger had dissipated. He purposely missed an easy shot and lost the game. Acting much drunker than he really was, he yawned and said he was leaving; he picked up his winnings and walked into the cold night air. The streets were deserted. It was after midnight and Gran was a solitary figure staggering down the lonely street.

Three men who had lost to him slipped out the side door and were following about a hundred feet behind. Gran felt their presence and was ready. To make it easy for them, he turned into an alley and leaned against the far wall as if he was going to take a piss. The biggest man filled the entrance and the other two separated on both sides, effectively blocking the way out. Gran had never bothered to learn their names because he didn't give a shit; they were simply an outlet for his pent-up anger.

Without preamble, the big man said, "You hustled us back there, you asshole, and we came to get our money back."

Gran turned to them and, thrusting his hand into his left coat pocket, he removed the neatly folded bills and said, "Here, fuck all; you take it." He threw the cash in the air and they watched as it scattered in the breeze and floated around the filthy alley and clung to the trash.

Feeling emboldened the big guy said, "Pick it up, asshole."

That's exactly what he wanted to hear, "You teensy wankers going to make me?"

The big guy went into a clumsy fighter's stance with his fists cocked; his buddies moved in closer.

"Teensy? I'm twice your size."

"Twice as fat maybe. How's that working for you? I'm quite talented."

"Let's fuck him up."

Gran pivoted and twisted to his left, kicking the leader's right knee viciously from inside out; the man buckled and dropped. From this position his right fist buried itself in the belly of the man to his left and, as he dropped his weight back to his right side, he kicked the remaining man in the head. It was over in a matter of seconds.

The fight gone, the men sat or lay in the alley. Nobody was seriously hurt—no broken bones or deep cuts. Gran was careful; the cops believed locals against outsiders. These losers were shamed. They'd recover. He didn't care about the money; he was stupendously wealthy. Finished here, he walked back to his motel for a few hours' rest, the men already forgotten. He did feel a little better.

Twenty-two

The man on the roof had spotted Brick when he entered the bar. He was two buildings over with high-powered binoculars. He'd been watching since yesterday. This was one of four locations given to him as possible places for a sighting. When he climbed down, it was dark and he moved to the street; he was looking in the window of a country store when Brick turned the corner and retrieved his truck. There were lots of people milling about. The shops were open with several bars and restaurants to choose from.

Brick left his room before dawn. In the darkened parking lot, he removed a set of Oregon license plates and exchanged them with the ones on his truck. Then he headed south to Sisters. The town was named for the three mountain peaks rising over the town. When the winds blew the mist and clouds free, the sight was majestic. They resembled three ice-cream sundaes with the white snow coating the top third like fluffy whipped cream and below the tree line the dark of rich, creamy chocolate sauce. The office was dark with a sign saying back in an hour, so he jotted a note requesting a room for a week and stuck it in the mail slot. He left the truck in the lot carrying a small satchel with a few essentials and started walking; he knew exactly where he was headed.

The skies were clear and bright as the sun fought its way over the mountains. The beauty of eastern Oregon was the number of sunny days far surpassed that of the valley. They still got their share of nasty weather, as it changes fast in the mountains, but it beats the valley by a mile. The horizon shimmered in heat waves, a promise of a warm day. Brick was a lone figure strolling through town. It was still minutes before dawn and only a few early risers salted the cafés. He had coffee and toast in a cozy spot he remembered and after chatting with the owner, bummed a ride to the Black Butte Resort and Golf Club.

The desk was manned around the clock and he commandeered a large suite for three weeks using a new identity and credit card. He walked around outside until the room was ready.

Feeling better with these precautions completed, he walked back to the motel a mile away. After the necessary check-in at the motel, he set off for his first visit. The watcher was relieved to have his prey back under surveillance but worried over where he'd been.

Twenty-three

I should have turned north from Bend not west. I was putting it off. I was afraid. Stupid, she's my sister. Not by blood but I adopted her and eventually so did Charlie. She was a wretched little waif when I rescued her. To say she had issues was the understatement of the year. I'm very proud of her. She has overcome more in a short time than is comprehensible. I have always been there for her. Until two years ago. That's when I left everything and everyone I loved … without a word.

Little miss Harry. I brought her home after rescuing her from the bully's. My mom would know what to do; she wouldn't tell me where she lived or much else, as defiant as any grown man. She would insist that her name was Harry and then seal her lips and cross her arms over her chest and puff it out. She was both precocious and ferocious. Not to mention cute as a bug.

My mom sent me back to my friends while she talked to Harry. Fed her a peanut butter and jelly sandwich, got her to take a bath, and brushed out the tangles in her hair. By the time I returned, she was dressed in a party dress and announced she was Miss Harry. I never knew how Mom did it, but she had a special touch with kids. Always secretly wanted a daughter and fell in love with Harry. Mom knew where she lived, her mother's name, and where she went to school.

Mom bundled her in the car and drove her home. She wouldn't talk about Harriette's mother, but you could see her disfavor. From that point on, Miss Harry was a regular addition to meals at our home. Mom bought her all new clothes and anything else she needed, and she loved her like her own child. Harry has been in my life since then and I love her dearly. It breaks my heart to know I've let her down with my abandonment.

Selfish.

Mason has been my best friend since kindergarten. Not like Charlie—he's more of a brother. But Mason, man … Mason is the man I wish I could be. He's like a fucking saint; he's always been there for me. No questions asked. His dad was a contractor and Mason worked summers during high school building stuff for his old man. He can do anything: build a house or an office building. He should have been an architect. He just had that eye for the thing missing, then built it. I love him.

I introduced Mason to my little sister. They were married in Minnesota before they moved to Oregon for me. Mason worked for me before I left. They should have plenty of money; I paid everyone well— they deserved it.

Leaving was a chicken shit thing to do, I admit that.

The truth is, I'm a coward.

Not from a fight. Sometimes I relish a fight, especially if the dude I'm fighting deserves it. It cleanses me. Frustration and boredom are my sworn enemies. I fight them tooth and nail. I'm a coward from emotion. A man I respected once told me, "Never apologize or make excuses and never, ever explain." I break the first rule; I'm not afraid to apologize when I'm wrong. Excuses and explanations, well no one cares really. What difference does it make if I have a reason? I was wrong and I'm sorry.

No, I didn't tell anyone, I just left. The problem with being right and always the man with the plan is simple. When you fuck up, it's a big one. At least it is for me. When it's your fault that someone you love gets hurt or dead, it's very hard to cope.

I hid … A coward …

And now I'm back and I find it extremely difficult to face Harriette. Not that Mason will be easy but like I said, Mason is cool. He will forgive me without explanation. There are others as well, but these two are hardest.

There is one other person, a woman.

Dawn wrote to me and was the only one who knew how to reach me. Do I trust her? Tough question. I want to—I really do—but when someone tries to kill you, you're leery.

Jocko? The answer is no. Jocko was a business partner. I set him up and watched over him. He's always been a loose cannon. He used too much of his own product and that alone makes him twitchy and unreliable. I've been gone two years; I can't imagine him stopping, so there is a better than average chance he's dangerous.

I need to start somewhere and I always follow the path of least resistance when I'm not sure of a situation. I still need to be cautious so this seems the best route. If she hasn't changed, it could be fun. I really like this girl.

Twenty-four

Brick drove to Dawn's log home and parked where he had a good view through the field glasses. He remembered the parties at this house. Dawn Lightner was from San Francisco, where her father, Samuel Lightner, was a big deal lawyer who made a name for himself as a criminal attorney and went on to form the famous Lightner, Chambly, and Knox legal practice; it became the premier criminal defense firm in the city.

Needless to say, he was filthy rich. Dawn, his only child, became a constant embarrassment—sliding from one mess to the other faster than Sam could reach his wallet. She became a career student, flunking out of every school around at an alarming rate. He couldn't seem to fathom the fact that his only daughter was crying out for Daddy's attention. Her mother died in childbirth back when Sam was building his firm and so Dawn knew an endless stream of nannies, housekeepers, cooks, and chauffeurs.

Jeremy, an arrogant older college kid, knocked her up when she was sixteen. After an elaborate screaming match with dear old Daddy followed by a quick abortion, she was shipped off to boarding school in Switzerland.

She broke free at eighteen and returned to the States and Daddy's mansion to begin her new career as wild child extraordinaire. She became a media darling locally for a short period because of Sam's notoriety in the city. From arrests for underage drinking and disorderly conduct, to DUIs, to hair-pulling fights at various nightclubs and whatever else would keep Daddy busy trying to rescue her and save face, Dawn did it all. Sam was losing the battle and growing weary of the game.

Sam turned her care over to one of his young rising stars to stop the bleeding. One of her major problems was the seemingly endless supply of money he sent for her to piss away. Sam loved his daughter to death and refused to let her languish poor and wretched, as he had worked his whole life for her benefit. He was sure she would grow out of her wildness, and that did eventually happen.

James Heckert was the attorney Sam tasked with his daughter's issues. Dawn thought he was cute, and at first she was determined to seduce him into submission and use this as another way to prove her father powerless over her life. But Jimmy was too smart for her. He was firm in his rejection of her advances. He didn't use her father as a prophylactic like she expected. Always gentle and kind, he didn't take any bullshit or accept her excuses. He would point out that her life was of her choosing and he didn't care if she was intent on ruining it. Jimmy was just doing the job assigned to him, same as any other. He told her that he admired her father and thought him a great man even more so with the burden she laid at the poor man's feet.

Two things happened, and the first changed her in ways she never dreamed possible. She was discovered at a supermarket in Seattle by a photographer from *Playboy* magazine. She was the epitome of the fresh girl next door with her long blond hair, perfect cheekbones, and large, natural perky breasts, high and firm. He planned to feature her in a special edition as the centerfold.

She was flown to Beverly Hills and almost overnight became a minor celebrity at the mansion. But being a centerfold and a working Bunny were two very different things. She soon realized that the Bunnies were no more than high-priced whores for the rich businessmen old Hugh courted. She didn't need the money or attention, but the notoriety she gained from that shoot followed her for a lifetime and she cherished the memory.

The biggest change for Dawn came when she moved to Eugene, Oregon, to attend art school. She loved the school and thrived in the environment. She still partied but the wild abandon was now absent. She never missed school and took responsibility for her life. She found the house in Sisters. Far from a shack, it had five bedrooms, three baths, and a spacious studio for her paintings and charcoals. A huge hot tub sat in a grotto surrounded by tall aspens along with a private road and seventeen acres of forest, with a full view of the Sisters surrounding her. It wasn't cheap—close to three million—but James recommended it to her father. At the time he was worth half a billion, and he bought it sight unseen and left James as the administrator.

Twenty-five

Almost exactly one year later, the boys came to town. The squad was intact; there were seven of them and they rented a vacant dude ranch while they searched for an appropriate site to build their compound. Only Brick's name ever appeared on any official documents; he was in charge from the start. By that time, all had left the military except for Charlie who remained until he retired. The dustup in Panama was over almost before it began.

Brick misjudged his stint in the service. He mustered out after six years as a colonel. Charlie remained in service until he became a brigadier general and set his plans for the security firm. It was political. Vietnam had been a complete fiasco and the party in power wanted a repeat in the Mideast. Noriega was easy and they thought Hussein would be the same. Charlie couldn't change it, so he got out. When the generals disagree so strongly with the politicians that they would rather retire than go along, the people of this country should pay attention. The corporations demand more hours for less pay, so who has time for morals?

Brick did the planning and, of course, they used Bucky as legal counsel. That was before the tragedy with Jesus.

It had always been Brick with the hidden plan. They were still young men; Nicky, the youngest and the oldest was Stoney James from Whites Creek, Tennessee.

Stoney was the only black man and undoubtedly the nicest of the bunch, even tempered with a laid-back demeanor. He was huge—6'6", 265 pounds—with a shaven head and coal black eyes. His scarred and calloused hands were like cast-iron skillets. His father had named him Stoney for his hard deadpan glare as an infant. Old Dad had racked his share of time and likened the look to the famous thousand-yard stare of hardened convicts.

Stoney never shucked the look and strangers gave him a wide berth, some crossing streets to avoid him. As a friend or soldier, he was loyal to a fault and would give his last nickel to a hungry stranger. He held a true soft spot for children; God help you if he noticed you being unkind toward kids.

Charlie stayed at the ranch that first month when they were still setting up but then left and eventually finished his career at Fort Lewis, Washington Charlie was making inquiries into his own private venture. His goal was to provide mercenaries overseas and security for those who could afford it. This was before he decided on a location and asked Brick for help on the business end.

Clint Shwegger hailed from Lost Corner, Arkansas, and was the joker of the group. Steady under fire but once back at the barracks, he would go to extremes to prank his buddies. Near the end of their enlistment, they had returned from one of their secret trips into Colombia and the men were left without a purpose for a few weeks. All were restless and while some of the guys worked out or partied in town, Clint was hell-bent on getting to Stoney. For some reason, his even temper was a challenge to Clint and he spent hours trying to figure out a prank to rile the big man. Clint was short and wiry with bright red hair and freckles. He barely made the height requirement for enlistment. His slender white hands looked more like an old woman's than a soldier's. Alongside Stoney he resembled a petulant child.

Clint was a driver and mechanic. Back home in Arkansas he raced stock cars and motorcycles, and he could reassemble a motor in his sleep—one of the best drivers/mechanics to ever hit the Rangers. Charlie and Brick recruited him for their squad immediately. It was rumored that Clint also ran bootleg whiskey in a souped-up Chevy.

Jesus knew an old snake charmer from his village and was telling stories about the incredible snake house with venomous varieties on hand.

The snake man's age was undetermined but he appeared ancient, and Jesus told stories of some amazing technics the charmer had discovered. Clint was mesmerized by these stories, and when he learned that the man held a little show on certain Saturdays, he pestered Jesus until he agreed to take him. Clint and Nicky were both snipers, with Clint being the steady one under fire, so Nicky became his spotter. The two formed a friendship, so when Jesus finally agreed to go to a show, Nicky tagged along.

The scene was surreal; there must have been over two hundred snakes in this tightly enclosed compound—snakes of all sizes and colors slithered over and around each other. Some were in baskets and glass cages, while many were loose and crawling over floors, furniture, and walls. Their yellow eyes seemed to glow with an unearthly presence as they slithered around the hut and each other. Nicky was so freaked out he had goose bumps crawling from his scalp to the bottoms of his soles, and his face had turned a sickly green. Finally, he ran from inside and stood panting and sweating in the heat of the merciless sun. These snakes were the ones who played mice with others. Those who didn't were kept in secure fastened glass boxes that allowed full view without the danger of an inquisitive hand making a deadly mistake. The old charmer they called Wahaka spoke rapid Spanish, and Jesus translated for his comrades. Clint was especially interested in the smaller poisonous snakes and when Jesus hinted that he had held several that had had their venom glands removed, Clint couldn't restrain himself and made Jesus interrupt to ask if they would still bite. The old man smiled a crooked little grin, as others had asked that question before and he knew the reason.

Clint bargained with the old man until he sold him a coral snake with its venom glands removed. It was about two feet long with bright red bands encircling its length at even intervals; it was also extremely deadly— or would have been with venom glands. It was known as the twenty-minute snake because, once bitten, you were dead in twenty. Clint wound up paying half a month's military salary to buy the damned thing.

One night the boys were out drinking, but after a while Clint snuck back early and put the sleepy snake in Stoney's bed. Jesus was home with his family, but the rest of the team eventually rolled in with Stoney. Clint was lingering close when Stoney crawled into bed. For years afterward, Clint told the story with glee as the big man came straight up screaming. Clint rushed to his side, grabbed the snake behind the head, and stuffed the evil devil back in the same burlap bag he kept it in and tied it tight. Everyone went berserk with the sight. They had all seen the videos of the poisonous snakes of Central America and the men recognized it immediately.

Nicky volunteered to go for the doc and rushed out of the barracks, then headed out to buy beer. Brick said they needed to cut his leg open and suck the poison out. GK said he would make the incision but no way was he going to suck the poison out. Charlie concurred that whoever had this poison touch their lips would die.

Clint consoled Stoney, holding the big man and repeatedly saying how sorry he was and how everyone loved him; he was crying real tears. It seemed that their friend and comrade didn't have a chance and there was nothing to do about it. When after almost an hour nothing happened, Nicky returned claiming the doc couldn't be found but at least he brought beer. Stoney said he felt fine, and Clint declared it to be a miracle; he had big Stoney thanking God for weeks. Clint got his money's worth out of that tired snake before GK got sick of the whole thing and killed it with his k-bar—cut the head clean off with one quick swipe and then wiped the blood off on Clint's camo pants. Stoney was never told the truth, as all were sure he would kill the little man.

Everyone was leery of GK, even Charlie, because you never knew what was lurking in his twisted mind. He was Brick's friend, which no one understood. They had gone to school together for a time at Harvard. Brick was auditing a series of business classes and GK had just transferred from Oxford when the two men met and hit it off. The special chemistry between them was as unlikely as cats and dogs swimming together. What initially bonded their friendship was that they were both younger than the other boys, with Gran being a hare's breathe the senior. They were ostracized because they were so young and privileged. .

Twenty-six

Through the glasses all seemed serene. Brick had parked in the woods, hidden from sight of Dawn's house, and now he walked in a loose circle in approach to the grotto.

The watcher was thwarted by this tactic and stayed in position, keeping an eye on the front of the house.

Brick was positioned in the trees just out of sight when an unexpected occurrence took place. Dawn stepped out the back door carrying a fluffy towel and a glass of wine. She was dressed in shorts, a tank, and running shoes, with perspiration still visible on her glowing body. Sitting on the step to the tub, she untied the shoes and then struggled out of the wet clothes. A pole shower like those they have at the beach was inset in the concrete slab and worked with a pull chain. First she piled the nest of honey blond on top of her head and, working blind, was able to tame the heap of hair tight with a series of pins and combs; then she stepped under the cool spray. After rinsing the sweat from her run, she fussed with preparations for a leisurely soak in the big redwood tub.

Brick was amazed as he watched the intricate hair hide. Magically she made three pounds of hair disappear in a makeshift nest. . His eyes moved down and were treated to an awful lot of that magic.

From time to time the Creator likes to show off. He starts in the womb with the perfect skull shape. Sets the eye sockets just so and leaves the proper spacing for the nose cartilage. Molds the cheekbones in a certain fashion and gives the jaw a hard, firm line. Enough room left for a full and generous mouth and move down.

The skeleton has to be a sturdy design to hold the curves he will sculpt next. The chest full enough to support the bountiful breasts, then narrowing to a long thin waist before flaring again in proportion to the chest. Add a wide enough pelvis to support femur and tibia. The feet made to hold it all in place, and add rich layers of flesh with flawless skin.

That is the creature they call Dawn. Untold thousands if not millions of adolescent boys have treasured the filched pictures of her and locked themselves away for hours. A similar number of businessmen have coveted the same pictures tucked away in desk drawers and only remove them once the door is locked.

Brick knew her as well as anyone, and yet coming upon her unaware stopped him short and he was lost for words. He hesitated, unsure of the approach. This was a violation of her privacy and he needed to tread carefully.

Finally, he cleared his throat and it startled her. "Hello," he squeaked.

She turned at the sound of his voice, searching the woods for the voice as she grabbed her towel and clutched it tight to her chest. Brick stepped into view not ten feet from where she stood frozen in time. He stood still and as recognition dawned, her face reacted in shock and her eyes just stared for a very long time.

Then the tears started falling; she dropped the towel and turned away, silently crying. She was shaking her head and muttering, "Oh no … not now, not like this. I can't stand it. I won't take it." She gave a quick look back over her shoulder to confirm who she saw and turned away again. Then, without a word, she stepped into the tub with the smooth grace of a proud woman.

"I'm sorry; it's just that I had to …"

"Shut up." She wiped the tears away with the back of her hand and mimicked picking up a telephone receiver and said, "Hello, Dawn. This is Brick and I'm in town and I really need to explain why I left suddenly like and then said barely a word to anyone for two long fucking years. I was wondering if I could come by and explain … is this a good time?"

"Again, I'm sorry. I'll leave and call and come back when—"

"Don't you fucking dare. Goddamn it, you are going to stay right here and talk to me or never come back."

He walked close to the tub and said, "I better start at the beginning."

"No, you don't Brick Winslow. I am not going to sit in here naked while you stand fully dressed and talk down to me. Take off your clothes and get in the tub."

"Can I use the bathroom first?"

"Make it snappy."

Once inside, he spotted her cell phone and looked through her contacts and call history. Mason's name was listed in the caller ID, and his number seemed to average two calls daily. Her computer was up and a quick check of her email told him all he needed to know. His suspicions confirmed, he used the bathroom, flushed, and washed his face and hands, raking them through his hair.

He was gone five minutes and came back with a towel over his shoulder and had a bottle of Beck's beer in his hand. "I found this in the fridge—is it okay?"

"Sure, put it in a plastic cup and bring me more wine. All of a sudden I seem to need it."

The clearing held her scent, a hint of lilac combined with the woodsy smell of the forest. Full blooming hydrangeas surrounding the redwood tub created a haze, erotic and hypnotizing in the secluded grotto as he settled in the spacious tub. He was careful to sit opposite her, as far away as possible. He sensed her anger fading; still he better go easy. He knew it was important he be gentle; the thought of losing her was unbearable.

He started with Jesus and how he had slid into a deep depression and couldn't face her or his friends. He told her everything, from the land in Wisconsin to the building of the cabin complex to keep his mind busy. He told her about Cassie and shooting her husband, the ambush at the cabin, and the price on his head. The only thing he left out was Laura.

He was visibly spent when he finished, so she moved close and held him to her breast and they both cried. He was drained and felt like a wet noodle. He tried to leave to spare her the drama. She wouldn't— couldn't—let him go. Stepping out of the hot tub, she led him to her bed because she loved him, had always loved him.

He made love to Dawn and ascended. Climbed lofty peaks, knew he was home. They fit, came together, a natural primitive rhythm. Hands and lips moved just so and melted the flesh until it became one. They rode the high crests and found respite in the gentle valleys. Bonded, melded giving and receiving in kind, so very perfect. Could this be the face of love?

He stayed the night and fought vivid and frightening dreams.

In the morning he tried to grill her about what was happening at the ranch, but she turned the tables. And before he could ask a single question, she started a rapid-fire staccato of insistent yet innocent inquiries as to where he was staying, how long he would be there, when would she see him again, and Charlie's whereabouts.

The planned lies rolled off his tongue smooth as butter. He announced that he was beat tired from the long trip and the unexpected lovemaking. Dismissed the offer of her house as a base and said he was traveling for the next few days. He would call her as soon as he knew his plans. He mentioned that he might go and visit Jocko at the ranch. He didn't mention Charlie and his plans.

She reacted with fear: "No! Whatever you do, don't go near him. Brick, you need to talk to Mason and Harriette first. Things have changed; you can't trust Jocko anymore. You need to stay far away from him." The panic was clear on her face.

"Okay honey, relax. I'll do what you say. I'm going to program my cell number into your phone before I leave, and I promise I'll stay in touch." He started to walk away and turned and looked over his shoulder, giving her his best sexy smile. He said, "Thanks for … you know, everything. Please don't give up on me; I swear I'm back."

Twenty-seven

The morning after the alley fight, Gran was at the garage bright and early. He was told upon arriving that there were a shitload of cars before his and they may not get to his until the next day. He asked for the proprietor and was ushered into in inner office where a burly almost bald man was screaming into the phone, "Fuck you, you cocksucker! I spend over ten grand a year with you fuckers and if I don't get those parts by the end of business today, I'll take my business elsewhere." He slammed the phone down and turned to snarl at the intruder, "What the fuck do you want?"

"Excuse me, sir, I can see that you are extremely busy but I have a matter of utter importance to discuss—that is if you're Jerry, the proprietor of this fine establishment."

Gran was smiling but it was because the red-faced Jerry had a perfect ring of brown hair circling his bald head and looked exactly like Friar Tuck, same as the bar. Jerry gawked at the Englishman, his jaw hanging down in the fleshy folds of his neck, so Gran continued.

"I am working as an agent of the British Air Force in conjunction with the Army Rangers on a matter of national security concerning our countries." Jerry still had his jaw in his throat. "I must arrive at command center in Fort Lewis, Washington, within a fortnight. The lives of many brave boys from both countries are at stake."

Jerry didn't have a clue what this man had just said, but he considered himself to be a patriotic American so he answered, "Sure, what can I do to help?"

Gran continued, "I am obviously on foreign soil and I miscalculated the weather conditions and the traction abilities of my vehicle and find myself stranded. Your man suggested new winter tires and chains to speed me on my journey to fulfill my mission."

Jerry looked out at the bay and parking lot overfilling with cars in for repair and stammered a bit.

Undaunted, Gran went on, "Obviously, you can't be expected to place me at the front of the queue without proper remuneration." He laid out five one-hundred-dollar bills in a line on the desk. "Allow me to compensate you for the privilege of moving up in the queue, as national security takes precedence. I shall purchase the parts and labor at your standard rate."

For a second Jerry was stunned but then jumped to his feet and opened the door to the garage and screamed, "Jimmy, move the Buick out and bring that black E-class in—now!" Jerry scooped the bills off the desk and shoved them deep in his pocket; he couldn't believe his good fortune.

"Her Majesty and I thank you, sir. I shall retain the key fob for the boot; you may have your man deposit the standard rubber in the backseat, please. I have quite sensitive equipment in the boot and it shan't be disturbed."

Twenty-eight

Back in the truck, Brick was laughing at himself. He had to admit that no matter how much he wanted to deny it, he was a sucker for a beautiful woman and this one, man, this one he called a friend. He couldn't bullshit this one; she was as real as they come. He had planned to ask questions and press for answers. But his mind went blank when she appeared and stripped off her clothes. One thing was certain: between his appearance at the Shoe and after this last encounter, things were bound to heat up fast.

He drove aimlessly, letting his mind clear and the flame in his loins subside. It was mid-afternoon and his little escapade made his stomach growl, so he found the Little Sisters Tavern—same as memory suggested. He ordered the blue plate special and had a couple of Henry Weinhard's to wash it down. The bar buzzed with a hum of activity. The scarred surface of polished mahogany held frothy glasses of foam-topped beer along with too many umbrella drinks and sweet concoctions of liqueurs and fruit.

The sun-scorched tourists sat with their plentiful rumps spilling over the sides of the stools surrounding the circular brass-tinged bar. Their voices rang with the high-pitched caterwauling of the already inebriated self-proclaimed winners.

These disgusting excuses for human beings always affected Brick the same way. Watching them threatened to ruin an otherwise special day. He laid bills on the bar and walked out into the sun-kissed fresh mountain air. He breathed deep, savoring the taste of freedom. So very lucky to be alive, but his thoughts clouded with doubt.

The late lunch and beers made him sleepy. With no real plan, he decided to drive to the no-tell motel. He took the usual precautions as he looped in a wide arc around the town but couldn't shake that feeling of eyes boring down on him at intervals along the road. Sometimes when either driving or walking he would make a sudden detour into an alley or behind a building, but if there were followers they were good and stayed out of sight. The sun was concluding its daily journey as the planet circled at dazzling speed. As it approached the tree line, Brick wanted to make his stop at the motel a quick one; he was anxious to return to the lodge, as night falls fast in the mountains.

The dread he felt when he pulled in the parking lot was palpable. The air was still, without a touch of breeze, which was unusual. The sky cast an eerie glow as a fog descended over the town, turning everything a ghastly dirty shade of yellow. He had seen this phenomenon before; when a cool front moves in from the West Coast, the atmospheric change is quite drastic. The most alarming fact? The lot was empty, devoid of any car, people, or motion. The office was dark and foreboding in the dimming gloom. Brick parked near the office at the opposite end from his room. The Kimber was in his hand before he opened the truck door. He peered into the office window but the blinds were closed and a "back in one hour" sign hung from the door handle. He walked all the way around the motel before approaching his room from the far side.

Staring at the bottom of the door confirmed his suspicions—his room had been breached. Someone had violated his space, and who knows what's waiting. *Fuck it, now's as good a time as any.* His key made a resounding click as it turned uneasy on unoiled metal, and he kicked in the door and charged in low with the big .45 held steady in both hands.

Twenty-nine

The sky cleared but the air still held crystals of frozen moisture that sparkled like a band of diamonds as the rising sun turned the dawn into a kaleidoscope of glittering light, reflecting off the hood of the Mercedes. Gran was in a good mood; he was always happy when he got his way. It had cost him some money as he watched the greedy garage owner rip him off. But he knew when to use force and when guile was appropriate. Money didn't really matter; it was just a way to keep score. When born with the silver spoon, it's a warped mind-set.

His head was clear and focused as he crossed the border into Oregon. He was confident and anxious to let fate run its course. Trouble was his drug of choice. The deep green of the fir trees towering overhead created a dark tunnel, winding and twisting higher as he rose to new altitudes. The vibrant green was in sharp contrast to the pure white of the fresh snow. The roads were plowed and with new tires and chains, he rode effortlessly into the cold air; the E-class proved again to be a worthy steed and he felt justified in his choice. He would always choose comfort over utility; the idea of bumping along in a drafty Jeep was distasteful. As he crested the rise and started to descend into the valley, he noticed the clanging of the chains on the dry roads.

Signs announced the location of food and gas in two miles, so Gran slowed to diminish the noise of the chains and watched for the stop. It came just as the road curved and started on its next rise. Several stores were encased in a natural clearing, sitting alongside a creek swollen with spring melt. The sound of the rushing water reminded him of home. Gran was a fan of fate; destiny and all signs significant spoke volumes.

He pulled to the station bustling with activity and friendly faces. If he expected difficulty or delay, he was disappointed. The stocky fresh-faced kid who greeted him said, sure, they could pull the chains right now if he would give them the keys; he would stow them in the trunk. His name tag read Guy, and he informed Gran that he was lucky he stopped when he did, as it was illegal to use chains in Oregon. Gran thought of Jerry, who knew he was headed this way but sold him as many accessories as he could. Gran just laughed; old Jerry had ignored all his bullshit and saw the money and knew he had a live one.

"Actually, you may retain the chains for future use. I won't require them further. Please change the tires with the backseat version and, as with the previous item, you may retain all for your trouble."

Because it was easy, he decided to have breakfast at the adjoining diner. The food and coffee were terrific, and Gran was on his way again in half an hour. The ride down to Bend was uneventful and the Brit was there before sunset. He marveled at the changes; the town had grown in size and scope, spilling into land that was originally forested and free from commerce. He drove about seeking changes and additions, then mirrored Brick's movements, finding a room and a nice dinner.

It was a balmy morning and the Shoe was closed when Zoe decided to do her paperwork early so she could enjoy the rest of the day—maybe spend it pampering herself, something she rarely did. As she walked through the deserted bar, she made a sweep of the kitchen to make sure the crew hadn't left the burners or ovens lit, a natural duty every restaurateur follows. Zoe was always diligent to check the stage and then the basement filled with the mechanics of furnace, water heaters, walk-in coolers, and all the expensive equipment that was bound to fail at the most inopportune times. With a sigh of relief that all was well, she wound her way to the office with the intention of accomplishing the boring task of paying bills and filling out the various unending forms for license renewals and the other detailed bullshit that no business owner relishes.

When she opened the office door, she flinched—sitting in her chair facing her desk with his back to her was a broad-shouldered man largely hidden from view. Before she had a chance to react further, a calm, vaguely familiar voice said, "A truly splendid morning … I've been waiting on you, my dear."

Her face lit with recognition when he turned to face her. "How did you get in here?" She was mad.

"No cheerio, Gran?" he said with his trademark grin. "I have arrived from a perilous journey and am tired and a trifle chilly, so I used some of my vast skills to gain access. I may assure you I mean no ill will; I simply wish to speak with you in private. Actually, I'm doing you a favor—your security is the shits and your code predictable. Were you aware, my dear mate, Brick and I are security specialists?"

"No, other than the fact that you were ranchers, I don't know anything about who you were before you came to town. You were all good to us, so I'm sorry if I jumped at you, GK."

He turned his head and hid the grimace on his face and the narrowing of the eyes. "I prefer Gran, as 'tis me name."

"I'm sorry again, but isn't that what the other guys on the ranch called you?"

"Quite a prank given by another mate of ours. Was administered during service in defense of our respective countries."

"Okay … what can I do for you?"

"I am looking for the aforementioned Colonel Winslow. I should imagine him a touch late; we were to meet here."

"Actually he was ahead of you; he was here two days ago and we had a nice chat. Funny, he didn't mention you."

"Typical of the old boy; a pretty face and he goes all a flutter."

Zoe blushed, as she didn't remember him as the type to hand out compliments. "He said he'd be back. Is there a message I could give him?"

Gran ignored her question and became thoughtful; finally, he said, "Have you seen or heard of Charles or any of the other lads about?"

"Brick said that Charlie was three thousand miles away in Indonesia, if I remember correctly. I haven't seen anyone else. Are you guys having a reunion or something?"

He laughed, "Precisely, good show. Should you catch a glimpse, a thoughtful mention would be appropriate I should think. Appreciate the gesture kindly, milady." He kissed her hand and got up to leave.

He disappeared as silently as he had arrived. Once he left, Zoe went through the club again checking doors and windows, but all was in order. She checked the security panel and nothing was tripped, no alerts. Very strange indeed, she thought.

Thirty

Sitting in the center of the bed with boots trashing the spread was Charlie, a glass of cracked ice filled with smoky amber liquid in hand. Brick didn't need to see the bottle to know it was J.T.S. Brown, but if there were any doubt it was perched on the bedside table. Through the open bathroom door, Brick could see a bag of ice in the sink with Charlie's pistol sitting next to it.

"I could have shot you! Damn it, Charlie."

"Settle down, buddy boy. You would never shoot me—you're too good. So, let's blow this shithole; take me where you're really staying."

Brick broke into a wide grin. "You mean you don't know? You're slipping, my friend."

"I'll give you that; you cover your tracks well and took the precautions, which I believe I taught you. We didn't have enough men to trail you effectively on foot."

"So who do you have? I've felt the presence but I haven't spotted him," Brick confessed.

"It's Keith; he flew into Fort Lewis a couple of days ago and picked you up at the Shoe," Charlie answered. "I'll call him in and he can drive us. I'm tired of walking."

"Have him follow us. I have my truck."

Keith Schmidt was Charlie's main man at McShane and Winslow Security in Austin, Texas. When Keith heard Charlie's request, he fell in behind the men in a nondescript Chevy.

Weather conditions changed while the men were talking, the balmy day disappeared in minutes flat. It was a damp cold—the moisture suspended in midair, small drops clinging to the branches, and leaves dripping steadily like a Chinese water torture. The wet chill seeping

142

through layers of protection until it froze your bones. Brick had the heater up high. Still spring this morning. Temperatures vary widely in the early seasons. One day you're sure that summer is here to stay; the next makes you do a 180. One thing you can count on in the mountains, it can turn on a dime.

They talked for over an hour, making a plan. Charlie said he'd been in contact with Mason and things at the ranch were bad. He'd taken Keith to the ranch by way of back roads just to give them both a lay of the land. Keith would be back on the hill next morning and Charlie would join him later. There was more, a lot more, but Brick needed to face it without advance warning.

Brick said, "Did you talk to …?"

"No way; she would have sensed the lie in a heartbeat. You're going to have to do your own dirty work. This way I didn't have to lie when I said I hadn't seen you. I won't lie to them for you."

"I know, sorry." He threw an extra room key to Charlie and left, both men agreeing to stay in close contact.

He called Dawn first and was relieved when he heard her voice. Keith had shadowed her and reported that when she left home, she went straight to Mason's house. Brick didn't give her an explanation, only pressing the importance of following his directions, which included calling Mason and inviting themselves over on Saturday. They would provide dinner and wine. He said he wanted to surprise them, so not to let the cat out of the bag.

Next he called Zoe and told her the plan. She balked at first, as it was already Wednesday and it didn't give her much chance to rearrange affairs on short notice. Brick insisted and her curiosity got the best of her, so she acquiesced.

It was two in the morning when Charlie got back to the suite and fell into bed. Brick was asleep already, but both were up before first light. They separated again and Charlie said he would see him at Mason's Saturday after he picked Dawn up. Brick would retrieve Zoe and shop for supplies.

They had set the time for five on Saturday, a bit early, but it had been two years and they had more than a lot to discuss. Brick was out and about again early; he had accomplished more in the last two days than expected but found an easy rhythm with details falling in place like the old days. His mind a computer, analyzing, adding, subtracting, making sense of the absurd. Having a purpose served to refresh him with new energy, so he worked feverishly trying to outrun the lethargy of his recent tragedies.

These last few days had been raining nonstop with a cold wind slewing down through the mountains, driving sleet like a nest of angry wasps. The skies were a swirling blanket of grey and black with a foreboding of impending doom. Perfect weather for the work the three men had divided between them. He couldn't deny that having Charlie back was the pacifier he needed to take the mountain to Mohammed. Leaving Dawn was hard for Brick. He knew that after what he had pulled the last time she didn't trust him, and he didn't blame her. He reminded her that some serious people were trying to kill him, which is why he hadn't been back to see her.

The weather had driven most locals and all tourists indoors, which gave the men more solitude to carry out their assigned tasks. It was still black and cold when he stepped into the main bar to collect Zoe. She looked radiant moving about the stage with the musicians preparing to perform that night. Adjusting amps and instruments, running sound checks, all as familiar as brushing her teeth. As if sensing him, Zoe looked up and smiled like she had just won the lottery. Something as simple as going out with friends and having dinner in a home with the warmth of loving friendship made her giddy as a schoolgirl; it had been too long.

In spite of the weather, she wore cotton Capri pants and a frilly loose and sheer blue blouse with a scoop neckline. Her dark brown silky hair covered her shoulders in cascades of waves and curls. She wanted to be alluring yet comfortable. It had been a while since she let herself feel like a woman rather than a business owner and performer.

Brick, of course, was the most handsome man in the place, the town, maybe the whole damned state. Dressed in grey wool trousers with a light blue Oxford shirt and dark blue blazer with gold buttons, he seemed out of place in the bar. His shoes were highly polished oxblood loafers with tassels. When she stepped close, his clean-shaven face and full lips seemed irresistible.

"Should we go?"

He smiled and held his arm for her, "Let's."

"I hope the car is warm. I dressed to impress, not the weather."

She scooped her jacket from the end of the stage and handed it to him. He acted the gentleman and helped her; lingering behind, he leaned close to her neck and breathed in her essence. In the full bloom of womanhood, beautiful girls seemed to create their own perfume.

His truck was right outside the door with the motor running and the seat warmer turned on. He helped her up the step and as she settled her butt onto the seat, she moaned at the warmth that was in contrast to the chilly wind. "I could live in this," she cooed, listening to the soft jazz emanating from all corners of the cab.

She couldn't resist—she'd dreamed of this since she was a very young girl. Turning his face to hers, she kissed him with passion.

It wasn't returned; instead he drew back. "I'm sorry if I gave you the wrong impression. I'm involved with someone, and she's going to join us for dinner. Zoe, you can have any man you want; I'm no good for you or, maybe, anyone right now."

"Who is she?"

"Dawn Lightner. She lives in Sisters and has for at least ten years; we've been friends since she moved there."

"Is she the pretty blond nude model with the fake tits?"

"She's a pretty blond, but you've got her all wrong. She's really nice and down to earth."

"Her model name is Dawn Light, right?"

"Yes, you're right about that … but they're not."

"What's not?"

"Her tits."

They both laughed at that, and he started to drive away; they rode in easy silence for a bit. In the warm comfort of the truck, Zoe took the opportunity to scrutinize her escort as he focused on the road and they chatted. He had aged, but gracefully as some men do, becoming better looking once the blooms of youth have settled into the character lines of experience and wisdom. His presence made her feel safe, the way she had felt when her father was strong before her sister had disappeared. She wouldn't admit it, even to herself, but she longed to have someone to depend on and take charge for a while. She also felt the force of Brick and his colleagues' return—something big—these weren't ordinary men. They were serious men with strong convictions. Life was different when they were near; danger and excitement trailed in their wake. Zoe felt her heart fluttering in anticipation of the night ahead. She couldn't resist turning the conversation back to what was really on her mind.

"It's not over, you know. I haven't seen any rings."

"What in the world are you talking about?"

146

"Men like you don't know about women like me. Of course I can have my pick. I twitch my ass on stage, and half the room stands up hoping it's for them. You tell me I can't have what I want, I just get more determined. We'll see if she's worthy competition."

Brick groaned, "I don't need this."

Thirty-one

Charlie was late picking Dawn up and he was dirty—dressed in camos slightly torn, his face and exposed forearms scratched and filthy. He was driving a Land Cruiser that appeared as beat-up as he was. Dawn looked like she just stepped out of a *Playboy* spread in a hot tube dress cut both low and high, showing off her ample curves. Her hair and makeup perfect, as though she'd spent hours preparing, because she had. She wasn't sure why she went to these pains but there was something in the air. It was the same feelings she had when these men were last in town. And, whatever happens, she just wanted to look her best and for her that meant sexy as all hell.

She was always uncomfortable around Charlie. He was nice to her, polite and all, but she felt as though he was constantly judging her and she came up short. The men walked softly when he was around. The bond the he and Brick shared was like that of identical twins she once knew. They finished each other's sentences and would pass a knowing look that conveyed their complete understanding without either of them speaking.

The men called Charlie "General." There was this cool confidence that he carried and if there was trouble, all—including Brick—looked to the General for direction. Dawn was a bit in awe of the man. He was normally well put together in a clean-cut tight wrapped style, but he always seemed cold, whereas Brick oozed warmth and sexuality. From day one, she had a hard time keeping her hands off Brick. She didn't like being alone with Charlie one bit.

Charlie didn't explain why he was late or the reason for his appearance but when she thought about it, Charlie never explained anything. In spite of that, she was high with anticipation for the night ahead.

Babbling on about nothing, Dawn couldn't seem to stop her mindless chatter; she was nervous. Charlie nodded and smiled. You could tell he was listening because he asked pertinent questions about whatever she said, but there was also a strange detachment like his mind was split in two until he suddenly interrupted her and said, "Be quiet!" He pulled over to the side of the road with his finger to his lips, shushing her. Then he got out and closed the door, leaving the motor running. He had his phone to his ear and was turning in a slow circle surveying the landscape.

Dawn knew exactly where they were; it was about a half mile from the turnoff to Mason and Harriette's house. The light was fading from the ashen grey sky; a light breeze had kicked up and it caught the clouds by surprise, turning the bright daylight dark with the flash storm brewing over the mountain. The swirling gusts parted the heavens momentarily, allowing thin streams of sunlight to filter through. She rolled her window down and the odor of the wet leaves and damp earth clung to her nostrils like vapors from a lost dream. The world seemed to rock unsteadily as she felt a wave of dizziness wash over her like the remnants of past events twirling across her brow. A faint sheen of sweat coated her upper lip. Charlie got back in and drove past the turn until he reached another small logging road; here he pulled up the trail until he was out of sight and turned the lights off. Rain pelted them with a sudden burst that blew through in minutes, clearing as fast as it arrived.

She giggled nervously and said, "Did you want to make out or something? Because, well I'm kind of with Brick, you know."

Charlie smiled in the faint light and said, "While that's an interesting proposal, we're waiting for Brick and Zoe."

"Zoe is with Brick?" She wasn't happy.

They sat in silence for a few minutes until the rear window flooded with headlights. Charlie left the Land Cruiser and walked back to Brick's truck. The two friends were outside and after a brief conference, Brick went to the passenger side of the Cruiser to retrieve Dawn. She was indignant at first, pissed that he had Zoe with him and not her. He tried to coax her out, but she became petulant and bitched about ruining her Jimmy Choo's in the mud. He was used to women's jealousies, so he laughed, reached in, and lifted her off the seat with a peck on her cheek. He carried her back to the truck and deposited her in the backseat, saying, "Chewy Jim's be spared." She didn't laugh.

When he was seated, both women asked at the same time, "What the hell is going on, Brick Winslow?"

"You're going to hear more of the plan inside the house. I need to tell Mason and Harriette, so I'm not going to do it twice. One of our employees by the name of Keith is here with some equipment, and he and Charlie are going to sweep the house for bugs before we talk."

Dawn said, "Bugs? Their house doesn't have any bugs."

"Employee? What kind of business do you have with employees?" Zoe seemed shocked.

"Listening devices, maybe cameras … those are the bugs I mean. Charlie and I own a security company and provide security to private firms and celebrities around the world. We have reason to believe that the house is under surveillance and we want to secure the premises before we all chat. If they have a video feed, I can't afford to show my face. We'll just sit here for a few minutes while they do the sweep and then they'll call us."

The women were both thinking the same thing. Here they had been looking forward to a nice evening with old friends, and instead they seem to be getting involved in some complex plot out of a cheap paperback. They exchanged a look as they sat in silence.

Brick got out once more to talk on the phone. Dawn said, "Fuck this." She held her shoes and maneuvered over the seat to the driver's side. "He can sit back there."

When Brick returned and saw her in his seat, he didn't protest. She knew the way better than he and she was already mad. He knew better than to push it. He climbed in back without a word.

Mason and Harriette were standing on the porch when the men arrived. Keith unloaded two large duffel bags while Charlie gripped Harriette around her wasp like waist, lifting her high off the ground and spinning her around.

"Set me down, you crazy bastard," she laughed.

"God but it's good to see you—you're more beautiful than ever."

"You lie as much as most men." She was blushing like a young girl, her head still spinning from the twirling. Plus the chemo had left her weak and thin. "Where have you been? Do you know anything about Brick? I've been going crazy trying to find him."

He kissed her again on the forehead and looked at his old friend Mason. While Charlie had called three days ago and twice since, they hadn't laid eyes on each other in two years. They processed the physical differences in the other in a couple of split seconds, and then Charlie walked the two steps and held his friend in a bear hug until Mason squealed, "Jesus, Charlie, you're crushing me to fucking death."

They both laughed and then for a moment all three stood looking at one another as thirty years disappeared; the kids born of memory replaced the older version. For the first time since Charlie had seen his family last, his heart was filled with love. He flashed on the reason for the visit and was suddenly pissed and silently vowed to kill anyone who fucked with any of his people. "Harriette, please just hold on a few minutes and all will be explained."

Back in the truck the girls exchanged a look; they were women really but Brick couldn't stand the thought of his past aging, so he thought of them as girls. These two trusted and believed in him, and yet he had abandoned all. Another ugly truth.

His cell started ringing and jerked him back to the moment. "Okay, we're coming in now." He leaned over the seat and said, "It's time."

Only Harriette was waiting in the yard when they pulled into the drive. Dawn stopped the truck ten feet away and even with her. Brick got out and stood stock-still. Dawn drove the truck around back and left them alone. Brick and Harriette stood staring at each other for a long time, each drinking in the other. Harriette had always looked like a fragile child, barely standing five feet tall and rail thin; she wore her soft brown hair short and her huge doe eyes watched the world with disappointment, as if she expected more. She certainly expected great things from her friends. In earlier days, her looks were always deceiving, as she had a sinewy strength both in muscle tone and determination—the personality and bluster of a giant compressed into a compact package. Now she appeared gaunt, a tiny wraith stretched around those incredible piercing eyes; she stared at him with an intensity that carried weight.

Finally, she ran into his arms and he scooped her up and twirled her, same as Charlie had minutes before. She had her legs locked around his waist and her face buried in his neck, and she was crying softly.

He set her down but still held her close. "I'm here, honey; don't cry."

She pulled back and started beating on his chest with both hands, tears streaming down her face. "Goddamn you, we tried to call and talked to people and I thought—I thought … Oh Jesus, fuck, I thought …"

He pulled her tight again and let her cry it out. "I'm sorry, so sorry; I've been a selfish ass." *Little miss Harry, how could I do this?*

After a minute, she started to laugh through her tears. "Come inside. Mason can't wait to see you."

Inside, the house was loud with laughter with a mix of voices all trying to talk over the others, fighting for dominance. The mudroom they entered was exactly the same as it had been the last time he was here, and Brick remembered laying the foundation so many years ago. He also remembered that Harry had looked in to supervise and said, "This is wrong—start over. It needs to be bigger, twelve by fifteen, and I want a big dump sink to wash in. With all you big, sweaty, stinking men traipsing around, I need to keep you out until you learn some manners."

On this evening, the group was clustered in the kitchen but when Brick and Harriette stepped through the door, they quieted and a beaming Mason got up to give Brick the biggest hug. The two men who had been close friends since kindergarten staggered in a drunken shuffle to the middle of the room, with Mason refusing to let go.

The house was a rambling single-level ranch built with the fir trees that dominated the land. It had six bedrooms and the same number of bathrooms. Mason had designed the floor plan and the crew spent five months building it to his specifications. Brick remembered how they all worked from sunup to dusk; how Harriette had flittered about changing the design on the go while cooking massive feasts and keeping iron washtubs full of cracked ice and beer. She seemed in constant motion back then, making endless trips to town for supplies while her husband kept the building moving. Mason's father had been a stern taskmaster, and proper

153

building techniques were ingrained in Mason from his years working for the hot-tempered man.

Drinks were made and dinner warmed as they all chatted amiably until Harriette sat everyone down at her big dining room table. She assigned the seating, with Brick on her right and Charlie on her left; as they ate, her gaze wandered between the two as if watching a tennis match in slow motion. Zoe felt right at home. She knew everyone well because of her sister's disappearance. Mason and Harry had opened their house to the search parties and had refreshments available at all times. Plus, in the years that followed, any night out for the men had included music and drinks at the Shoe.

Without a word spoken, Mason, Dawn, and Zoe began clearing the table when the meal was finished. While they were in the kitchen, Keith stood and said he was going to take a look around; then he slipped on his coat and went out the side door. Keith was on the clock; he didn't drink and he stayed in the background. If the truth were told, he would have worked for free just to be around his mentor and employer. He had more respect for the General than any other man he knew. He learned more every day from Charlie than he would from a month in training.

"You've been sick," Brick stated, looking at Harriette somberly. "And you knew," he said, turning to Charlie.

"You should have," Charlie shot back.

"Shut up a minute, Charlie," Harriette interjected. "We tried to find you when we learned, but no one had a clue, and Charlie disappeared at the same time. You're right, of course. I've lost twenty pounds and both the girls are gone," she said pointing at her chest.

"Breast cancer," Brick stated the obvious. "And now?"

"In remission but I'm still so sick from the chemo; that's why I can't eat much. At least my hair is coming back.... We needed you—I needed you. You've always been like my big brother and when I didn't hear from you, I thought you must be dead."

"He's been fucking hiding," Charlie chirped.

"I haven't been fucking hiding; fuck you, Charlie," Brick said before jumping up from the table and charging out the back door.

A few minutes later, Harriette followed and found him shivering and looking up. The skies had cleared and the moon was high. She walked to him and slid her arm around his waist. "He's just upset because of me," she said.

"No, he's right … I have been hiding for over two years now, but it's over. I was happy here—I don't know why I left." His mind was focused on Jesus, but he couldn't bring himself to say the name.

"Come on, big brother; let's go back inside. There's more you need to know."

The group was already back around the big table when they sat down. It was quiet; Keith hadn't returned—he seemed to know instinctively when to let these old friends have some privacy.

Dawn was the first to speak and she directed her words straight at Brick. "They're broke, and now it looks like they will lose the house and everything they've worked so hard for. Mason has gone back to working for Jocko just to put food on the table."

Brick looked at Mason and said, "But you had millions …"

Mason shook his head and replied, "But no health insurance and I insisted on the best treatment possible. This has been going on for two years. I flew her out to the Mayo Clinic, and thank God they saved her life … I couldn't believe how expensive it was though. I had to take out a mortgage and now I can't make the payments. I'm sorry."

"Fuck," the word hissed out slow and labored from Brick's lips as he looked at Charlie. Charlie nodded his head so slightly the others

155

couldn't see the tiny gesture, but they had been communicating like this for most of their lives.

Brick put his arm around Harriette's shoulders and said, "Good news, Mason; we never took you off the payroll and you have health insurance through us. We're going to reimburse you for the hospital and doctors' bills and will be taking care of them from now on. You're also entitled to back pay, so I'll have a check for you tomorrow. You will not lose the house. You still work for us, is that clear?"

"No, it's not clear at all. Who do I work for?" Mason asked.

"McShane and Winslow Security—McWin is what we named it—based in Austin, Texas. You, my friend, are a security consultant and quite highly paid." Brick grinned as he said the last.

Harriette couldn't stop crying and now Mason joined her, and then the two women joined them. Finally, Charlie said, "Enough already! My business manager has been lax in his bookkeeping so you can blame this sorry prick," pointing at Brick. "I have an early day."

Charlie hugged everyone and said his goodbyes, and when he walked out the door, Brick followed him. Keith was in his car waiting with the motor running and the heater on. The two men stood on the back deck.

"You good on the money?" Brick asked.

"I don't give a flying fuck about the money; do what you want with it. That was the right thing you just did. No one deserves to be bailed out more than those two."

Brick said, "I know, but it's your money too. I've been giving some away for a while now—I don't know what else to do with it."

Charlie smiled and looked at his friend and said, "I've never cared about the money—that was your thing. How much is it, anyway?"

About the economy of a third world country, around a quarter of a billion" Brick answered. "But I've made some moves and the market is strong and it keeps growing. I would like to keep the principal and give the interest to people. Good people—friends and friends of friends."

"Do it. You know, you've changed—for the better I might add. It's really good to see. I could use some help and you could use a purpose; are you back for good?"

"I think I am."

Charlie gave him a quick hug and started walking toward the car. Before getting in, he turned around and said, "We're going to need more men. We need to protect our friends and our flanks exposed."

"Do it," Brick answered.

When Brick reentered the house, the group had composed themselves and Harriette had put on a pot of coffee. When the coffee was done brewing and Mason laid out cups and accoutrements, Brick began again: "There's a lot more you need to know—the main reason we're here and what's going to happen next." He then proceeded to explain everything, starting with where he'd been and the visit from Cassie and her dead husband. He told them in brief detail about the shoot-out at his cabin. The only thing he omitted was Montana and Laura.

He looked defeated when he admitted he needed help, a lot of help. He asked Zoe if she could keep an eye out for strange characters, as most people tended to visit the Shoe. He had a role for all of them to play. He hated looking weak and needing help, but it endeared him more than he could imagine. He had always been the strong one, the one who gave and gave. They felt honored to be of service.

It was late when they asked their questions, and all knew the dangerous game they played. Just by being associated with the men put them all at risk. So each was lost in their own thoughts weighing the danger in their minds. Harriette finally announced that it was late, and she insisted that they stay at the house and get some sleep. This was met with mild resistance, but she wouldn't hear of it. They house was large and sprawling with more than enough room. They built it when they thought they were rich.

Harriette chose a large bedroom with a king-size bed and double shower and vanity for Dawn and Zoe. She knew Dawn and she understood men and their physical hungers. By putting the girls together in one room, they would keep each other subdued for the night. Before she left them, she admonished both by saying, "I don't know what you girls had in mind for tonight, but keep it in your pants. I'm going to keep Brick in the room next to mine, so everyone can get a good night's rest."

Zoe was about to object when Dawn gave her a nudge and a stern look. She was right; all that could be accomplished by arguing was to set Harry into a lecture that would last all night. She was a mother hen when it came to her precious Brick, and she just got him back.

Thirty-two

Charlie was ensconced in a blind halfway up the hill behind Jocko's ranch. He was in full camouflage, hidden in a small tent and holding a steaming cup of coffee in one hand and binoculars in the other. Near the top of the next ridge, he caught a glimpse of another glass peering at the ranch. Charlie had dug in hours ago in the dark and the hill was now becoming visible. He smiled to himself, reliving the feelings of love he felt within the cozy house last night with friends.

Knowing he wasn't alone confirmed his suspicions and he changed tack. He began sliding sideways away from the watcher and heading for higher ground, moving infinitesimally slow until he crested the hill, then worked his way back until he was above the man. Charlie was good at this, liked it. Surveillance was a calling; it took incredible patience, but Charlie always found it rewarding. It was a question of who blinked first.

Training his binoculars on the back of his prey's head, he waited for recognition. He thought he knew the dude but held steady for confirmation. Spring was winning the battle with winter, and the morning held promise of a glorious day. The ground was drying as the sun crested the mountain and warmed his back as he stared westward. He was getting hot and realized he was too far above his target to be of any use. The watcher was in perfect position to see the ranch awaken and follow the activities.

Time to make a move. Charlie found a suitable rock, not too big and well rounded. He judged the right distance and lobbed the rock behind and to the side of the watcher. It had the desired effect and the man turned enough so his face was in profile for a second. Charlie almost laughed out loud when he recognized another from their past, someone impossible to forget. The man, once an ally; still so? *We'll soon find out,* he thought.

Knowing he couldn't accomplish anything else from this position, Charlie worked his way farther to his right and topped the hill and then started down the other side. He made it about a third of the way down when a voice from behind stopped him in his tracks.

"Why are you here?" The voice cracked like rusty metal parts moving without lubrication.

Looking over his shoulder, he saw a large grizzled man of undetermined age who looked like a bum in torn jeans and a frayed flannel shirt. He had long brown hair; it looked greasy. His beard was even more impressive, with touches of grey. He was big and filthy, but what drew the eye was the axe resting on his shoulder.

Charlie tried to look past him, but the man moved to block his view. He feinted right and when the man moved, this time he noticed a small opening in the outcrop of rock behind the man. It was invisible unless you knew it was there.

"It's none of your fucking business what I'm doing. This is federal land not your backyard, asshole."

The statement took the big guy off guard and he thought for a second and then said, "Wrong, motherfucker! Federal land stopped 100 feet back." Then he asked, "Somebody with you …? You a soldier?"

"I am a soldier and I carry the authority of the US Army. My partner and I own the ranch on the other side of the hill, asshole."

"I've never seen you before."

"Because we lease that property and now I'm checking on it. That makes us neighbors."

"I don't give a shit. Get off my mountain."

Charlie looked over the man's right shoulder and nodded his head. It had the desired effect; the brute couldn't help himself from twisting to look. In that moment, Charlie flipped his body backward and rolled behind some brush, effectively disappearing from view and continued downward. He had a bad feeling about this guy and wasn't going to banter with him anymore. As he continued down the hill, he made a new discovery. The abandoned miners' shack had been replaced with a well-built sturdy house, garage, and storage building. Maybe Charlie should check the ownership.

It was late when Zoe woke from her dreams and blinked the night away as the room came into focus. Dawn was still sleeping, her breath slow and smooth with a slight whistle. Zoe needed to pee something fierce and leapt up in her panties and one of Harry's old ragged, too small T-shirts, then scurried into the bathroom. Harriette had set out clean towels and toothbrushes still packaged from the drugstore. She lingered and took a hot shower. After she dried her hair and dressed, she glided back to the room only to find Dawn missing.

She soon found Dawn bustling around the kitchen, making pancake batter and frying bacon in a heavy cast-iron skillet on the commercial stove. The aroma was tantalizing and made Zoe's mouth water in anticipation. She had lived alone for so long, she almost never cooked, taking most of her meals from the bar and eating in her office or room at the top of her stairs. Dawn looked up when Zoe walked into the kitchen and gave a big smile and cheery good morning.

"I've got bacon and flapjacks; do you want some eggs?" Dawn inquired. "How did you sleep?"

"Like the dead. Jesus, that smells good. Sure, eggs too. Where is everybody?"

"Harriette's still in bed and it appears the boys are gone—just us chickens left. I always sleep so sound here; there's something about this place that's very comforting." Dawn seemed at home in bra and panties.

"You seem to know your way around here pretty good. I suck at cooking. I can barely boil water." Last night's startling news seemed to draw them closer.

Dawn laughed and appeared genuinely happy. "I've been here a lot taking care of things while Harriette's been sick. She taught me to cook, but Mason's the real chef—he's a food god. If I was here all the time, I'd look like a hippo. Harry's the housekeeper and this place is always immaculate, even though she's been so sick. Fucking kitchen makes me nervous; I'm afraid I'll make a mess and little Miss Harry will yell at me. She's not too sick to yell her ass off. No matter how many times I've made meals here, she still finds something I didn't clean quite right. If I didn't love her so much I'd tell her to fuck off."

"Hey, what are you two laughing about? And who needs to fuck off?" a sleepy Harriette asked as she walked in wearing a light blue ratty flannel nightgown, her hair a fright.

The women ignored the questions; all three were soon eating and chatting away like sisters. Soon the conversation turned to what was on everyone's mind.

Zoe was the one who kept asking questions, until Harriette told them both to shut up and listen. "When I was just a little girl, my mother and I lived across the street from the Winslow's home. We were in the only apartment building in a nice neighborhood. I don't know how my mother managed to stay there, because she was a waitress and we were always broke; she drank most of our money away but somebody always helped her out, probably sniffing around her pussy. She was very pretty when she was young and always had a guy around. I never knew my father. School was torture for me. The other kids bullied me because of my threadbare clothes, tangled hair, and they called my mother a whore."

"Kids can be cruel; they tortured me because I *had* money," Dawn said.

Harry continued, "My life was hell until one day when I was seven and two of the mean boys that always picked on me were chasing me home and hitting me with tree switches … That's when this beautiful boy came out of nowhere and beat the two boys bloody. From that day on, he's been my protector and my best friend. No one ever picked on me again. He brought me home and his mother found me clothes, and they had over me for meals and treated me like a princess. That boy was Brick, of course, and I've loved him like a brother and father rolled into one." Harriette was glowing with the memory.

Zoe said, "That's a sweet story, but what has it got to do with—"

"Just shut up and listen. I met Charlie through Brick of course, and you have to understand that those two men love each other and would die if necessary to protect the other. Brick was and still is the smartest man I know, and Charlie is the toughest. Together they seem invincible and now I'll tell you the whole story.

"Cassandra was always a bitch; we grew up in the same town. She was a lot younger than me, but from the first time I met her I knew she was bad news. But somehow, she blinded Brick and he was crazy about her. All she thought about was money and prestige, and she constantly pushed Brick to make more money. He could have done anything, but he concentrated on a career where he could earn the most. His career path was leading him to Wall Street, all because of that bitch.

"After she left him, he gave up on Wall Street—like I said, that was never his dream—and he drifted for a while until he got an idea. Charlie had always been military and became a captain or something in the Army Rangers and was headed for Panama. Brick had no interest in the

163

army, but he still wanted to get rich just to prove to Cassie that she made a mistake in leaving him.

"Charlie had no interest in money but was willing to help Brick with anything. So Brick joined up and did the training. He was always a tough kid so soldering was easy for him, but he only joined for one thing. Panama was close to Colombia and the large drug cartels had fortunes. The plan was really simple: go in and take it away from them.

"Brick chose this location in Oregon for the main distribution point, but things got shipped all over the country and some to England, courtesy of Gran. That's what was happening in the days when you two met all the guys. Brick bought the ranch where Jocko lives now, and the guys used it as a base until Brick said he was finished with that life. Many of the old crew are still in business, because they pissed away the money Brick made for them."

Dawn said, "Everyone had a nickname back then, so I didn't know them all by their real names, only Brick. Was that part of the plan?"

"Not originally," Harriette said, "but it became useful, so Brick pressed the names on all the locals. It was his name on the property. This was before he set up false identities and the network to wash the money, so they could spend it legally. Do you two remember Clint—we called him the Joker?"

Zoe and Dawn shook their heads yes.

"Clint named everybody. Remember, they were a military squad so some of the names came from combat. Charlie was the General; Gran Harlow was called GK for the Gentleman Killer; Nicky was PB for Pretty Boy; and Clint was the Joker. Hey-sues was Jesus, and Stoney remained Stoney. Clint said that he tried to come up with a nickname for him but later admitted that nothing was better than Stoney."

"What about Brick?" Zoe asked.

"Clint said at first they called him GG for God's Gift, but Brick squashed that. Clint changed it, first to the Banker and then the guys shortened it to the Bank," Harriette answered. "You saw what he did for us last night. That's Brick—he fixes things and he likes to be in charge; he really is the Bank.

"Clint said he went to Charlie once to ask for an advance, and he thought Charlie was going to bust him in the mouth. Charlie told him to never question Brick about money and to never question him about tactics. No one knows how much he's stashed away for Charlie and him. He saved my life again last night. Mason and I didn't know what we were going to do…. I was afraid that Brick was dead."

Zoe was starting to feel uncomfortable sitting fully dressed while Harriette stayed in her housedress and Dawn was practically naked. It was now afternoon with the sun pouring in the big kitchen, and they were getting hungry again so Harriette set about throwing together some sandwiches when her phone rang. Harry walked away and the girls could see her listening and nodding her head.

They were alone and Zoe couldn't resist asking Dawn, "So what's the story on you and Brick?"

A knowing look came over Dawn's face. *Was Zoe poaching on her turf?* Now wary, she said, "We're a thing; two years ago, I'd have said a forever thing, but he gets weird-like spells or something and his mind goes far away where he can't be reached. Not even Charlie can shake him out of his trances when they happen. But never mind any of that—he's back now and he's mine. I'll scratch the eyes out of any bitch thinks different."

The look on Dawn's face scared the shit out of Zoe. "Whoosh, just asking—never mind," she said. *Maybe I should back off. She looked like she would kill me if I went after Brick.*

165

Harriette hadn't said much on the phone but when she hung up, she glanced back at the two women with a quizzical look on her face and then headed to the back of the house. When she came back into the kitchen, she was holding an envelope in her hand and shaking her head.

Harriette was still shaking her head while she made a call. Dawn and Zoe heard her ordering a cab to come to the house and take them to Bend. When she hung up, she said matter-of-factly, "When we finish eating, we're going to town to buy me a car and rent furniture for a six-bedroom farmhouse."

Thirty-three

When Charlie made it to the road at the bottom of the hill, he was tired and pissed off. He couldn't stop wondering about the guy with the attitude. *Why was he so willing to mess with a stranger just for being on that hillside, and who is he?* He called Keith to pick him up but when he called Brick, it went to voicemail. He called Harriette and was given directions to a house and told to meet Brick there.

Brick had spent the morning with a pretty auburn-haired real estate agent who had shown him three of the four properties he had selected in her office. He was dressed in jeans, dress shirt, and sport coat—the way he dressed when he wanted to impress, and she was. He could tell by the twinkle in her eyes after viewing the second property. They were in her three-year-old SUV, and she was dressed similarly to Brick. Her loose hair covered the shoulders of a white cotton blouse thin enough to show her bra straps beneath. Tight-fitting jeans revealed a shapely figure and her blue blazer was tossed carelessly in the back seat. She had a nervous habit of spinning the wedding band on her finger, and she chatted as she drove. He had the same effect on her that happened to most women in close quarters alone with Brick—she was self-conscious.

Kelly Knowles jumped in her seat a little at the mention of her name. They had been riding without speaking for the last several minutes and she wasn't comfortable with the silence.

She kept fiddling with the stations on the radio until his warm fingers covered her own, and he said, "Do you mind if we turn this off?" He was smiling at her in his usual seductive manner and she was nervous as a cat in a tree. "Stop someplace so we can have some lunch. I'm starving and I'm buying," he said.

She had to smile back; he was so direct—turn here, go there—like he was used to giving orders. He hadn't told her much, just said he wanted to rent or lease a large farm or ranch with some property around it for a few months. He mostly gave one-word answers to her questions, but she liked him so what the hell, she decided to show him whatever he wanted. *It's not like I have any big sale coming up and I'll make a few bucks from the lease,* she thought.

Kelly was loose and relaxed after a sumptuous lunch where all stops were pulled and he took over ordering. She was about to select a salad until he took her menu away. He told her she was skinny and needed some meat on her bones, so he ordered fried razor clams with rice and asparagus along with a basket of bread and a half bottle of chilled sauvignon Blanc for her and a Newcastle for himself.

After lunch, they had barely arrived at the last of the properties when he told her to go back to number two. There, he left her in the car and wandered around on his own, checking places where no one else would think to look. When he finished, he came around to the driver's side window and leaned in close. "When did you leave your husband?" he asked.

Her jaw dropped and she stared at him. "How did you know?" she asked.

"You've lost weight and your wedding ring is very loose. You keep twirling it and lifting it almost off, staring at it. You're tan without a line around the finger, so you only put it on when you're meeting a man and don't want the hassle. I'll take this place; you can leave me here and I'll come to your office tomorrow to sign the papers and leave a deposit."

"You want me to leave you here on foot?" she asked.

He just smiled and said, "It's sweet of you to worry." Then he turned and walked into the back door of the house.

Charlie and Keith turned into the driveway, with Keith at the wheel, when Charlie motioned him to stop. When the truck slowed to a crawl, Charlie was out and running toward the front as Keith thundered up the drive and skidded to a stop. Both men had guns drawn and pointed at the house when Brick walked out to the yard to greet them.

Everyone was jumpy. The events of the morning had set the men on edge and their senses were on high alert. Brick led them on a tour of the house and grounds, pointing out the strategic reasons for his choice. Charlie silently agreed with the assessment. The eastern edge was lined with a thick stand of young fir trees, and beyond was open field for at least two hundred yards. They could conceal the motion detector cameras in the firs. The farmhouse itself sat on a high hill that gave good visibility in all directions; the north and western borders were once ploughed fields for crops and had since grown over with scrub brush and weeds, making it hard terrain to cover without ATVs. The eastern edge led to the county road and provided the only access in or out of the property. Brick had made the agent drive him around the perimeter and there were working farms surrounding them, which would inhibit trespassers.

But the best attribute was a full basement foundation, rare in this part of the country. At the eastern wall a heavy wooden door concealed a fruit cellar that extended underground for at least twenty yards toward the fir trees. It would be an easy task to extend it farther and bring it to the surface in the trees. This would only happen if the worst came calling. These were all precautions that weren't necessary until they were.

Until they had the furniture delivered, there wasn't anywhere for the men to sit, so they went to Keith's truck; he had traded in the Chevy he was driving earlier. Brick called Mason and asked him to go back to Jocko's to spy while they got settled. Charlie and Keith wanted to give

Brick a report on their morning reconnaissance missions there. Keith reported first.

"There's another watching from the far hill. He's hard to spot but if you stare long enough, you can see a glint off his binoculars. There seems to be two separate crews working the ranch. The first one is doing mundane farm work—moving sheep, mending fences, and shoveling shit out of the barn. They come and go, but I estimate that there are maybe ten or twelve hands working the ranch. They have the main house, a bunkhouse, barn, livestock pens, chicken coop, and a six-car garage. Lots of cars and trucks moving all day."

"Tell us about the other crew," Brick said. "The layout hasn't changed since I had it and that's good to know."

Keith continued, "These are hard men. Ever alert, they patrol the property in shifts day and night. They work like a military squad and they're armed to the teeth. They don't touch any of the ranch work and seem to be waiting for something to happen. There are two enormous Quonset buildings that must be divided into several rooms. There are some heavy-duty power lines coming in and at least ten gas generators visible. I'm pretty sure they have a fleet of panel and delivery trucks that are kept inside … lots of activity at all hours. Oh, and a thirty-foot crane for loading pallets."

"I can confirm the watcher; what did I tell you, Brick?" Charlie said.

"GK?"

"You bet your fucking britches," Charlie said.

"That confirms Zoe's story. Makes it more interesting, that's for sure," Brick said.

Keith looked back and forth between the two, wondering about this new twist; he didn't have to wait long.

Charlie said, "He's an old mate of ours, name of Gran Harlow; he was with us in the squad in Panama. I had a feeling he would show his face. Back then, he was on our side, a Brit … now I wonder."

Keith said, "What's with the GK?"

Brick laughed and said, "That was his nickname in the squad; everyone had one. Clint named all of us. He was with Gran on the third raid at this cartel camp at three in the morning. Hey-sues dropped us from the chopper three miles away because they had tough security. We called Clint the Joker … so anyway, GK and he were crawling through the jungle close to the cartel camp. Gran came up behind their outmost guard and grabbed him with a hand on his mouth and his k-bar under his chin, and the fucker bit him on the thumb. I heard him groan in pain under his breath—"

Charlie cut in, saying, "Tell him what the Joker did when we got back to the base."

Brick continued, "We all got pretty drunk celebrating … Turns out, Gran's father is a lord in the English Parliament. So Clint goes into the barracks and comes back with a blanket around his shoulders and a cardboard crown on his head with a broom shoved through his belt loop and has all of us stand in a circle around Gran, and Clint does this little skit.

"Clint says, 'Sir Granville Harlow 111, kneel before thy king.' He doesn't move, so Stoney puts his big meaty hands on Gran's shoulders and forces him to his knees. Clint pulled the broom out, holding it by the bristle end, and touches Gran on first one shoulder then the next and says, 'I dub thee GK, the Gentleman Killer, henceforth and forever. Rise, Sir GK; it is an honor and a privilege for these humble peasants to serve you, squire.'"

Charlie takes over the story, saying, "We're all laughing our asses off and Clint finishes his story with the sentry.

"Clint says, 'This fucking narco is going to bite Gran's thumb off and we can't risk him giving us away with a shout, so he pulls the k-bar from under his chin and slides it in his mouth alongside his thumb and pries the guy's teeth open enough to get his thumb out.'

"Gran says, 'Sir that was quite rude and truly unnecessary. There are consequences to such behavior.' Then he drives the knife up into the little fucker's brain."

Charlie says, "There you have his personality—he's a ruthless man and very talented. He was our communications expert in the squad. This guy was into computers before the rest of us ever heard of them. He was the surveillance expert for the Royal Air Force for many years. There's nothing he doesn't know about the latest gadgets in technology or spyware. After Clint's skit, Gran laughed right along with the rest of us, so the guy's got a sense of humor and he's a pretty good guy and a great soldier once you get used to the bizarre. Brick and he have been friends since school."

Keith asked, "So, do you want me to bring him in?"

Charlie and Brick smiled at each other, and Brick said, "Sure, go ahead; bring him here."

After he left, Brick couldn't help but laugh, "I got a hundred bucks on Gran."

Charlie said, "I should probably give you the money right now, but I think a lot of Keith, so you're on."

Thirty-four

Harriette bought a three-year-old Toyota Land Cruiser for cash and dropped the girls off at their respective homes. It was late afternoon when she drove to the furniture store. After three calls to Brick with questions, she had worked out a deal on a houseful, rented for two months minimum. The store made out like bandits, receiving four thousand dollars for a couple of grand worth of beat-up crap, but Brick didn't care; he just wanted it now.

She was getting tired but felt exhilarated from the excitement and the pace, her world changing by the minute. Following Brick's directions, she stopped at his new place before returning home. Brick took her through the house, pointing out where he wanted certain items that would be delivered in the morning. She was charged with making the place livable while the boys were busy elsewhere. He sent her home to rest around five and said the boys would be back by seven with dinner and to hear Mason's report.

Charlie slept until 2:00 a.m., the next morning or the same night depending on your perspective. Now he was dressed in full gear, complete with night-vision goggles, and positioned on the far side of the hill. He crawled in a zigzag approach as he crested the hill well before sunrise. He had told Brick about the hillbilly and what happened. "Fuckin guy braced me and wasn't worried about consequences—why? He definitely didn't want me to see something."

From the top of the hill, the cave was impossible to see or even suspect. The hill caved in on itself and left the slight depression and small entrance invisible. The dead bush in front of the opening camouflaged the cave entirely.

But … Charlie knew something was there, had seen it two days ago. He tried all the tricks, tossing pebbles, birdcalls; not a hint of movement. Fuck it … he pulled the bush away and charged, keeping low and alert, pistol in his right hand and flash in the left.

He didn't make it far; blocking the entrance loomed a large boulder. There was no way it could have been moved outside the cave, which meant it has always resided within. It wasn't here the other day—he was sure of it—so how had it moved? His hands roamed along the sides of the boulder and cave opening; nothing.

The owner of the house was Henry Johnson. He bought it at auction when he settled here about ten years ago. He was a logger. Nobody seemed sure where he came from. Charlie did his best to find some dirt, but he appeared squeaky clean. Reportedly not real friendly but that's not a crime. The information was public record and Charlie didn't find any discrepancies.

There used to be an abandoned miners' shack on the property; that's what Charlie remembered. When Henry bought the property, all twelve acres, he tore down the shack and built a house and large barn at the bottom of the hill. He built it strong with heavy locks and thick glass windows—his fortress.

Charlie wondered if this Johnson guy and the big guy were one and the same. He'd have to investigate.

Thirty-five

Just before dark, Charlie gave up the wait and headed back to his car. He noted the house and pole barn just below the cave and wondered. *If that brute lived in the cave, then Johnson had to know. Something was very wrong about this place.* He called Brick but was pretty tight-lipped until he knew more. Brick was good with trick latches and engineering, so he could help solve the boulder mystery.

Back at the rental house, Brick was putting together a new plan. Stoney was flying into Bend in a couple of hours and he needed to pick him up. When Charlie called, he sounded strange; something was off—his friend was hiding something. Brick was pacing and thinking; he couldn't sit still, so he made a pitcher of ice tea and went out to the deck. Harriette had included a couple of Adirondack rocking chairs with her load of furniture; he smiled when he thought of her efficiency. He noticed a small plume of dust starting at the eastern horizon and sat and watched it grow.

As the dust drew nearer it became a dark shape, which morphed into a car, and when it turned into his drive, it became a black Mercedes E-class. The car slowed to a crawl, then came to rest parallel to the porch with its ass end nearest the steps. It was parked on the sparse, yellow scrub grass of the lawn. The driver stepped around the car, climbed the short staircase to the porch, and stood four feet in front of Brick's chair.

"I just made ice tea. You want a glass?" Brick said.

"I'd fancy one, thank you."

Brick set his glass on the table and returned in a minute with a fresh glass and handed it over. The man took the offered glass and set it on the table next to Brick's. The two men stared at each other for a full minute. Slowly the man's right hand rose from his side and he waited. Brick looked at the hand like it was a foreign object and then, as a wicked smile crossed his face, he grabbed the hand and the two men embraced. They were both aware of the thumping sound that had been coming from the trunk of the car ever since Gran parked.

"Would you let him out, please?" Brick asked.

Gran pulled the key fob from his pocket and opened the trunk, then sauntered down and, as the blade flashed open, he neatly sliced the duct tape from first his ankles and then his wrists before quickly stepping back. Knife in hand.

Keith leapt from the trunk and ripped the tape off his mouth. "I'm going to kill you, motherfucker."

Gran stood his ground smiling.

Brick moved fast and covered the distance so he could restrain Keith. "Easy, big guy; he'll cut you to ribbons. Deep breaths, walk it off. Go get some tea from the porch."

Keith stared with murder in his eyes until he was drawn to the wicked-looking blade still in Gran's hand and finally stalked off toward the deck, yelling over his shoulder, "He fucking Tased me."

"He yours?" Gran asked.

"Charlie's really but he's part of the team, so play nice," Brick said.

"Charles sent this bloke rather than a personal appearance?" Gran asked.

"Charlie's here," Brick said.

"Blimey, missed him clean," Gran said.

"He's seen you." Brick said.

"Well fuck me, that crafty bitch still with a trick or two. The kid damn near shagged the pooch. How did Charles acquire the mutt? Never glimpsed Charles but managed a bit of juice from an old mate," Gran said.

"First off, you need to tell me what you're doing here," Brick said.

"I've come to save your sorry arse. I was in New York working a wee touch of dodgy business for her Ladyship. I have a tracker on odd blokes here and about. Electric gizmos you Yanks aren't on to yet. 'Twas near the goal when old Wingate got his self switched off. Close he was, on your cunch was the shout—coincidence I should imagine. I selected a path to locate me lost mate. Coincidence is either a fickle bitch or a lying whore, and the cock up in Chicago sounded spot-on. Might I assume?"

"You might."

"You require old Gran's assistance. If you feinted left, you'd go right and this the logical spot." Gran smiled, pleased with himself. "I spied the Wild West, gobsmacked to find a mouth and no trousers. Not a bloody farthing here to Denver?"

They were interrupted as a truck approached. They waited until Charlie arrived before continuing the conversation.

"As I live and breathe, if it isn't the devil himself," Charlie said when he stepped onto the porch.

"You got that in one, mate," Gran said. They shook hands.

Charlie looked to the front door and a dejected Keith stared back at him. He reached into his front pocket, removing a wad of bills and handed Brick a hundred.

Gran looked incredulously at Charles. "You bet against me? I'm shocked and shamed."

Thirty-six

Harriette was feeling much better; her nausea had subsided and she was starting to eat more every day. She felt like a fog had lifted from her brain and her reality turned upside down. Brick was back and, like usual, had made all her problems disappear. They would keep the house and now they had what had been lacking for so long … Hope.

It felt so good to be productive with people around her again, so she wanted to do something nice. A party would be good—food and drink and, most importantly, love and laughter. She started to think about who to invite, Zoe and Dawn of course and maybe a few of the friends that she and Mason had made over the years. She better check with Brick first and make sure it was alright. She couldn't get over the fact that he was really back and in charge. Nothing made her feel safer than he did. She almost swooned and looked to the heavens and screamed … *Goody!*

Brick didn't feel that confident. Bringing the crew back after so long was riddled with issues, but he had to start somewhere and it felt good to have Charlie back. If there was going to be a fight, these were the guys to handle it—the toughest group of men he knew. He could always see several steps ahead; it made him a good chess player but there were innocents to consider.

Stoney was waiting by the curb when Brick pulled into view. He carried a small backpack and medium suitcase, both black. Brick activated the rear hatch on the Suburban. Earlier in the day, he had rented the big SUV they would need now. Stoney was grinning from ear to ear. He looked exactly the same, the years seeming to have little or no effect on his angular ebony face. Brick moved to shake hands, but the mountain of a man ignored his gesture and grabbed him around the waist, lifted him off the ground, and spun him around like a child.

"Man, oh fuckin' man ... I didn' know I ever lays eyes on you 'gain. I hear you was dea. Da General here too? I can wait. I've miss you boys."

It took a while, but Brick finally got him in the truck and they headed to the new base.

Before Brick could offer more, Stoney began his rambling again. It was hard to understand him when he talked fast with that heavy southern drawl, but Brick could make out snatches of phrases that made sense.

"Yees suh, I spoke wit ol Clint yestaday an he be in 'marrow roun eight. Hir Jesus gone; how bout Nicky? Hey GK roun?"

"Sorry man, but Nicky's gone; GK is at the new ranch. I'm going to need you to pick Clint up tomorrow. It's good to have you back."

They chatted for the rest of the ride about their lives since their last meeting and when they arrived, Gran was sitting on the porch fiddling with his knife. "Hey you big dumb nigga, how you been?" Gran said.

"You honky bitch, Im take dat pig sticker and whittle dat faggy ass down some."

Both men laughed and embraced. Despite Gran's assertions of nobility, he held no prejudice and loved the man dearly. Gran never judged a man on race or religion, only on honor and loyalty. They had bonded when they first met years ago. Stoney had covered his cookies many times, as he had all the men. He was as tough and kind as God ever made a man.

The three walked into the kitchen and Keith was sitting at the table glaring in their direction. Brick took Stoney back to show him his room and Gran sat down across from him.

Keith couldn't help himself; he was still pissed and embarrassed that Gran got the best of him. "I don't know you but I thought we were on the same side—you sneak up and Tase me? I don't work for you guys; I'll wait till the General gets back and take my orders from him."

Brick was heading back to the kitchen and Charlie was standing on the deck listening when Gran spoke.

"You ignorant bloody cunt, you don't even know who the fuck's in charge. I didn't have a fucking clue who you were, just some arsehole tramping through the fucking woods like a twat. You're lucky I didn't cut your throat. You made enough bloody fucking racket to wake the dearly departed and you stink. I watched you for two days and you never had a clue. I smelled your deodorant. Fuckin animals took a runner, not a rabbit twitching. The bloody twits had a brain they'd have shot your stinking arse off the fucking hill."

Keith came off his chair with fists clenched and looked as if he would reach for his gun. Just then Charlie stepped through the door and in his most commanding voice said, "Stand down, soldier. I won't tell you twice."

Brick walked calmly over and sat next to Gran, then motioned for Charlie to sit. He did but his cold glare never left Keith's face. Stoney heard the commotion and walked into the room. Brick said, "Sit down; you can get settled later. I think Charlie has something to say."

Stoney felt the tension and nodded in Charlie's direction. "General," he said and sat at attention.

Charlie looked from face to face before he spoke. "This is my fault; shit's been fast, uncertain. I need to explain it to you, Keith. Gran's right; Brick's in charge, always has been. He'll defer to me if and when we face a firefight, but make no mistake: it's his plan. He's my brother and I'll die for him. He's smarter than the shitload of us put together. These men we're assembling are the toughest, the best you'll ever have the honor to serve with, so you have two choices. Either stop acting like a whiney little bitch and start being the soldier I thought you were, or go back to Texas, draw your pay, and send Dave. Decide now."

Keith was red as a radish as he looked from face to face. He swallowed twice, then said, "I apologize. I'm here to serve and was out of line; it won't happen again."

Gran broke the silence by saying, "Alight, gentlemen, anything worth drinking around this shite hole and not that bloody fucking swamp water of Charles?"

Brick rose and retrieved five lowball glasses and then opened a cupboard and, just like she promised, found that Harriette had purchased a bottle of thirty-year Glenkinchie, Tanqueray, Grey Goose, and Charlie's bourbon. Brick removed the bottles, two in each hand, and set them on the table. Each man poured a measure of his favorite—neat. Brick stood, and so did the rest, and said, "Here's an old Irish toast my granddad was fond of: To success and may we all be in heaven before the Devil knows we're dead."

After getting the approval, Harriette made plans for the party, starting with the guest list. The guys of course, Dawn and Zoe, Rick and Joann—friends from Bend—and maybe the real estate agent, and whomever else Mason wanted. She also made a list for food and drink; when she finished, she sent email invitations to the people she could and called the rest.

Thirty-seven

Jocko paced the great room of the ranch, worrying. Next week would be the biggest score since working on his own. A huge shipment that created multiple concerns. Logistics seemed in order but he always fretted over security. He had brought in three new men, virgins. They made him nervous. This shit made him jittery, got to lay off the blow. Brick always handled this part; he personally lacked the confidence and knew it showed. That fucking Cisco looked at him like a vulture at roadkill. He was still waiting for confirmation; just the thought of it made him sweat. He'd been promised that Brick would be dead by now—what the fuck happened?

"Sit down, for Christ's sake; this pacing is making me nuts." Nadia was irritated; she complained that he always made such a big deal out of every little thing. Plus, right now she had cabin fever. They hadn't gone anywhere in weeks. She had warned him that if she didn't get out of here soon, she would explode and Jocko didn't want to see that. When she lost her temper, it was a shit-show. She was capable of mass destruction. Her fuse was lit and it was very short.

Fun loving by nature, Jocko had grown up in the outback of Australia and normally he had that easy, whatever attitude; he wasn't cut out for the pressure. Drinking beer, chasing pussy, and bar fighting—those kind of things were more his style. Jocko Neilson joined up in '89 and got stationed in Panama during the Noriega crap. That's when he met Brick and Charlie's crew. They got along well enough. After they were discharged, he went to work for Brick and was placed in Oregon. You went where Brick said, if you wanted in. By then he had developed a strong craving for a certain Polish whore and wanted to bring her along. These days he had too many cravings.

So Nadia Matczynski found herself living in a small Oregon town and she wasn't happy. This was a woman of serious appetites, and she was ultra-hot and knew it. At 5'9" she was long and willowy with jet-black hair reaching the bottom of her breasts, and what spectacular breasts they were. Jocko took her to Switzerland for the perfect 36Ds and they were glorious. Eyes big as B&B plates, black and smoldering, the most exotic woman Jocko could hope to land. Holding onto her was iffy.

She was his, for now.

Action, parties, booze, drugs, orgies—a big nasty life. She craved sex the way men did and was bisexual. She loved being a whore, but sticking with Jocko meant she had the means to unlimited luxury. She was smarter than Jocko and it wasn't long before she became his most trusted adviser. When the call came, she lobbied and finally demanded Jocko agree to Brick's elimination; after all, what had he done for them lately?

When Raoul contacted him about the hit on Brick, Jocko was against it. Brick was hard enough to take, but what about Charlie? Nadia, who grew up in Poland and Russia and had been turned out as a very pretty whore at the age of fifteen, thought different. The men who ran her were large and swarthy; they carried guns and violence was always in the air. Nadia never understood why everyone was so afraid of Charlie. She would say, "It's simple; you walk behind and shoot him in the head. What's the problem?"

He tried to explain that Charlie was different; many tried to take him out and they died. When Jocko voiced his concerns, Raoul said Charlie was a world away and Brick had gone missing; Charlie wouldn't be a factor. They kept at him until he agreed.

First he was told that Brick had been killed in Chicago, yet now he might be back, a possible sighting in Bend. Nadia said it was just rumors, but ... Brick made Jocko millions before he quit, leaving Jocko manager of the ranch—managing fucking sheep? Nadia was a disease and had expensive tastes; she could burn through money faster than a comet. He had to keep working. He resumed pacing.

Thirty-eight

Kelly Knowles was a little confused when first Brick called and then an hour later a woman who said her name was Harriette called back. They invited her to a party on Saturday. She had sounded sincere enough and it did sound like a lot of fun, the way Harriette described the party as a big outdoor barbecue—with music, dancing, and some interesting guests, some from a movie company.

She had thought about Brick these last few days. When they had lunch, he touched her arm to make a point, and little tremors ran through her. He was the most interesting man she'd met in a long time, mysterious. He exuded confidence and knowledge without the ego that usually accompanies his type. He seemed kind and gentle and actually listened to her. He made her feel important and respected and … and … like a desirable woman.

He was upbeat and funny, thanked her repeatedly for her help, and confessed he was the leader of an advance group looking for locations to shoot a major motion picture. He swore her to secrecy, as he didn't want their competitors to steal their plan. So she had a new task—looking for available land in the area that met his specifications for movie scenes. She would be well compensated. That had worked out pretty good. She already had a fat check and an unexpected cash bonus for a few hours' work, and now he invited her to a party and who knows what else?

Friday night Brick and Charlie held court in the kitchen around the big oak table. Brick reiterated the details of the cluster fuck in Wisconsin, including his ex and Nicky. He didn't want any confusion about the mission. The contractor, supposedly Raoul, wants Brick gone and he forked over serious cash to make it happen.

185

Clint asked, "Do you know why? It covers several states, so it's got to be a big deal"

"It's easy; follow the money. The who is still unclear. I have a couple of theories but I'm not sure yet. From the raid in Wisconsin, we know Raoul set it up. He's had a hard-on for me from the beginning. We know Jocko knew and agreed, the two asshole buddies.

"I know you're not here for the money, but it's all I got. I think I know why and I'm touched, thank you. I had to tell you now in case … well, you know the stakes. Just remember we built that ranch. We know it as well or better than they. Odds are in our favor."

"'Member in the jungle? The General always said number one rule, protect the Bank. We never forgot and you was good to us," Stoney added.

"You're right, Stoney; I'm still the Bank and if you stick with me, there's benefits—remuneration, as Gran calls it. Keith, I don't speak for Charlie, but I've got you; everyone in my squad gets a taste."

"And Gran?" he queried.

"The pleasure; you couldn't stay away, so don't give me any shit. You own half of England. We good?" Brick quipped.

"Point taken; shall we carry on?" Gran answered with a smirk.

"Alright gentleman, Gran has eyes on the ranch, so we have good intel and visuals. Now Gran is going to go over the details of what he found and give you the location and range of audio and visual devices he planted. Charlie will handle the plan going forward and assign roles and duties; any questions?" Brick looked at each face. "No questions? Things will come up as we progress so make sure you understand each aspect. I'm going to sit and listen as they explain their parts and see if I can find any fault in our thinking. If any of you are unclear or have something to add, don't hold back. This is a group decision so jump in with anything you can think of."

Gran explained that as he placed listening bugs around the property, he picked up that a nasty Mexican thug had a thing going with Jocko's woman. When they were alone, he would squeeze her ass and kiss her hard on the mouth. A little something maybe they can use later. They would be going in hard and fast, so the more knowledge they had about what they might face, the better. This thug obviously had a hidden agenda.

The group had done this kind of work before, and they all knew that daily and even hourly briefings would make the difference between success and failure. Communication was the key to success and this squad of men were the best at early preparation.

Thirty-nine

Dawn was in her hot tub luxuriating in the steam, pondering what to wear. She anguished over the party. When he left, she had hit the pause button on her life and now he was back in play. Yes, he seemed to want back into her life, but she wasn't sure she could trust that it was really true. She had noticed that Keith had been checking her out; he was cute and about her age. Brick was the target but maybe if she could make him jealous … well, she could hope. There was always plenty of competition— the bitches queuing around him like puppies with a new ball. She needed an edge. She didn't care if it was a barbecue; she wanted male attention, Brick's attention, so dress to impress was her motto. Damn it, why wasn't he falling in love? Every asshole in town was after her.

Making love with Brick was like finding a favorite shirt after believing it lost. Worn flannel, soft and warm, a perfect fit. They proved it again. Easy relaxed, so familiar. Every touch, caress, locked in muscle memory. No thought or awkwardness. As natural as breathing. He sensed her body's needs before she knew them. He held her tight and his big hands caused ripples along her spine as he read her like an ancient scroll moving to her rhythm, changing positions before they became strained. The forceful thrust when needed and the gentle touch when stated. Damn him.

At that moment Laura was at the resort bar back in Montana; employees were allowed to drink after their shift if they weren't in uniform. This was the only place she felt comfortable drinking alone, because here she wasn't really alone. She knew the employees and was good friends with Vicky, the bartender on duty. She only paid half price, if Vicky charged her at all. It had been ten days since he left, and he'd warned her not to expect to hear from him until his thing was finished—whatever. She tried his cell; it went to voice. Still she was lonely.

The party was rocking; Zoe had hired one of the best local bands named the Rhythm Cats. They were jamming to a Mellencamp cover. Drums, base, rhythm and lead guitars, a raspy male vocalist who played rhythm guitar—not too shabby. Zoe said she might sit in on a couple of numbers if the mood struck.

There were twenty to thirty people milling about in the yard and house. They had set up a temporary bandstand on a raised platform, and currently three couples were dancing on the lawn. It was early; later, the more they drank, it could get interesting. Mason saddled in behind Harriette, slipped his hands around her waist, and pulled her tight, nuzzling her neck. He had tears in his eyes, filled with emotion. A year ago he was scared shitless he might lose her, and now to see her beaming and happy like when she was a girl tugged at the strings of his soul. They would long remember this night, for many reasons.

Everyone had pitched in to decorate the yard with strings of white lights and paper lanterns strung from tree to home. The large cherry tree looming over the crowd was all a twinkle, as Clint had climbed like a spider monkey and draped a thousand tiny white lights in and around the branches. The night was perfect, with balmy breezes filtering through the group, refreshing the sweaty dancers. As Harriette worked the crowd, her face lit with joy; she kept repeating, "What a great reunion!" A piss-eyed Clint teetering on a beer keg said, "Sweet."

Dawn cornered Keith and was flirting, looking to see if Brick noticed. Keith was relaxed for the first time since the men came to town and enjoying a beer, grinning from ear to ear. Dawn exuded sexuality, dressed to the nines in a low-cut sleeveless white tube top that hugged her figure like a second skin, fishnet stockings covered by a slip of purple chenille barely stretched over her fine ass, and five-inch black stilettos; she created quite a stir. Wives chastised their husbands and gossiped. Brick smiled when he saw her nibbling on Keith's ear and whispering something, his face glowing.

Sitting in the kitchen was the unlikely pairing of Zoe and Kelly. Kelly knew Zoe from the Shoe; everyone did—she was the town's only celebrity. Zoe, to her credit, had seen Kelly around and even knew she was a sales agent. Right now they were arguing whether Elvis or the Beatles had the greatest influence over rock and roll.

As casually as she could, Kelly asked, "So what's the story on the guy they call the Bank?"

Zoe laughed. "Pretty hot, isn't he?"

"Sizzling." Kelly almost blushed.

"That being the standard reaction, I've had a crush on him for the last ten years. The guys used to call him GG for God's Gift; it embarrassed him. I mean, he's like a total chick magnet. He's nice. Some people here work for him. They say he's smart—it's an understatement. They call him boss. People owe him, including me. He staked me when I took over the bar from my dad," Zoe said.

Brick and Charlie sat on either side of Gran, watching the split-screen monitors he had arranged in the spare back room. There was a flurry of activity; it was a cloudless early summer night, visibility premium. They could make out the faces of Jocko and Nadia as they stood on the porch that ran the length of the front side of the ranch house. They noted the new men and started to wonder.

During the years of absence, Gran had continued to work with the RAF and was current on the spyware. The technological industry had grown by leaps and bounds, but the military applications had really skyrocketed. Spy craft technology seemed to change by the minute. Gran had placed sixteen visual bugs around the house, split four to a screen, with all displayed in full color. "Placed" was a misnomer, as the tiny infrared cameras were shot from an air rifle and stuck to any surface; they were top quality. Anticipating his needs, Gran had arrived with two large suitcases filled with goodies. The cameras he used resembled tree knots, as if a limb had been severed.

The compound had grown over the years, not by much, but a shed or small storage bay scattered where needed. The ranch encompassed sixty-five acres of rich, green pasture. Water was plentiful and the setting picturesque, dwarfed by Shadow Mountain that drew the name from its location, sitting in the shadow of Mount Rainer to the west, whose encompassing presence obscured it entirely as the sun sank into the fertile valley below.

The ranch house was a long, single-story rambler laid on a grid designed to capture the best elements of the landscape. It traversed front to back forty feet and at the end, laid like Legos, were two perpendicular branches on either side, exactly the same only twenty feet. This gave the structure, when seen from above, the sense of a perfect letter T.

The house faced south, so they had full sun most of the day, but as the sun began its descent behind the mountain, the light soon faded into an eerie gloom—still sunlit from below but almost twilight at the ranch. The house itself was constructed with fir, painted a dazzling white with dull red trim. A hundred yards west were two Quonset huts, each the size of a football field, and any given time in the past there could have been as much as a thousand kilos of cocaine stored within. In addition, a large barn and seven-car garage were positioned to the east of the house.

Jocko appeared to be giving orders to the group; soon four men left in a black Suburban and three more headed to a black Escalade. After what looked like a heated argument, Nadia stormed off the porch and joined the last three. Interesting, they would try to track their route.

Gran had attached a parabolic microphone to the front bottom window that looked like a fly; working off the vibrations of the glass, it delivered a crisp, clear audio of all conversations in that area of the house. Unfortunately, everyone at the ranch spent the afternoon on the grounds and only went in one at a time, so they hadn't heard the plans.

Forty

As night overtook the festivities, it brought a slight chill snipping at the heels of the reveling troop. Halfway between the house and bandstand, a fifteen-foot fire pit lined with river rocks was stacked with wood waiting for a breath of flame to ignite the seasoned kindling, thereby bringing the pine logs to a blaze. Brick and Charlie finally left the screens in the competent care of Stoney and ventured into the crowd. The scene they just witnessed was disturbing. Something was up. They talked about sending a scouting party to check, but decided to hold off for a bit because Harriette would be disappointed.

They wandered over to the bar and joined three couples who were standing, drinks in hand, discussing the latest violence in the Mideast. Charlie went directly to the bottles aligned in neat rows behind the bar and instructed the bartender on the composition of his favorite libation: J.T.S. Brown poured over cracked ice in a shaker that slightly bruised the bourbon into submission till thoroughly chilled, then slowly dripped in a lowball glass filled with more cracked ice. Charlie liked it ultra-cold.

One of the couples standing next to the display was enthralled with the performance by Charlie and the bartender. Dave, of Dave and Janet, inquired as to the choice of liquor, which he hadn't heard of.

Before anyone had a chance to answer, Brick arrived and said, "It's a 100-proof Kentucky bourbon that's oaky, harsh, and bitter. Paul Newman drank it in the movie *The Hustler*. Charlie is a fan of the actor. He thinks he's a combination Fast Eddie Felson and Cool Hand Luke."

Charlie laughed and said, "There is that."

This got the couples talking on the subject of little-known yet superior attributes of rarified spirits that each was familiar with. That segued into movie and celebrity gossip as Brick and Charlie drifted away.

They walked easy within the crowd and both men felt the glow that ran through the party; it was fun.

Charlie said, "This feels pretty damn good; I haven't felt like this since the last time I was home with my tribe. Harriette deserves this after what she's been subjected to with this disease." He paused and turned Brick to face him. "It's pretty nice to have you back again too, brother."

They embraced and then Brick worked his way into the throng of dancers and revelers, wearing his content and satisfaction in his body language. He was oblivious to the looks of admiring females turning from their husbands and boyfriends to stare openly in his wake. Brick was tired; ever since that fateful day when Cassie stepped back into his reality, except for Montana, he had not stopped moving or thinking. It only now dawned on him why he had become a recluse. The death of Jesus set him off, but the pressure had been building for a very long time. Two years alone were a blessing. Ever since he could remember, he was in charge of so much, so many people dependent, and now he was back.

It didn't feel bad and in many ways good. Suddenly, he realized an important truth—he liked being in charge; he was born for it.

Charlie wandered back in the house on a new mission; he was looking for Kelly. He found her in Zoe's company. The two women were heading back from the rear of the house and it looked to Charlie like Zoe was giving a tour; it made sense—after all, Kelly is a real estate agent. She was making noises like she was getting ready to leave when he interrupted the women and asked Kelly if he could talk to her alone for a minute.

Zoe said, "Uh oh, be careful! Charlie isn't big on talk and alone with a woman is suspicious." She was smiling when she said it, but it was true.

It's not like Charlie didn't like women; he liked them just fine. To tell the truth, the big, bad warrior was just shy. He grew up in a family of men, didn't date in high school, and then went into the military. His biggest exposure to the opposite sex was with prostitutes overseas.

Now he drew Kelly outside and then led her to a small table on the perimeter of the crowd where they could hear each other. "I know the boss doesn't like to give away too many details because he's paranoid about others poaching his ideas. But I'm the one who's been scouting shoot locations. I do stunt work and choreograph the action scenes. I really like the one that he mentioned to you—good lighting and camera angles. Can you tell me what you know about it?"

So she did, including the man's name who owns it and the company he works for, even his boss's name. "I spoke with Tony, the owner, and he said that Hank was working a landslide clearing trees. He should be back in a week or so. I could try to contact him if it's important."

"No, no, don't do that," Charlie said. "When people know we're really interested, they raise the rental price and the boss would kill me if I spilled the beans. Let's keep this between us, okay?"

It was after midnight and the crowd had thinned considerably. After checking with Harriette and making sure that she would have her bedroom in the house alone for the night, Dawn went in to make preparations for her seduction.

The guys were wrapping it up. Stoney had already shepherded a drunk Clint to a vehicle, and Stoney drove him back to their rental. Gran sat with Keith reviewing the footage at the ranch before they buttoned things up here and moved back to their house.

Dawn was pretty tipsy as she went back outside looking for Brick. The fire had subsided and most lights were extinguished, so it was quite dark. She removed her shoes but was unsteady and stumbled along.

She couldn't stop from giggling as she roamed, calling his name in a drunken whisper louder than intended. She saw movement over in the far corner of the lot and headed toward it. A dark form separated itself from the trees and she said out loud, "Peekaboo I see you; you can't hide from me, honey man." Then she continued in a lopsided gait to the trees.

As she drew near, the dark figure dressed all in black stepped out, wrapped his arm around her waist, and clamped the other hand over her mouth. A second dark form, smaller and thin, stuck a scarf in her mouth and wrapped the ends around her throat. Dawn felt the sharp jerk as her head snapped back and she was caught in a bear hug by the big man. She struggled with her assailant, but her arms felt weak and useless as she tried in vain to fight him off. The pressure around her throat increased; she couldn't breathe. She was drifting, losing consciousness, her body going limp. Her attacker threw her over his shoulder like a sack of ripe melons and headed to a waiting van.

It started again, fast, thrumming until his head was sure to burst. He just knew it was Dawn, the feeling as strong as a riptide urging him to action. He turned in a slow circle, tracing every face in memory for the hint of yellow in her blond hair. Harriette walked out the door at that minute. "Is Dawn in the house?" Brick demanded.

"No, no ..." she stammered. She could read the fear clouding his features.

"She's gone, I know it," he said.

He turned and set off at a run, gun in hand. For the party, he had opted for the small brother of the big Kimber, concealable and just as deadly. If she wasn't in the house and not visible in the open yard, there was only one option left—the stand of trees along the back ridge. He had to wait for his eyes to adjust when he entered the thick stand of fir and aspen. He heard a faint gasp off to his right and moved toward the sound with caution.

Then a muffled cry of his name and he turned to the sound. A tree fell hard on his left arm and the gun went spinning off. He raised his right arm in defense and another whacked him in the ribs. A Mack truck came racing through the clearing, hit the back of his head, and the world turned black.

The men spread out with flashlights. Charlie found him and spotted the gun some ten feet away. They rigged a stretcher of sorts and brought him to the house.

Harriette had tears in her eyes when she said, "But this can't be happening … I mean, who?"

Brick came to hours later to find a strange woman lifting one of his eyelids and shining a bright little light directly into the pupil. He grabbed her wrist, his grip weak and feeble. She gently pried his fingers off and set the hand down under the covers.

"Does he need to be in the hospital?" Harriette asked.

"Probably. His vitals are good and he seems to focus, but he took a nasty hit to the back of the head, so he should be checked for concussion," she said.

"No, no hospitals," he whispered. "Is she gone?"

It was Charlie who answered, "Yes, but we're pretty sure we know where she'll be and we have eyes on the joint, so you relax. I've got this."

Charlie overpaid Jane Ferguson and thanked her for coming out and taking a look. Harriette had called her. She was Harriette's nurse practitioner for the last year and could be trusted. Brick spent the next few hours at Mason and Harriette's until Harriette finally deemed him strong enough to leave.

Forty-one

Think Brick ... think it through. It's what you would have done ... it makes sense—strike first, first and fast. I should have anticipated it, but I wanted Harriette to have her party. Okay, it happened; now think it through. They won't hurt her. Jocko's too smart for that; he knows the repercussions. He still doesn't know about Charlie or he never would have tried. Use that to your advantage. He was back in his suite at the lodge, needed to be alone. There was too much commotion with the guys around to think clearly. *I'm too tired; I need sleep. This doesn't change the plan; it just gooses it up a notch. This might be better; I'm starting to see it.* He lay down on the big comfy bed fully dressed, staring at the ceiling. *In the morning ... I always think better in the morning.*

He awoke to the sound of his phone buzzing. It was Stoney; after he left the party, he had taken over the night watch while the others slept. He reported that a white panel van had arrived at the ranch and pulled into the first of two Quonset huts and no one had come out. As soon as he ended the call, Brick knew exactly what they would do. He fell back into a dreamless sleep, his computer-like mind finally shutting down. They had until at least noon, but he would have the soldiers ready by nine.

Hours later, he was back with the guys drinking coffee at their rented house. Everyone had some sleep and they were gathered for the next phase. He had already talked to Harriette twice and assured her it would be alright. She would still worry; she and Dawn had grown quite close over the last year.

Charlie was pacing, not good with waiting. Brick sat with Gran studying the monitors. As the morning broke, the ranch came alive in slow motion, beginning with the worker bees who set about tending to the livestock and chores. The hired guns were resting, secure in their sentry patrolling the perimeter. Nadia woke at ten feeling great, powerful. Last night had been exciting; it made her wet. Danger aroused her sexually like nothing else, pain and pleasure so intrinsically linked. Inflicting pain on others was best, the best high ever.

She strode into the living room dressed in her finest rags and announced she was going shopping. Jocko looked at her over his coffee cup and said, "Are you fucking nuts? What you did last night was stupid—I never authorized this. Since when are you giving orders to my men?"

"Since you became such a pussy. Why are you afraid of these people; they are nothing. I took Cisco, mucho mano; we stole her right from under their noses. It was fun. I would do it again. You need to show some balls, Jocko, or maybe I find another man not so afraid of everything."

Jock sprang from his chair quick as a lightning strike and slapped her hard across the face, knocking her down. "You fucking bitch! Don't ever talk to me like that again or I'll feed you to the wood chipper. Polish whores like you are a dime a dozen." It was true—he feared what her stupid actions might cause, and he was furious.

She wiped a small trickle of blood from her lips with her tongue and smiled wickedly. Then she crawled across the floor until she was between his legs, and looking up at him with those smoldering eyes said, "That's my Jocko; fuck me now."

He scooped her up and did just that; violently, rough, just the way she liked it. Their sweating bodies glistened from the intensity of the raw, uninhibited sexual romp and Nadia now laid spread eagle under him stroking his face and cooing at him. She had talked so dirty while he pounded her.

She was working him now that his lust was satiated and he seemed docile. "I have to go shopping, baby—just for a couple of hours. I need some women's things and you ripped my favorite panties ... please, baby ... please."

"Okay, take the Suburban and take Cisco, and have him pick two others to accompany you. It's noon; you be back by six or I'll beat the skin off your back. Now go before I change my mind."

Cisco was Francisco Eduardo Suarez; he was an enforcer for the Sinaloa cartel. They all worked for the cartel—once in, never out. They were the men who created nightmares for the cops and terrorized the land. The chainsaw their favorite tool, they were famous for beheadings, torture, and mass slaughter. Cisco was the head monster.

He was used to taking what he wanted and was placed here six months ago to make sure the cartel's interests were protected. He had been fucking Nadia for the past two months. She teased and flaunted until he couldn't stand it anymore. Lately the cartel and he were wondering if they still needed Jocko at all. After this next big shipment, they would reconsider his worth.

Forty-two

Juddiah was hot. He was balancing on the joists of the second-story while setting the tresses for the roof. A new bank, as if Redmond needed another. That wasn't his problem; it was the heat. The sun had been relentless since they started the work. He estimated that if they could hold this pace, it would be another two, maybe three days until they completed the framing. Let the finish carpenters do their thing and he was out of here. He hated working out of town and bunking with other men. Sure he drank with them and they all considered him a friend—a big, amiable, good-natured guy; that was the image he strived to portray but if they even had a clue, he'd be finished.

The sky was a deep blue cloudless expanse that seemed to go on forever. At eighty-five degrees, it would be a perfect day on the water or sipping a cold one on the dock. The only good thing was the dangerous nature of the job wouldn't let his mind wander. They all needed to stay focused. A slip would send you on a nosedive to your grave; pay attention or suffer severe consequences. He grabbed the struts as the framing gun jacked the staccato rounds of nails in an even pattern.

At night in his bunk before passing out from fatigue, he would lie there masturbating and have the most delicious thoughts of some naked little bitch on her hands and knees while he pounded her firm young body, defiling her dirty little holes until no longer small. He could imagine her red welted flesh squeezed between his fingers and the greenish purple bruises covering her body. The best part was the screams echoing off the walls. He loved the screaming and crying best of all.

First, he would need to buy the shoes; he decided that for her a bright blue satin with six-inch heels would be perfect. He would buy the shoes before he left town. Oh the fun he would have, just a few more days.

He wanted to make this one last, maybe even weeks, but he knew there was no guarantee; he had tried to limit himself before, but the blood lust blinded him.

Away from the unbelievable horrors of these animals, fortunately unaware, Harriette couldn't stop worrying. Mason consulted with Brick, and had driven to the ranch under the guise of needing work, only to be dismissed by one of the underlings as if he were a gnat. Jocko didn't want any unnecessary spectators today. The guards seemed on high alert and appeared jumpy before they recognized his truck. Harriette ignored Brick's warnings and started calling his cell every hour and was ignored. She was about to drive out to the rental when he finally called back.

"Is she okay? Did you find her—how is she?"

"Do you trust me?"

"Of course, but I'm …"

"You either trust me or not. I said I'd get her back and I will, but you can't keep calling. Stop it … clean the house, anything, get you mind off this. I'll call when I have her." He hung up.

Nadia slammed the door as she left the house and took long strides to the hut. She unlocked the door to the room and closed it behind her. Dawn was on a thin dirty mattress atop a single metal bedframe. Her hands were cuffed in front of her and her ankles were wrapped in duct tape. She had a piece of the grey, sticky tape covering her mouth. Nadia stepped close and ripped the tape free, causing Dawn to cry out in pain. She was clad in only her bra and panties, her clothes having been cut off, and she was shivering with cold. While normally the sight of another woman would give her hope—in this case, hope that the woman would be compassionate and maybe at least give her a blanket—the image of this woman immediately crushed any such optimism.

Before Nadia entered the room, she had grabbed a cold bottle of water from the cooler. Now she stood in front of the woman helpless on the bed and asked, "Thirsty?"

Dawn said, "Yes, please."

Nadia handed her the bottle and watched as she worked her constrained hands to twist off the cap, then drank half the bottle in one gulp. "You're a pretty little slut. Too bad you're on the wrong side, the losing side." Nadia sat on the bed beside her and inspected her body from top to bottom, her long painted fingers touched then kneaded the firm flesh beneath her hands. She pinched her nipples savagely and when Dawn cried out, she slapped her hard across the cheek, remembering her own slap not long before. She moved her hand between Dawn's legs and squeezed her sex as hard as she could. "I'll be gone for a few hours and when I return, we'll see to you. If you're not submissive and responsive, I'll let the men have you until you beg me to kill you."

Back at the rented house, the three men were watching the monitors, staring with intensity and listening to every word between the sexually charged couple in the living room. This was good; they were back on track with Brick's plan with a few minor adjustments. The three foot soldiers were already in place, and they wore headsets locked on the same frequency so communications would have a direct flow in real time.

Forty-three

A pair of dark brooding eyes stared at Laura as she sat chatting away with the bartender. He recognized her right off; they'd been watching for her since the incident. He never drank at this bar—it was too upscale for him. It was only chance circumstance that had him standing in the lobby of the resort.

He was bored waiting for so long and a little pissed.

He needed a drink. Ever since that sneaky bastard tricked them and put Billy out of commission, his life had gone in the shitter. They were big men around this town and people were afraid of them, or at least they used to be. Billy was finally home, but he was using a walker. He could have used crutches but the broken wrist made it impossible, even with the cast. Big Ansel kept moaning about the cost of home health care. They used to take what they wanted … but without Billy, it was all gone and he was almost broke.

Fuck it, Danny's late. He headed into the bar; he had enough for a beer or two. That's when he spotted her, sitting there pretty as can be with her little upturned nose and perfect hair.

He stood in the entranceway staring at her. The tap on his shoulder made him jump and it hurt like hell. "God damn it, don't sneak up on me like that! The bitch is here; we need to follow her when she leaves. I don't want her to see me." They waited over two hours, but she never left and they finally gave up.

Jimmy bitched all the way home. They didn't have any money and now his mother's car was broke and he couldn't pay his cell phone bill and they had canceled service and he hated the crummy little trailer park where they lived and goddamn it why did everything bad happen to him? Getting a job never crossed his mind. At least they had a landline, so he wasted no time and called Big Ansel. They had been searching for the girl for weeks, and Jimmy was sure Billy's old man would give him some money for finding her or at least for knowing where she hung out.

He was too stupid to think of trying to get her name or find out more, which Ansel pointed out after he heard she'd been spotted. But yes he would pay; he rubbed his sore nose, thinking he had more than one debt to settle. This girl was the key and at least they had a starting point.

The Escalade sat idling in front of the Quonset hut with Diego driving, Cisco riding shotgun, and Philip Ortiz in back. Nadia took long strides to the truck; her cheeks were a blazing crimson in contrast to her long, silky black hair trailing in the breeze. She was flushed, feeling sexy and powerful. Let Jocko feel in control for now, but she had plans.

She felt reckless and safe with Cisco and the other men. Soon she would be issuing orders and things would be different. She would use her power and be viscous in business. Her goal was to be free and rich beyond belief; she was close, just a little longer. Diego drove fast through the twisty blind curves on the back roads, a shortcut to Bend where the black whore could raise hell; that's what she was good at. The men knew what was going on with her and Cisco. He was the man they feared and took orders from. The Aussie and Polish pussy were just a nuisance. They were all waiting on the shipment.

The sky was crystal clear this afternoon without even the wispy clouds that dotted the horizon most days. Three fighter jets appeared in formation, their jet streams trailing in unison as they headed south. They originated in Fort Lewis and the Escalade followed in the wake. It was still cool with the western breeze washing over the Cascades fresh from last night's gentle showers. A good day to die.

Four miles down the road, just before the juncture onto blacktop, there was a severe curve that forced them to slow way down or risk flipping the top-heavy vehicle. As they completed the turn, Diego hit the brakes hard, sending his passengers lurching forward and straining against their seatbelts. Nadia, of course, wasn't buckled in and went flying over the seat back landing on top of Cisco's head. She came away with a cut on her forehead, swearing like a mad sailor in Polish. Fucking trees in this area were always falling on roads, houses, and cars. Old trees with shallow roots gave way in the rain-soaked earth.

At that precise moment, flanking either side of the car, Stoney and Clint appeared with Keith covering the front. They were dressed in white cotton coveralls, wearing gas masks and face shields. Stoney and Clint carried long tube-shaped rifles and, firing simultaneously, pierced the back two windows of the SUV. The canisters were bullet shaped and exploded on contact, filling the interior with military-grade tear gas. Keith held a machine pistol in case one of the occupants reacted fast enough.

As the passengers rolled out on the ground choking and blinded from the gas, the two soldiers set down the tubes and drew their Beretta 9mm pistols. Now the three men opened fire and the bodies bucked and lurched in their final dance. The operation was over in seconds. They left the woman writhing on the ground, screaming and frantically rubbing her eyes with the heels of her hands.

Picking up the chainsaws lying by the side of the road, Keith and Clint cut the tree into short rounds they could move, while Stoney threw the bodies like rag dolls back in the SUV, dumping them on top of each other. The gas dissipated in seconds with the doors open and both rear windows shattered. Clint climbed behind the wheel and drove away while Keith retrieved one of the five-gallon jugs of water from their truck and poured it over the still-screaming bitch.

He liked Dawn … he liked her a lot. Along with the water, he had brought a dirty burlap bag that he now pulled over the woman's head. It reached to her ankles, which he secured with duct tape. Stoney wasn't gentle either as he threw her in the back of the pickup before they drove off. Stoney liked Dawn too.

For the first time since she was little, Nadia was scared. Her eyes burned and watered, and she feared she might be permanently blind. She couldn't draw a deep breath, couldn't stop retching and choking. The filthy bag smelled like shit and added to her gag reflex. It was picked on purpose—a farm fertilizer bag, fresh. Keith felt responsible for Dawn's disappearance—it was on his watch, a black mark. He was carrying a world of guilt. He had been so confident when Charlie picked him. He had planned to show his boss how good he was in the field, but this group of men made him seem ineffectual by comparison. These guys, Jesus, Joseph, and Mary, he had never in his life been around guys like these.

He had underestimated every one of them, starting with the Englishman. And Brick, the pretty boy with all his charm and slickness, the leader. He'd planned this a week ago. He seemed to know in advance what could happen and had a contingency alternative ready. *How the hell did he do that?* They said he was smart, but it was more than that. Keith was properly chastised; he would follow orders. Brick had assured him they would have Dawn back by nightfall, and he believed him now.

Dawn was frozen with fear and chattering from the cold as she lay near naked on the small bed cursing her fate and wondering when or if the man she loved would find her in time. She was sure that the Russian bitch or whoever the hell she was would do as she had promised. While she certainly didn't want to be raped, she was tough and knew she would survive whatever happened. But then what would be her fate? Her mind reeled at the thought of what could happen. She tried to block the images. She couldn't let herself dwell on the consequences—survival was all that mattered for the moment.

The door opened and a subdued Jocko walked in and sat next to her on the bed. He carried a warm Indian blanket and a bag, which he set on the floor. He wrapped the blanket around her shoulders and produced a key from his pants pocket that he used to free her hands from the chafing handcuffs. Without a word, he then removed the contents of the bag and handed her a hot steaming cup of coffee and a warm croissant sandwich.

He sat there staring at the floor between his feet while she consumed the delicious ham and brie croissant, washing it down with the equally great coffee. He had doctored it with cream and sugar, and it soothed her raw throat and warmed her insides as the blanket warmed her outside. He hadn't said a word since he walked in; he seemed lost in deep thought, like he couldn't decide how to start.

After she finished eating, he pulled a napkin out of the bag as if he just remembered it. "Did that help? I didn't … I mean, it wasn't my intention to … Well, you're here now and we must make the best of it. Nadia, she's upset and probably scared you, but I'm in charge and I mean you no harm. I need you to help me find a way out of this mess."

Dawn looked him over and noticed that he seemed contrite, so unlike the crazed woman. He spoke with a heavy accent similar to Gran's but a little different. Maybe it would be okay.

"You know he'll kill you?" she said.

"You mean Brick?" he asked.

"Yes, he's been my friend for a long time. I know who you are. Mason worked for you and Harriette is my best friend. If you know Brick, you know he won't rest until I'm back and you're dead."

"Well, you and I must figure out a way for that not to happen. Taking you was a mistake and I'm sorry. Brick and I used to be mates; we can work it out with your help. We'll just call him and I'll explain…. Do you know if Charlie is about?"

A fresh wariness entered her mind; her instincts told her she needed to be careful with information, so she said, "There were a lot of people at the party, but I don't remember anyone by that name."

He seemed to sigh with relief, and with a brighter mood said, "Alright, I think we can fix this. Here's my phone—call him."

Dawn dialed the number from memory, but after five rings it kicked over to voicemail and a generic female voice gave instructions about leaving messages. Dawn said, "Brick it's me and I'm ok …"

Jocko snatched the phone out of her hand at that point and continued the message. "Hello mate, it's been a long time but there's been a mistake and we need to fix it before it goes any farther. The girl is fine, and I want you to know that you will get her back as soon as we can work out arrangements. This is my number; call as soon as you get this message."

Keith and Stoney had returned from their rendezvous with Nadia and friends, and were now out on patrol. The others gathered around the table listening to the message. It made Brick feel better to hear the fear in Jocko's voice, and he knew Dawn would be safe—Jocko wasn't crazy. This would just take a little longer before it was over, and not the way Jocko envisioned. It made him crazy to think of how frightened and lost Dawn must feel. He wished he would have answered the phone and offered her some reassurance before Jocko took the phone away. Brick knew she was smart and tough; he only hoped she would react accordingly when the opportunity presented itself. The operation snatching Jocko's woman had been a success and would provide the leverage they needed. Now it was time to set the next phase of the plan in motion.

Forty-four

It was 6:00 p.m., after dinner, and Molly Sherman was at her small desk in her room doing homework. It wasn't a frilly pink room like so many of her friends had, but it reflected her own unique personality. She was a cross between tomboy and debutante, and at thirteen she knew what her likes and dislikes were. On most days, she liked blue jeans and either T-shirts or sweats, depending on the weather. But if it was something special like a birthday party or class play, she loved to dress up like her mom, who favored simple dresses and a casual yet feminine appearance.

Molly was struggling with her math assignment. She was a good student, not the best, but she worked hard and did well in science and English; it was just math. She got so frustrated that she clenched her fists and yelled "Mommm" at the top of her lungs. Her mother hated it when Molly lost it like that but she remembered that puberty, with all its raging hormones, was a tough time for a young girl. She had just started her period and her place in the social pecking seemed tragic. Her equally screwed-up friends set Molly's teeth on edge these days. Francie was sympathetic, as she herself had been an outcast at her daughter's age.

Lately, Molly had been on a makeup kick that never ended: "Just tell me why not? My friends all wear it, it's no big deal, you're ruining my life, etc., etc." And then the whining: "Please, please …" and then "When can I …?" It was driving Francie crazy.

When she walked into the room, her only daughter was pulling at her long hair and gritting her teeth. She was doing math, the new math that didn't make sense to anyone who had learned a much simpler method. Francie was at a loss, so she now yelled along with Molly and dual cries of Ed and Dad mingled together in a rebel yell that brought Ed Sherman out of his own thoughts and to his daughter's room.

Ed was a gentle man by nature and loved his life. He never wanted more—a loving wife and his precious daughter. Ed worked as an electrical engineer, so math was a snap and as he eased into the bedroom, he said, "What's going on in here? Sounds like you're slaughtering chickens."

Molly was still yanking on her hair and almost in tears as she looked up at her father and said in her most dramatic voice, "This stupid problem, I hate it! I hate this class and the teacher and I just can't do it. I can't wait for summer vacation to be here already!"

Lifting his wife by the waist, he helped her stand and said, "Why don't you go back to what you were doing and me and pumpkin here can solve the world's problems." Then he gave her a loving pat on her rump followed by a little rub.

"Gross, why do you guys have to do that in front of me?" Molly whined.

"Sweetie, when you grow up, you can be gross too. Now let's take it from the top."

Juddiah was in Seattle at Pike Place Market eating a sumptuous lunch of fried oysters and a pound of steamer clams and feeling much better—the job finished and his wallet fat with the bonus money. He was aware of the heat in his loins and he felt himself growing tumescent. His thoughts keep drifting to his new fantasy and it was difficult to stay focused in the present. He had just purchased the shoes sitting in the shopping bag at his feet. He guessed at the size, a nine medium; over the years he had developed the knack of accurately sizing up a girl.

Once he settled on the shoes, he got impatient. His mother used to wear these types of shoes when they had sex. Because of their religion, she only wore plain, simple clothes while engaged at the farm, but she secretly longed to dress in flamboyant clothes and party like when she was young.

The shoes were a huge turn-on for both mother and son. Sex without the shoes seemed shallow and incomplete. This is when the obsession started to churn in his belly—whenever he had the shoes, it wouldn't be much longer.

The fear and anxiety Jocko felt was like a vise squeezing his head in a tight embrace that threatened to stop his heart. It was almost 9:00 and no one was answering the fucking phone. He kept pacing the big room with his cell in a death grip. Dawn sat in the corner nursing a vodka and soda. By 7:00 Jocko had been so distraught and frustrated, he needed a drink to calm his nerves so he had three fingers of Booker's bourbon in a rocks glass. He didn't like to drink alone, so this was Dawn's second drink and his third.

He had brought her to the main house after he rescued her from the hut and now realized it was more for the company than anything else. He left two more messages for Brick and his nerves were shot. It was bad enough that Nadia had ignored his warnings. Cisco missing was a major cluster fuck—the cartel man was necessary to the confirmation call. Jocko was already concerned about Cisco's presence. The scary bastard worked hard to undermine Jocko's control. Maybe it was time for him to think about an alternative plan before this one crumbled. He had money stashed but needed this last big score; they all needed it.

Charlie was fast asleep, taking a long nap before they moved. This was a talent he had learned in combat. When in a conflict you went days without rest, so he'd mastered his body to sleep on command. Clint and Stoney were in their rooms, and Keith remained on patrol. He had napped earlier and was now breaking the others. Only Brick and Gran sat at the kitchen table studying the plan. Gran would make the call. Jocko didn't know his voice; it would fuck with his head. Jocko never knew the whole crew, only Brick and Charlie. Brick had only brought him in after the raids, when he was starting the business end. Jocko could be an asset and give them contacts in Australia and New Zealand. He was never much of a businessman and Brick had to guide him through most transactions. A rounder and not the brightest so when he learned Nadia was gone he was lost.

Harriette was beside herself with worry and Mason wasn't helping. Their world had been turned topsy-turvy once again. It seemed her life was comprised of huge swings: First disaster, then redemption. The horrible disease followed by financial ruin. And then Brick, her savior, appears out of the mist like an apparition and they are saved only to face another crisis. Drive a girl nuts!

Mason had always been steady, a calming influence especially to his wife. He'd lived in Brick's shadow since they were kids and was good with it. He wasn't a brilliant thinker or a lady killer like his friend, but he liked to think of himself as loyal and a good provider. Give Mason a task and he would always strive to do his best to accomplish it, but worry got you nowhere so he didn't indulge. He knew it pissed his wife off, but he didn't see how it would help. Action usually helped, so he told Harriette he'd drive over to the rental and see if he could lend a hand and would call to let her know of any new developments. This had the desired effect and Harriette seemed to calm down; he always knew what to say.

Laura felt eyes on her and looked around in a bit of a panic. She had this feeling of being watched. It hadn't been that long and he'd warned her, but she missed him. It was crazy she knew; he was a man and men are selfish brutes—they disappeared. While she knew this in her head, she could still feel him, smell him. He shook her world, rocked her out. He was exciting with that cool confidence. Not the macho pig she usually met.

The real problem was, he had changed her, showed her a glimpse of life outside Glendive and opened a world of possibilities. Truth be told, she was bored. There weren't any other suitors clamoring for her attention. She went to work, had a few drinks with the girls, listened to their shit-show, then went home, watched television … and did it all over the next day. It sucked.

But she didn't have a way out right now—she was stuck here for the season. She needed the money for school and knew she'd be fine after the summer and she resumed her old life back home. Without a distraction, though, this was going to be a long, boring summer.

Meanwhile, Jimmy watched and followed her. He was as bored as she was. She didn't do much, mostly hung around the resort. He finally figured out that she lived on the grounds. He stayed in the shadows but wasn't very adept. Ansel wanted to know if the man could be found through her. As long as Ansel was keeping him in booze and cigarettes, Jimmy would keep an eye on her. Ansel had given him a good set of binoculars, so he watched from afar. At least he didn't need a car.

Forty-five

The call came in at 11:00. Nadia's name appeared on his caller ID, so Jocko answered with a combination of relief and anger. "You were to be home by 6:00, you bitch," he spit into the phone.

"Good day, mate" came the reply from a voice that he didn't recognize. Although he didn't know the voice, the accent was familiar—an Englishman or even New Zealander.

"The bloody bitch don't listen so good," the man said, followed by a short laugh.

"Who the fuck is this? I'll kill you, motherfucker," screamed a frustrated Jocko. His nerves were singing like telephone wires; all the waiting had made him half crazy.

"Alright mate; I'll just cut her fucking throat." He hung up.

"Oh shit, oh shit, what did I just do?" Jocko cried to no one but himself. He called back, three times; no answer.

It was a tense fifteen minutes later when the phone rang again. "Are you listening, cunt?" the voice asked. "Bring my girlfriend to the deserted motel off route 16 by the dead lake at midnight and we will have a simple exchange of bitches. You come alone, understand?"

Jocko's mind was racing and this guy wasn't even giving him time to think, so he said, "Yes" and the man was gone. He wanted to ask about his men. Nothing made sense. Why did Nadia have to be so rash, take the girl without asking and what about Cisco? He said midnight, so he only had minutes to act and this wasn't Jocko's strong suit; he didn't understand how far under water he already was, so he made another stupid mistake.

They were already set up, of course. Brick was near the back of the burned-out motel. It was his land; he'd bought it back when he bought the ranch and property. It was a good way to launder cash, according to Bucky. His corporation took care of the taxes. He got it dirt cheap because after years of toxic runoff from the big logging companies clear-cutting forests—the spillage had killed the aquatic life and polluted the lake forever. It was a perfect dumping ground for his own toxic waste and bodies stayed lost.

No one knew if it was lightning or arson that destroyed the motel and land for a square mile, but it remained dissolute and austere. Brick's crew had set heavy logging chains across the dirt road that led to the entrance, but kids looking for a place to drink and screw still found ways in, so the grounds were littered with condoms and beer cans.

Tonight, the chains were down and the team was in place. Counting on Jocko not to follow instructions, they were anticipating his rather obvious counter play. They weren't disappointed—at five minutes to twelve Jocko's big lumbering white Escalade, his personal car, began to slowly traverse the rutted trail leading to the motel and, true to form, almost a mile back the Suburban followed loaded with hired guns.

Dawn was numb with shock and despair. After the last phone call came in, Jocko had leapt into action and knocked the drink from her hand; then he grabbed a fistful of her hair and dragged her to the floor.

"You fucking bitch, this is all your fault!" he screamed at her. "You stay right there; you move and I'll kick your teeth in."

She knew he meant it. He was in a blind rage; he threw his drink at the fireplace, where the glass shattered. He ran into the yard screaming orders; most of them were incomprehensible, but the tone of his voice had the desired effect. Sleepy-eyed men began straggling out of the bunkhouse, still buckling belts, naked from the waist up. They got the message and were on the move. In less than fifteen minutes the men stood dressed and armed, ready for action.

Dawn watched from the window as Jocko stood in front of the assembly and paced back and forth giving orders. Then, after listening to comments or suggestions and finally making up his mind, he told the men to move out. He was calmer when he reentered the room and looked at Dawn as if to say, "What are you doing on the floor?" He helped her up and then sat her down in a chair, looking concerned. He said he wanted her to clean up and offered her fresh clothes. Dawn knew it was to make her look better when they made the switch, but she felt dirty after the day she'd had; the clothes helped, even if they belonged to that viscous woman.

Now sitting in the butter soft beige leather seat of the Cadillac, she felt as if she had been transported to another reality, a spaceship in a different dimension. Everything surrounding the car was barren and white-grey, like aged bones stuck in the earth with broken and splintered teeth. The black char of burnt and molded vegetation covered the ground like an ominous fog hugging and obliterating the low features of the landscape in the pitch-dark stillness. The smell of decaying fecal matter and black mold seeped into the interior of the richly appointed car, a foreign and intolerable intrusion. She glanced at the dashboard of soft blue lights and dials, reinforcing the image of soaring weightlessly in their spaceship through a strange and repulsive land.

As the soft ride of the Caddy smoothed the ruts and holes in the trail as designed, they floated along the distant and twisty road at a snail's pace. Dawn was nervous, and shivers and chills began exploded in a rash of goose bumps over her body. Her forehead oozed sweat that ran in her eyes and made them sting and burn.

The fear and apprehension she felt was heightened by the faint soft lights lining the road. She longed to see the dawn of a new day. She turned to look at Jocko; his eyes danced with the same intensity she felt, darting to the side of the road. The thing that remained steady was the ominous dark hole of the barrel of the big pistol in his right hand, pointed directly at her belly.

The distance shrunk and now the lights were clearly visible, solar lights spaced at intervals on both sides of the road leading to the dead motel and lake directly behind it. The water as stone black in daylight as it was now at midnight. At fifty feet, Jocko stopped the car and sat with his bright lights shining across the gutted string of burnt ruin. After a few minutes, Nadia stepped out from behind a break in the charred motel and walked a few feet before she was stopped by the chain attached to the studded dog collar around her neck. She looked like crap. Her hair a rat's nest of tangles and snarls. Her makeup smudged and smeared like the broken doll of a demented child. Her clothes torn and filthy. She was wearing a single shoe, like a Halloween freak. Smiling like he had just won the king's crown, Granville Harlow III stood holding the other end of the chain. He moved directly behind Nadia, making a shot impossible.

"Out of the motor arsehole and we'll sort the slappers," Gran directed.

"Fuck you, the bitch can leave but I'm not moving," Jocko said and motioned Dawn to step out.

She was hesitant at first, cautious as she exited the vehicle and made her way past the front grill and started forward.

Now Brick stepped out of the trees on Jocko's right with his Kimber held with both hands, pointing directly at Jocko's head. He didn't say a word, just stood steady, the threat obvious. Jocko pressed the button on the remote in his left hand and waited.

Dawn continued a slow, determined march toward Gran. As she walked toward her, Nadia started forward as Gran played out the chain. When they reached the middle point, Gran let go of the chain and the two women stood shoulder to shoulder for a long moment. Nadia opened her mouth to say something but before she could form words, Dawn threw a vicious right hook to the woman's face, her body's weight behind the fist. Nadia dropped like a chunk of concrete broken loose from a construction site.

Moments later, an explosion erupted behind the Escalade that lit the night sky. It rocked the Caddy on its springs and a huge fireball engulfed the road. The Suburban was consumed in flames and the smell of burnt flesh fouled the night.

Forty-six

Juddiah was cruising again past the familiar Walmart and along the street where the school was located. It was mid-morning and the streets were quiet. The kids sequestered in their respective classrooms, a normal day in most respects. Juddiah was sweating profusely and could hardly sit still in his seat. He had the low rumble in his belly and was as hard as iron. This needed to be the day—he knew this was the last week of the school year. Then he couldn't be sure when he'd find her again. Besides, if he had to wait any longer, he felt he would go mad with lust.

School let out at three and it was only ten now, so he had five hours to kill. He drove back; the shoes were sitting inside the entrance on a tall black box he'd built for just this purpose. He walked through the rooms of the cave, fondling the trophies lovingly.

Souvenirs …

The cave opened to a series of three descending rooms, starting with the largest and dwindling from there. The first were living quarters, furnished with items that were basic, cheap—either found or bought from Goodwill.

The second was the bedroom. Two pallets were arranged together with a foam mattress and covered with rags that may have once been a quilt. Chilling when the horror became reality.

In a niche above the bed a line of human skulls was meticulously arranged. The walls were covered with pornographic images so base and disgusting that they couldn't be conveyed with words. The depictions were of violent sexual and sadistic images that degraded and humiliated the young female victims. There were hundreds of these covering the walls and ceiling.

The worst was the last chamber, smaller than all the others—the trophy room. A series of ledges and niches were carved in the walls; few were empty. Shoes … maybe fifty pair, each arranged neatly on a shelf of its own. And below each pair was some article of a woman's undergarments. Most were stained a brownish red, dried blood. Ripped panties, bras cut with a ragged edge …there was too much to comprehend. At the very top of the cave was a cherry red stiletto shoe standing alone. This was to be Molly's new home.

At two he was so restless that he drove back toward the school and stopped at a burger joint for something to eat just to pass the time. He played with the food, too restless to eat; his hunger revolved around something far more enticing than a burger. Finally, he threw most of what he'd ordered in the trash, grabbed his cup of coffee, and headed back to his truck.

He was smart enough to know that he couldn't keep hanging around the school or he was bound to be noticed, so he went back to the Walmart, but as he drove along the back row he saw a kid in a Walmart uniform walking along writing down plate numbers from the cars without the employee sticker in the window. *What was up with that?* A shiver of fear ran through him and he pulled back on the street.

He went over three blocks and up two to the Home Depot, parked, and went in. Took a cart and sauntered through the aisles picking up a few things he could use. He glanced at his watch constantly, as he was again killing time waiting, and the longer he waited the more his hunger grew. At ten minutes after three he paid for his purchases and drove past the school. She was with the same gaggle of girls so he passed them and drove to the 7-Eleven, parked, and went inside.

He was in the back pretending to look through a copy of *Field and Stream* while watching the front door out of the corner of his eye. He'd seen them stop here on many occasions. Sure enough, four of them came into the store, chattering away and picking up some sodas and snacks. He was listening intently to the gossip when he heard Molly tell her friends that she couldn't hang with them today because her mom wanted her to come straight home and help with the quilt she was finishing.

They all left together but soon two of the girls split off and went in a different direction. She still had one companion for a couple of blocks, and then that girl waved and went up another street off to the left. Now she was alone; she stopped to put in earphones and now became oblivious of her surroundings. They were on a deserted street with woods on the right. Juddiah's pulse increased and he was ready—*this was perfect.* He checked his rearview mirror and saw a lone car approach; he panicked.

The explosion captured their attention, mesmerized by the flames shooting twenty feet in the air. Clint had rigged the C-4 along with two packs of cat-eye marbles, and in typical Clint fashion he didn't spare the explosive. They had delivered the package to the roof of the Suburban via an experimental drone that Gran had brought along, courtesy of her Majesty's service.

While Jocko stared in disbelief at the towering fire, Brick moved up to the passenger window with the big Kimber pointed directly at Jocko's head. By the time he noticed Brick, it was too late. His driver's side door was flung open and a big meaty hand grabbed him by the throat and yanked him from the car, knocking the gun harmlessly aside. When he looked into Charlie's hard eyes, he had his first real taste of fear. The gun he'd been holding lay close to his head and his eyes rested there.

"Do it," Charlie said, "if you think you're man enough."

Jocko shook his head but didn't speak. He knew that with Charlie he could only make it worse; Charlie was cold as ice.

While this drama was taking place, Dawn had crumpled to the ground in a heap. When Brick noticed her lying there, he thought she had been hit by shrapnel. He raced to her side and, upon examining her, realized she had only fainted. He lifted her in his arms and carried her over to where Charlie now had Jocko bent over the hood of the car and was securing his hands behind his back with zip-ties. Gran retrieved the chain and was reeling it in as the woman regained her knees.

Brick said, "I'm taking her with me; it's my fault. Follow the plan and I'll call tomorrow."

He carried her to the passenger side of his truck parked behind the deserted motel, covered her with a blanket, and fastened the seat belt. Taking the back roads, he sped as fast as he dared push through the curves. She appeared to be sleeping and he drove straight to his suite at the lodge. Parking in back, he carried her through the back door using his key card for entrance. Once inside the suite, he laid her in the king-sized bed in the master bedroom.

Forty-seven

After closing the door, Brick went to the living room and switched on the gas fireplace. After he poured three fingers of vodka over ice, he paced the room. *What happened to Dawn was my fault! Thank God she wasn't seriously hurt, physically at least. Emotionally, she'll be scarred for life.* Brick knew he had fucked up again; first it was Jesus, now her. He felt he was better off in the woods alone where his plans and ideas couldn't hurt the people he really loved. Brick felt he deserved whatever he got, but his friends didn't deserve any of this.

He finished the first drink and poured another. A little calmer now, he sat in front of the fire and thought about Harriette and Mason and the rest of the people he cared about. Before, he knew he had abandoned them but only now were the true consequences of that action really sinking in— how they were hurting when he was gone, how they were taken advantage of by the system, how they were changed by the evil he had exposed them to. He knew he couldn't hide and was probably going to fuck up again. *Stop playing God and stop pretending to always be right,* he told himself. Still, he couldn't deny that he did possess the ability to see further ahead than most, and he knew that was needed right now. He sat and let that thought roll around his head for a while. Feeling a little better, he lay down on the couch and soon drifted off to a fitful sleep.

Dawn woke just before daybreak in a panic; she was disoriented and confused. She didn't know where she was and started shaking with fear. The last thing she could recall was a certainty that she would die. She remembered the flames and the bleak, desolate grounds of the motel and those awful people. She rose with trepidation and went to the door, sure it would be locked and surprised to find that it wasn't.

Stepping through the bedroom door, she looked around the opulent suite in awe. She tried all the doors, finding two bedrooms, and then stumbled into the master bath that was heavenly. The large Jacuzzi tub and shower area were most appealing to her, as she wanted nothing more than to be clean after the last few days. Turning from the bathroom, she felt rather than saw the fire flickering in the living room. Taking a tentative step into the darkened room, she saw that the only light came from the fireplace; it took a moment for her eyes to adjust.

On the couch turned away from her was a form covered in a duvet. She looked for a weapon and spotted the ornamental fireplace poker. She grabbed it and the weight gave her confidence. With it raised high above her head, she tiptoed over to the sleeping form and with her free hand pulled the duvet away from his face. A strangled cry erupted from her body when she realized the man on the coach was her beloved Brick. The poker fell with a clatter and she threw herself onto his sleeping body.

Brick woke smothered by her near naked body, as he had stripped her down to her underwear when putting her to bed. She was sobbing and had her head buried in his chest, holding him around the neck in a fierce embrace. She started shaking and he realized that she was frozen with fear. Trying to soothe her, he started rubbing her shoulders, arms, and back but she continued to shake. He tried to pull away but she wouldn't let him so, wrapping her in the warm coverlet, he gently rose with her in his arms and carried her into the bathroom, sat her on the commode, and started the hot water running in the tub.

She stared at him with a blank expression as he went about preparations. The lodge had thought of everything; he found a bottle of bubble bath and added a little to the steaming water. When he thought the temperature hot enough without being scalding, he stood her up and stripped her of bra and panties and led her to the side of the tub. She stepped wordlessly in and sank down to her neck, moaning all the way.

He kissed her on the forehead and assured her he wasn't going far and would be right back. Moment later, he returned with a glass, ice, and the bottle of vodka. He handed her a full glass of the clear liquid and she downed it straightaway. He poured her another and set it on the side of the tub. She settled deeper into the water when he turned on the Jacuzzi jets and the force massaged her into a gentle relaxation. He sat next to the tub and told her where she was and that she was safe and would be from now on. She protested a little when he said he was going to leave the suite for a few minutes, but he assured her once again he wouldn't be gone long.

He slipped out of the room and went down to the bar in the lobby to find some bubbly. It wasn't open at five in the morning, but he located and bribed a manager with a hundred to get him a bottle of Dom Pérignon from the wine cellar, chill it, and put it on his bill. The man was only too happy to palm the cash and oblige.

He was only gone about fifteen minutes, but Dawn was already getting nervous being left alone. She was sitting on the edge of the tub running more hot water when he entered with the bubbly in a chilled wine bucket and a crystal glass. He was rewarded with a big smile when he pulled the bottle up and showed her the label. Seeing her beautiful smile made it worth the effort.

She asked him to join her in the tub and he couldn't refuse her anything after what he'd put her through, and so he stripped off his clothes and sank in the swirling water next to her. She had taken only a sip of her second drink of vodka, so Brick confiscated it for himself and declared the champagne ready to drink. Dawn had never been a big fan of hard spirits, but Brick knew she needed something to soothe her frayed nerves. She loved good champagne and was quick to refill her glass.

It soon became apparent that Dawn now needed some physical attention, and they left the tub and showered together. There were several new toothbrushes still in their packaging in the medicine cabinet and they both brushed and she insisted he shave. Then she took him by the hand and led him back to the living room, where she closed the drapes to block the rising sun and threw the duvet on the floor in front of the fire.

Grabbing a pillow off the couch, she lay on the duvet and pressed him to her. "Make love to me, honey, slow and beautiful love like I know you can," she cooed.

She was a sexy and alluring woman in her prime, and he knew she needed this to feel alive again after the harrowing experience she had been through the past few days. He couldn't deny her anything, not that he wanted to. Starting slow, gently caressing her sore limbs, he kissed her forehead and nose, then nuzzled her neck, nibbling on her earlobes, which drove her crazy. Brick started to move down her body and paused when he reached her magnificent breasts to pay homage to her growing arousal. He intended to tease a little, but her need was great and she put her hands on his shoulders and pushed him where she needed him most. As soon as his tongue separated the swollen folds of her sex, she found her first release. For the next two hours, she was insatiable and used and abused him to exhaustion.

The recent brush with death drew their mortality into sharp focus. The lizard brain reverted to primal survival mode, driving them unconsciously to mate and reproduce. The raw emotion of being alive overwhelming them in scope and desperation.

Finally satiated, they lay together wrapped in a cocoon of sweet embrace, the passion dissipating like a gentle summer breeze. This is what was needed most—the warmth and comfort of the human touch, sharing the fears and anxiety of the unknown. Brick wrapped her tighter in his embrace, never wanting the moment to end. They drifted off like that into the land of unconscious revival.

Dawn awoke once again in panic, her dreams clouded in shadows and struggling to breathe. It was dark in the room and her heart fluttered as she fought her way back to reality. She was still wrapped in her lover's arms. Her emotions were fragile and she started to softly sob. *Don't wake Brick,* was her main thought so she wept silently. She reflected back on the night of the party when she had tried to make him jealous; she had only made a mess of everything. She loved him, always had, but trying to keep him was like holding smoke. It was too much to contemplate, so she melted deeper into his embrace and drifted back to sleep.

It was almost noon when Brick awoke alone in the dark bedroom. The events of the previous day and night were vivid in his thoughts. Sudden fear enveloped him like a tightly wrapped blanket—*where was Dawn?* He made long strides to the door in the semi-darkness, opened it, and was bathed in warm sunlight. All the drapes were drawn open, and Dawn sat at the table by the bay window with the remnants of her meal still on the table.

She was wearing a fluffy robe and when he appeared naked in the doorway, she giggled like a schoolgirl. Then she got up, shucked off the robe, and walked into his embrace. They stood together wrapped in each other's arms and held tight for the longest time without a word.

Brick finally broke the hug and said, "I need to pee."

She laughed. "Okay, you go and then I'm going to clean you up. You smell like a whorehouse."

A short time later, they made slow, sweet love for maybe the last time. Brick was worried this could be the last time he did anything. He didn't kid himself; he knew this could all go south fast. He was brought out of his reverie when Dawn announced that she had nothing to wear. She said the clothes she had worn the day before should be burned—she couldn't even stand to look at them. As for Brick, he was hungry. But, ever gallant, he helped her back into the bathrobe, dressed, and left the suite, headed for the clothing store in the lobby. He bought her new underwear and a pink matching sweat suit combination that cost a small fortune in the trendy lodge store.

She was dressed in her new garb by the time the food arrived and he devoured his breakfast. Dawn said she couldn't leave the lodge looking like a witch. He gave her a room key and some cash, and she headed to the beauty shop to have her hair and makeup done.

He took the opportunity of her absence to call Charlie. Dependable as always, Charlie had done as they planned and now had the two prisoners sequestered in separate rooms at the farmhouse. Gran had held his knife to Jocko's eyes as he made the call back to his ranch and talked to the two remaining guards. They had until tomorrow to act; Brick assured Charlie that he would be back early that evening.

Brick knew this beauty ordeal would last hours so he used the time, first to work the phone and then to clear his mind by going for a run. He was gone about an hour and the suite was still empty when he returned. He took another shower and was dressed and ready to leave when Dawn came back. She had been coiffed and buffed and once again looked the part of a *Playboy* centerfold, stunning really. They left together arm in arm, and as they crossed the lobby heads turned to admire the attractive couple.

He explained to Dawn that she couldn't stay at her place in case there was more danger lurking. He had spoken with Harriette, who told him she would be delighted to have Dawn back as a houseguest for as long as necessary; Brick assured her it would be for a few days at best. He would have one of the guys watch Harry and Mason's house. It would be easier to have them all under one roof.

She agreed to go to Harriette's but insisted that he take her back to her house first for clothes and other essentials. He made her stay in the truck while he searched the house, leading with the .45. He kicked open doors and went through every room and closet, but the place had a barren feel, cold and musty from being closed so long. They opened doors and windows to air the joint out, as it had turned into a fabulous warm, sunny day. Dawn poked around and packed one bag with clothes and another with bathroom supplies. It was almost dark and he was starting to get anxious; they had been at her house for almost two hours. While he waited for her to finish packing, Brick went into her studio and sifted through dozens of her charcoals and paintings. He was more than impressed with her work. This woman was good … really good.

Forty-eight

We were quiet on the drive to Bend, both lost in our own thoughts. I was conflicted at best, confused by my emotions as usual. After everything I had been through, I couldn't shake the guilt. Then the pure joy of her rescue. Conflicted and confused, still struggling with my emotions, I was afraid to admit how I felt about this woman.

All I could think about was holding her and never letting go. The warmth and quiet of her presence. The smell of her hair. The comfort of sharing a bed. She was alluring as always, but now there was more … much more.

I thought back to when we first met. She was beautiful, of course. Sexy and fun, but was that all I saw? I wondered; there was more to her—I was sure of it—but I didn't see it at the time. She acted like a wild child, party girl, but underneath there was this vulnerability. It seemed men exploited her sexuality and I was no different. Let's face it, I was just a cheap thug justifying my every move as some higher calling. My life a lie.

Dawn was so young when we met, just twenty years old at the time, but so gorgeous it made my teeth ache with longing. We made love often, maybe the best I've ever had and I've had a lot. First girls, then women—they've always liked me, been drawn to me. I never knew why but I took advantage of it. If they wanted me in the sack, who was I to question it? And then I would leave and not often look back. She's thirty now, ten years younger than me; this would never work, would it?

What was I thinking? Laura's fifteen years younger than me; I must be crazy. If you think I feel guilty about the time I spent with her, you're wrong. We needed each other. I never promised to be faithful; I only said I'd be back and I will when this is over … If I'm still on the green side of the grass. I owe her that, to fix the trouble I caused. Laura could never be a long-term companion, and I'm pretty sure she wouldn't want to be—I was a summer romance. Dawn is a different story. I've never felt anything close to what I feel with Dawn. Maybe a little of this feeling with Cassie, but Dawn has become more. Why can't I say the words?

Dawn took care of Harriette and Mason for years—who does that? Her art is fantastic. I never looked at it before; there were many things I overlooked in the old days. But my eyes are wide open now. She was lost in her own thoughts; her brow wrinkled as she stared out the window and watched the landscape speed past. I thought about what she'd just been through. I saw the determination and resilience, how she cared for the people she loved, the kindness and warmth of her heart. God but she's beautiful, a woman in full.

For the first time since Cassie, I think I'm in love …

Forty-nine

The visit with Harriette and Mason was short and he had to struggle to break free. They had received the wire transfer that morning and were in shock—rocketing them from poverty to sudden riches—and they showered Brick in adulation and praise. Harriette fussed over Dawn, amazed at how good she looked, and kept insisting Brick stay for dinner. He reminded them of the recent problems and practically ran from the house.

Dusk was descending by the time Brick pulled into the farmhouse driveway. Keith and Stoney were patrolling the grounds, and Clint was working with Gran in the basement. Charlie walked outside when Brick arrived, and the two men had a beer together on the deck. There had been an overnight sprinkle and with the temperature rising and the rain in remission, the grass was a vivid lush emerald and the deciduous trees were leafing. In the short time they had been in the mountains, the seasons had transformed and spring reigned once again. Unfortunately, they weren't able to fully appreciate the weather, as there was much to be done.

Charlie reported that Jocko had been subdued and seemed to accept his fate, but the woman was another story. She kicked and bit and screamed, throwing herself around the room knocking over furniture. A real piece of work. It ended when Gran went in with his knife.

Brick and Charlie were reluctant to leave him alone with her, but he insisted. "I know the bitch; she's fearless, been used rough, and detests weakness. I'll treat her to a bit of the wicked. She fancies you boys pussies. She's a pretty little brass nail. She'll respect the blade, can't lose the pretty; she'll come around quite proper."

Gran told her he would hog-tie and gag her if she didn't shut the fuck up and to convince her, he drew a thin line down her cheek with the tip of his blade and then laughed as blood spilled down her neck. She shut it proper enough.

Charlie waited for Brick's return to question Jocko. Now Clint led their captive to the kitchen and sat him at the table. His eyes were taped shut again, as they were on the drive. Gran sat on his left and Charlie the right. Brick was at the head of the table and he reached across and ripped the duct tape from his eyes, tearing some skin and eyebrow in the process.

Brick slapped him hard forward and back across the face and said, "You tried to kill me, motherfucker. After all I've done for you and that's how you repay me?"

"No," he sputtered. "I had nothing to do with that; you have to believe me!"

Brick was polar cold when he said, "Maybe not directly, but you knew and approved. We've been listening for days—you want me to play the recording back?"

Jocko couldn't form a reply; he stared at his hands.

"You and Raoul have been working together, and he sent a hit squad to take me out. Why does he feel it necessary to kill me after all this time?" Brick asked.

Jocko sprang to his feet with both hands flat on the table and said, "No, you've got it wrong! There's a contract out on you, that's why."

Quicker than a snake, Gran drove his knife into the back of Jocko's left hand, pinning it to the table. "Who?" he spat in his ear. "Who the fuck would purchase a contract? Sit down. I didn't tell you to stand, you cunt. I'll cut your fucking hand off!"

Jocko was sobbing. The knife had cut through nerves and tendons; it would take a specialist to repair it … maybe. He managed to scream out in anguish, "I don't know; he won't tell me."

Gran pulled the knife; the cut spurted blood. He walked to the sink and wiped the blade on a dish towel, then threw the towel to Jocko who wrapped it tight around his hand and laid it in his lap. Gran was brutal but very effective with interrogation. You can question his methods but not the results. Jocko was rocking in the chair and moaning.

Now Brick leaned in close, grabbed a handful of Jocko's hair, and turned his head so he had to stare into Brick's cold eyes. Stone blue when angry. "Listen to me, you asshole. These guys all voted to kill you and that bitch of yours, but I'm going to give you a chance to live."

Jocko sobbed out a grateful, "Thank you."

Brick said, "You're going to do exactly as we say. We know you have a big shipment coming in from the cartel any day now. Cisco is dead, so we need a cover story with these assholes. You're going to help us suck them in. If you do it right, I'll let you live; don't ask for more."

Jocko said, "Alright, I'll do what you say."

Brick looked at Gran as he said, "Bring the woman here; at least she's afraid of you."

Fifty

Hank pulled over and stopped. That's when the grillwork on the bronze Charger lit up like Christmas morning. Red and blue filled the rearview mirror in the truck and for a moment he panicked. Nothing happened and Hank figured the cop was probably calling in the plate number. Still his palms were wet and slick as he fumbled in his wallet for his license and insurance card.

When the cop emerged from the unmarked, Hank noticed he wasn't in uniform. He wore a cheap rumpled green suit and his tie was askew; in dark aviator glasses, this was a detective and a prick. It was then that Hank realized this was no routine traffic stop. The cop walked close to the truck, his right hand near his hip. The window was open and before he could ask, Hank had his hand out the window with the documents. The cop ignored this gesture and said in a loud, clear voice, "Please step out of the vehicle, sir."

Definitely unusual, but Hank complied without comment. *I know that look,* he thought; *he's got a hard-on for me.* The cop made him assume the position and did a quick search, but it was obvious that his only concern was a weapon.

"I'm Detective Riley, and I would like you to come back to the patrol car, please."

At this point Riley took his cards and placed them in the clipboard in his left hand. He opened the rear passenger side door and gestured for Hank to get in back. The backseat was like a coffin and his knees almost touched his chin.

"May I ask what this is about?" Hank said.

The cop ignored the question and instead asked one of his own: "What are you doing on this street, sir?"

"I'm trying to find one of my employees. His address on record doesn't seem to exist, and I thought he might have made a mistake, so I was combing the entire length of the street trying to spot his truck." It was a good lie and Hank could back it up if necessary; Dean Gordon lived around here somewhere and Hank could always say their secretary must have given him the wrong information.

Detective Riley turned around in his seat to stare at Hank, his eyes hidden behind the dark shades. "I've got my eye on you; you've been reported seen in this neighborhood before, twice. I'll be watching you. Now get out."

Hank reached for the door handle but it was missing, the cop purposely fucking with him. They sat for a minute before Detective Riley opened the door. He stayed very close, invading the big man's private space, making a statement.

Hank drove away as fast as he could without breaking the law. He tried to act cool but this confrontation shook him to the core. *Fuck, fuck, fuck,* he'd been reported, twice before. He drove home thinking and sweating.

It was only a few days later when he decided to take a drive and watch for a tail. As he topped a ridgeline, he heard a strange buzzing sound that became more insistent as he climbed. He was frantically looking in all directions and finally looked up. Drone was a foreign word for the time, but he had seen radio-controlled planes and helicopters before, and this looked like a larger version of the helicopter. He took a small pair of binoculars from his coat pocket and focused in on the small aircraft; it looked as if there was a camera mounted underneath it.

The paranoia was overwhelming, like when he first arrived ten years ago—a man without identification. He'd felt safe for so long, he was forgetting to take precautions. Now he headed for home, where he locked all the doors and had two stiff bourbons to calm his nerves. His first instinct was to pack a bag and flee, but the bourbon calmed him and he continued to drink and think. He roamed the house staring out windows in the dark until almost midnight when he finally went to bed. Juddiah's last thought was relief that he had the presence of mind to hand over Hank's ID instead of his own. Quick thinking gave him the alibi that would stand up later.

Fifty-one

The lights were ablaze and the fragrant aromas of rib roast permeated the air. Mason had been hard at work for the last couple hours whipping up a celebration feast. There was a tear in his eye, and he wanted to hug everyone he saw and bring 'em on home tonight. Brick had made their financial foes disappear. Harriette went to the doctor that morning and had been declared in remission. Dawn was back looking perky and they were as toasty as butter biscuits hot from a wood oven.

After the delicious meal, the three of them went out on the front porch and sipped wine while they contemplated dessert. The conversation soon reverted to Brick and the other men. Dawn chronicled her harrowing experience with the proper embellishments. Earlier, she had shared her seduction of Brick with Harriette; she avoided details but spoke of her needs and the masterful way Brick had fulfilled them. Harriette was secretly jealous because she had just got Brick back—the man she considered a brother—and really didn't want to share him with another woman. Still, she understood and was happy he had been so good to her friend. Dawn didn't share her true feelings for the man and of her expectations for the future, afraid he would disappear in vapor once again.

They speculated what the men would do next and how long the crew would last. Brick never shared more than they needed to know, so their next move was a mystery. Mason had only been told that he would never have to go back and work with Jocko, and Harriette was grateful for this above all. She desperately hoped for a safe and speedy conclusion. She prayed they could continue their reunion. She kept repeating what a wonderful party it had been. No one mentioned the end result. *Let little Harry have this memory,* they thought.

Dawn was yawning and her eyes were shutting, so Harriette shooed her off to bed. She had had a rough few days with very little sleep and the ordeal was catching up with her. She would wind up sleeping twelve hours straight.

Once Dawn was tucked in, Harriette rejoined Mason on the porch. He had foregone dessert for a glass of port, and when she appeared, he poured her one and beckoned her to sit on his lap. She nuzzled into his neck and he squeezed her tight and kissed her cheek and the side of her mouth. She turned her head and they kissed with hearts full of hope and joy. They cuddled like that until it started to get chilly. Both were aware of how lucky they were and counted each blessing before turning in for the night.

Fifty-two

Brick opted for a walk in the cool night air. It had been the first sunny warm day of the year and he recalled the gorgeous summer days he had once spent in these mountains hiking and laughing. It seemed like a lifetime ago … After a while, his thoughts turned to Gran. Gran was an enigma. When they were alone, Gran was a loyal friend, even kind. The bullshit slang and British wit disappeared, and he spoke perfect English with an Oxford arrogance. But Brick found Gran's quick temper and flares of sudden violence disturbing. Granted, Jocko deserved rough treatment, but sometimes Gran's actions depressed him.

He left his cell at the lodge, preferring to use the encrypted one Charlie had provided. When Dawn went to the beauty shop, he had retrieved it and checked the log—three voice messages from Laura. The first was a general "I miss you," but in the second she said that she felt someone was watching her. The third was disturbing; she explained how she had been cornered after work by a big man reporting to be the father of the boy Brick had the altercation with and he threatened her. He said if she didn't cough up Brick's location, he would make things very rough for her. She was afraid.

He called her and she answered on the second ring. Although he didn't think they would ever resume their relationship, he did feel a duty to protect her. After all, he was responsible for these crazies in her town bothering her. Laura told him about the father's cut and swollen nose, that he blamed some English guy looking for Brick. Brick made her look up the father's name, address, and number and assured her the harassment would stop; he said he would make damn sure.

Best to deal with it now, he thought; he went back into the house and found Gran sitting in the kitchen sipping scotch and sharpening his knife. At first he feigned ignorance when asked, but then suddenly remembering, he admitted to the act, making light of it as if it were the guy's fault for not being polite in the first place. All he wanted was to ask a few questions, he said.

Brick could just imagine the conversation Gran would have— threaten to kill his family and burn his home to the ground. Better for Gran to deal with it; comparatively, he was milk toast. The dumb slob better get the message; Gran was a pisser to underestimate.

Bright and early the next morning, the men formed a caravan of cars and trucks as they drove to the ranch Charlie was driving the lead car; Jocko rode shotgun with his arm in a sling and Brick in back. Stoney had done a competent job sewing the gash on Jocko's hand and disinfecting it. Gran insisted no pain pills; he wanted him on edge and didn't get an argument. They were cruising in Jocko's Cadillac.

Gran and Stoney were in the next truck, a four-door Silverado, Nadia in the rear with Gran. Clint and Keith brought up the rear. They drove a Suburban, large enough for their shit without the ostentatiousness of the Caddy. The crew was armed with AK-47s and Uzis. They went over the plan in detail that morning before they left the farm. They were fairly confident that Jocko would hold up, but the woman was the joker; she could queer the deal and it would lead to bloodshed fast.

There were only six remaining guys left in Jocko's original crew— the two guards and four ranch hands—and they were shaky.

When they arrived at the ranch, Charlie got right in the faces of the guards, glaring as the rest of the crew surrounded him. To Jocko's credit he played his part perfectly, yelling orders to break up and spread out to the perimeter and patrol the grounds. He didn't try to explain the changes, as he never did, but he did stop them and point to Charlie. He said, "This is

Charlie. I fought with him in the army. He's in charge of security starting now. You take orders from him. The rest of these men will be bunking with you sorry pricks."

Charlie led the way into the main house with Jocko behind and then Nadia with Gran on her ass and Brick bringing up the rear, head swiveling and eyes darting. Brick did a quick scan of the rooms while Charlie held the couple in the living room. Gran was unloading the contents of his bag, preparing for an electronic search for hidden bugs. Brick wasn't surprised that nothing had changed since his last visit and concentrated on the interior bedroom without windows that would serve as Nadia's cell.

Once the men were convinced they were alone, Gran led Nadia to the designated room and made her sit. He held the blade to her neck and, snatching a fistful of hair, pressed his lips to her ear and said, "One snivel, a whimper, and I'll slice your bloody whore throat open quicker than you can say, God save the queen." He slapped her hard across the face and asked, "Are we clear?"

She gave a strangled cry and said, "Yes." As he closed the door, she spit at his back and kicked at the wall.

The door opened a crack; in an icy tone Gran said, "If you don't shut the fuck up, I will drive a boot up your arse." The lock snapped shut.

Jocko was respectful and afraid of Charlie, and now he seemed to cover him like plastic wrap. He was docile, the fight gone and mere survival the goal. Charlie wasn't cruel, just efficient. If Brick wanted Jocko alive and kicking, he must have some need for him. He let him roam in the kitchen under a watchful eye. There were knives there but Charlie wasn't worried. Water was all the man wanted and then he sat and said, "Now what?"

Brick walked in with Gran and they heard the tail end of the conversation, so Brick replied, "Now you tell us all about this big shipment and when and how this is going down." Gran sat close to make the point. So Jocko spilled the beans hoping to spare his life, then blurted, "It wasn't my fault Jesus turned on you, man."

"What the fuck did you just say?"

"You didn't know he sold you out?"

"Fuck all you say," Gran said.

The shock of Jocko's statement was an avalanche of emotion for Brick. All of it spinning past his eyes in disbelief ... Eventually, a quiet peace settled on his features as he assimilated the new revelation.

The next morning was another kind day in the mountains; a light balmy breeze was blowing out of the south in a cloudless sky when Brick and Charlie crested the ridgeline. Brick wanted to get Charlie alone, and Charlie wanted Brick to take another look at the mysterious cave on the other side. It would be an all-day trip, but nothing would happen before nightfall.

Gran was in charge, and both Clint and Keith were watching the crew and patrolling the grounds. Brick had Jocko make the call and the message came back that they would talk on the secure satellite phones at 9:00 Pacific Time; Raoul was a night owl. There had never been any love lost between them. Raoul was Juanita's son, born in Puerto Rico and kidnapped by his birth father when he was a child. When he was a teenager, his dad died in a gun battle in Colombia and Raoul ended up living on the streets of Old San Juan until his twenties. When he finally decided to look for his mother, he found her living the good life with her new husband in Panama.

His stepfather, Jesus, welcomed him into their home as his own, but Raoul immediately resented him. He was a military man and had these American friends that the boy didn't like or trust. Raoul's only skill was as a pickpocket in the streets of old San Juan, preying on rich American tourists. His mother forbade him of plying this trade in her village, as she was a respectable woman of her community. So he lived in the shadow of the successful and proud man of the house and resented every minute of his miserable fate. It soon took its toll on the family, as Juanita and Jesus also had two beautiful daughters in their early teens and an older son of Jesus's who was a prominent businessman in the city.

Raoul took an immediate dislike to Brick the first time they met. This Anglo pretty boy had the respect of the village, plus he was military; Raoul hated the Anglos and how they forced his people to embrace the American lifestyle. This belief wasn't anchored in reality; the ideas and ideals propaganda came from the slums. Raoul's grasp on truth was distorted, his young mind formed by a psychopathic father who stole, raped, and maimed with impunity. He was raised in a den of vipers, the worst scum old San Juan festered in its ghetto gut.

It was always tense in the house when Jesus and Raoul were together, so they both made an effort to stay apart. Juanita loved her son and was infected with guilt over his childhood. To stay with his father was suicide, as Marco beat her when drunk and he was always drunk, so she ran with her infant son. Marco found her after a few years and stole the kid back. It was pure meanness because he didn't really want the kid; he only wanted to deprive her. Now that she finally had Raoul back, Juanita couldn't bring herself to say no to him when he asked to borrow her car to look for work. His stepfather was a pilot and flew planes and choppers. Raoul knew he worked for the Americans and made a shitload of money, as the family lived well.

As Raoul set about pickpocketing in the worst part of town, it didn't take long to be noticed. The man whose territory he was invading, La Serpiente, and two of his thugs caught the boy one night and beat him senseless. Instead of whining and begging, Raoul pulled himself off the pavement and said, "I want to join you; I'll do anything you ask." La Serpiente liked the balls the kid showed and they took him to a house where The Snake interviewed him.

Raoul worked as a gofer for three months until on a grey, wet afternoon he made a drop—a quantity of heroin. He got jumped by a fat, ugly bastard with a broad scar down the left side of his face from forehead to lips. Raoul was small comparatively but fast, wiry, and he managed to squirm away. His attacker caught him by the throat, but the knife went in his assailant's belly fast. When he stepped back, Raoul ripped with a viscous twist of the wrist and the fat bastard's intestines spilled out in a hot, steaming stink painting the sidewalk a putrid yellow pile of guts, bile, and blood.

He made his bones that day, and in the blink of an eye Raoul rose to the top of the organization. Known as the enforcer, he earned the nickname Pequeno Gato, or Little Cat. He worked with Jessepe in the beginning, a big bruiser with ham-sized fists. Once he gained the rep, he worked alone—small, mean, and deadly. The bad blood with Jesus and the Americans would come later.

Fifty-three

The pink and purple tentacles of dawn turned to wispy fingers and faded as the sun burst over the mountain. Charlie and Brick had reached the hill above Jocko's ranch and the bright glare caught them with a steely stare, raising sweat under the collar. They found stumps the size and height for perfect stools. Charlie shouldered off his pack and sat, signaling Brick to take the opposite stump.

After taking a drink from his canteen, Charlie tossed it to his friend and asked, "How's the girl?"

Brick stared off into the distance for a few seconds before he replied. "She's tough, a lot tougher than she looks, but I don't know … she was petrified."

"Listen to me, Bro, you couldn't have seen this coming; don't go into your shell again over this."

Brick said, "What do you mean?"

"I mean, don't let this be another Jesus and disappear on me. Nobody but you thinks that Jesus's death was your fault. You couldn't have seen that coming any more than this." Charlie hesitated before continuing. "You heard Jocko … and I checked it out. It's true and it hurts me as much if not more, but face facts. He set up a shady deal on the side and got burned. You can't shoulder the blame for every fucking thing that turns to shit. Stay cool, old buddy. We're going to clean this up once and for all."

"From your lips to God's ear," Brick mumbled under his breath. "Did you know he worried about going alone and asked me for an escort? I guess he didn't want a witness. He let me think I sent him to his fucking death—did you know that? And now I almost got Dawn killed."

"Yes I knew; he asked about going alone, but can't you see it was a ruse to make you back off? It was a trap and it blew up in his face. Stop this shit! You are the smartest man I've ever known, maybe smarter than all of us together, but you're not God. Stop beating yourself up, goddamn it—I need you." Charlie said this quietly, almost with reverence and Brick heard him.

Charlie walked on and was quiet for a minute and then asked, "Where is Dawn now?"

"I dropped her with Mason and Harriette."

"Alone."

"No, of course not. I left Stoney there until we need him."

Charlie stopped and gave his friend a smile—he needed it—and said, "Good choice. Stoney would tear the arms off anybody crazy enough to try and harm our friends. He could take two in the gut and still destroy a squad."

Brick grinned and said, "I can't abandon those I love, and it hits me in the heart knowing you guys are with me. I'm finished hiding and off the pity pot."

At that, the two friends threw their arms over each other's shoulder, laughed, and continued their journey. As they came to the spot where Charlie had the run-in with the grizzled mountain of a man, they went silent. Charlie made a beeline for the cave and Brick took the high ground, coming in from the top. The hillside was deserted and Brick examined the boulder for all the tricks but couldn't break the code.

Brick said, "Are you sure there was an opening here, or was it just a trick of the light?"

"No, it was clear. I could see into the front, maybe ten feet or so."

They walked the rest of the way down and circled the house, but nothing stirred and it felt empty. They gave up for now and called Gran to ask for a ride back. They expected him to send Clint or Keith but when the Mercedes pulled up twenty minutes later, they were happy to ride in comfort. The three of them wanted to check on Harry, Mason, and Dawn. Soon they would have to pull Stoney off guard duty. Brick was intent on convincing them to move to the resort.

At the house, the two women kept Brick busy, while Charlie and Gran had a short conference with Stoney and Mason. They discussed the situation and made provisional plans for any contingency. They didn't expect trouble here, but after the kidnapping they couldn't be too careful.

Juddiah had left his apartment three days earlier and drove to a campground north of Redmond. While Charlie and Brick were watching the hillside, he went in search of a new truck. As far as he knew, the authorities didn't suspect him of any crimes but he'd needed a new truck for years. He figured it couldn't hurt his chances to change trucks. He called Marsh, his boss, and said he could use a couple of weeks off; since there wasn't any job looming, Marsh agreed. The weather was improving by the day and a little camping would be a nice change of pace. He felt safe at the campground.

He was haggling over the price of a three-year-old Silverado with a camper, but the manager was starting to piss him off and he said so. He stood up to use his size as intimidation and leaned into the man's face. "Don't you dare treat me like some rube off the streets," he said. "I'm no kid and I know what this fucker is worth, so stop dicking me around or I walk."

The man backed off and tried a more reasonable approach. This scary looking dude had made a good offer, so he gave it up and the deal was done. An hour later Juddiah drove off the lot in his new black truck, smiling at having intimidated the intimidator. He was feeling good and it was getting late, so he stopped at a strip club and promptly got fifty dollars in one-dollar bills. He would have a few drinks and enjoy a bit of fun.

The more he drank, the more reckless he felt and hostility wafted off him like a black cloud. He got louder and more aggressive with the girls. He elbowed the men on either side of him and before long two of the larger bouncers approached with short heavy clubs and told him that he was done. He wanted a fight—oh how he wanted to crush their faces and break their bones—but he knew the consequences and he had too much to lose. He stood abruptly, knocking over his chair as he put his shoulders back and walked slowly and deliberately to the exit.

Mitsy was fourteen … this was the third time she had run away from home and she planned it to be the last. It wasn't that her parents were bad people or treated her like crap. It was more about who she was. She was a slow learner and despised school. She was awkward, gangly, and the other kids made her life hell. She had to get away—*anything would be better than this shit.* She wore her older sister's hand-me-downs and it pissed her off. *Why can't I ever have anything nice of my own, something new for a change, not the used crap of my siblings?*

She would join a circus and travel all over the world and the ringmaster would fall in love with her and they would get married. She wouldn't have children; she would be selfish and her life would be wonderful, she just knew it. These were her thoughts as she walked along the dirt road past the campground.

Fifty-four

Harriette talked the men into staying for dinner. Brick sat in the middle between the women, with Harriette asking questions and Dawn trying to get frisky under the table. Brick wasn't having any of it. He ate fast and then stood to relieve Stoney, sending him in for supper. It was quiet and uneventful; the men finished and left to make preparations for the call to Raoul.

After they were gone and Mason went out to smoke a cigar, the two women were cleaning up when Dawn said, "You are always so nice to Stoney, and you go out of your way to treat him special. Is there a reason for that? I mean you're nice to everyone, just a little kinder toward him."

Harriette gave a low chuckle and said, "Did I ever tell you the story about when I cussed him out for no reason?"

"No, I don't think so."

"It was back when we were building the house and all the men from the Ranger squad were here helping. Mason worked as general contractor. He and I drew the plans—our first house, my dream. I was horrible and kept changing my mind and adding shit hourly. I know I made everyone nuts, but we had money for the first time in my life and we were building the first house I ever owned, so I guess I got a little power crazy.

"The house was almost finished and I started cleaning, and you know how I am about my kitchen, so I spent the morning scrubbing and waxing the floor. I wiped down all the cabinets and woodwork, and cleaned the cupboards, inside the refrigerator, freezer, and stove. I was tired after all that, so I took a nap in our bedroom at the back of the house. When I woke up, Stoney was outside the bedroom door yelling my name. I didn't know him very well then and I admit I was a little afraid of him. I mean, he is really big and imposing.

"Anyhow, I flew off the handle. Here I woke up to yelling, and then when I opened the door, I found he had tracked mud through the house and my wet freshly waxed kitchen floor. I just lost it and called him names I regret. I didn't want to hear any excuse; I loudly insisted he clean it up and wouldn't listen to a word. The man stared back at me and he is one scary dude. Suddenly, I panicked and looked for a way to escape. He shook his head, took the muddy boots off, and started scrubbing. I followed him like an old shrew until he finished. It must have taken him two hours the way I carried on. When it met my satisfaction, I finally asked him what the fuck was so important.

"He kind of shuffled around and finally said, 'Mr. Mason fell off his horse and broke his arm and mebe some ribs. Mr. Brick sent me to fetch you and drive you to the hospital.' I felt so damn bad when I heard that. I guess I'm still trying to make up for it, so I treat him like a king."

Fifty-five

Nadia was like a caged monkey flying from corner to corner in frustration. She had underestimated the Americans. She knew men and she counted on them being predictable, simple basic beasts, coarse and needy. She knew she was a whore. As she saw it, men were all about their cocks. They had it mixed up with power and money, but at the end of the day they wanted sex, sex, and more sex. This worked for her—she had the assets, but there was a shelf life and she knew it. She was already twenty-seven, so maybe eight years left at best and then the men would look for younger; it was the way it was.

She understood the Russians; they were ruthless but predictable. Jocko was a pussy—that's why she picked him. Locked in the room, she made herself sit and think, but before long her nerves had her up and pacing again. She had to escape, so she reviewed her possibilities. The Englishman was like the Russians but with no desire to screw her; no room there. Brick and Charlie were too smart. After an hour she made her choice; now she needed an opportunity.

It presented itself sooner than she thought. There weren't any windows but sound traveled well, and early the next morning she heard them outside preparing to leave. Only one car and it sounded like an SUV. An hour later her door opened and the English looked in; he didn't speak, just looked around and left. She decided to ignore him and he laughed at her.

The day dragged by with nothing to do but think. Lunch was served by Keith, another cold prick; no opening there. She was allowed to eat and use the bathroom but nothing else. Her body was going through withdrawal from everything—booze, cigarettes, and coke. She was a jittery mess. For Nadia, this was an existence worse than hell. If she could get

Clint interested in a blow job, she might get his weapon; it was a thought. When she heard the car pull out late in the afternoon, she was sure it was the smooth sound of the Mercedes and her spirits rose. She waited an hour before pounding on her door and it was Clint who answered the call. Perfect.

He led her to the bathroom and here she turned and, in the sweetest voice she could muster, asked if she could please get her makeup case from the bedroom. She used her eyes and tried her best to look innocent when she pleaded with him, saying how ugly she felt without any makeup.

Clint was shy around women; he stammered when he said, "You look real pretty without any." But then he caved.

He followed her and watched as she retrieved the case. Just before she closed the bedroom door, she leaned forward and rubbed his crotch, smiling and beckoned him in. With a sigh and a groan, he plucked the bag from her grasp and she held her breath as his thick fingers rummaged around and dumped the contents on the bed. She almost cried in relief when he handed the empty case back.

"I could make you feel real nice ... I bet it's been a long time since you've had a woman, all shut up in this stinking farm." She tried.

His eyes did the roving dance along her curves blatantly for the first time and surprised them both by saying, "I know you're a whore and all, but I just can't take a chance." Then he shut the door in her face.

She only had one chance. She worked her fingers along the top of the lining, found the invisible pocket inside the makeup case, and slipped the lock picks free. One of her scams back in the day was to sneak back after her john had drifted off, pick the lock to his room, and take the rest of his money and valuables. She hadn't lost her touch—she had the door open in thirty seconds.

Creeping along the hallway, she caught snatches of light from the high windows topping the hall. It was almost dusk, perfect for her escape, but later than she thought. Someone would be bringing dinner soon. She was carrying her shoes and staying to the edges of the floor, so the boards wouldn't squeak as she crept through the empty space. She crouched below the windows in the kitchen, bobbing up now and then to check her progress. She caught sight of Keith talking to a couple of dark-skinned men who were Jocko's ranch hands. The men soon moved off; Keith headed back to a car and the men back to work.

She made it out the door and to the edge of the deck when the sound of a car moving up the drive made her leap down to the ground and start running. She abandoned the shoes, hiked up her skirt, and took off for the trees. The throaty roar of a powerful engine split the silence as the woman changed course to get off the road. She headed for the dirt path behind the first Quonset hut, but the car altered its course as well and drove up the other side of the building to cut off her escape.

Quick as a mouse, she ran blindly into the thick stand of trees and brush. The branches ripped her clothes as she pressed forward. She was frantic, not knowing which direction she was heading but desperate to escape. Her ankle twisted as she missed a depression in the soft earth; she fell, the brambles tearing her blouse and drawing blood from a long scratch on her now exposed left breast. She scrambled away on all fours.

Gasping for breath, she pulled herself up the steep, slope breaking fingernails in the process, then crouched behind a large oak. She took one step and fell again; the ankle had to be sprained at least. Determined not to stop, she crawled along the ground until she spotted a clearing where she could reorient. A suitable branch lying nearby provided a makeshift crutch. It made her wince in pain, but she could walk with a pronounced limp and tried to put most of her weight on the good leg and branch. She detected footsteps behind her on her ascent up the mountain, but soon they receded and finally disappeared. She made a frightful figure as she broke into the clearing and paused to evaluate.

If she could make it across the open space, she'd reach a path that led to the road where she could flag a car. What she really needed was a phone, but she thought it might still work out. The light was fading fast as twilight turned a rosy bronze hue that cast a hallo around her head. To an observer she would appear as a crippled black Madonna limping toward the Promised Land.

She had almost crested the hill at the far end of the clearing when Granville caught sight of her. She was too far for a throw and by the time he fumbled for his pistol, she had disappeared into the trees. Jocko used to like to walk and talk to her as he wandered the hills. As much as she had hated it, she was now grateful for the knowledge she had gleaned from those excursions. She recognized the way; the brush thickened and straight ahead was a series of bramble bushes too dense to traverse. To her right was a series of old game trails, now impassable. To the left, a short distance away, was a clear path to an old logging road that fed into the paved county road. If she followed that she would be able to entice a car to stop for her and she'd be in the city within hours. Gran tried to pick out her route to no avail.

It was full dark when Brick and Charlie returned to the rental house. Keith was the first to greet them and delivered the news of the missing prisoner. Gran stood in defiance behind Keith, waiting. Gran might have been a psychopath, but he wasn't a snitch and would never give up Clint. Charlie looked to Brick as if to say, "Now what?" but remained silent.

Shaking his head, Brick said, "Nobody tells Jocko; we need to make that call." As he figured it, they couldn't change things now, so what would be the sense of recriminations? This was a dangerous game, but these are the cards they were dealt. He looked at the men and nodded; they'd live with the consequences. Brick thought, *there's a bigger test down the line and loser dies. Stay sharp.*

It was black as Christian sin when Mitsy came abreast of the campground. The flickering lights of the campfires and gas lanterns were a welcoming sight. She was cold and hungry and if she allowed herself to admit it, maybe she hadn't thought this through completely. She reacted like a typical teenager and just went with her first desire—escape. The big man sitting by the roaring campfire seemed oblivious to her presence, but he snuck glances under hooded eyes as the girl drew nearer.

Fifty-six

There were three law enforcement agencies in the county: the two separate police departments in Bend and Redmond and the sheriff's department—responsible for a hell of a lot of open space. Detective sergeant Gill Riley sat at his cluttered desk in a cubicle just large enough for the big man to turn around. He was forty-seven years old, twice divorced, and he'd been around, the years and experience evident in the creases and lines that defined his broad face. His black hair was thinning at the back and freckled with grey, but his soulful brown eyes were alert and watchful.

This wasn't his first rodeo, not by a long shot. He spent twenty years working sex crimes in the Bronx and had been interrogating child molesters for so long they came to him in dreams. This guy was definitely hinky; he could see it in his eyes—something not right with the wiring in his head.

Gill was a no-nonsense cop who left the big city for a quieter, peaceful existence in this small community. He imagined it would be traffic stops and vandalism, but in the first month he learned that the fucking crazies were everywhere. When he thought about it, he had to admit that this was still nicer than city life. He went home most nights, had every other weekend off, and slept better. Still … this Hank Johnson bothered him. He checked him out and ran his picture and description through every cop database available, including the FBI's. Before he picked up his trail in Oregon, he didn't seem to exist. Definitely hinky …

He was assigned to investigate the rampant meth cooks springing up all over the county like bottle flies on a corpse, which seemed to flow in an endless river of pain and misery. It was the new cheaper drug of choice that was quick to addict and destroyed faster than most of the crap they'd seen. It was made exclusively from toxic chemicals, so no sane person could believe it was harmless. Gill saw it as a scourge on the beautiful countryside of his adopted home.

This was what he was working on full time when the news of the latest victim reached his desk. It hit him like a blow to the belly, almost took his breath away. For the two years that he'd been on the force, this was what kept him awake at night. These poor girls were taken so young, before their lives even started. They were adolescents and died in horrible fashion. The absolute terror they faced made the bile rise in his throat and chills blanket his back.

He tore the notice off the teletype and headed to his Charger, lights and sirens all the way north to the site of the latest tragedy. There were three cars, an ambulance, and too many people tramping through his crime scene. He had to caution himself to be cool before he pissed off everyone assigned; charging in like a wild bull was a bad habit that didn't endear him to his peers back in the Bronx and it wouldn't fly here either.

He remem7bered being told of the red shoe case, still unsolved, from years before his arrival. Most of the cases since then were reports of missing girls never to be found. He assumed they had met a similar fate and been buried. This had been the pattern, but now it seemed that his crazy has escalated and he raped, killed, and left them as debris to be hosed off like roadkill.

They were a hundred yards off the dirt road that branched off from County Road 26. The area had been cordoned off with yellow crime scene tape, and when Gill arrived there were two uniformed cops guarding the road and scene. Gill badged his way as close as he could and when he stepped to the edge of the road, he saw the coroner and crime scene techs down a slight embankment maybe twenty yards in.

They surrounded the tiny frame of a female figure sprawled face down in the tall grass, her skimpy T-shirt torn and her jeans tangled around her ankles. There was a hollow feeling in the pit of Gill's stomach and he needed to brace himself against retching.

Juddiah looked down on the scene through field glasses. He left the campground hours ago and drove here. It was too fast; he knew that. It took the edge off 'cause he was wound super tight but wouldn't quell the hunger for long. After a last longing look, he started his new truck and headed out. He'd been lucky with that cop when he turned just in time and the pig grabbed another truck. He was feeling a recklessness he didn't deserve.

Back in his office Gill grimaced when the distraught couple headed toward his desk, the woman carrying a couple of glossy pictures. He took them into the sheriff's vacant office. He tried to stall, offering coffee or soft drinks, then sat them on the sofa and pulled a desk chair around. He hated this part of the job; it never got any easier no matter how many times he'd done it.

Yes, he confirmed, the victim matched the photographs; it was Mitsy Whitlock in the posed school pictures. The mother's name was Gwen and she screamed her anguish and despair while Don, the husband, seethed in anger. Gill could relate to that rage; he felt it each time another helpless victim fell prey to a monster. He vowed, foolishly perhaps, that their daughter's death wouldn't go unavenged.

He sat there alone long after the parents left and thought about Hank and what he'd seen hidden in those black eyes. Fuck the meth dealers and cookers, this was more important. He didn't have a shred of proof, but he trusted his gut after all these years. He couldn't get a warrant but he had the right tools. And he may be a little rusty, but he could still pick most locks … and he had just the one to try first.

The patch that Gran wired into the phone line worked perfectly, and there wasn't any feedback on the line with the other three men listening. Brick insisted they wait until 9:20 before placing the call, not to sound overly anxious. He also didn't want the little prick to demand his way, not this time. They were at the ranch, soon they would abandon the farmhouse.

Of course, Raoul didn't answer the phone. Brick was sure he was standing next to it but he needed to have control; it was all a dramatic play starring his bloated ego. Finally, someone picked up.

Jocko was great. "Put him on," he snapped.

"May I ask who's calling?" the female replied.

"Stop this shit right fucking now or I'll hang up."

Raoul's high-pitched voice said, "You're late."

"Too fucking bad, where's my shipment?"

Something wasn't right; Jocko never talked to him like that. Raoul was the boss and when he snapped his fingers, everyone jumped. In reality, this was a partnership and they needed each other to make this shit happen, so until he could replace him, Raoul needed Jocko. He tried another dodge, "Where's Cisco? I can't reach him."

"Since when is Cisco running my operation?" There was a long pause, maybe thirty second of silence ending when Brick gave him a nod, and Jocko continued. "Cisco is no longer with us; he's gone to the big shithole in the sky. He was screwing my bitch and skimming money. They have both ceased to exist. I fired his men and sent them packing back to whatever rat hole their whore mothers gave birth in. I have a new crew, men I can trust. Now where's my fucking shipment?"

Raoul was stunned, lost for words; never in his wildest imagination could he have seen this coming. He needed to stall for time to think, so he said, "Let me make some calls; I'll get back to you tomorrow."

Brick was shaking his head, and Jocko picked it up without missing a beat. "No, get back to me tonight or I'll make different arrangements. After Cisco's betrayal, I've looked into other sources. I need to hear back within the hour. I have important customers that can't be kept waiting, so either produce or I change suppliers—I don't give a shit." Brick disconnected the call.

Shock left Jocko drained, all color leeched from his face. He had planned so carefully. This last shipment and then the betrayal wouldn't be some stupid whore; it would be complete.

Cisco and his men were going to eliminate Jocko and give Raoul control of the operation. Now Raoul had to regroup in a hurry, so he made the necessary calls and got back to Jocko within the hour, saying the package would arrive in two days. Before he hung up, Jocko asked Raoul if he had found Brick. When he said he hadn't, the arrogant prick had the nerve to say that maybe Raoul was slipping.

Brick was up early, having spent the night at the ranch. Charlie, Gran, and he were having coffee in the kitchen while Brick explained what he thought would happen next. They took their time, made plans and then contingency plans, and briefed the guys to the double cross.

Nothing would happen that day; they knew Raoul would need time to make changes and set forces in play. He had to react and he was now on the defense, which is what Brick wanted. Perhaps he would move the next day and they would be ready, but Brick doubted it. This wasn't a little change, and he knew Raoul wanted to set a surprise attack. He probably didn't lie when he said two days, but you never knew so they were looking for the kink.

Fifty-seven

Brick drove back to his suite at the lodge, careful to dodge into side roads now and then and watch for anyone on his tail, but it seemed clear. It was a gorgeous day in the mountains, still cool and dry with a brilliant sun. At this altitude, the sun appeared perched on his shoulder like a tight shadow and currently squatted on the left through the open window. He needed to think the situation through and required complete solitude without interruption to achieve the prescient state when clarity of vision encapsulated his mind. Charlie would only call if something drastic occurred. It was a secure feeling to be back with the one man he could count on to be his rock.

He parked in the back and entered the rear entrance with his key card. Once in the suite, he stripped down to his shorts and sat in an easy chair facing the golf course. He would prefer water but you make do. He inserted himself inside the problem and let his computer like mind and his experience triangulate the various possibilities and come to a logical conclusion. Another thing he just couldn't share with others.

"Remember what the dormouse said, Feed your head, feed your head."

He soon entered a trance state where he appeared to be moving down a long tunnel lined with symbols and strings of words written on the walls, but he was moving too fast to discern the meaning. He was a four-year-old child sitting in the backyard of the family home in Saint Paul. He remembered his father's voice screaming at his mother and her hysterical replies. The reel fast-forwarded through his formative years and finally settled on his high school days, throwing the winning pass into heavy coverage for the state title. It seemed to stall there as it collected the stored knowledge of his early years and paused as it shifted to Cassandra.

Cassandra, Cassy, Cassie, Cass—she loomed large in his mind ... The moment he changed from an adolescent to a man. He wanted to understand how women thought and why they did what they did. Sensitive men since the dawn of time strived for the same solution. He never came closer than admit they were indeed strange creatures.

Blackness as he looked inward and his body tensed. The hair on the back of his hands rose as with an electric charge. This was the point when his mind tried to block the images; they were painful. Not this time, he forced himself to remember—it was important. He was at Harvard, Cassie was home, she had decided that she would pursue her degree in fashion and was supportive of Brick and his ambition. At least that was her public face, the one she showed Brick whenever they were together or with others.

The real Cassandra would be bored to death with that life. She was a schemer, a sexual deviant, a cheat, a thief, and possibly the devil incarnate. She needed to consume everything she lusted after. She liked older men and went to fraternity parties and enjoyed sex. At one party it got late and she wound up being the only female left. The air was so sexually charged that she just stood in the middle of the great room and slowly stripped. Everyone had her. When she left near dawn, she was exhilarated.

She was still sore days later when Brick came home and would only have sex with him in the dark while the red marks from slaps and bites receded. Then she would become silent and morose, staying in bed all day and refusing to eat. He never knew; he was so wrapped up in his studies, determined to make the money she desired and build a wonderful life for the two of them. It only depressed her more, that he was book smart but stupid in love. The more he did to please her, the more she grew to despise him. Screwing her boss and taking him away from his happy little family was thrilling.

In the chair Brick winced at the memories, but then the reel fast-forwarded through all of the misery, his drunken ramblings, the bar fights and reckless behavior. He had wrecked his car, smashed it into a tree, blind drunk and in a rage after a bloody bar fight. He was arrested, the charges dropped because of his parents' standing in the community and his outstanding grades at school.

That was the event that changed him. It was Charlie who got him through and, later, assigned to the same unit and eventually under Charlie's command. They were in Panama; the war was short lived and a bit of a joke. They handpicked their crew composed of a hard and seasoned class suited for the life of mercenaries. At first when Brick talked about making big money ripping off the cartels, it seemed another joke. But the more Brick planned and worked to gather information, the more the plan became a possibility, eventually a probability. This was what Brick was good at—planning. In his mind's eye, he could see it like a chess game and predict a dozen moves ahead. He put it on paper and it became reality.

The hardest part was convincing Charlie. He was the ultimate warrior, not interested in wealth; home was the military. Eventually, Brick was able to convince him with a simple argument. These were bad guys and wasn't Charlie here to battle bad guys? Charlie also knew how important it was for his friend to have the kind of money Cassandra envisioned, even if they were no longer together. He had something to prove. After the first raid, Charlie used the thrill of the fight to sustain him; the next time became easier and then progressively easier after that.

Brick was in his glory; he was using his mind again. He worked out the network to move the drugs into the States, and Granville moved them to Europe. Between the two of them, they had the contacts from Harvard and Cambridge to make it successful. They weren't selling to the poor and downtrodden—quite the opposite. Their customers were the rich and successful businessmen who used coke and pot with associates on golf courses and the private clubs throughout America and Europe. Business was good and they took advantage of the military to move most of their product. Jesus was their ace in the hole, a Spanish-speaking native with contacts and access in the countries of Central America that Brick could never achieve. Plus he was a pilot; Jesus could fly anything and was good. He became Charlie and Brick's close friend.

Charlie hated Cassandra. He always referred to her by her formal name; to give in to calling her Cassie would admit she was a friend—and she would never be anything but a disease to him. Shortly after the big fraternity orgy with her in the starring role, one of the frat brothers told Charlie about the incident. Charlie told him that if anyone ever told Brick, he was dead meat; nobody wanted that shit storm on their head, so it never got leaked, though Cassandra was known to have shared it with a number of her friends. Charlie would never allow his friend to be hurt that way. He was the most loyal friend anyone could have. Charlie didn't made friends easy or often, and Brick was his brother. He loved him like family.

The reel slowed and paused when it reviewed the raids—this was pertinent information. The culmination of the review sorted itself into a separate file folder in his mind that allowed easier access. This happened on a subconscious level. His computer like mind would only recognize the conscious information provided as a possible solution. This was another quirk, like the tingles, that he could never express to others.

The reel moved forward, slower now. It paused on the incident and then moved on. It wouldn't help to dwell on Cassie. He had to force his will into reverse and deal with it; like it or not, this was important. He went further back. It was really about his relationship with Jesus many years ago when Raoul came into the picture.

He knew that this was maybe the most important part. Brick and Jesus were at the peak of the business at the time of Raoul's arrival. The kid practically lived at the compound. It was a sprawling six acres that had been in the family for forty years. The main house was an adobe-style ranch with curving arches and whitewashed stucco design. There were several outbuildings and an airport-sized hangar with a helicopter landing pad fifty yards from the hangar. Ironically paid for by the good old USA.

Raoul had that sly, sneaky look about him that said ghetto trash. They were moving most of the goods in the warehouses and were both absorbed. Jesus and Brick ignored this skinny stepchild as an inconvenient interruption. Neither of the men had any trust in the kid and they tried to hide what they were doing. The kid sensed the deception.

During this period, Brick was the only conduit that Raoul ever saw to his stepfather's business. He heard stories of a larger-than-life figure they referred to as the General, but the boy never heard his real name so he never knew about Charlie. Raoul made it clear to both Brick and Jesus that he would be willing to do anything, but they never trusted him with more than scut work. His resentment festered to irrational proportions.

While Raoul stewed, the partners were making plans managing and organizing a vast network of distribution throughout multiple countries. The wishes of a throwaway street kid weren't relevant. This proved to be a big mistake now. Everything comes clear with time.

That's where and when the hatred began. The reel didn't show this but his mind added it to the equation. The reel continued through the death of Jesus in a fiery crash on a mission that Brick had sent him on alone … that was the hang-up. That was what he hadn't been able to get past. Hence his self-imposed reclusion to the solitude of his Wisconsin cabin for two blessed years while he healed. He faced it. He let it enter his private place and touch him deep. He knew that wherever Jesus was, he forgave him and wouldn't want his wife's child to win against the best friends he had ever known. Brick forgave him the indiscretion. Another hang-up was Charlie: Jesus was also Charlie's friend and Brick knew only too well what it meant to be Charlie's friend. Brick's sin against Jesus was nothing compared to the feeling of failure in his buddy's eyes.

Brick was sweating profusely when he finally stirred from his trance. He was physically and emotionally drained, but he recognized a cognitive breakthrough. It wouldn't take long now, just waiting for a killer from Central America. The shipment was here but they were leery of making the delivery. Cisco was the inside man and he'd been planning on cutting Jocko out. Brick knew with a slight tingle that he was right in his assessment and had a day to secure his plan.

The hair on the back of his neck stood stiff and chills enveloped his body; he was scared. He sat back heavy in his chair and as the feeling subsided, he broke into a sweat once again. He flashed back to high school and the big game against State for the title. The fear that took him before the game was unbearable. An hour before kickoff, he sat in a stall in the boy's toilet with an uncontrollable case of diarrhea. His heart was beating so fast, he was sure of an attack. The room was empty when Coach came looking for his star quarterback.

Brick remembered standing on rubbery legs as he made his way to the field. As soon as he came into view, the home crowd stood cheering for their beloved star. He was stunned and looked into the stands where he saw family and friends who were counting on him to make them proud. He was sure that instead he would shit his pants before he ever stepped onto the field. But he somehow stumbled out for the coin toss and almost cried in relief when he lost and the other team took possession of the kickoff.

He was dismayed when his defense held them to three and out and the offense took over. He was scared he would somehow fuck up. Brick was sweating then as he was now when he cozied up and placed his hands under the center's ass. But as soon as his fingers found the laces and he dropped back, an icy calm settled in his bones and the world slowed to a fraction of normal time. Now it seemed he had all the time in the world. He was quick and sure in his delivery of that first pass and easily completed it for a first down. All the fear and nerves disappeared once he started. He went on to have a magical game and was carried off the field on the shoulders of his teammates.

From that moment on, he knew that fear was good. Fear sharpened your senses and focused the mind. Back then it was a fear of losing, of disappointment and despair. Now it was the fear of death, not merely for himself but for his friends and comrades—the brave men who had suspended their lives to help him and who were willing to put themselves in harm's way for the sake of a man they hadn't seen in years. Fear for those who weren't soldiers—Mason and Harriette, Dawn and the people he loved back in Minnesota and Wisconsin, all were at risk.

They'd been both good and lucky so far, but Jocko and his crew were rabbits in a field of foxes compared to what they would soon face. Raoul was a stone killer and he was strong in numbers and resources. This was a very serious game and the stakes were as high as he had ever faced. If Raoul had the backing of the Sinaloa cartel, they were fucked. They had billions and an army of troops. His sorry little band wouldn't have a prayer. *But why would the cartel be involved?* The Jefes of the past were long gone and they never knew him or any of the men by name. All they knew was the US Army ripped them off. Simply the cost of doing business.

Exhausted, he entered the shower and let the water run hot, washing away some of his fear while he came to grips with the next forty-eight hours. He stayed in the hot water long enough to revive his body, but his emotions were taut and conflicted. He walked into the spacious bedroom and there, carefully arranged on his pillow, was a black, lacy thong. Next to the bed on the nightstand was a vase with a single red rose and centered on cream-colored custom stationery was a note in perfect script.

Brick, just call

D

He longed to be held and to hold before a battle. The human touch as necessary as air. His past looming large, but his hunger insatiable. He dialed her number.

She answered after the second ring and just said, "Thanks."

"I found your present and note," he said.

"Did you like it?"

"Yes."

"I'll be right over."

She was there within minutes and they came together with need and lust, not in love as love is perceived, but as desire melds with love to form a force greater than the whole. This was a physical release that was borne of fear of death and the simple life force that provokes humans of a certain order to bond through their sexual strength.

They poured their fears, hopes, and dreams into one another as they mated and found temporary comfort in the flesh. It was the cleansing of the body and soul that finally flushed them clean and pure as they both drifted into a deep, dreamless sleep. They had admitted their love. Not to each other, but at least to themselves. It was a start.

When Brick woke, it was to an empty bed. He shook the cobwebs from his brain as he surveyed the room. It felt empty and he knew without checking that he was alone. His paramour gone after she had accomplished her goal—providing comfort to a love in need.

Fifty-eight

I just can't think about it too much. We both needed this. I refuse to keep beating myself up; we all like sex—maybe I just like it a little more than most. I'm not kidding myself either … this next phase is a bitch. Jocko was complacent and sloppy, so that went smooth; this will be different. The men coming are cold-blooded killers, not drugged-up losers.

I need to be cool, think it through. Get Harriette and Mason over here at the lodge with Dawn. They should be safe where they are, but that's not a chance I'm willing to gamble on. They will love it here—hot tub, pool, and golf for Mason; beauty shop and spa for the girls. It'll be like a mini-vacation and no one would think to look here, if they look at all. I can't underestimate Raoul though; he's smart and cunning. I just can't make any more mistakes with my innocent friends in this drama of mine. By now that whore of Jocko's will have gotten word to him and he'll know it's me; I just hope that Charlie will still be a surprise.

While I still have a little time, I better put my affairs in order. Harriette will be taken care of—she's a principal in my will—but I need to add Dawn. I better check to see if Digger and his family have enough. Shit, I can't remember half of what I put in there; when was the last time I changed it?

This was the conversation that Brick often had with himself. It was his way to calm his nerves so he could focus. He realized he had some time this afternoon and thought of Bucky. It had been months since his last chat with his old friend and attorney, Bruce Buckstein. They were friends back at Harvard and he'd been Brick's lawyer since before he even passed the bar. Bruce started building his client base the day he set foot on campus.

Bucky's father was the founding partner of the Buckstein, Freeman, and Manis law firm in Manhattan, star criminal defense attorney.

274

Bucky was his youngest son with his third wife. Saul Buckstein was old to father a son but thanks to a busty young showgirl, he proved to still be potent enough. Sherry Fox, her stripper name, had signed a prenup and wasn't happy about it, so she lied and said she was on birth control. When she found out she was pregnant after spiking the old man's orange juice with enough Viagra to harden a horse, she hid the pregnancy until it was too late to abort.

So here was Bucky entering his first year of law at Harvard and the old man, already a retired, rich eighty-five-year-old. When he kicked the bucket a few years later, he left Sherry squat, except what she got in the original agreement. Bruce inherited the lion's share; there was plenty to go around. Bruce was the only child of Saul's to replace his dad at the firm and was rewarded for the effort. Saul made Sherry comfortable, but not to the level she had envisioned. Bruce figured out his mother was a slut and gold digger before he reached puberty. They weren't close and Bucky was raised primarily by Martina, Saul's longtime housekeeper and cook.

Bucky was raised in wealth and opulence, so money was important. Saul had always been a hustler, and the apple didn't fall far from the tree. Bucky loved the law and was committed to becoming the best in New York to honor his dad. He was fascinated with how he could manipulate the legal system for nefarious purposes.

Later, when Brick, Gran, and the others were making a small fortune, Bucky was a natural to not only represent them but to help launder the money through sham corporations. It was a union of conspiracy condoned by the power brokers of New York who used his father's law firm for the same purpose. Money was the Holy Grail they worshipped.

When Bruce heard it was his old friend Brick Winslow on line three, he put the CEO of Chase Manhattan on hold and then, thinking better, told him he would have to call him back.

"Brick, you old outlaw ... what's up, dude?"

"I'm in a bit of a fix Bucky and I need to get my shit together, so of course I think of the crookedest Jew shyster on the planet."

"Honored to have a master criminal like you call. What can I do you out of today?"

"First off, has my bitch ex-wife contacted you?"

"Yeah. of course. Not her, but Danny Lockhart, the big blow-ass California tort guy."

"And?"

"Two mil, claiming you fucked her on the original divorce decree and hid assets that should have been community property, plus interest and whatever else the fuck Danny can think of to pad the bill. Unfortunately for you, it's California and the liberal pricks pick a man's pockets clean when the poor abused woman cries foul. I planned to call you in a couple."

"So what's the bottom line here?"

"She can prove the income that shows you can afford a little trimming, so I guestimate a couple of hundred or so. Can I assume you don't want the publicity?"

"Yes, especially now. Do you really think it would hit the Hollywood rags?"

"Of course. When Lockhart farts, it's news."

"In that case, I want this to disappear. I'm in some serious shit right now."

"Ooh, something I should know about?"

"Only if you want the cops camped on your door."

"Who are you again?"

"Are you in a gambling mood today, Bucky?"

"Always my man, what you got?"

"Anything under three hundred grand, and you keep the balance or you do the work pro bono."

"Pro bono was Dad's filthiest word."

"Yeah, but Saul was as smart as he was mean, so he knew better than to gamble."

"Damn straight, make it four and you got a deal."

"Okay, Bucky baby. I know the drill, three and a half. I've got some will shit to discuss and I suppose I'll lose my fucking shorts in fees you fabricate."

"You are catching on, Brick my love, why I love the law. Deal. Talk to me, brother."

Fifty-nine

Nadia made it down the mountain, her clothing torn by thorns. The deep scratches and cuts inflicted by brambles and branches left her leaking blood. Her left breast was hanging most of the way out of her blouse. She looked a lot like an abused Daisy Mae with her skimpy dress and heavy breasts. A circus freak. So when she stood by the side of the road with her hip cocked and her thumb extended, the first cars couldn't believe their eyes. They passed her by, at least the families and women did.

It took a certain type of man to stop and check her out. That man, as fate would have it, was Dave Martin, fifty-three, recently divorced, and horny. She was thrilled when he stopped in his ten-year-old Chevy pickup with a shell topper; a quick scan told her he was perfect for this part. He seemed to be sensitive as a gnat and smelled like a goat. His eyes mapped every square inch of her body. His food-stained jeans were partially hidden by his overhanging belly. Yes, he was just the type of man Nadia needed.

An hour later she was driving the truck as she tore through his wallet. She had scored a driver's license, two credit cards, and eighty-seven dollars in cash as well as four condoms, two of them scented and ribbed. As she had predicted, once he picked her up he drove a short distance and then pulled onto an old logging road. The pretense was that he had to urinate, but after he stopped the truck he twisted his body sideways and openly leered, the lust in his eyes evident.

"You know, I was thinking ... I'm taking a chance here helping you out. It's plain to see you're in trouble and this is a lot of effort. Maybe I should at least get a little kiss for all the pains I'm taking to save you."

"Yes Dave, I agree. You're quite handsome; I could go for a guy like you. I want to show my appreciation."

She scooched closer and threw her leg over his and brought her lips down hard. His hands started the strip search of her body and she responded lustily, pressing his face into her breasts. It was better than his foul breath swallowing her oxygen. As he clawed her tits and slobbered on her ruined dress, her eyes roamed the cab of the truck searching for what she needed, but she couldn't find anything suitable. As she leaned over him looking behind the seat, his fat, dirty fingers moved down lower; he was now kneading the cheeks of her full ass.

"Lay back here, bitch, so I can fuck you real good."

"No, there's not enough room. Let's go to the back of the truck and I'll bend over the tailgate and you can do me doggy style."

"Great idea! I'm going to fuck you so good."

Nadia was out the door in a flash, heading around to the back much faster than Dave could get realigned with the door and pull his bulk out. He was afraid she had run, so he bellowed a curse as he rounded the back of his pickup, but she was there. She had already dropped the tailgate and was bent prone with the top half of her hidden in the well of the camper top; her left hand was hitching up the back of her dress.

"Ooh, you want it bad, you filthy slut, and old Dave is gonna give it to you good. Pull down those panties."

"No, don't you want to rip them off?"

Dave gave a lewd laugh and stepped behind her. Her face and shoulders were obscured from his view in the shadows of the camper, but he lowered his pants and stepped directly behind. He placed both hands on her hips, grabbed a full handful of material, and yanked at her panties. Her legs spread and her body was turned as her right arm broke free of the camper. She swung the heavy tire iron into the side of his face with all her weight, crushing his eye socket and cheekbone.

He fell like a wet noodle, both hands clutching his face. He was trying to form words, but his mouth wouldn't function. He was squirming on the ground, kicking his legs to no avail. Nadia already moved; she was standing in front of him now looking down at the top of his head. She was aligning her target and when she was confident she had the angle and distance, she swung the tire iron back and high, gaining momentum as she brought the heavy end squarely down on his head, crushing the skull and sending shards of bone and brain matter bleeding into the ground surrounding his twitching, lifeless form.

She was out of breath and had to slump against the back of the truck to keep from joining her victim at her feet. After she regained her composure, she found an old rag in the back of the truck and wiped the tire iron, removing all fingerprints. There was a canvas tarp in the back she pulled out and spread on the ground; then she rolled the body onto it, dragged it to the ditch at the side of the road, and kicked him in. She found a branch and swept the ground, obscuring the blood and carnage.

She now had a truck, cash, and credit cards. She was headed to Bend. She also found his cell phone in the glove box. It was a smartphone, so she looked up the address of the women's shelter in town. It was late and she didn't know Raoul's phone number, but she was free and it had all been so easy peasy.

She parked two blocks away and walked to the shelter. It was two in the morning, but there was a bell on the gate in the fence surrounding the shelter. The fence was eight feet high, made of metal. It was the third they constructed. Abusive husbands and boyfriends didn't take no for an answer and running away constituted a cardinal sin, so they often came to haul their property back. Average police response time: four minutes.

She hadn't cleaned up, so her appearance was frightening but she had composed her story. She would claim to be too afraid to reveal her abuser and wouldn't deal with the cops. She wiped the truck of fingerprints, then removed the battery and SIM card from the phone and concealed it under the right rear wheel well on top of the tire. She was confident that the body wouldn't be found for weeks or months. She had no remorse for the pig she had killed; she'd done it before.

She pressed the buzzer twice before lights went on in the house. It was only a few minutes until the blazing spots illuminated the yard bright as day. A middle-aged woman in a tan housecoat appeared with a flashlight. She realized Nadia's appearance left little doubt as to the nature of the late-night visit. She hurried to the gate and unlocked it, hugging Nadia to her breast.

"Oh my God, honey, come in and sit down."

"Thank you," Nadia croaked, trying to work some spit in her mouth.

The woman scrambled into another room and returned with a glass of water, for which Nadia was grateful.

"My name is Martha; what should I call you?"

"Call me Liz." Nadia used to love watching Liz Taylor movies in Poland, where they played long after their release.

"Should I call the police?" Martha asked.

"No, please ... I'm too afraid; he'll kill me."

Martha was familiar with this attitude. Most of the women were used to the abuse; 85 percent returned to their abuser and sometimes they were killed. The shelter didn't involve the police if the women insisted. This had to be a safe haven for women and to betray that trust would defeat the purpose of the shelter. Instead of making a call, Martha went about the business of making her charge comfortable.

Nadia said she would prefer a bath to a shower. Many of the women did, as they felt soiled inside and out. Next was ointment for the cuts and scratches. An Ace bandage for ankle support, a clean gown, hot tea, and finally chicken soup. Nadia was grateful, though she would have preferred a shot of whiskey to the tea. It was after three when Martha led her to a large room with six beds. Three were occupied, but when she crawled under the clean, crisp sheets in the bed under the window, she found that having roommates didn't bother her. She was dead tired and immediately fell into a dreamless sleep.

Sixty

Gill hadn't made any headway on the Mitsy Whitlock investigation. Like most of these cases, it seemed to be one dead end after another. He used his tools and entered the back door of Hank's house. His careful search bothered him. Not that he found anything—the opposite. Nobody is that clean, especially a man who lives alone. No porn or condoms, no booze or drugs, not even a joint; no way. He's hinky, Gill would bet a month's pay. Still he didn't have a fucking thing to go on. For a minute Gill considered bringing something in; there was a couple of juicy items in the evidence locker that would give him cause. It wouldn't be the first time. In New York they did what was necessary, but he sensed that wouldn't fly here.

He pulled out his cell phone and was surprised when all bars lit up; he had a strong signal. His intention was to call Lucy at the department and have her run a search on cell phone providers and give them the name Henry or Hank Johnson.

Lucy Foley was an enigma. She was a graduate student from Penn State working out her internship in criminology. At twenty-three, she was a bombshell by anyone's standards. What she was really doing in this sheriff's department was beyond him. She would look more at home as a Victoria's Secret model—a tall, statuesque beauty, long silky brown hair hanging below her shoulders. A shapely figure and huge brown eyes that sparkled with a secret mirth. These attributes were offset by square, fashionable glasses, lack of makeup or other additions. She became more alluring in the process. Her goal was to become a technical advisor at Quantico. She was smart as a whip and made a difference in the small department. And ... she was a total nerd.

Her sexuality was a favorite subject of the force, especially among the young guys. There seemed to be an endless supply of suitors. To the best of anyone's knowledge, she always declined with a smile and gentle manner. Behind her back, she was known as Juicy Lucy or sometimes Juicy Fruit; even the women used the nickname. Lucy was aware of the interest in her private life, but was a firm believer in never mixing business with pleasure.

Plus, most of the young men she met at work were adolescents, still enthralled with dick and "she said" jokes. If she were to become involved with someone, it would be a man not a boy. What she did with her free time was nobody's business, something she had been heard saying more than once.

Gill didn't usually have a signal when in the hills, so having such a strong one was weird to him. He checked his Wi-Fi and saw that he had internet service—*how the hell do I have a signal and good service out here?* He barely had it in his office at the department. Like everything about this hinky Hank character, this was another mystery that made Gill more and more curious.

Gill was turning in circles in the spotless living room, wondering what he'd missed when a sudden flash of recognition hit him like a hammer blow. *I am such an idiot! He's been gone a while; he must have snail mail.*

Gill walked down the long driveway to the end and opened the mailbox. A flood of envelopes and flyers tumbled to the ground, a treasure chest of information. He knelt and sorted the junk first, then took the stack of bills and as he began leafing through it, his eyes lit up. The jackpot—an internet bill. He hadn't seen a computer or modem, so he tore the envelope open and sure enough, it was a bill from a satellite service.

He stuffed the mail back in the box but kept the internet bill. His eyes were focused on the trees as he made his way back to the house. There wasn't a dish on the roof or the yard; he had checked. When he got back to the Charger, he retrieved a small pair of binoculars and started a slow survey around the grounds. There were hundreds of trees, but he imagined it would be close. He thought about his own satellite dish and realized it faced southeast, so he narrowed his search to the trees that were the closest and aimed in that direction.

Craning his neck to an almost painful position and focusing in on an area too far away for the naked eye to see, he could make out the shape of a dish exactly where it should be. *Who would ever search that high? Duh, he's a lumberjack; climbing trees is second nature.* The cable was threaded down a deep crevasse in the trunk that blended in to the bark. There at the base, the cable snaked into the ground. He looked in a direct line to the house and it led to the back bedroom. It wouldn't take much for a man like him to trench the cable.

He studied walls, ceiling, and other possible locations, finally settling on the closet. It was a spacious walk-in affair, with clothing hung on a long rack and shelves lining two of the walls. Most of the garments were work clothes, jeans and flannel shirts. Several pair of work boots were lined along the wall that held his dressier clothes. The interior walls of the closet, same as the house, were lined in knotty pine panels fitted together on seamless joints. He noticed a small space at the edge of one panel abutting the corner.

He was running his hands along the edges looking for a release latch of some sort when he stubbed his foot on a box, and when he leaned against the wall near the edge, the panel popped open. Behind it was an eight-foot width running the length of the house. The narrow room held a series of modems, with colored LED lights stacked on a shelving stand. Gill was no techie but he knew a sophisticated internet system when he saw it. There wasn't a computer, but it was certain that the man owned a laptop or two and took them with him. A grin spread out across Gill's face. *I'm getting closer, motherfucker. I'll get you yet.* He didn't have grounds for a warrant, not with an illegal search, but Gill felt certain he had him by the short hairs.

Sixty-one

Paco was transported through one of many tunnels used by the cartel. Ricardo came along as his guide and interpreter. Ricardo wasn't happy; he was a mid-level player and resented babysitting this turd, but orders aren't questioned. Paco was a filthy little psycho who didn't speak a word of English, but was arrogant and loco as a rabid pit bull.

Ricardo was twenty-eight and Paco only eighteen, but it was rumored the kid made his bones at thirteen and was said to have twenty-seven kills. One thing was true, he was cool. He brought a MAC-10 machine pistol in a burlap bag tied with a piece of twine and a sling of the same material that he looped over his head so the gun hung down the middle of his back as they walked. He was small and thin, with a wispy little hint of a mustache. He wore wraparound sunglasses day and night and seemed to survive exclusively on flour tortillas.

Ricardo's job was to transport him to Oregon in thirty-six hours, no small feat. It was more than a thousand miles from the Mexican border to the mountains of Oregon. A car was out of the question, so they had to rely on the small single-engine Cessna. They needed to land twice to refuel. Ricardo feared landings. The kid never traveled and asked nonstop questions. He was an irritating little prick and Ricardo tried to tune him out. Still, it had been made clear that this was important, so he tried to suck it up as best he could; he prayed for it to be over, fast.

Paco finally shut up and Ricardo returned to being nervous. He didn't like to fly even in big jets, and this little puddle jumper dipped and rose with the wind; his stomach convulsed and stuck in his throat at every bump and turn. Any turbulence and Ricardo gripped the seat back so hard his knuckles glowed pure white. He told the pilot he thought he might throw up. The man handed him a bag. A bag for fuck's sake, he wanted to land the fucking plane and jump out, but the stone-faced pilot had orders too and so he never said another word. Ricardo worried about the return trip alone. In his eyes, Paco was expendable.

Brick was getting ready to drive back to the ranch when his cell chirped. He picked up and heard Zoe's soothing voice at the other end.

"I thought you should know, there were two Spanish guys in here last night asking my customers questions about the area and Jocko's ranch in particular. I should say, only one was asking questions and the other, a mean-looking little dude, sat stone-faced. He wore shades in the bar and seemed to only speak Spanish. I know a bit and could make out what sounded like threats," she said.

Brick asked if she could be specific.

"Well, he was swearing in Spanish and it sounded like he was pissed off and hinted that there was a problem with either Jocko or someone at the ranch," she said.

"When did they leave?" Brick asked.

"Around midnight," she answered. "I followed them but they walked down the street and turned at the next block, so I didn't see a car or anything. Don't you lease that place to Jocko?"

"Thanks, hon; you did good to call me. I've leased it since I left town, but it's still in my name and as owner I need to know what the hell happens."

"When are you going to come by and see us again?" she asked.

"Soon, I'm just wrapping up some details on my old business dealings. I want to hear you sing again," he replied.

"Brick … I spent the day with Dawn and Harriette, and I'm sorry for what I said before about Dawn—she's really nice and obviously crazy about you.… But if it doesn't work out, I'm still here."

As she hung up, Zoe sighed; the crush she had on him was still there, like a pilot light. It had been a long time since she'd been with a man and the itch was distracting. She was still a young woman and had her needs. Time to find a scratching post.

He was kneading the back of his neck, the muscles in his shoulders stiff, strung tight. Brick willed himself to relax and let his shoulders drop. *It's begun,* he told himself; *the shooters have arrived and time is precious.* He drove methodically up one street and down the next, trying to get a glimpse of the boys Zoe reported. After an hour he gave up and headed out of town.

He was traveling north on County Road 6 when he felt the first tingle. His truck slowed with his mind, nerves jangling. The light dulled to a pale yellow and cast an eerie sense of foreboding with sepia overtones as he drove in what seemed like slow motion. Around five miles south of the turn to the ranch, his attention was drawn to a cluster on the hillside off a logging road partially obscured by a thick stand of pines. It was a fleeting glance.

He couldn't remember a time when the premonitions came more than every few years. He was always grateful for the warning. At the same time, driving while under the influence of a spell was challenging. He needed to stop.

The road began a steep incline as it rose on the mountain and he had to drive almost two hundred yards before he came to another road heading in the right direction. He made the turn and crept along until he was approximately even with where he thought the scene was. He stopped until his head cleared, then climbed out of the truck to look down the slope. When he came abreast of the stand of fir trees, he had to climb on top of the cab to get a clear view at what he thought he had seen. Through the lenses of his fifty-power Leupold binoculars, the scene swam into sharp focus.

What had appeared to be a sugar cube surrounded by ants morphed into a white semi-trailer. The ants proved to be swarthy small men with rifles and machine pistols. In the middle of the men stood Nadia, looking defiant as ever. She didn't have a way to contact Raoul earlier, so had she waited in her stolen truck outside town on County Road 6 until she spotted the convoy with the two SUVs and the semi. Now she was waving her arms and talking to the tallest of the group. He had a Pancho Villa–style black mustache and held a cell phone to his ear. He soon handed it to Nadia; she turned in circles, gesturing wildly. A moment later, she handed the phone back and was ushered into the backseat of one of the SUVs.

Brick hopped off the roof of the cab and walked down the slope through the trees until he had a clear vantage point, then sat and called Charlie. This was an unexpected development. Raoul had never been to the ranch and now he had inside information as to the layout and an advantage Brick wasn't expecting. He should have let Gran kill her. He sat patiently watching and waiting until it was clear they weren't moving anytime soon. Then he walked back to the truck and drove straight to the ranch.

The sun had cleared the mountain peak and the last rays of daylight were turning to dusk as he pulled into the drive. Gran told him that Charlie was patrolling the grounds while Clint, Keith, and Stoney slept. He was in the kitchen with Jocko when Brick entered the room. Jocko sat in a straight-backed chair caressing his injured hand and looking sullen. They sent him to his room while they made plans. Jocko seemed resigned to his fate and held on to the promise Brick had made to let him live if he followed orders.

Outside, Brick gathered the remaining four guards around the bunkhouse and explained what he thought would happen that night. He retrieved a fair amount of cash earlier through wire transfers arranged by Bucky. They agreed to his plans just as Charlie returned. Brick told the men to get some sleep, and then he sat with Charlie on the porch and went over alternatives. Any plan would fail in part so they played the what-if game. The men wouldn't sleep tonight and Brick said a silent prayer that they would all still be alive come morning.

The call came at nine that evening. Charlie answered on the fourth ring and simply said, "Yes."

"Who is this?" the caller asked, irritated and impatient.

"This is the person who answered the fucking phone—who did you want?"

"I thought it was Jocko's fucking phone, asshole."

"I'll get him."

They made him wait a couple of minutes before Jocko's voice came on the line and said, "Yes."

They all knew he wanted to rage, scream, cut a throat, but Raoul had a scheme to sell so he was subdued when he replied: "I wanted to tell you, there's been a slight delay—it couldn't be helped—and the load will arrive around noon tomorrow."

"Fine, just so it's here tomorrow; I'll call a crew to unload," Jocko lied.

"Good, I'll only have a couple of men along with the shipment; they'll need help to unload and distribute," Raoul lied back.

Gran entered the kitchen as Jocko hung up. "He'd nick his own mum for a farthing and you take his shit like a twat?" Gran prodded. "You're a bloody poof."

Jocko knew better than to take the bait—he knew what a crazy sonofabitch the bastard was. He felt his hand throb; provoking him would be suicide, so he kept his mouth shut.

At midnight they assembled the men and assigned positions. The guards had agreed to provide support as sentinels but didn't want to be involved in a firefight. They were simple ranch hands, not soldiers, but the money Brick offered was hard to resist. They were positioned along the road starting at the turnoff and hidden in the ditches alongside the road every fifty feet. Their cars and trucks were parked at the turnaround in the clearing just past the entrance to the ranch. When they left, Brick paid them and they could have split then but thought better of it. They knew these were serious men, hardened veterans; *why take the chance?* After watching these guys operate for a while, they didn't relish the idea of pissing anybody off. Take the money and keep your mouth shut was the consensus.

Clint and Keith left together; their job was to guard the backside at the crest of the hill that covered their ass end. With Nadia involved, Raoul had the players and the whore was their guide. She knew the area better than anyone other than Jocko and Brick. Charlie brought them up and positioned them in the only spot where the intruders could pass. The cliffs and terrain made it all but impossible to trek elsewhere.

Charlie equipped them with Kevlar vests, automatic weapons, night-vision optics, and water. Brick warned that it could be hours before they were hit but to stay alert. At first they held their positions in silence, but Keith was curious. He'd settled down and gave each man the respect he now knew they deserved, but he had to wonder why they came to fight in this desolate spot after not having contact with Charlie and Brick in so long. Keith worked for Charlie; he served with him in the military in Afghanistan and had been an operative of the company in several locations around the world since coming to work for McWin Security. He was here as an employee and getting paid but was loyal to Charlie. Clint was an anomaly that Keith couldn't figure out. He wanted to ask what his story was but never had the chance, as Clint spoke first.

"How long you been with the General?" Clint asked.

"I did a two-year tour with him in Afghanistan when it started; man, what a shit show that is. The fucking people hate us; the Taliban are like termites—they just keep popping out of cracks in the fucking rocks and it's all rocks. This is like a golf course compared to that shithole. The people are living in the Stone Age and their religion is harsh and cruel. They remind me of the right-wing Christians in this country who would just as soon kill anyone who disagrees with them. It's crazy how people can devote their whole life to some ancient story about God; it seems every country has one. I don't know if I even believe in God. I'll tell you, if I did, mine would be truly loving and compassionate. He sure as shit wouldn't be a hateful prick like most of the ones I've seen.

"When I came back to the States I finished my tour in Texas, which is my home, so that was cool—easy duty but you get bored. Afterward, I couldn't get a decent job and was working on a farm pitchin' hay when the General called. I been working for him over a year now; he's real good to me and the work is cool. I've protected movie stars and dignitaries and all kinds of shit. Charlie likes me working the domestic trouble, the cheating spouse or blackmail. He uses the hard guys for overseas stuff. I think I've proved myself."

They were quiet again for a time, then Clint said, "I'd follow the General anywhere. We did some serious shit down in Panama and quite a few years after. We were a family, if you know what I mean. Every family has a head and people who are good at different stuff. Charlie is the best soldier I ever met. We're all Rangers so I don't have to tell you what that takes; just to make it, you're special. I never thought I could do it, but the

General had faith in me like no one ever has—even my family—and I would give my life for the man."

Keith was touched; Clint had such a look in his eyes when he said that, you knew what loyalty meant. They were quiet again listening; there hadn't been an interruption in the night sounds. Even insects sense the difference when a man enters the woods—perfect silence.

This was the first time he'd talked alone with Clint and now he couldn't resist. "So what did you think about Brick? Was he there from the start of your tour?"

"Oh yeah, the Bank was always there, 'cept we didn't call him that then. He was a lieutenant you see, and he and Charlie acted more like equals than officers of different rank. After a while you learned that they were brothers—known each other all their lives growing up—so you treated Brick the same as the General, except for titles. He looks like a movie star, so you don't realize how tough he is. He was a first lieutenant in the Rangers and that ain't easy. I would fight alongside that man any day; he can hold his own with anyone. You should see him hand to hand, no one better 'cept the General."

Keith mulled that over for a bit, but couldn't let it go; he asked. "You mentioned his looks; that's the first impression I got. I didn't take him seriously at first, big mistake. It's just his looks are so disarming."

Clint gave a soft chuckle. "Don't go chasing pussy with that boy— the chicks never see you. Sometimes all of us would be celebrating and would go out to some shit-kickin bar and mix it up a little, you know? We'd find a big table and Brick would start ordering all the best booze and shit that they had. He would ask for all this top-shelf stuff none of us had ever heard of, and once in a while, they would have a bottle of like this really great bourbon at a fucking ridiculous price and he'd say, 'Bring the bottle.' He just knew all this shit; he's really smart. Soon the owners,

294

waitstaff, and the best-looking broads in the joint would be at the table talking to him. I would look around the room and every single chick in there was staring at him, whether they were with a dude or not. It's a wet-panty party when that boy walks in … It's getting to be time; we better shut up and get ready."

Stoney was farther down the hill; he was the fail-safe in case they got past Clint and Keith. He wore all black, not camouflage. With his coloring, black clothes, and black rifle, he blended in perfectly with the trees. He was ageless, one of those black men who is tougher than most men half his age. His exact age was anyone's guess, but probably around forty-five or so. He was big and strong, but most of all he was good. He learned at an early age that a black man living in a white man's world has to be twice as good to survive and Stoney wanted to thrive, so he worked harder than most. He was a motherfucker in battle.

Growing up in the hills of Tennessee was no picnic for a black man. He was born in a dry county and moonshining was a white man's business. His granddaddy, old Amos, started shining when he was young and it became the family business for generations. Amos was known for making the best shine in the state, a recipe he was very selective and secretive about; he'd only repeat it to the oldest male descendant and that tradition was passed down. Amos was a mechanic by trade and the Cajun blacks who were his early relatives were known for their potions and formulas. As a mechanic, he had a passion for fast cars and he worked on the white shiners' heaps until he built his own hopped-up Chevy, three hundred and fifty horse, fat sway bars, stiff springs, and a fifty-gallon shine tank.

Amos's firstborn, Chet, was the driver. Chet drove the way only a black man from the hills of Tennessee can; he was used to being chased. With a superior product and faster car, first Chet and then his brothers made more net profit than any white shiner in the state. They ran four cars in four years. It took that long to prepare the cars and the boys. Stoney's daddy was the youngest of the boys and the smartest. He saw things the way Granddaddy Amos did and branched out into drugs, gambling, and smuggling.

His daddy was known as Smoke; he never learned his real name. Smoke was the most feared black man ever seen in those parts. He paid the law and gave tribute to the Clearys who ran the county. Smoke greased everyone who mattered—he knew what it took. When his son returned from the service with the best contact in the whole fucking country, the business was practically printing cash. Stoney didn't need the money. This was his family and he felt most alive living on the edge.

While these three waited, the General took a position with a Mouser mounted on a tripod with a .556ML belt feed, set on the hill across from the bunkhouse. He was entrenched in a dirt bunker behind an old window air-conditioner with the barrel of the rifle clearing the top of the unit by inches. Charlie always felt a sense of calm focus just before battle. It had been a while since he was in a firefight; in fact none of the others had seen action of this intensity since they parted. He admitted he missed it, missed the preparation, the intense flow of adrenaline, but most of all the challenge—us or them, life or death. It didn't get more real.

Gran wished Mister Sullivan was here. He would appreciate this; there was a dark period in his past. He hoped Sullivan was proud of the man he had formed over the years under his tutelage. The thought made him smile. He wore the vest Charlie provided and carried the weapon, but he liked the wet work best. He would look for his opportunity. He was positioned on the other side of the hill from Charlie, higher and south. They would create cross fire, both men firing down so they didn't get caught in the mix. His pulse was strong and steady, forty-seven beats a minute.

The crew left Brick alone in the house with Jocko. They sat facing each other in the kitchen.

"What happens to me?" Jocko asked, considered the possibility that Brick would shoot him now.

Brick just stared at him for a solid minute, his eyes cold and hard. "I should kill you for your betrayal. You're lucky I'm not that man, not like Gran. You're going to stay here alone and wait for them. They'll try to draw you out and find our positions. Try not to get your ass blown straight away. If you do this like a man, you might live—I'm not promising anything."

His mouth was so dry, he had to work some saliva in before he could speak; Jocko was shaking from fear. "What will you do? Will I be able to get away?"

"Yes, if we're alive you can drive away."

Brick walked him to the door and pressed his Beretta F9 into his hand along with two full magazines. He turned to leave and then as an afterthought said, "Nadia will be with these men; she betrayed you."

Sixty-two

When Ricardo took the phone back, he spoke rapid Spanish that Nadia didn't understand. He led her into the back of the truck and when he dropped his pants, so did she. He couldn't believe his luck. The way this beautiful whore had dropped into his lap, it had to be a good omen. Raoul laughed when he told him they had found her. Raoul said she was a whore. "Treat the slut rough so she knows who's boss; she'll be a great guide. She knows the fucking place better than that prick Jocko."

After he screwed her, she would tell them how best to invade the ranch. She understood; men had always treated her this way. She longed for revenge against the Americans and was dumping Jocko. She would become Raoul's mistress in her fantasy and her life would blossom. She could live in a big city again. She never liked it out here in the sticks. She was young and hot and needed action.

As he traversed his long, winding trail, Juddiah felt a wave of relief. The familiar surroundings comforted him; his cave was his sanctuary. The apartment he rented in Bend over the liquor store was just a place to crash and keep his stuff. But the air smelled strange; he couldn't put a finger on it but different somehow. Yet nothing seemed to have been disturbed. He'd heard the cop came by Tony's office asking probing questions, none specific; he kept saying it was just routine, but he was sniffing around the edges hinting at more.

Well fuck him. That cop didn't have anything and he wouldn't find anything. If he came around again, Hank would confront him. *Arrest me or stay the fuck away.* He would file a report, go on the offensive. He was going back to work in a couple of days and thought he could stay on the straight and narrow for as long as necessary.

All the heat was on Henry, so Juddiah was in the clear to move freely. He wanted to cruise the hillside before dark. When he rode past the entrance to the cave, his face flushed; it took an effort to keep moving. He crested the top of the hill and turned on the powerful lights on the sides and top of the four-wheeler searching the grounds. Combing the hillside, feeling a little better at the lack of activity, he parked out of sight. The cave was too much to resist and he needed to make preparations. He had the shoes with him.

Hank left his bedroom and went back to the living room with the glass and bottle. He was sitting in the dark watching the hill and the trail to the cave.

He fell asleep in the chair after midnight and woke when he heard muffled voices and saw flashlight beams playing across the yard outside his window. Nadia, dressed in grey sweatpants and a flannel shirt courtesy of the women's shelter, led the way. Ricardo wasn't in shape to make a long trek uphill in the middle of the night, so he sent one of the smugglers who spoke English along with Paco on this mission. The two young men weren't used to trailing behind a woman, but the sight of her attractive rump in the tight sweatpants made it tolerable. It also distracted them from the task at hand.

That's why nobody noticed as Juddiah slipped behind them with his shotgun and ax. Nadia knew the way but Juddiah knew it better. He was able to stay above and slightly ahead as they made the climb. His watch glowed in the faint light as shadows hovered along the towering trees and played hopscotch between the boulders and small rocks.

Hank thought of following them, but was half drunk and not sure what he would accomplish; this didn't concern him. It was his asshole neighbor's problem; he drifted back to sleep.

It was time; the convoy would arrive at the ranch a little after three. Nadia had assured the smugglers that it was just a few old ex-army men protecting the ranch, so they had a false sense of security. It seemed simple; catch the crew in their sleep so they would be groggy and in skivvies. Ricardo was in the driver's seat of the cab with a trailer of twelve men. The Suburban would stay 100 yards back with three more to cover the rear. It was a good plan and should have worked.

The guards hidden in the ditches along the road spotted the invaders as soon as they rounded the final bend, before they ever turned on the ranch road. Cell phones chirped and clicked; they did their job and split.

The semi was a tight fit and both sides brushed along the trees and brush; it was slow going when they entered the yard. The drugs were in back with the men: two hundred kilos of cocaine packed in ten-kilo bundles in crates marked asparagus. There were also five hundred kilos of high-grade marijuana and five hundred kilos of hash destined for the local market. This was a drop point and would be offloaded into panel and step vans for distributors along the northern Pacific and western states.

Raoul had expanded the operation over the years. Originally this was the main drop and as many as four semi loads would arrive at timed intervals and fill the two huge Quonset huts to the brim. Back then, the coke would be in shipping containers six times larger than the current packs. They needed a construction crane to lift the containers and load them onto big furniture delivery trucks. They never used to include marijuana on these drops, as the odor was detectable by dogs. This was before the dogs could identify coke.

It hadn't been mentioned, but of course there would be an exchange of money as well. This was a cash-and-carry business, and this load was six million for the coke alone. That was Jocko's. The pot and hash went to a dealer in Washington, his profit three mil on the cannabis and nine on the coke. This was serious money; it made everyone except Brick's crew jumpy.

Brick started searching for the money stash as soon as they took control of the ranch. He found it in the second Quonset hut and moved it. No one knew. Jocko was counting on them overlooking the cash. He would play it off as though the distributors would pay directly. That way when they confiscated the load by force, he would be in possession of the money and the coke. He knew this was his last chance, so he was still hoping to come out of this with a small fortune for the load he paid a million six for. He already had three million stashed, and with Nadia gone it was time to call it quits.

The money had been concealed in a false wall in the second Quonset hut locked in a steel vault. It took Clint two days to break in and then he, along with Brick and Stoney, moved the cash to a rental locker in town. Brick had plans for the dope but he was keeping that to himself. First they had a truckful of hardened shooters to dispatch, but he liked their odds.

Ricardo pulled in front of the ranch house and parked with his bright lights shining on the front door. The interior was dark and whoever came out would be temporarily blinded by the brilliant halogen beams. He stepped out of the truck, keeping the open door between him and the house. The men in back of the semi had orders not to show themselves before his signal. The rear doors had been rigged so they could be opened from inside and there was an access door in the middle of the passenger side of the truck, so the men would be split in two when they attacked.

The pistol was in the waistband of Ricardo's jeans behind his back, within easy reach. "Hey Jocko!" he yelled.

It was eerily quiet in the still night air; a touch of cool breeze filtered through the tall pines. Even the insects had stopped their insistent buzz. Behind him was the sound of a diesel motor coughing to life. As Ricardo whirled to look, Jocko stepped out of the dark at the far side of the ranch and shot him in the head. The name Raoul was the signal for the men in back, but he never had the chance to utter another sound.

The gunmen had no leader and were confused by the sound of the roaring engine and the single gunshot. Both sounds were muffled in the back of the trailer. The giant construction crane swung into position. With its mighty jaws, the claw attachment ripped through the top middle part of the trailer and started to lift it off the ground. Brick sat in the operator's seat high above them. He started the arm in motion and it swung back hard; as it lifted off, the trailer came loose from the cab.

At ten feet off the ground, the doors flew open and men tumbled out like fruit from a torn shopping bag. A few landed with broken arms or legs and two with broken necks. From the cab of the crane, it looked like a puppet show with the strings cut and marionettes left crumpled and broken. Then the scene exploded in a chorus of automatic weapon fire with bullets peppering the air like popping corn.

The crane swung in wide arcs back and forth, so slow it was as if the scene had been set to a millisecond speed until, with tremendous momentum, it reached its end of the fulcrum and he released the claw. The trailer hit the side and roof of the house like a bomb. It crushed in the front right side and part of the right roof, tearing lumber and concrete into splinters. It ripped wires and left water pipes torn, with jagged ends spewing a torrent of steam. In the ensuing madness, electric sparks flew in the night hissing and crackling under streams of steaming water, making a spectacular and dramatic light show in the black sky. In seconds, the shadows were climbing the hillside like erratic shimmery vines. Hearing the gunfire and explosion, the men in the Suburban rushed to the scene and were cut down by machine gun fire.

Sixty-three

Laura was dismayed and depressed. It was almost mid-summer and she was bored senseless. Work, maybe a couple of drinks with the girls or a show—that was about all she did. She went to the rodeo with her mom last week, *how lame was that?* She was about to give up on Brick. Or at least, she wouldn't sit and pine for him any longer.

The next week when a nice-looking young man asked her out to dinner, she said yes. He was a guest booked into a single room for a week. On the guest registry, he had listed his occupation as sales, and he drove a blue American sedan. Laura would see him leave in the morning, wearing a dark suit, white shirt, and narrow dark tie. He was in the same getup when he collected her for the drive to the restaurant. She expected him to go to the bar and then probably have dinner in the restaurant at the lodge.

Instead he walked her out to his car and drove her to the local bar where she and her girlfriends usually hung out. She was a little disappointed, only because of her previous date, but decided to make the most of it. He seemed surprised that she was known here, as most of the employees and some of the patrons greeted her by name. They took a booth along the back wall and Rosy greeted them and asked what they'd like for drinks. She ordered a daiquiri and he had a beer.

She asked about his job and found that he sold advertising for the monthly magazine in Billings. He said that he was here to pitch the resorts and golf clubs and that the trip looked promising. They made small talk about their jobs and friends for a bit. She had her usual for dinner, and he just had a burger. After they ate, the conversation faltered.

Finally, he said, "I have an early day tomorrow, so we should get back."

"I don't start my shift until noon and it's pretty early." She checked her watch; it was 8:30. "So if you don't mind, I think I'll stay for a bit. I can catch a ride home with one of the girls."

"I do mind actually. I take a girl to dinner, I expect her to stay with me."

"My dates usually last more than an hour. I spend way too much time in my room and at the resort, so when I get dressed to go out, I want to make a night of it. I'm sorry if that offends you. I can pay for my own dinner if that's what's bothering you."

"I thought we'd go to my room when we got back."

"Look, I just met you and we haven't even had enough time to get to know one another. I don't sleep with men on the first date. And I only sleep with men I choose."

He sat there with his mouth hanging open for a minute before saying, "What a cunt."

She slapped him across the face, stood, and marched to the bar and took a seat. He got up red-faced, looking like he could kill and started to follow. That's when Rosy intercepted him with the check. He fumbled for his wallet, paid, and left a paltry tip.

By now he had the attention of most of the customers in the bar and all the staff. He started for the door, then swerved and headed for Laura with murder in his eyes. He never made it to her. Two of the larger men seated on stools rose as one and stepped in his path. No one said a word. It didn't take long for him to change his mind and leave, muttering obscenities under his breath. After some laughter, the bar resumed the easy atmosphere that normally prevailed.

Laura remembered how Brick had made gentle sweet love to her, treated her like a queen, and defended her honor against those awful local boys. She longed for him to call, especially now. Some of the girls she knew came in a few minutes later, and she stayed until they left, catching a ride with them back to the lodge. It turned out to be a fun night after all.

Later, her mind wandered and she considered how many women Brick must have slept with to acquire the skill he possessed as a lover. She was committed to this job through Labor Day, then back to school and her mom. Not so bad when she thought it through … she knew he was never long term and there would be tons of hot guys back at school.

Gran picked off the cripples, those injured from the fall and crabbing sideways across the yard searching for cover. He got two confirmed kills. Charlie shot two more as they spread into the trees and was confident they were finished. Now they were under heavy return fire. Brick was shooting from the cab of the crane, bullets ricocheting off the steel beams of the immense structure as they zeroed in on the cab.

The men in the trees were confused and disoriented. They had never seen country like this and their ambush turned on them before it started. This was supposed to be easy—pull in, spill out, and massacre everyone in sight. Most of these kids weren't even good shots. They counted on automatic weapons and a spray of death, killing without aiming. But in this unfamiliar ground, they were dumping ammunition by the carload at shadows.

Some were already looking for an escape, but without cars or trucks what could they do? Even if they had transportation, the drivers had been killed—where would they go? One thing they knew was that if they didn't kill all these men soon, they weren't leaving this foreign place. They spread out into the trees until they formed a line spaced roughly equidistant apart and stayed behind cover. They weren't trained for this kind of work; unfortunately for them, their adversaries were.

Stoney worked seamlessly through the trees. The invaders never felt his presence until a bullet pierced heads and hearts. Gran was in his glory, up-front and personal. He slung his rifle and went to pistol and k-bar, saving the switchblade for more intimate victims. Charlie covered Brick with a torrent of machine gun fire as he clamored down from the cab of the crane. Four highly skilled Army Rangers were now combing the woods doing what they had been trained to do, search and destroy.

After Jocko shot Ricardo, he retreated to the house and barricaded the doors and windows. He only had a Beretta 9mm pistol and would try to defend the interior as best he could. At this point all he could do was hope for the best. He was conflicted as to whose side he was on, but knew the men from the squad and the talent they possessed—they were his best bet. Brick had said he could leave but all these guys were pissed at him. Still, he really needed to get the fuck out of here. The money still worried him; it shouldn't but it did. He wanted to live, but not poor. He had been poor and couldn't face going backward in life. While he pondered, the world exploded around him.

He was huddled in the far corner of the back bedroom watching the windows when the front of the house blew apart. He peeked around the corner of the hall and was met by a blast of fire and water. He ran back through the bedroom and tossed a nightstand through the window and leapt out after it. Rolling into a ball he rose, pistol ready. It was pitch-black behind him and an inferno to the front. He froze like a deer in the headlights until a shot sizzled past his ear; he rolled sideways into the brush.

Paco was at the choke point at the crest, but stopped to sniff the air. His instincts were finely honed, as only those of a stone killer can be. His accomplice was lower on the hill and a little ahead when the first shot fired and the diesel engine sounded. They both froze and went flat to the ground. Clint and Keith were forty yards in front of them flanking the road, with Clint on the high side and Keith the opposite. They had a brief view of the gunmen before they fell to earth, but held their fire not wanting to give away their position. They stayed still as possible, knowing that the first one to move loses.

Juddiah, hidden high above Keith and Clint, fired both barrels of the shotgun near the gunmen, causing them to scurry like cockroaches and dive in different directions. Keith opened fire at the nearest one, Henrico, and his short life was finished. Paco was unbelievably fast and accurate. His first shot caught Keith in the chest, knocking him to the ground and the breath from his lungs, the vest saving his life. The second bullet caught him in the right middle thigh piercing the femoral artery.

Clint rose from cover and sprayed the area where the shots originated with a full clip, the bullets ripping apart small trees and brush, but again Paco was too quick. He returned fire, driving Clint behind boulders; one shot tore through the sleeve of his shirt and grazed his upper arm. Then like a ghost, the tiny Mexican disappeared, zipping past him like a chipmunk on meth.

The blood was spurting from the femoral wound with each beat of Keith's heart. If Clint didn't act fast, he would bleed out in minutes. Clint ran across the exposed ground without a thought to his own safety. Juddiah could have taken him then, but he still didn't know the lay of the land and who to root for.

Whipping off his belt, Clint wrapped it around Keith's upper right thigh and pulled as tight as he could; the blood slowed to a trickle. Clint carried a small pen light in his pocket, which he now held in his teeth as he examined the wound. The bullet was embedded deep in Keith's flesh, pressing against his femur and causing an ache in the bone that made his teeth hurt. Retrieving his pack, Clint located the packet of congealing powder and poured the contents over the wound. Selecting a compression bandage from the kit inside, he pressed it firmly in place, then wrapped the thigh with tape. Stoney was really the master of this technique, but they could all do it in a pinch. It would hold for a bit, but they would have to get him to a hospital soon.

The cacophony of gunfire and smell of burnt powder reached them, and Clint thought it best to bring Keith closer to the fray. He took Keith's right side and looped his arm around his neck and shoulders. "Okay buddy, we're going to stand up. Put your weight on me as I lift you up."

Keith needed a minute to catch his breath and shake the nausea as he gained his footing, got a determined look on his face, and said, "Let's go."

They set off, Keith finding his balance and using his strong left leg with his other side limping, but supported by Clint they ambled along at a good clip, both men ready to fire at the first sign of the enemy.

Paco slipped past Stoney as he was stalking a lone gunman, his full attention focused on the man creating the direct threat. The kid could have shot him in the back, but he was on a mission. He was a solemn ghost as he slithered his way through the sea of men as silent and deadly as a snake in the forest, heading ever downward toward the house. He was looking for a specific someone—that was what he was getting paid to do and he had a reputation for doing just that.

Nadia had snagged her sweatpants on a branch and it tore a small hole in the butt. She was worrying it with her finger, not wanting to give the men following her any more reason to flame their desire. She paused to inspect the breach in her derriere when she recognized the sound of gunfire.

She moved downhill into the trees and threaded her way forward just as the attention was focused on Keith. She knew where the money was stashed and she was determined to get there first.

Juddiah noted this exchange with a sneer; he knew this woman as a wanton slut, too old and used for his tastes, but knew her to be devious, unstable, and dangerous—a wild card to add to the mix. In general, he was pleased with this turn of events in the area; it would certainly take the heat off him and create a new focus for law enforcement. He would have left but was curious to see the outcome; he enjoyed carnage.

The superior training was turning the tide against the greater odds, and the Rangers had decimated the drug runners' numbers to five. They still didn't know about Paco. Guys were dug in to their positions and the only way to end this was for someone to work their way around behind; otherwise they were just wasting ammunition.

Stoney was weaving his way through the trees to a position above and behind the two gunners who had Gran pinned down. Everything changed when Brick lit the sky with a series of flares he retrieved from the farthest Quonset hut. They had been stored for ten years but they were dry and still worked. He found five of them and loaded each into the flare gun, sending them either straight up or at a slight angle. When they reached the crest, the shell opened and a piercing light burst forth and each floated gently back to earth on a small parachute. There was no way to fire them all at once, so they created a timed illumination.

Those still wearing the night-vision goggles tore them off and paused to let their eyes adjust. The lights helped Clint to evaluate the scene and join the battle. He settled Keith between a thirty-foot fir tree and a boulder. There wasn't anything else Clint could do for his injured mate until the firefight was won. He left him with his weapon and plenty of ammo and then infiltrated the woods behind the enemy. It was slow going, but the squad, including Keith, kept in touch through their throat mikes.

Nadia threaded her way along the deer trail to the back of the house and arrived just as Jocko was rolling out the bedroom window. She was only twenty feet away as he stood. He smiled at her; in response, she lifted her arm and pointed the big revolver at his head.

"Wait, it's me—Jocko. Come with me and we'll be safe," he pleaded.

She stared at him with cold fury in her eyes and said, "You're a pussy. I'm moving on." And she fired.

She missed by a mile. Jocko started moving, weaving, pleading with her to stop but she wouldn't. She kept advancing, now holding the gun in both hands and firing blindly. She was getting closer and so were the shots. The next one tore through his shirt and creased his left shoulder, plowing a deep gash through the flesh. The Beretta came up as if on its own volition and he shot her in the face. She was dead before she hit the ground.

Charlie used the diversion and abandoned the Barrett, pulling the firing pin first, then ran a zigzag course closer to the house and stopped at the left corner of the back bedroom. The flames were rising and the wood at the back of the house was hot as he pressed his cheek tight to peek around the corner. In the faint illumination from the flares, he saw a shadowy figure stalking a much larger stick form that emerged from the brush and became a man. As the man rose to his full height, Charlie could discern the difference in size between them. The crouching man when erect was almost a foot taller than the shadow and as the light caught the side of his face, it revealed Jocko.

Paco recognized him in the light from the flames as the same man in the picture he carried—the man he was paid to kill. He raised the gun and swung it to bear on his head when his right arm went numb and the fingers sprung open, leaving the machine pistol clattering to the brush. Charlie had jabbed the butt of his rifle into the back of Paco's elbow where the nerves are most vulnerable. The pain made the arm useless. But the kid still had the presence of mind and the fast reflexes to react. He reached across his body with his left hand where a pistol and knife were stuck in his belt. The kid was fast, but Charlie was faster. Charlie swept his legs from under him and he crumpled to his knees. Then Charlie used the rifle butt to smash the bridge of his nose flat. Blood gushed from the nostrils, soaking the sweaty shirt until Charlie slung the rifle and, using both hands, snapped his neck. Paco hung limp as a rubber chicken.

Jocko realized how close he had come to death. The small figure looked childlike in the flickering flames of the fire that now consumed the house in an inferno of sparks and heat as Paco lay twisted and broken at Jocko's feet.

Jocko's gaze met Charlie's eyes and he silently mouthed, "Thanks."

Charlie nodded and then moved back up the hill. The shooting had stopped and with slow deliberation, one by one the men stepped into the clearing and started poking bodies.

Juddiah had watched the squad decimate the drug smugglers and he was watching now with his eyes glued on soldier-boy. The slow burn in his belly stemmed from the hatred he felt for this one man who had had a glimpse of the cave; he saw it happen. Juddiah had had enough and faded back into the mountain

Brick surveyed the damage and gathered the squad around him for instructions. "Keith needs a hospital, so Charlie will drive him to the base house and call in a military chopper from Camp Rilea to take him to the vet's hospital. Stoney, Clint, and I will burn the Quonset huts and all cars and trucks that aren't ours. There's kerosene in the first Quonset, so let's start with those."

Jocko couldn't stand it and almost yelled, "No, don't burn them yet—I need to get something personal."

Brick continued, "Stoney, retrieve the kerosene." Then he turned to Jocko and said, "The money's gone; I moved it days ago."

He couldn't think of a reply. Jocko's mouth was moving, but he wasn't making a sound. Then, recognition filled his eyes and he resigned himself to the facts. All hope of leaving with the money was gone, along with Nadia and everything else.

Charlie helped Keith into the truck and they left. Stoney set off to take care of the Quonset hut fires, and Brick brought Clint into the decimated trailer to help rig the fire. He wanted part of the coke and pot to burn but wanted most of it left intact. If the drugs disappeared, neither Raoul nor the cartel would rest until they were found. But if the cops confiscated it, there wasn't much they could do.

Jocko was leaning against the hood of the Escalade, thinking he would just sneak off and was patting his pockets looking for the keys. Gran sat on the back bumper of Brick's truck watching him. Clint went up to where Stoney was to get his supplies for the fire and Brick just stood beside the trailer watching Gran and Jocko.

"I thought you were leaving with Charlie," Brick said to Gran.

"I want to know what happens to this bloody piece of shit first," Gran said.

"I'm leaving," Jocko asserted.

"Not in the Cadillac—I'm taking that. You plan to walk?"

Jocko still had the Beretta stuck in the back of his jeans and felt bolder when he said, "I've taken all the shit I'm going to from you."

Gran held up the keys to the Escalade he had snatched from the ignition. "I asked how?" then he threw the keys in the dirt at the Aussie's feet.

"Fuck you, I'm leaving in my car." Jocko was spitting mad as he leaned down to retrieve the keys with his injured left hand and reached for the gun at his back.

Gran said, "You're a cheeky cunt for a tout." Then he took three long strides, twisting his body to the right. He jumped into a spin on to his left side, with his left foot missing Jocko's chin by a fraction of an inch and as his right came around, it kicked his head up and was followed by the right hand with the knife, slicing through his carotid artery so deep it took part of the larynx with it. Blood spurted out in a stream, covering the hood of the car. It continued to pump with every beat of his heart until Jocko lay dead at Gran's feet.

Gran looked sad when he met Brick's steady eyes and said, "I know you said he could split … but mate, he was yanking a pistol. A gun you gave him. He fucked us—a sniveling twit. He'd have cocked it up your buff. Straight to that treasonous chippy Raoul or done up like a kipper. I'd bet a tenner the peelers nicked em at the bum of the hill."

Brick sighed. "I know, I made the promise; you didn't. Let's finish this shit and get the fuck out of Dodge. Cops are minutes behind."

Sixty-four

Brick drove to the airport in Bend with Clint and Gran. They left Clint there; Stoney arrived with the rental they returned before they boarded flights. The men said a brief goodbye; then Gran and Brick continued on to the rented farmhouse where Charlie was waiting for the chopper with Keith. Charlie still had the juice to have a little bird land without authorization in the bare field behind the house and airlift Keith to the vet's hospital at Fort Lewis.

Brick left the other two to wipe down fingerprints and clean out the farmhouse, with directions to regroup at Harry's. It was late when Charlie and Gran drove separate vehicles into the yard. All lights were still ablaze, with the occupants glued to the TV coverage of the fire and massacre at the ranch. Gill was the lead investigator and the news vans showed glimpses of his back as the various stations strove to gain ground for breaking coverage. The big network outlets had helicopters in the air, but the space was being protected by police choppers. Every available police and sheriff's department from fifty square miles were in attendance, along with all available ambulances and hearses.

As usual it was to no avail; it was already over, just the cleanup and investigation left. It would keep Gill and all pertinent police personnel busy for weeks, if not months, focused on this event without a possible conclusion other than the obvious. The roadblocks and traffic stops continued for four days, but with hundreds of secondary and logging roads in the area it was about a 1 percent chance that it would be fruitful. It was national news for three days, so the networks felt the excessive coverage was justified.

Gill had been to this ranch several times in the past year. It had always felt wrong. All these hard Latinos standing around. This wasn't how

Bend was. He had nothing against immigrants; they were usually good people. He knew bad guys, seen plenty in his time. These were very bad motherfuckers. But he was the new guy. The ex-sheriff said he knew the owner and it was cool; they were good guys. Of course, Casper hadn't been out since Brick left, so he didn't have a clue. Now Gill wished he would have ignored the sheriff's advice.

They stored the Suburban with all the guns and gear in the garage, and Mason covered it with a canvas tarp. The next morning Brick drove Charlie to the airport, where he would catch a ride to Fort Lewis with an army unit. Brick and Gran both stayed a week at Mason and Harriette's. They ran together each day challenging the hills, competitive still, with their bond stronger from the experience. They spent time roiling with laughter at their days together at Harvard and recalled images of carefree times and camaraderie, the follies of their youth reminding them of the brotherly love they shared.

Sixty-five

It should have been a mellow week. Half the job finished, at least from this end, but the next step would be much harder. I was an emotional wreck. I talked to Laura. The boys I had the altercation with followed and threatened her—all my fault. And then there was Dawn here every night in the flesh and what lovely flesh. In my bed and in my head. Nights were filled with guilty passion and days with guilty confusion. I owed them more; leaving when they needed me most was a chicken shit thing to do. I had to finish what we started and the men were waiting. Dawn wanted to go with me; Laura wanted me to come back. Sometimes I thought, *Great, I'll take you both and we can all die together.* How do I get myself into this crap? I should take a vow of celibacy, but I know I wouldn't keep it. I love women, but I always seem to fuck it up. I wasn't sleeping.

Without the pressure and a crisis to keep him occupied, Granville was a different man—carefree and funny. With his dry sardonic British wit, he kept Harriette and Mason in stitches whenever he was around. After a few days, he started disappearing each night without explanation. The mystery remained until one morning just after dawn when Harriette was up making a nice breakfast, and a tall woman with long auburn hair walked past her kitchen window. Peering out, she saw the woman was wearing baggy sweatpants and a man's dress shirt and carrying a dress and high heels. Harriette walked out on the front porch and intercepted her as she rounded the house.

"Good morning! I remember you from the party ... Kelly, right?"

She was heading for Gran's Mercedes, so it was pretty obvious why she was doing the walk of shame at dawn. "Yes, you have a good memory. Thanks, I was just ..."

317

"Yes, I can see but don't go; come in and keep me company. I could use another woman to talk to, seems like we're the only ones up this early. There's so much testosterone around here lately, I need a break and you look like you could use a good breakfast."

"Well, I should probably go."

"Nonsense, this is a guilt-free zone; nobody's going to judge you."

Kelly wound up spending the day and was treated to a great dinner that evening. The only one in the house with a bad attitude was Brick. He couldn't relax; the idea of a hit was like an itch he couldn't scratch. He went for long walks thinking back to who besides Raoul could have a reason to put a contract out on his life. Going back over every detail about those days ... the drug lords and their minions were the obvious answer. The only way they could have gotten on to him was through Raoul, but he didn't really know much; Jesus kept him in the dark on all their business dealings. Plus, if it were the cartels, they would have come down like a swarm of locusts and destroyed the town. He knew Raoul was working with at least one cartel in order to have a steady supply chain. His problem with Raoul was personal, no reason to get the cartel involved. They expected Raoul to clean up his own problems. Who could it be?

Charlie had called to report that Keith was healing and all was well. The boys from the base were treating him to a good time and soon Charlie would head back to Austin to catch up with the security business. They were all waiting for the smoke to clear and things to settle down. It was then that Brick got a call from Bucky. The authorities wanted to question him regarding the ownership of the ranch. So one morning he strolled in to the police station and put on a show for Gill, playing the pissed-off property owner who got fucked over by a tenant. He ranted on about the damages and bitched that now he couldn't sell the land with the horrible reputation. He practically accused the police of causing the damage and wouldn't shut up about his loss. Gill was happy to see him go.

A week later the two men said their goodbyes to their friends and headed east in Brick's truck. Mason promised to bring the Mercedes to Fort Rilea, where Charlie would have it loaded on the next C-130 headed back. It was the end of June and the roads were perfect. The two men settled into an easy silence as they took turns driving. The job at hand, a reconnaissance of the enemy's lair. This stage would be next to impossible. Raoul's complex was formidable, a fortress. First, they had a stop to make it right with Laura.

Dawn made it easy for Brick when the time came. She'd done her best to wear him out the previous night, but said she understood he had to go, even though she didn't. It was hard to leave; he worried about Mason and Harry, but promised to stay in touch. Dawn was the toughest; she wasn't the flighty scattered girl he once knew. She had grown into a lovely and intelligent woman, but he couldn't think straight with her around.

Gran waxed philosophical as the miles passed: "Can't toss it off, mate. There be dragons and like it or not, we be slayers. Some cower under the shadow of the beast with fear of the flames. We're the black knights and we stand against oppression with spears and swords, rusty though they be. Tis in the blood I tell you. You worry too much. We'll get the punters sorted right quick. Look about, mate—is it not a glorious day to die?"

Sixty-six

The new day was clear and China blue. Cloudless without a trace of white when Brick and Gran rode into Glendive. The first days of July in Montana made the term big-sky country fact—the horizon stretched to heaven. They spent the day scoping out the town and made sure that Laura was at work. They were careful and, to be as inconspicuous as possible, split up and did the reconnaissance of the town on foot. When they were sure of their anonymity, they made their move.

Ansel was pissed. He stormed into his kitchen with Billy trailing on his ass. They had wasted the entire afternoon at the clinic waiting on a doctor who, two hours late, was claiming to have been in surgery. After a sleepless night, this day was pure shit for father and son. Ansel wasn't used to kissing ass and the morning had been a colossal cluster fuck. As usual it was Billy's fault; the fucking kid just couldn't leave the bitch alone.

He'd been warned many times to leave it, but it wasn't in his nature. Billy had snuck out of the house three days previously and took the truck that Ansel said was off limits and confronted the girl outside her work, right in front of several witnesses. Someone called the cops and after hearing the witnesses and Laura's account of his threats, they hauled him straight to jail. Once a bully holding most of the town in his twisted grip, Billy felt his loss as if he'd been gutted. He was in a walking cast now and the right wrist had a hard shell to protect him from himself.

Ansel's trip to the jail this morning was disheartening and demoralizing. John Bauer, the sheriff, had been a buddy growing up—hell, they played hockey together since they were kids. Now it seemed like the whole town had turned against him. John wouldn't stop yelling obscenities.

320

He blamed Billy for most every shitty thing that happened in the area over the last few years, and then he blamed Ansel for allowing it.

This time the kid stepped in it. The broad was claiming everything from attempted rape to terroristic threats and assault. Billy ended up spending three days in the slammer, and Ansel had to call in every chit he was owed, kiss ass for a mile, and still post a fifty-thousand-dollar bond. He was released into Ansel's custody at 8:00 this morning. Today they had tried, unsuccessfully, to convince the doctor that the medication from Billy's injuries confused his mind and led to hallucinations. Billy was facing serious time.

This had been their home for twenty-five years. Billy was born here; his wife, Emma, had died here; and Ansel considered this his castle and sanctuary. It made the invasion after jail seem like a rape. In fact, at first it was surreal—like a bad trip on acid along with the jolt of Kickapoo Joy Juice—and they both froze, not believing their ears.

There it was again: the mocking British voice that stunned Billy and made Ansel's blood pause. It was clear enough and came from the other room. The kitchen was at the back with an entrance door, a pantry, and two doorways, one leading to the living room and the other a hallway to the bedrooms and den. The voice definitely came from the living room.

"A mistake, laddie, a big fucking beautiful mistake," said Gran's voice.

He walked into the kitchen holding Emma's picture in his hand. It was a dismal scene—dated yellow linoleum floors and chipped Formica countertops set off by the olive green appliances; it screamed seventies.

"A fine-looking woman." He laid the picture facedown on the worn counter. "Poor lass must be shamed at what trash her family has come to." It was said with the trademark smirk. "I'll just lay this down and spare the lass the sight of you wankers."

Billy reached into the drawer at his side and pulled an old Army Colt revolver, pointing it at Gran's head. Ansel went to the broom closet and found it empty. He tried to exit through the door they had just entered but was blocked by Brick waiting with the missing shotgun.

Billy fired from point-blank range. Click … click, click. Gran opened his hand and the bullets clinked on the dirty linoleum.

Ansel tried to rush Brick, but the stock of the gun sunk into his sizable belly and he fell, curling in a ball on the floor.

Billy opened another drawer and extracted a large kitchen knife.

"It's to be knives then, is it? Bloody good show; come teach old Gran some tricky moves, laddie."

Brick said, "I'll warn you once; don't do it."

But of course he did. He lunged at Gran's chest, which the Englishman sidestepped with ease and then pushed his face into the wall. Billy roared like a caged lion and came at him again with the knife raised over his head. Gran laughed, his hands empty. The two men circled each other, Billy furious; with eyes seething in rage he lunged, the knife slicing through air and sticking in the door frame next to Gran. His left fist was still holding the knife against the wall from the momentum.

With lightning speed, the switchblade clicked open and was driven through the left hand, pinning it to the wall. Gran moved behind him, kneed him in the small of his back, and used his free hand to gain purchase on Billy's right forefinger sticking up from the cast, yanking it back until it snapped and the kitchen knife clattered to the floor. His hand was pinned fast to the wall.

"For a wanker, you're a sniveling cunt. Listen up, trash. I do this shit for a living, but I fuck arseholes like you up 'cause I fancy it. We're pros—you can't win; you can only die, I guaran-fucking-tee it. Last warning … let the bitch be." Gran pulled the knife free and swept his legs, leaving him crumpled at his feet.

Brick pressed the barrel of the shotgun into Ansel's throat. "Are we clear, old man?"

A weak reply: "Yes."

"I should shoot you both right now. What do you say?"

"I'm sorry."

"And your dickhead son?"

A squeak from across the room, "Yes, damn it; yes, it's over."

"Next time you're dead."

Gran kicked Billy in the ribs. "Are we clear, you fucking cunt?"

He weakly nodded his head and Gran kicked him again. As they walked out the back door, Brick swung the shotgun against the jam, breaking it in two. They both drew handguns and emptied the clips in the windows and tires of the tow truck. When twenty feet away, Gran threw a match at the trail of gas, and the garage and shed billowed into fireballs. He looked at Brick and said, "Making a point, mate; don't fancy the punters dismissing a harsh nip—thick cunts, the lot." They walked off.

They spent the next two days at the lodge, where Brick explained to Laura well as he could why the mission wasn't finished. There was never an option of her going with them. After two days in the company of the Englishman, Laura was convinced that the man was nuts and she didn't argue. It wasn't Brick's reassurances that convinced her but rather the chilling look in Granville's eyes that did the trick. He made it clear that she wouldn't be bothered again or someone would die. She realized that she didn't need the drama. This wasn't the life for her. Brick was fun for a romp but it was over.

Sixty-seven

It had been two weeks since the activity on the hill slowed to a trickle. The asshole detective had been by twice with probing questions that he made sound like accusations. Hank remained stoic throughout the ordeal; all Gill had was suspicions, no facts. Hank thought it funny how he wasn't accused of the crimes he'd actually committed. He was becoming overconfident, which made him ripe for a picking.

Molly was in tears as she walked home alone. Janie was so stupid and mean sometimes. She was supposed to be her best friend, but was flirting with Ben in the malt shop. When Molly confronted her, she became a total bitch and said she could talk to whoever she wanted. She knew that Molly was sweet on him; she could have picked any other boy in town but she had to choose dear, sweet Ben.

These were the thoughts that preoccupied her mind as she headed down the country road around the woods. It was a long walk this way, but at least she wouldn't have to face any snooping, gossiping kids she always seemed to run into in her worst moments. Her folks were going out and her mom said she'd leave a casserole in the fridge for her to warm for dinner. Her brat brother was at a sleepover and it was Friday night. Her only companions—depression and teenage angst.

She'd lingered so long at the malt shop that now on that deserted country road, the shadows were long and fading with the sun. It was late, much later than her curfew, but she knew her house would be empty; besides, she was tired of being a goodie two-shoes. Her own shadow appeared to be nine feet tall and freakishly distorted as she trailed it along the edge of the road.

As she rounded the last long bend before the trees thinned and blocks of houses began to form, she saw a pickup truck with a camper shell covering the bed. The truck had pulled in at the shoulder without lights. It was a common occurrence along these roads; people stopped for a multitude of reasons—to pick wildflowers, walk the paths, or even (in the case of men and boys) to relieve themselves. Molly had been lost in thought, but now something caused a chill to ripple up her spine and spark her lizard brain, releasing a rush of adrenaline that shook her from her trance.

For a flash moment she considered turning back, but it was a very long detour and she craved the comfort of her home. It was so quiet, almost as though the normal rustlings of woodland creatures had ceased with the wind. So, crossing to the far side of the road with caution, she inched her way along the opposite shoulder with her head on a swivel as the hair on the back of her neck stood stiff and her upper lip coated with sweat. When she came abreast of the driver's side window of the truck, her steady gaze could have melted the glass. No one there. With a sigh of relief, she quickened her pace and soon was well past it.

Like an ancient bird of prey swooping from the sky, a dark presence suddenly wrapped her arms and torso with iron talons honed by past victims that rendered flesh and pinned her tight as a shroud. One horned claw clamped her mouth immobile in a vise and trapped the scream rising from her throat. Then she was airborne, light as a butterfly across the road, and thrown in the bed of the truck as a gag replaced the brutish hand. Her arms were trapped behind her back and cold metal bracelets secured her. Her legs were bound with what felt like wire and she was hog-tied, unable to move. She was invisible from detection as the camper shell was windowless. It was over in twenty seconds. The pain and agony painted her features a mask of horror.

With a face filled with heat, detective Gill Riley sat in his office with the steaming coffee matching the steam rising from his head. As soon as he walked into the station this morning, he was summoned to the sheriff's office, where he sat like a petulant child while dressed down, as his shortcomings were arranged like a grocery list: The lumber guy, Tony was his name, had complained that Gill was harassing him and his employees without reason. It followed from there to the war that left half a mountainside burning and littered with drugs and dead bodies. No suspects and no leads, and it was all Gill's fault—the unchecked meth trade that scoured the countryside on which he had made zero progress.

The frosting on this morning's cupcake was the missing girls that Gill had practically been accused of ignoring or at least giving a milk toast effort. Never mind that the girls were what kept him up at night. Gill knew shit ran downhill and the sheriff had been in the middle of the shit storm from the county commissioners and the mayor, but still … he didn't deserve this.

The drugs were a part of the modern culture, the same here as Brooklyn. It was this way for longer than Gill could remember, and it would be with them until some sensible laws were passed. It was like prostitution—it had always been and would always be. Most cops wouldn't cross the street for a pot bust unless it was a career maker. No … what hurt was the girls and their families. He was positive the innocent girls suffered unthinkable horrors at the hands of some animal, but the pain of their loss would last a lifetime for those left behind.

So fuck the lumber guy and fuck the mayor. If they think they could do better, then he would surrender his badge and they could kiss his ass. But until that happened he would follow his gut and pursue his only good suspect. This wasn't just the job; it was personal.

Sixty-eight

Charlie was vague about his plans and whereabouts; he said he was taking care of business and had pressing issues with the company in Austin. His current location was a mystery. He assured Brick that he'd be there when needed, but didn't they have some reconnaissance and research before pinning the rodent in a cage? Brick knew he could count on his old friend, but wondered what the wily old warrior was up to with all the secrecy.

Yet he soon forgot about Charlie when after four days on the road, not counting the time in Glendive, he reached the verdant river valley of his hometown. The corn and barley fields were planted and Minnesota was in full bloom, her glory released from the bitter constraints of the ancient glacier that had once threatened all of North America. With its ten thousand lakes, swollen rivers, and multitude of streams and creeks, fresh, pure water had never been in short supply in this state. This was the Midwest, breadbasket of the country, with agriculture dominating the economy since the first settlers had stopped on their journey westward to make their stand.

It was also a natural playground for later generations of outdoor and sportsmen featuring some of the finest hunting and fishing land in the country. Along with both summer and winter sports, there were plenty of other activities to keep the residents of Minnesota busy year-round, despite the frigid winter it was so famous for.

The long drive had been a bit of a blessing. The Englishman became subdued and made for a good companion. Both men were comfortable with long periods of silence, so Brick's mind wondered ... He still couldn't make sense of the supposed hit; Jocko had seemed so confident about it. If Raoul hadn't been stroking the man and it was true, then who would have issued the contract? His mind would pause as he tried to think past Panama and Mexico. Colombia was out of the question; as far as the cartels knew back then, it was the US Army who ripped them off. Nothing to be done—unless there was a mole. It had to trace back to Jesus. Still, if that was true, a squad of fifty armed men would have descended on the cabin like a wet blanket.

The one piece of reliable intel they gleaned from Jocko was the approximate location of Raoul's compound in Minnesota. Brick smiled at the thought. Raoul must have learned this information from Jesus. Having the base in his home state was intentional. The reasons were threefold. The south and west were the natural locations for such an operation, but they were saturated with cartels with planes, tunnels, and trucks. Most drugs entered from the south and the entire area was covered. Minnesota was in the middle of the country and a large plane or chopper headed north from Oklahoma was invisible to the drug cops. The Canadian border was less than five hundred miles from the Twin Cities. Canada was a brand-new marketplace for cocaine and Raoul saw the possibilities.

The two friends stayed in a Radisson in downtown Saint Paul for a couple of days as they pored over aerial and land maps trying to determine Raoul's exact location.

The name Hazeltine was common in Minnesota There was the Hazeltine National Golf Club, where PGA tournaments were held every few years. The most famous Hazeltine, though, was actually Hazelden—as in the Hazelden clinic, where world-famous drunks and junkies came to dry out. Hazeltine or Hazelden, outsiders didn't know the difference. Both were situated in remote and spacious locations. This made the whole areas ideal for a sprawling complex of buildings that could easily house drugs. The constant movements of semi-trailers, cargo vans, and light truck traffic tended to blend in.

From the aerial images, they were finally able to pinpoint a cluster of large nondescript buildings without any known designation. They changed their base the following morning to a Best Western on Highway 7. For the next week they discreetly mapped the back roads, interconnecting trails, and footpaths. They took hundreds of pictures and gathered the reconnaissance gear they didn't already have access to.

Gran had another drone sent out, but they still had to get close enough to control the damn thing and that was a challenge. Back at the army supply post, they were very lucky to score a couple of ghillie suits. So at two in the morning the two men climbed the highest rise and crawled on their bellies to as close a vantage point as they dared. It took them two hours but they were in position when the sun rose and they blended in with a clump of bushes. This wasn't their first rodeo, though the real pro at this was Charlie; they managed without him. They had water, energy bars, and optics for observation and the drone. The call of nature was the biggest deterrent, but again they were prepared.

Once settled they needed to stay put for nearly twenty-four hours, but it was worth it—they were able to map the buildings and follow the traffic flow. There were six structures clustered around a huge colonial-style house with white pillars guarding the entrance that they assumed was Raoul's residence, though they never saw him that first day. Another ranch-style rectangular box housed the permanent staff, and five solid concrete warehouses with sixteen-foot-high double steel doors were an indication of stored goods.

The complex sat on roughly twelve acres of land that was mostly flat with grass, bushes, and scrub. There were a few sparse windblown trees, nothing big enough to provide cover. It was a perfect location isolated enough from any known landmark that might draw attention. During the course of the day, the grounds were searched twice. The same six men both times spread wide. A lot of ground to cover, so it was mostly superficial. The men looked bored and Brick could tell they were loafing and did a half-assed job. They'd been doing this so long without incident, they had become sloppy. On one pass, a man walked next to Gran's position without a second glance. He could have reached out and grabbed his ankle, he was that close.

After that first day, Brick and Gran took turns. The routine was predictable and within a couple of days they had a schedule. On the third day, Brick was on watch when Raoul left the big house. The car pulled in front of the house with two Mexican-looking toughs. Both men looked formidable, larger than most Mexicans with the heavy bulk of body builders, their suit coats stretched tight across the shoulders and the telltale bulges of weapons under their arms. Raoul had put on a lot of weight. He was at least a foot shorter than the bodyguards. His hair was thinning and all traces of youth had disappeared and the sneer was better. He started barking orders in Spanish. Good to see he was still a prick. After ten or so minutes, he climbed into the back seat of a Bimmer, the driver and man riding shotgun accompanied him, and they left by the only road in or out of the compound.

There was a narrow trail used by animals and hikers leading across the back of the property, but it lay exposed for at least two hundred yards. The options for a frontal attack were slim, nearly impossible. The only viable alternative was by air, but both men dismissed that idea because of the attention it would draw from the locals. They would have to make their move at a time like this when he left the site and could be intercepted in a remote spot.

Brick risked a quick text to Gran: follow and observe. They prepared for this contingency when they agreed to split their watch. Gran was parked on a side road out of sight waiting for them to choose a direction. He allowed two cars to pass before falling in, keeping a respectable distance. When they stopped, he would possibly have an opportunity to attach a bug under the BMW.

They drove at a steady pace, staying within the speed limit for almost thirty miles. Technically, their location was in Chaska, but the designation between townships was slight, so most of these western suburbs were like a drunken picket fence. The narrow lanes and twisty country roads were a pisser. When Gran saw the signs for Chanhassen, the lead car slowed and shifted to city streets until they came to a large modern complex with a discreet sign announcing Paisley Park Recording Studio. They approached the famous artist's studio, where Prince made legendary recordings and was known to throw pop-up concerts. The grounds were surrounded by a chain-link fence ten feet high. The gates opened and the Bimmer drove through; the gates closed.

Gran watched from a distance as Raoul exited the car parked near the front door. He was obviously expected, as a smartly dressed black man came out to greet him. The two men went inside while Raoul's guards turned the car around and waited in the driveway next to a smaller building. They waited for an hour until he returned. The trip back mimicked the drive in.

Sixty-nine

Molly struggled against her bindings, tossing her body a scant few inches from side to side in a desperate effort to escape but to no avail. The restraints held fast and true. They'd been moving for over half an hour, but to her it seemed like an eternity. They left the smooth blacktop ten minutes ago and the truck was bouncing along a bumpy road until it finally stopped inside a clean modern garage. She heard a door open and close and the sound of receding footsteps echoing on concrete. Her mind reeling, body frozen with terror, she strained against her bonds with the tendons in her neck standing taut as wire, her heart thudding and about to burst.

She forced herself to settle down; gasping for breath, she twisted her head as far as she could. In the faint light emanating from the garage, she noticed a hard ridge in the bed of the truck protruding with a slight fragment of a nail head or something sharp next to her right cheek. She rubbed the edge of her gag against it and felt the gag begin to slip. She felt a glimmer of hope as it moved an inch. Her neck began to ache with the effort, but she redoubled her struggle and at last it came free.

At first her dry raspy throat failed to produce sound, but as she worked her saliva to moisten her lips and throat, she found her voice and screamed as loud as she ever had: "HELP ME! PLEASE, SOMEONE HELP ME!" The sound echoed in the empty garage and came back to her ears weak and feeble. She lay in the back screaming like that for over an hour, maybe two, until her throat was so raw and sore, she collapsed sobbing with snot covering her mouth and chin. Her total despair was draining what little energy she had left.

She heard footsteps coming in her direction and continued to scream even as her sore throat protested in agony. *Bang,* the tailgate of the truck opened hard and the lid of the topper raised as she continued to beg,

"Please help me, help me!" Her feet were untethered and two strong hands pulled her free. Now she was looking into the wild eyes of her captor; his bushy beard and long greasy hair sent another cold chill of fear rippling along her spine and a sinking desperation into her heart.

He threw back his head and roared his laughter as wild as a lunatic. "Go ahead—scream you're fucking head off. No one can help you now, you little bitch."

She kicked at him with a fury she had never felt before, but he was ready for her. Trapping her legs in one mighty arm, he slipped the flex cuff over her ankles and rebound her feet. He replaced the gag and lifted her out, light as a feather, and deposited her in the cart hitched to his ATV.

"We're going to the cave now and have us some fun, at least I am." His crazy laughter trailed after them as he hit the lights and they left the garage and bumped toward the cave.

As night descended over the open field, Brick made his way back and the two men rendezvoused at the motel. They agreed the best way to approach this was to take Raoul when he was away. He obviously didn't think he was in any danger, so he wasn't on high alert. This might not be so hard after all. Their call to Charlie went unanswered, so Brick made contact with Stoney and Clint and they agreed to come out in five days to help. *Where the hell is Charlie?* They went to dinner and pored over their plans and the surveillance photos until Brick had it all memorized.

The next morning Brick tried Charlie again; still no answer. He went to Prince's website and found reference to a spontaneous concert he had planned for the following Saturday, which was only six days away. They hadn't been able to get close enough to Raoul's lair to plant a listening device, so they were in the dark as to what he might do. But the men agreed that Raoul attending this event seemed a good bet. The timing would be tight, but it was doable. Brick committed but would have felt a lot better if Charlie were by their side.

Charlie had been busy. When he left them, he went directly to Fort Lewis in Washington outside Tacoma to check on Keith and touch base with some old cronies who helped him out occasionally. Keith was recovering remarkably well and things seemed in order. Charlie then left for Camp Rilea in the far northwest corner of Oregon near Astoria. It housed an Air Force base and a sprawling airport with a wide range of planes and choppers. He wanted to secure a few rides to bases around the country, especially to Fort Snelling, the old stronghold overlooking the Mississippi at the eastern edge of Minneapolis.

The Air Force and Rangers had been an enormous help to the security company he co-owned in Austin. Washington wasn't aware of the cooperation, but the network of loyal friends figured, fuck-em. The trips are scheduled; if the passenger manifest isn't complete, who's to know?

During this time his friends were driving back to Brick and Charlie's hometown, but Charlie couldn't make himself available to them just yet. After taking care of his business obligations, the warrior had a nagging feeling haunting him. He caught a jump on a Black Hawk and headed back to Bend. He had posted alerts on his phone to signal certain events in a few select places. This one hit a panic button in his heart and he was speeding toward it.

Raoul had his own concerns. The raid at the ranch had shaken him to the quick. Not only had he lost a great deal of money and some trusted associates, but now Don Carlo was crawling up his ass and demanding to know how this happened and what he would do to fix it. He had learned the hard way that it wasn't wise to piss off Don Carlo. The most frustrating thing for Raoul was he didn't have a clue as to what had gone wrong. It seemed under control, easy even. That fool Jocko must have somehow fucked it up.

Now he was expected to work for free until the Don had recouped his loses. Raoul was impossible to be around. He ranted and raved at his men, babbling incoherently at times and shouting senseless orders at others. His only solace was in his friend Jimmy Natchez who was working with Prince's crew; artists liked their weed and coke. That was Raoul's in with the musicians and Raoul loved hanging with celebrities.

He had scored an invitation to the impromptu concert next Saturday, so he set about rounding up the best-looking Putas to use as eye candy. He saw himself arriving in a white stretch limo with a car full of hot women and drugs. Perhaps the great man would take notice and include Raoul in more parties with celebrity friends. He hated to lose at anything, but could afford the loss. The party was a good distraction, but soon his mind would return to Oregon.

The greater mystery was what really happened at the ranch and who he could blame. His drugs weren't missing or he could have followed the trail. They were in a locked room probably in the custody of the DEA. *Had anyone been captured? Are men ratting him out now to save their sorry asses?* If the authorities were planning a raid, he needed to clean house until squeaky.

When Gill received the call from Molly's parents, his heart froze. *Not another one, not on my watch!* His gut was tearing him to pieces. He stored bottles of Tums in the office, car, and home, devouring them like candy. Every man on the force was out combing the back roads and hillsides to find the girl. Overtime be damned, he had to find her before he went insane. He just couldn't face telling another set of parents the horrible news of their daughter's fate. If he could only find her before it was too late. *Fuck a bunch of protocol!* He headed to Hank Johnson's place. It was late but he was going to roust that fucker until he squealed like the pig he was.

Seventy

Charlie was dropped back in Bend and his first stop was Harriett and Mason's place. An army colonel lent him a car and he skidded into their drive; they confirmed his information—another young girl was missing. After explaining his plan and enlisting their help when called, he checked his gear and headed to where he was convinced he was needed. The question was, would he arrive in time?

The ATV bumped along the hillside at a slow, deliberate pace. Juddiah had learned from experience that a bound, helpless girl in the cart could be bounced out if he tried to move too fast. It was hard to go slow—his lust was at a fever pitch—but he forced himself to be patient. He stopped several times and killed the lights and engine, then listened to the night sounds. All seemed as it should be.

When they were near the entrance, he stopped, turned off the lights and motor, and waited for his eyes to adjust to the surrounding darkness. When they did, he got off and did a wide search of the area. He checked above and below the entrance and made a couple of circles moving farther out as he went. When he convinced himself that all was quiet, he went back to the ATV. Attached under the right handlebar was a compact remote control. He pressed a button and the boulder guarding the entrance rolled silently back.

He went to the opening and lit a kerosene lantern. Moving through the rooms, he lit candles and checked to make sure all was in order before returning for the girl. Stepping back out of the cave, he looked at his four-wheeler and had to blink his eyes—he couldn't accept what he saw. A man dressed in camouflage was bending down releasing the girl. He had already cut her ankles free and was removing the gag.

Juddiah roared his indignation, *How dare he interfere!* At the sound, the man turned to face him and recognition lit Juddiah's features—*the fucking soldier boy was back!* He grabbed an axe he kept by the cave entrance and started his charge. He was brought up short by the pistol now pointing directly in his face.

Charlie said, "Give me the keys to the handcuffs."

"Fuck you," he replied. "If you want 'em, come get 'em."

Charlie leaned down and spoke softly in Molly's ear: "Walk down the hill. Go slow so you don't fall. When you get to the bottom, hide. I'll come for you in a bit and take you home. If I don't, hide till morning and then make your way to the road. Go now."

Molly started walking away in a slow, careful gait still sobbing.

Juddiah made a move to follow and Charlie raised the gun again. He didn't bring his rifle, just the Sig .40 caliber and the long K-bar military issue knife, the scabbard strapped to his leg.

Juddiah said, "If you were going to shoot me, you would have done it already, so fuck you, soldier boy."

Charlie holstered his weapon. The big man summoned a wicked grin and reached back in the cave for another axe. He hefted them both and, deciding, threw one at Charlie's head and charged in behind it. Charlie grabbed it out of the air one-handed and ducked just in time to avoid the axe blade as it whistled over his head.

The man was faster than his size would indicate. He moved with quick, guarded steps. He was up on the balls of his feet, holding the blade in expert fashion. Charlie feinted right and spun left looking for an opening; there was none. Juddiah had anticipated the move and countered. Juddiah went on the attack, moving deliberately slow, almost dancing in a choreographed method meant to keep his opponent off balance and defensive.

Charlie would bet his pension that Juddiah won every battle this way. His massive size was intimidating; a longer reach with the axe gave him a physical advantage over most men. Plus, he was at home in his environment and the axe was an extension of his thick forearms and deep chest. He handled an axe with sure hands. It was held without effort, the way another man would handle a jackknife. Charlie took note that the axe Juddiah kept was longer and double-bladed, sharp. Charlie was given the shorter weapon whose single blade and blunt hammer-like back were nicked and dull.

Within seconds, all these impressions were recognized, analyzed, and tested against the great storehouse of knowledge of hand-to-hand combat residing in the soldier's computer-like mind. He countered by doing something that no one had ever tried before. Instead of backing away, he moved in with lightning speed too close to swing at and, using short jabs with the axe's head, pummeled Juddiah's midsection knocking the air from his lungs.

Feinting left, Charlie's body unwound to the right as his right boot came whistling through the air and landed with a solid thump against the big man's jaw. Juddiah fell back, shocked and hurt for maybe the first time in his life. Recognition brought a fresh bout of fury to the beast's face. He charged again, determined to finish his opponent, but then Charlie had disappeared only to reappear behind him and he swung the hammerhead into the left kidney.

Juddiah dropped to one knee and Charlie kicked him in the face, breaking his nose. With blood pouring over his lips and chin, Juddiah somehow managed to stand and turn; Charlie moved inside again and drove the head of the axe into the soft folds of his belly once more. This time the air whooshed out in an audible gasp. Still, somehow he stood. The man looked beaten, but he seemed to have found an inner strength; a moment later, he produced a hunting knife and came at Charlie, opening a long cut above his shoulder.

Now it was Charlie's turn to be surprised, but the expert soldier immediately went to work with renewed effort and brought all of his speed and training to bear against his larger opponent. He feinted and spun, threw a devastating kick to the other kidney. Juddiah screamed in pain and Charlie used the hammer side to smash his right kneecap. Juddiah went down but to only one knee, leaving the intact one raised. He swung his double-bladed axe wildly and Charlie responded by smashing the other kneecap.

As he gasped in pain, his attention was suddenly diverted. Juddiah's face lit in recognition. "Noah, thank God, finally. Kill him."

Charlie turned to look: standing not more than six feet away was Hank Johnson with his shotgun aimed at Charlie's belly. Without time to think it through, Charlie threw his knife; it caught Hank in the throat. As the big man sank slowly to his knees, the shotgun fell to the ground. He couched once and a spurt of blood erupted from his mouth; he died on his knees.

Juddiah thrashed on the ground screaming obscenities at the world. Charlie responded by breaking both of Juddiah's elbows. Juddiah could no longer move and lay broken. Confident that his opponent was finally incapacitated, Charlie went into the cave and explored its depths with the kerosene lantern. When he again appeared outside, he was in anguish. The nightmare images and ghastly souvenirs stored within the bowels of the cave were unbearable to see. The sick minds that had caused so much misery, despair, and loss lay crumpled before him, defeated at last; one still alive, barely. It was not enough.

Charlie drew his Sig and pointed it at the monster's head. He cocked back the hammer but his steady hand wavered, his vision blurred, and he lowered the gun. He started walking down the hill, then stopped, started, stopped again. He shook his head at the thought, his mind racing— killing was too good for him … but was this enough?

Charlie stood like a statue for a full minute and then, building his resolve, he returned to the prone figure before him; he steeled his nerves and removed the bootlace from one of the monster's feet. He knelt with gloved hands and pulled the k-bar knife from Hanks throat and cut away the Juddiah's pants to expose his genitals. The long, thick penis lay like a bloated sausage covering the large testicles. With renewed resolve, Charlie wound the bootlace around the testicles and formed a tight knot, cutting off circulation. With fast, sure moves, he slit the sack and speared each ball with the tip of the knife, then flicked them into the woods.

Afterward, Charlie quickened his pace back to the house where the monsters had lived. As he drew close, Gill stepped out from behind the dwelling with his pistol raised in a two-handed stance. Molly was visible behind him.

"Stop right there," he ordered.

"I don't think so," replied Charlie. "The men you want are lying on the hill in front of a cave. I think they're brothers; they look almost the same. Probably why they avoided capture so long. You need to call a full forensic team and an ambulance," he finished.

Molly broke free and raced to Charlie and clung to his leg, sobbing. "Thank you, you saved my life."

Charlie said, "Get your teams here in a hurry or that man won't make it. I'm going to take Molly home."

Holding Molly around the shoulders, he walked past Gill and headed to his car. Gill holstered the weapon and grabbed his cell phone.

Seventy-one

When the cops got a look at Juddiah lying in the dirt, half-dead and unconscious, they sent out a bulletin on the man they believed did it, although the details of his appearance were sketchy. Gill claimed he didn't really get a good look at him, and the man had the drop on him. Once they had a look in the cave, interest in the man who was clearly Molly's savior waned.

Two days later, dressed in the uniform he wore for commendations, replete with general stars on the collar, he walked into Gill's office. Charlie stood at attention and waited.

"General, thank you for stopping by. I didn't expect to see you again, but I'm glad you're here. I have some information you might be interested in ... Yes, I know who you are and your many accomplishments in service to our country; I salute you." Gill stood and did just that. "Please have a seat and I'll explain what we've learned.

"I got this from Jeff Potter, sheriff and lead investigator on the case. Sheriff Potter located a former member of the church and he supplied details of the lives of the family. You were right, the boys were brothers, the Utterdahls; the oldest was Juddiah and Noah was two years his junior. Their father was a preacher who started a cult religion outside Falls Church, Idaho. He was an old-time fire-and-brimstone kind of guy, also big and strong, and he ruled his congregation with an iron fist.

"The church was based on free love, mostly sex. Every Saturday after services, the congregation dissolved in a free-for-all of sexual abandonment. Everybody screwed everybody else in the church; it was the number one rule. Small children were in attendance, so they all grew into deviants like their parents. They started sexual relations at the beginning of puberty, the age of twelve or thirteen; boys like them were broken in by their mothers and then the older women took turns.

"The girls, young, some very … were a prize for their fathers and then eventually the other elders who felt it was their right to do whatever their twisted deviant minds fantasized. As head of the church, the father, Jerimiah, had the option of deflowering any girl of his choosing. All the men, and especially his oldest son, resented the preacher for always picking the cream of the crop for his prize.

"Turns out, their mother, Grace, had a thing for shoes—flashy stiletto heeled and nasty looking. The dress of the group was plain and simple, featuring drab colors, so when she had sex she always wore a pair of the type we found. That must be where the boys got the fetish. Seems this ex-member was very close to the family and especially Grace, spent a fair amount of time in her bed.

"The rest is mostly speculation: Juddiah heard some kids singing about a woman named Lizzie Borden. It was a catchy tune and he loved how 'axe and whacks' had a magical ring. He was very good with an axe—had been chopping firewood since he could remember. It seems he liked the tool; he liked it a lot.

"Sally Crouthers was out picking a bouquet, fifteen years old and well developed for her age. Juddiah was sick of the worn-out older women and needed to experience fresh, young pussy. So he took her there in the middle of those flowers. He ravished her over and over. She fought him and he loved the fight, but it got out of hand and he wound up strangling her to death. He left her torn and bloody body lying in a field of beautiful yellow flowers. This was well documented by several of Sally's friends hiding nearby

"He was whistling the Lizzie Borden tune when he walked back into his yard three hours later. There were four of the largest men from the church and his father holding a horsewhip. He lashed the boy until he was unconscious and then locked him in the barn. Again members were reluctant witnesses to most everything that happened. This all came out during the investigation.

"Juddiah woke in the middle of the night and was in so much pain, he cried. The ex-member said they could hear him all over the compound. Then he saw the axe—they had locked him in with the axe. He stood tall and powerful as he towered over his sleeping parents, axe in hand. Seems he loved that too, forty whacks. The first took his father's right arm, the one he used to beat him. That was the nice thing about an axe, he thought, you could take pieces when and where you wanted.

"He didn't leave Idaho empty-handed. Besides the axe, he took his father's hidden cash—over $100,000 in a money belt around his waist— and the Caddy. He drove to the summer camp and plucked his younger brother, Noah, from the bunkhouse in the middle of the night and they were off before anyone discovered the crime. The members were so intimidated by the crazed brothers and fearful for their own lives that no one intervened.

"The killings led to the sex cult posing as religion and made national newscasts across the country. They posted numerous pictures of the two boys, but a massive multistate manhunt for the fugitives proved fruitless. Relatives of young Sally Crouthers posted a twenty-thousand-dollar reward, to no avail.

"Juddiah was crafty and very strong. He established himself in Oregon with a new identity—he was now Kirby Quinby, construction worker, living a quiet life in his apartment in Bend. This was after he killed the drifter for his ID. He saved his money, kept to himself, and pursued his hobby at the cave. He found the cave while wandering the hills looking for shelter, and after flushing the bats and a badger that he killed with the axe, he made it his own. He and his brother stayed hidden in the cave until they grew their hair and beards, becoming unrecognizable. After a couple of years, they were able to buy the land and build their base right below the cave. It was perfect for many years … until you came along. We discovered this in the last 24 hours.

"Yesterday I dropped in on Zoe at the Shoe and told her that her sister's killers had finally been brought to justice. She knows you quite well it seems, and I left a hint at who deserves credit, so don't be surprised if you hear from her. I felt we as a community had an obligation to tell her the truth."

Zoe was heading there now. Charlie had been staying with Mason and Harriette since he started surveillance at the cave. She caught him packing to leave. Her voice cracked with emotion and the tears were brimming in her red swollen eyes.

"Gill, I mean sheriff now, told me everything … I don't know what to say—thanks seems petty in comparison to what you did. You saved that poor girl and who knows how many others. Most important, you stopped those maniacs for good and solved my sister's murder."

Overcome with emotion, she broke down completely and sobbed hysterically. Charlie gathered her in his arms and held her tight as she buried her face in his neck. Once his shirt was soaked in her tears, the sobbing ceased; she kissed him hard on the lips. "It's okay, honey; now you can put Audrey and your demons to rest. Time to heal … and time for me to rejoin Brick; his ordeal isn't over until it's over." Charlie left soon after.

Seventy-two

The five Rangers were reunited on Wednesday, just three days before the planned concert. They all stayed at the same motel owned by Jimmy Stilton, an ex-serviceman who welcomed them and thought the squad was having a reunion. The first night of their stay, he bought them all drinks at the bar.

The plan was simple enough: they would arrive in two cars, with Brick and Gran in one, and Charlie, Stoney, and Clint in the other. This was a tricky mission; the timing needed to be perfect and the whole thing might need to be aborted. Find a better location. Play it by ear. They didn't expect trouble, but it usually found them.

They were two hours early and drove separately around the complex several times to establish specific intel on the layout. This concert was to be an upscale casual affair, a party atmosphere. They didn't want to attract attention with innocent people at risk. It would be dark at party time; that worked for them.

Charlie dropped Stoney and Clint off at the back of the complex with a set of wire cutters, then ditched the car and rode with his friends. The two advance men were dressed in slacks and collared shirts covering Kevlar vests. Sport coats concealed either hip or shoulder holsters. Silenced pistols and knives would be enough. Knives were best; fortunately Gran and Charlie excelled with their use. This wasn't some kamikaze massacre; it only involved one man.

There was a large crowd gathered in the courtyard before the concert. Prince was known for starting these events late. He was an artist and he'd start when he was good and ready. Those who knew him well lingered outside; many of the crew and guests smoked in the designated area.

The line of luxury cars was interspersed with a few limos as they queued up outside the gate. Stoney wasn't out of place in this part of Minnesota, he blended in with a number of large black men and women in the crowd. This was a diverse group, with many Spanish honchos and hotties peppering the throng. The only one who looked a little out of place was Clint, the little man with flaming red hair; he was the shabbiest of the lot, but his self-assured confidence made him seem a natural fit. As an adept pickpocket, he became essential to this mission.

As expected, Raoul made a grand entrance in a snow-white stretch limo with four beautiful blonds and two bodyguards in the front seats, one the driver. He was followed by an Escalade with four more bodyguards. He looked impressive in white tails and matching high hat. The two-car procession made quite a stir in the crowd who gathered around expecting another celebrity.

Brick drove a black Mercedes E-class sedan, which Clint had "borrowed" from a nearby corporate lot. It was a better choice than leaving a record of a rental company, and they planned to return it before anyone realized it was missing. Charlie and Granville were in the back of the Mercedes wearing designer suits with ties, Gran's treat. Brick wore a black suit with white shirt and a skinny black tie. The chauffer's cap on his head was the clincher. The previously used invitation that Clint had lifted and passed to them through the hole in the back of the fence was barely examined and they were waved through.

Raoul sat in the back with the girls drinking champagne, smoking reefer, and snorting coke until it was show time and then the six bodyguards formed a circle around the entourage as they were escorted into the studio. This was all for show, as there was no perceived danger. Raoul and the women sat near the front of the concert hall.

Brick stayed with the car like a proper driver, and Charlie and Gran went in and took seats near the rear. Stoney stood near the exit door acting like security and after checking the layout, Clint went to join Brick with the car. They expected to all leave together. Things don't always work out as planned.

For the first hour the band warmed to the music as they started easy. Prince made a grand entrance and gave the crowd a sample of his genius as he moved from instrument to instrument jamming with the band while they rocked the house. He worked them into a sweat before the break. A full complement of his greatest hits had the frenzied crowd on their feet swaying and clapping.

When the music stopped, Gran and Charlie rose as one and were first to exit. Raoul stood and stretched, waving the girls back to their seats. He said he'd return with treats; he wanted to smoke alone.

When the parking area was deserted, Brick and Clint walked up on either side of Raoul's limo, opened the front doors, and shot the two men in the head. Then they flipped their bodies over the seats into the back.

The four bodyguards from the other car were milling about smoking and joking; they never knew what hit them. They were clustered two per side by the doors, chatting over the roof. Brick and Clint came down opposite aisles smiling, and as they drew even with the SUV, they opened the back doors to the Escalade. One of the men laughed, thinking it must be a prank. He said, "What's up?" Brick shot him in the head and then quickly shot the other man. Clint repeated the act with the men on his side. They loaded the bodies in the trunk and back seat, then walked calmly away.

Raoul exited the club and made a beeline for the limo; he wanted to smoke and talk to Ramone, his head man, about the arrangements for the women after the concert. He planned a hot sexual romp with those putas.

As he got close enough to see into the front seat, he wondered where his men were.

As he came even with the driver's door, Brick sprang out of his crouch by the back bumper and kept the gun low; he pressed it into the smaller man's abdomen. "Tell me who put the hit out, you piece of shit."

He was standing very close and, keeping the gun pressed tightly against his belly, he wrapped his other hand around Raoul's throat. "Who hired you to kill me?" Brick demanded.

"Fuck you, bitch. What for I tell you?" he said with a laugh.

"Because if you don't, I will take you someplace quiet and cut off little pieces of your fat little body."

Raoul laughed again and said, "My men gut you, gringo."

"Your men are dead, asshole."

For the first time the diminutive Puerto Rican looked worried. He said, "What you give me, I tell?"

Charlie and Gran were just coming up on the scene when someone two aisles over yelled.

Brick turned to look.

The thrumming in his brain was so intense it distracted him; he was careless.

The knife seemed to come out of nowhere as Brick's mind remotely registered the distinctive click. It felt like a punch as it entered his stomach just under the vest, traveling up and cutting deep.

"Yes," Raoul screamed in glee, "the fucking win!"

Those were the last words he ever spoke, as the bullet Charlie fired an instant too late entered his right eye and exited out the back of his head, lodging in the hood of the limo.

Brick fell with Raoul, holding him until his hand released the knife. It was a switchblade about four inches long, buried to the hilt in his belly.

Charlie was by his side in a second and held his friend off the ground. Gran gave a hand as the two friends helped Brick into the back seat of the stolen Mercedes. The men knew better that to extract the knife; the blood loss alone could kill him.

Gran drove slow and deliberate until they cleared the gates. He had programmed the location of the nearest hospital into the GPS as they exited the lot, and he now raced through streets ignoring traffic signs and blaring horns. It was a wild, erratic ride but the trauma unit was waiting when they arrived at North Memorial hospital, thanks to Charlie's call.

Stoney and Clint loaded Raoul into the back of the limo and Stoney drove the three dead men out the gates while Clint did the same with the four men in the Escalade. They left the cars six miles away and Clint stole a scooter to take them back to a safe car. A call to Charlie let them know that their friend was being airlifted from North Memorial to Regions in Saint Paul where they had a proper trauma unit, the knife still embedded. If Brick lived, infection could be the next enemy he faced.

Seventy-three

Remnants of vivid dreams troubled my mind when I woke. My eyes were crusted and unfocused, but I knew something was horribly wrong. I tried to work some saliva into my mouth; it was too dry to speak and I had a painful stitch in my side. When I blinked and my eyes began to focus, a new sense of panic arose—I didn't know where I was. I could make out a large window and a grey, cloudy sky; it was raining. A snatch of the dream remained. I was on a train, the destination unknown to me, but there was a kindly old woman who comforted me and told me it was fine; she would guide me on my next journey.

There was a loud moan from somewhere distant; then I realized it came from me. A young woman in a nurse's uniform scurried around my bed, checking machines and dressings. There were tubes and wires in my arms and something attached to my chest. I moved slightly and a red-hot blooming pain seared my belly. The nurse drew a syringe from her pocket and shot it into the IV in my left arm. As the pain melted away, I sank back into the pillows and my body relaxed.

The nurse said, "There, that should make you feel better." Then, speaking to someone else, she said, "Keep him quiet while I tell the doctors he's awake."

I realized someone was holding my hand. I looked up into the crying eyes of Dawn siting in a chair by my bedside.

"What happened?" I croaked.

"You were stabbed by a mugger," she replied.

My foggy brain started working again and it came back to me: Raoul with his fetid breath in my face claiming his victory with a win … the knife in his hand.

"Where are my friends?" I managed.

Dawn was still crying and it was hard to hear, but she managed to say, "Your friend Gran was here with Charlie, but once the doctors said you would survive, Gran said they had something important to do and they left three days ago."

"How long have I been here?"

"I don't know for sure … over a week, maybe nine or ten days," she said.

"How did you—" I stopped as she talked over me.

"Gran had your phone and he called and told me you had been stabbed and could use some help, so I came. He's been great; he flew me here first-class and put me in a suite at the Radisson just downtown. He gave me your credit card and I take taxis here every day."

I noticed she had stopped crying and was smiling now. I needed to process this information so I told her to take a break, I needed to rest. She was getting up to leave when a man in a long white coat arrived. I assumed he was a doctor, but he looked impossibly young.

"You're awake! So how are we feeling?"

"I don't know how the fuck you feel, Doc, but I feel like shit."

He was nonplussed but continued to smile and said, "Well, that's to be expected; you took a rather nasty cut to your abdomen. Nicked your liver, punctured a lung, sent your heart into A-fib, and caused massive internal bleeding as your intestines were severed in two places. We've operated three times, but you seem to be out of the weeds now." He said this like it was the greatest experience of my life. He was smiling all the way through.

I said, "It feels like you put a damn zipper in my gut and the broken glass is on the move. I need to get out of here. Where are my clothes?"

"Very funny … you are not going anywhere, tough guy; that's up to me. You walk out of here and all our work is for nothing. You'll tear the stitches and bleed out before you make the lobby." At that, the doctor turned and started to leave.

"Okay Doc; how long, a week?

The doctor came and sat back down. "Listen to me. I know who you are and your record. You think because you're tough it will be easy, but this isn't a paper cut. This is really serious. I don't know how long you're going to be here, but at least a couple of weeks. Maybe because you're in such good shape I could release you to a private health care facility then."

He seemed to be on a roll and kept talking. "I was a brand-new doctor and did my residency in the sand box. I saw more boys and men than I could count; missing limbs, eyes, gutted like you and every one of them asked the same question: When can I get back to my guys?

"I understand the mentality, but you need to stop thinking weeks and months; think years, at least one."

When he got to the door, he turned one more time said, "Mugger? Bullshit."

After he left and I was alone, my mind drifted back to the scene at the studio … *I wonder what happened to Clint and Stoney. And where in the hell had Charlie and Gran gone?* I don't like mysteries. The pain in my side started again and the same nurse came back and gave me another shot. Panicked, I suddenly remembered my phone.

"Do you know where my cell phone is?" I asked the nurse.

"No, I imagine one of your friends has it; they were very thorough with your possessions, said they would keep them safe for you."

There was a landline on the bedside table and I tried to reach it but couldn't. I realized I didn't remember their phone numbers anyway. I felt lost without the phone. More precisely, I felt lost in general. It seemed like I had done battle with one enemy or another for years and yet the supposed puppeteer of this staged farce still remained a mystery.

The next day my mind was clearer, though still somewhat foggy from the narcotics invading my bloodstream. Dawn returned bright and early, but she didn't know more than what she had told me already. Midmorning a parade of white coats crowded my room; I counted five in all. They introduced themselves and gave their specialty, but the information left my fevered brain as soon as it was given. All I wanted to know was when I could leave. I wasn't to gain any satisfaction from the answers they gave.

"Well Mr. Winslow ..." the first of them began. "You had major internal damage and the wounds are very fresh. Sudden movement could tear the stitches and you could hemorrhage and bleed to death, or infection might be a contributing factor. We believe another week or two of bed rest and around-the-clock monitoring will give us a clearer picture of your recovery schedule." It was a confirmation of what my head doc already told me. I was starting to believe it and it made me cry.

Some of the other docs made comments and suggestions, but I had already tuned them out. *Another week or two? Un-fucking-believable.* And so the time passed in slow motion. After another week, they got me up and sitting. The next day I walked to the door of my room and back.

On Saturday of what I believe was the third week, Harriette filed in the door with Mason and Dawn in tow. They all hung around for hours each day and it was driving me crazy. I could feel the love, but I was still in the dark as to the aftermath of our mission. My friends by my side remained clueless. I was pissed off at the two men who might have answers, yet they remained elusive.

Seventy-four

It was Tuesday morning around ten o'clock on the fourth week of my hospitalization when Gran and Charlie strode casually into my room. What I had come to think of as Dawn and her accomplices were there along with an older, rather plump nurse.

I tried to catch Charlie's eye but he wasn't having it; he stared resolutely at the ground. Gran spoke up bright and cheerful. "Everyone out," he said. "We need to discuss matters of extreme importance with our colleague. The Queen's own business, if you will. Nip out, there you go, good show; take a breather, have a bite, but sod off."

When the nurse lingered and continued to fuss, he shouted at her: "Are you bloody fucking deaf? Out, you silly cow—now." She left.

"Okay, where have you been and where is my fucking phone?" I was losing patience.

Gran continued to smile brightly. "Now, now, laddie, give us a minute. Charles has the fucking phone and we have been confronting your nemesis."

"What do you mean—how could you know who it was? Raoul never told us." I was mad.

"Of course he did," Gran persisted.

"All he said was that he won," I protested.

"Not so fast, it was that the ever-quick and nimble Charles papered his fucking brains on his limo as he began," he said. "The fucking win, had Charles hesitated he would have said, it's the Wingate bitch. Your ex arranged for the nasty, mate."

I looked at Charlie and this time he met my gaze. "You've always been blind when it comes to Cassandra," he said, "but I was suspicious the minute you told me she had come to see you."

"You talked to her?" I asked.

Gran took over again. "We took tea in Montrose, California—not a shack, I might add. She wasn't in, a pity; we took a look about. Obscene security, fucking Yanks. I had a gaze at her computer, cracked like an egg in less than a twiddle. It's all there, dear lad—chats with Raoul, the insurance, the lot of it."

"What's he talking about, Charlie?"

"We waited until she came home, about an hour after we arrived. Gran grabbed her when she came through the door, a hand over her mouth and that fucking dagger at her throat. Six months before she came to see you, she upped the life insurance on Jonathan to three million. She just brought him there for you to kill him. She tried twice to suffocate him after you shot him, once when you went to fetch help and again that night in the hospital; then she saw you sneak in to finish the job. All along, she wanted you back, said she came on to you but you rejected her. She couldn't take your rejection. So she put out the hit to Raoul."

"I don't believe you."

"Brick … she admitted it all to us," Charlie finished.

Gran jumped back in. "Very cool bitch, I rather fancy her. Didn't flutter an eyelid. Surprise visit, knife at her throat and she smiled, fucking chilling, knackered me off kilter a might bit. Wouldn't mind running her up the old royal flagpole for a fortnight or three."

I threw him a look and Gran added, "Charles warned me you would get your knickers in a twist, so I backed off, mate. It's like the fop-haired boys used to sing, let it be. Still, a fancy little piece of tail—very cool and collected when we braced her."

I had to ask, "What did you do?"

"We didn't do anything, Brick; I know how you are about her. You've always had a soft spot where she's concerned. So we came back here to see what you wanted. But the good news is that it's over. There wasn't anything to tie Raoul's death to Paisley Park. No one is after you and it's finished, except for her," Charlie said.

Gran again: "I get not voting elimination; she's too fine a filly. Here's another twitch: I said I had a peek at her finances. While there I snuck in a wee bug. We could loot the lot with a few clicks of the wee mouse."

I sat there staring off for a long time and the room was silent. Finally, I said, "Do it; leave a couple hundred thousand and park the rest, and we'll see what she does."

It was six weeks total before I was released from the hospital. When I finally got out, Dawn and the others left for home. It was a tough goodbye with my friends from Oregon. Tears and promises to stay in touch. Once again, parting with Dawn was the hardest. She put as much passion into her kiss as she could muster and everyone could see her determination. The love was bleeding from her heart as she stifled her tears and said goodbye. She would be back soon, but after everything that happened she admitted she was afraid that when she left, it would all slip away.

Then I was transferred to a nursing home until I could arrange for equipment and full-time nursing care at my cabin in Wisconsin. Alone again, I had plenty of time to think. It didn't help. *Now what? Stop running and hiding, once and for all.* It was cold and would soon be bitter. September already. The summer disappeared in a fog of delirium and pain. A sudden chill ran up my spine when I considered it could have been my last. I'd been cleared of danger and was able to finish recuperating where I pleased. I called up Dawn and invited her to spend the winter with me in the islands. She didn't hesitate, said she'd be back tomorrow.

Back in Wisconsin, I invited Digger and Lisa to join us for dinner and drinks. It was interesting to watch Lisa circle Dawn in silent appraisal. Two beautiful women, each used to all the attention. Digger followed Dawn like a lovesick puppy, and Lisa shot daggers from her eyes at their backs. Hoping for an agreement to take care of my place, I suggested we arrange a payment schedule and as usual Digger was agreeable.

Lisa said, "I don't know … we can't run over here every day. Maybe once a week or twice a month might be doable."

"Okay, I thought you might be interested but I understand, Lisa. I know this real estate woman and I can have her arrange care."

Dawn kept her eyes on the other woman's face, and she smiled with a wary knowledge. Lisa was jealous.

Lisa caught the look but pushed forward. "I'm also a fucking real estate agent," she said. Then, glaring at Dawn, "We could move in here, but the kids would tear this joint apart; it's too fancy for young children. Next summer we can talk. For now, we live free at our place and you pay the mortgage and our utility bills; in return, we'll take care of things here. Digger will fix whatever breaks until you decide if you want to come back; if not, I sell it at my usual commission. Digger gets paid extra for any work."

"Now wait just a fucking minute—" Dawn was pissed; this woman was playing her man.

"Shhhh, both of you. Digger's done a lot for me—a lot you don't know, Dawn—so I'm willing to agree to the arrangement."

Turning to Dawn, I continued, "We can stay on the islands through the winter then come back here or live at your place in Oregon while you decide what you want to do. It will give you a chance to think about whether you might want to keep this place. We could come here from time to time; it's quite pretty."

Her wide grin told me what I needed to know; she was in this for the long term and I decided right then that I was too. I would leave it up to her. She started to cry. "Okay, whatever Brick says; you've got a deal."

Epilogue

It was the week before Christmas and we were at the house on Jost Van Dyke in the British Virgin Islands; we flew out three days after Thanksgiving.

I had invited our friends here for the Christmas holidays, asking them to stay until after the New Year. Harry and Mason were flying in today. The airport is in Tortola and then it's either a ferry ride over or, like today, they could be picked up by boat. Dawn was on her way over in the boat. Hitting the chop of the waves in the ocean is still a little more than my sore guts can handle, so I'm staying here to do my exercises while she goes alone. That girl is so much more competent than any of us ever gave her credit for that I'm ashamed of selling her short.

I stared off at the beach below. White Sand beach sat nestled in the little cove with the crystal blue waters of the Caribbean stretched out as far as the eye can see. You couldn't see the cruise ship, as it was docked on the other side of the island and the tourists were bused over. We stayed away when the ships were in port. The people dotted the sand like exclamation marks without a foot between them.

I wasn't here for the beach. I turned my attention to the hill, my new nemesis. This is the hardest part for me, the beginning. Last year if you asked me to run down and back up, I would have asked, how many times?

I've learned a lot in the last few months. I've known a lot of guys who have been hurt and hurt bad. You never think about what they go through after the pain diminishes and you start to heal, that is until it happens to you. It emasculates a man. Probably everyone, but maybe more so for a soldier. Strong to weak, healthy to sickly in the space of an eyelash. The bullet, the knife, the damage so quick and incredibly lasting.

So I stand here afraid to start because so far I haven't finished. The hill, almost a mile down and then, of course, back up. The down is not bad, not good, but not too bad. My goal is to finish one down and up without stopping to rest. Haven't come close yet. I steeled my resolve; when I would whine as a boy about something being too hard my mom would say, "Brick, if it was easy, anyone could do it. That's why it was given to you." I never could think of a good reply.

I do this every day. The first few times Dawn would follow me in the Jeep. The very first time I tried I only made it down and about twenty yards back. She picked me up and we didn't speak on the ride back. Yesterday I made it back up halfway before taking a ten-minute breather. My heart rate was over 100. Dawn doesn't follow me anymore. Today she was retrieving our friends, Harry and Mason. Thank God they don't come this way.

At the bottom of the hill I checked my heart rate, 75. My old resting rate was 47. Turning, I headed back up without pausing. Slow and steady, a mantra ringing in my head. I focused on one thing only—one step in front of the other. If I thought about my breathing or the pounding of my heart, I'd be lost. Nearing the top gasping for breath, I pushed off the balls of my feet and kept inching closer. When I finally crested the ridge, I wanted to scream in elation but had nothing left. Instead, I crumpled to the ground panting like a thirsty dog and waited for breath.

I must have been there at least fifteen minutes, but that was fine. You couldn't wipe the smile off my face with a Brillo pad. People walked around me with concerned looks, but the smile must have reassured them because they let me be. I thought of another truism of my mom's: "Brick, life slaps everyone down, some more than others. The measure of a man

362

isn't the shame of his defeat; but rather the resolve he shows in how he gets up, overcomes, and moves on."

Finally picking my sorry ass back up, I headed to our temporary home with a new spring in my step. My thoughts turned to Dawn, loving her, living with her. The joy she'd brought to my heart. The loving care in which she slowly helped me heal.

She had gone back to work. After setting up a studio in our back bedroom, the one with the morning light, she started drawing again. It was a series of charcoals depicting her kidnapping. The one that kept me mesmerized was the scene at the motel at the dead lake. It was of her; clothing tattered, half naked, but the terror on her face was chilling. When I looked at it, everything came rushing back and my scalp crawled and my upper lip was covered in sweat at the memory. I can't imagine what it did to her.

Now I stared in disbelief at the scene before me. Six people circled the pool. The house sat high on the hillside overlooking the beach. I was still thinking about the hill and my goal. This was another Bucky investment, but it served its purpose. Five bedrooms, four baths. Garage and private drive.

I had expected to see Mason and Harry, not the rest; they sat in lounge chairs around an umbrella table. The next table held a defiant Gran with Kelly, the real estate woman. She no longer wore the wedding ring; Gran wore that "I dare you" smirk.

And last but never least, Charlie sat in the company of an attractive brunette. Dawn introduced me to naval commander Betty O'Malley, retired, of Sisters, Oregon. Charlie smiled up at me grinning like the Cheshire cat who just ate the canary.

The next week was the happiest of our lives. Harry was like her old self, all traces of cancer gone, hopefully for good. Mason smiled and beamed at his wife with love and unbridled pride.

We played in the surf, took long walks together on the beach, and ate seafood by the armload. It was sad when Mason and Harry left for home, but already the group had made plans for our next rendezvous back in Oregon.

Dawn told me that Charlie had called her before they arrived and asked her to pick him up alone.

"We have something to talk about, and Charlie didn't want you to drive him crazy with questions."

"Since when have you two become so chummy?"

"You don't know everything about me, Mr. Winslow. A girl has her secrets." She kissed me on the cheek and resumed eating.

"If I wanted a mystery, I'd write one."

Dawn shook her head and muttered, "Men."

The next night the six of us went to White Beach for dinner and drinks. Betty had Charlie dancing on the shore to a steel band playing soft tunes. I had never before seen my old buddy dance; he was great. Should have figured. After a while, we broke away from Kelly and Betty, leaving the two women at the Soggy Dollar Bar. Dawn led the way to Ivan's with Charlie and Gran on her heels. I was left to tag along in a befuddled state.

Ivan's was a quiet little bar sitting on the beach, mostly a series of thatched-roof cabanas with a table surrounded by mismatched wooden chairs. The only way to reach it other than by boat was a short walk over an outcropping of rocks. For years a small army of wanderers had left dozens of pairs of worn sandals on both sides in case you were caught barefoot on your walk. The rocks were sharp.

Once we were settled with drinks, I asked, "So what's this something you want to talk to me about?"

"Steady there, lad. Old Gran's never had the pleasure of a wee visit to my islands. Allow me a glimmer of reflection," Gran said.

Dawn said, "Your islands?"

"Absolutely, lass—the British Virgins no less."

I said, "Gran thinks that if it's British, it's his."

"Spot on, old chap. We need to educate this beauty to me heritage."

"I'll fancy a stroll and perhaps this rare darling will walk me about. We'll be wanting a pint or two to loosen the limbs. Serious business afoot."

We were gathered under one of the huts. Charlie cleared his throat and began: "Later. Please, I want to get this out. Dawn and I have been chatting about what the agency needs, and I've put together a plan. We've proven that we're great together time and again. I need someone like an office manager." He looked at Dawn. "Gran would add a level of technological experience necessary in today's world. Brick, you're the smooth talker and my partner; we need to be together back in Austin."

Dawn reacted first, "I've told you before, Charlie. I'm not moving to fucking Texas! Look if you want an office manager, that's not something I could do remotely. I have to be nearby to field calls, assign work, and many other things. We really need a physical presence. Otherwise we look like a fly-by-night cheap detective agency. Sisters is my home and everyone loves it there. Plus you guys will travel for work, but you still have to come back to base from time to time. Wouldn't it be easier if we moved everything to the West Coast?"

Charlie said, "You know, I'm really not sure why I decided on Austin."

"Do you have a pertinent reason for keeping it there?" Dawn inquired.

"Not exactly. Shit, the army was my home for most of my life. When I left, I felt lost and security is all I know. I didn't think it through, I just had to do something and Brick was off—plus he had his head up his ass, so maybe I fucked up. I am capable of it, you know."

I chimed in: "I hate fucking Texas. Never had any luck there."

Gran said, "Sounds ridiculous, Charles. Sand and shit kickers, the lot."

"Well. Shit," Charlie said.

Dawn started again in a softer tone. "Look Charlie, you don't have much of a physical investment in the location. Brick told me it's just a leased office in a crummy part of town, and who the hell wants to travel there to hire you? No one, that's who. Why not be someplace nice? Everybody who comes to Oregon loves it. I drew up an alternative plan. Do you want to hear it?"

"By all means, lass, do tell. I'm all atwitter for the post," Gran commented.

Charlie shot Gran a cross look but said, "Yes, of course I do. Tell us what you think."

The moon was full and the bar had emptied, only a few tables left. It was a pleasant night with the waves gently lapping at the shore and not a trace of a breeze. The clean smell of the ocean and quiet waves the only background.

Without pause, Dawn began, "We move the operation to Sisters. The old newspaper building is for sale. They moved to a larger space. It would be perfect. It's freestanding in a great location, plenty of land. And Sisters is a picturesque little town adjacent to Bend, now a destination for the California jet set. We also need to change the name of the company. Honestly guys, McWin sounds like a cartoon dog; it doesn't convey confidence."

Dawn turned to me now and said, "We'd need a plane."

I laughed and said, "Why?"

Dawn continued, "The Learjet 70 is perfect. With an altitude of 45,000 feet and range of 2,000 miles, it has luxury and style. It seats eight comfortably and will impress the living shit out of prospective clients. I know of a slightly used Lincoln Towne Car that will complete the journey from the airport to our offices."

Charlie asked, "How much for the jet? And who could fly it?"

Dawn shot right back, "Eleven and a half million for the jet; we could look around for a used one, so maybe eight or nine. I'll have to get recertified on the Lear, but that's not a big deal. The car's another fifty grand, and I already have my chauffeur's license. I can take care of everything."

The three of us stared at her in disbelief.

I finally broke the silence when I asked, "How?"

She laughed and explained, "Rich man's daughter. Riding lessons, flying lessons, driving lessons. Daddy didn't believe in idle time. I was treated like the son he never had. I drew it all out on a corporate chart." At that, she withdrew a large folded paper from her purse and opened it up on the table.

Listed in order, it read top to bottom:

ISS: International Security Specialists

Offering a broad range of technological and physical security and protection.

CEO: Brigadier General Charles McShane, Retired US Army Rangers

CFO: Colonel Brick Winslow, Retired US Army Rangers

COO: Group Captain Granville Harlow III, Retired British Royal Air Force

TAO: Dawn Light

Again, Charlie and I stared at her. Charlie was the first to speak: "TAO ... is that supposed to be a joke?"

"What do you think it stands for?" Dawn asked.

Gran was laughing. "I should imagine tits and arse. It would be fitting."

"Actually it's Transportation and Acquisitions Officer. The double entendre is intentional. I'm a girl who believes in using her assets to the best of her ability."

She continued, "The acquisitions part includes courting the Hollywood jet and Playboy sets. I ran with that crowd and by using my modeling and stage name of Light, I open doors you could never hope to breach. I will acquire all supplies and essential equipment needed for a smooth operation, with the exception of arms. I'm sure you should be able to handle that little detail alone. The fact is, you gents can't do this without me."

"Spot on, lass. Bloody good show. Here, here."

She continued, "It would be a four-way partnership with Charlie as tie-breaker if any disagreements should arise."

"You're a cunning one, child, and a beauty in the bargain. This bloke's count seems short in the rankings," Gran said, pointing a finger at me.

"I'll invest; in fact, I insist," said Dawn.

She looked at me now. "What do you say, moneybags? Can you swing the cost of the plane, car, and office building?"

I was bewildered, then laughed and said, "Hell yes, just to work with you. You're a girl with many hidden and obvious talents, with a touch of eye candy for the shop, an added benefit."

"You bet your sweet ass, baby."

"I'll toss in a match," added Gran.

I said, "Let's iron out the details and I'll set it up with Bucky as a corporation with the benefits and breaks. For the investors, we'll set aside a portion of the profits as return on investment. Charlie and I are equals in everything."

"So are we decided, mates? Shall we give it a go and let the devil steer the course?" Gran seemed jubilant.

As one, we laid hands atop one another and nodded our heads. Gran spoke again. "We drink to this unholy alliance and God help those who stand against us."

The Beginning

Thank You

I have strong feelings about storytelling. There is only one point of view and that is the authors. If the author is honest with themselves you the reader is the only opinion that matters. I don't believe in writing groups or collaborations with others. True, honest writing is done by your muse. This subconscious genie knew the story before it ever popped into the writers knobby little head. The writer's job is to shut up and listen. I feel this is best accomplished in a serene and remote location. Distractions are the enemies of the muse; telephones, meals, thirst, sleep, comfort and any and all unrelated activities must be avoided. The muse becomes irritated and snarly when he doesn't have the writers undivided attention. Mine sure does.

Publishing doesn't have anything to do with storytelling. That's why it takes a village. Nobody can be good at everything and I'm not good at most of what it takes to get my story told. There are many people responsible for finalizing this story. I hope I don't miss any, but if I should it was purely unintentional.

Kate Ellefson and Susan Lauer are my biggest fans and have read every word I've ever written. I have sent them complete crap and even my rough first draft they lavish with praise. Nothing I say can change that, but we love and support each other all the same.

Mindy Logan thinks I'm the finest writer she's ever read and that this book is going to make me rich, I hope she's right.

Peggy Schumaker for not only taking my pictures, but helping me be comfortable in the process.

Jim Lundquist for his professional advice and most constructive criticism when I needed them most. He was never cruel or harsh, but pointed out inconsistencies and plot holes with an honest editor's eye.

My Beta readers; Tammy Thomas, Harry Felsenthal, Rod Aird and Patty Pfoser. More thanks to Patty for final proof reading duties.

Denise Burton for sharing her team of professionals when I was starting out.

My editor, Cathy Bromberg who made this a much better story than when she agreed to take me on as an author. I knew she was good when she auditioned me and insisted on reading my work before she agreed to accept me as a client. This wasn't easy. I don't like to be edited or censored and I definitely hate it when anyone messes with my prose. We fought over a lot; a word choice was of worthy of biblical proportions and we fought like warriors over some. As much as I argued my case, she still won most. I can't argue with reason. I now consider her a friend and wouldn't think of using anyone else for future books.

Celia Wirth for my website, cover layout and trying her best to help me struggle with the computer. I barely know how to turn it on and she's a master. She has done amazing things I didn't even know needed doing.

Finally my friend for over 40 years, Erik Dolson an accomplished writer, publisher, editor and great guy for leading me by the hand through this labyrinth of self-publishing.

Made in the USA
Monee, IL
06 April 2023

31457273R00205